MOONLIGHT ANGEL

Cord's mouth went desert dry as he watched her. Her high-necked frilly nightgown covered everything but her hands and face. Her golden hair fell halfway down her back, swaying from side to side when she moved.

Trixie crossed before the window and the moonlight turned her gown transparent. Cord slammed his eyes shut. Too late. He'd branded her shape on his mind's eye. Breasts that'd overflow a man's palm. A waist he could span with both hands, and shapely legs that'd wrap around a man's flanks and hold on for the long, hard ride to glory.

One Real Cowboy

JANETTE KENNY

ZEBRA BOOKS
Kensington Publishing Corp.
http://www.kensingtonbooks.com

ZEBRA BOOKS are published by

Kensington Publishing Corp.
850 Third Avenue
New York, NY 10022

All Kensington titles, imprints, and distributed lines are available
at special quantity discounts for bulk purchases for sales promo-
tion, premiums, fund-raising, educational, or institutional use.

Special book excerpts or customized printings can also be created to fit specific needs. For details, write or phone the office
of the Kensington Special Sales Manager: Attn. Special Sales
Department. Kensington Publishing Corp., 850 Third Avenue,
New York, NY 10022. Phone: 1-800-221-2647.

ISBN-13: 978-0-8217-8146-3
ISBN-10: 0-8217-8146-4

First Printing: March 2007
10 9 8 7 6 5 4 3 2 1

Printed in the United States of America

ACKNOWLEDGMENTS

To my mom, my first reader, avid listener, and loving shoulder to lean on. She believed in me from that very first rough draft, taught me tenacity and patience, and encouraged me to never give up my dream. Mom, this book is for you!

To Amy Knupp, Allison Brennan, Karin Tabke, and Sharon Long—exceptional friends as well as talented authors and awesome critique partners. When we teamed up, magic happened. We all buckled down for that wild ride to publication, and we all did it.

To Edie Ramer, Liz Krueger, and Michelle Diener. Thanks much for the pearls of wisdom, the laughs, and the friendship.

To my editor, Hilary Sares. When you called me to say you loved this book and offered to buy it, you gave me the best birthday present I've ever had.

Lastly, to my dad. He was one real cowboy at heart, and was an inspiration for this book. Dad, I know you're looking down on me from the heavens with a big old smile on your face.

CHAPTER ONE

Revolt, Kansas—1893

Cord Tanner crossed the dust-choked street, the jingle bobs on his spurs clanging louder than a dinner bell inside his head. Waking up dead broke and sicker than a bull on green pasture had put him in a real sour mood. Until he figured out how deep a well he'd dug for himself, it wasn't apt to sweeten none.

He hefted the saddle he was packing, gripped his rifle, and stepped into J. A. Zachary's law office with a passel of regrets riding his shoulders. The four folks in the room gawked at him.

A glassy-eyed gentleman garbed in a black suit and gloves stood by the door and greeted Cord with a stiff nod. A matronly lady dressed in black sat on a settee by the front window. Cord spied a fringe of frizzy hair the color of carrots peeking out from under her black pot hat. He nodded to her.

The matron turned up her nose, as if she got a whiff of fresh shit on him. So much for being neighborly.

James Zachary presided over the room from behind his desk and didn't appear any happier to see Cord either. After giving him a long, hard look, he snorted and pushed to his feet.

"Let me know when you're ready, Miss Northroupe," Zachary

said to the other lady, who perched on one of the armless chairs angled before his desk. "I'll be in the next room."

"Thank you." Her British accent surprised Cord.

As Zachary left, Cord shifted the saddle's dead weight, which was wearing on his sore shoulder, and eyed Miss Northroupe. So this was the lady boss his old friend Ott had roped him into helping. He'd seen her before. But where?

In that faded mourning dress and ugly black bonnet topped with a godawful black feather, she reminded him of a little prairie chicken guarding her nest, feathers fluffed, chest puffed out, and head up. But a shadow of fear lurked in her wide eyes and he knew she was putting on a brave front.

Miss Northroupe had good reason to be skittish. Some cowpokes didn't cotton much to working for a woman, especially a young one like she appeared to be.

Cord didn't care one way or the other. A boss was a boss. He'd worked for good ones and more than his share of bad.

He inclined his head Miss Northroupe's way. "Name's Tanner. Ott Oakes said you had a job for me."

"Indeed, I do." Miss Northroupe favored him with a shaky smile. "I trust Mr. Oakes explained the details to you and stressed the position in question is a temporary one?"

She had him there. Truth be told, Cord recalled Ott saying his boss lady needed Cord's help. Other than Ott mentioning a herd of horses, the rest of last night was a blur. Cord didn't even remember agreeing to do the job, though Ott swore he had.

Zachary and Miss Northroupe appeared to be expecting Cord, so it must be true. He wished to hell he knew what he'd gotten himself into. Since he didn't, he decided he'd best play along.

"Yes, ma'am, the temporary job you're offering suits me just fine." That was the God's honest truth.

He'd hire on for a month at the most. By then, he'd have a horse and a helluva lot more than two bits in his pocket.

Then Cord aimed to put this town and its heap of bad

memories in a cloud of dust behind him. Miss Northroupe could hire another cowpoke to ride herd over her outfit.

"Excellent." Miss Northroupe motioned to the empty chair beside her. "Do leave your equipage by the door and be seated."

He obliged her, then eased onto the chair. She smelled of lavender water and high hopes. Wisps of golden hair escaped her bonnet, curling this way and that around her face. Her blue eyes put him in mind of a clear prairie sky. Farm-girl freckles dusted her nubbin of a nose, and her mouth had the prettiest bow to it. Inviting lips, the kind a man hankered to taste.

She cleared her throat, and her mouth puckered up, like she'd eaten something sour. "Mr. Oakes has great trust in you. Though I usually agree with his character assessments, in this case, I shall reserve judgment until I'm convinced you will undertake this short-term task with dignity and respect."

He didn't blame her none for being wary of him. She had a ripe woman's body and a sweet face that'd tempt a cowboy into settling down, something she clearly didn't want from him.

"I'm just a rambling cowpoke with no notions of sticking around these parts. When the job's done and I'm paid for my trouble, I'll be on my way."

Miss Northroupe frowned as she eyed him again. Her gaze wandered to his belt buckle, then ventured lower.

Cord tensed up. Usually, he didn't mind a pretty woman looking him over. But Miss Northroupe had him feeling like a plug horse at auction instead of a young stud. He leaned forward and braced both arms on his knees.

Their eyes locked. She let out a whisper of a gasp and sat back, cheeks turning bright red. Cord reckoned she was embarrassed because he'd caught her staring at what a proper lady had no right to look at.

Maybe whoever she mourned had kept her away from the

corrals and the wranglers. Poor little gal probably didn't know the first thing about men and not much more about horses. If that was the case, he aimed to put her mind at ease on one score.

"Don't mean to brag, but I'm real good with horses." Cord leaned back and angled his buckle up. "I won this in Oklahoma last spring for being the best bronco buster."

She sucked in a sharp breath. "Bronco busting, you say?"

"Yes, ma'am. Ott told me that you run horses on your outfit. I reckon breaking them will be one of my chores."

Miss Northroupe pressed a lace-gloved hand to her bosom and went pale as milk, as if he'd said something downright vulgar. "I'm sure your award was justly deserved. However, it isn't an attribute to someone who raises thoroughbreds. We don't break our horses. My stableman trains them to be exemplary hunters."

"You don't say?" Though it riled him that she didn't want the likes of him breaking her fine thoroughbreds, the notion of a woman running a stud farm spurred his curiosity.

"Indeed. I should have several hunters finished by now, but I've suffered the loss of my father and, ultimately, my ranch hands. Those remaining in my employ can't attend to the various tasks at hand, which is why I'm forced to tread this path."

The old gentleman by the door hunched his bony shoulders, cleared his throat, and stared holes in the floor. By the window, the matron folded her hands and mumbled to herself.

Cord shook his head. These highfalutin British folks were making a mighty big fuss over hiring a ranch hand. Didn't they know that cowboys drifted like tumbleweeds from spread to spread?

"That is why, before we proceed any further," Miss Northroupe said over the matron's mutterings, "I must have your word of honor that you'll obey all my orders without question."

He bit back a laugh, wondering if her bossy ways had been

what sent her former cowhands packing. "Short of breaking the law, I'll do anything you ask of me."

Miss Northroupe took a deep breath that strained the thin cloth covering her bosom and looked him square in the eyes. "Very well, Mr. Tanner. You now work for me."

"You won't regret hiring me, ma'am."

"I sincerely hope you're right."

Miss Northroupe nodded to the old gent. He shuffled to the connecting door Zachary had left by and knocked on it twice.

"After you sign the contract which details your duties on the Prairie Rose," Miss Northroupe said with the slightest quiver in her voice, "we'll get on with finalizing our common bond."

"Yes, ma'am." Cord had worked for demanding bosses before but had never signed a contract.

As the old gent moseyed back to his post by the front door, Zachary stepped into the office. He placed a paper, pen, and inkstand on the desk before Cord, then stood by the bookcase.

Seeing as he'd worked every ranch job, Cord only gave the contract a quick scan. Nothing peculiar jumped out at him.

He dipped the nib in ink, ready to sign. "Just tell me what you want me to do and I'll get right on it."

"Very well. Your first task is to marry me this afternoon."

Cord strangled the pen so hard he nearly snapped it in two. He shook his head and looked her over, certain his ears were playing tricks on him. "Come again, ma'am?"

Poker-faced, she said, "You will marry me this afternoon."

"Like hell I will. I'm looking for a job. Not a wife."

The matron commenced chattering like a squirrel, and the old gent set up a racket clearing his throat. Zachary coughed— like he was trying to hide a laugh—and turned his back on them.

The prim, proper, and clearly crazy Miss Northroupe sent Cord a patient smile. "Moments ago, I gave you a job. You promised to do whatever I asked of you, excluding breaking the law."

Cord snatched up the contract and read every blasted word. It was there, all right. Tucked in amidst the list of dos and don'ts. Husband. Short-term marriage of convenience. For his *services*, she'd pay him and give him one of her fine horses.

The headache Cord had tried his best to ignore since he'd rolled out of the hay this morning reared, kicked, and bucked like an outlaw horse. Ott couldn't have known his boss lady aimed to hobble Cord into marrying her. His old friend wouldn't have pulled such a dirty, low-down trick on him.

But the old gent and matron knew what their boss lady had up her faded sleeves. Judging by their down-in-the-mouth expressions, they didn't cotton to this idiotic idea any more than Cord did.

Same with James Zachary, who seemed mighty interested in gawking at a row of books on a shelf. Cord would bet good money the lawyer had drawn up this asinine contract, but the man had the sense to turn his back to them so as not to embarrass the lady when Cord tore her contract in two and walked out.

Cord was fixing to do that when he glanced her way. She was doing her best to hold back tears. His head commenced pounding. Hell, it was easier to rope the wind than deal with a crying woman.

"No offense, ma'am," Cord began, intending to let her down easy like, "but I don't want to get married."

Miss Northroupe buried her gloved hands in her skirt. "Neither do I, but I must if I'm to retain my independence."

That didn't make a lick of sense. Cord ran a hand over his face and cursed the fact that his hand shook. "Pardon me for disagreeing, ma'am, but getting yourself hitched is a surefire way to lose your freedom."

Miss Northroupe swallowed, and the high, stiff collar on her dress bobbed. "Not if we agree to abide by the terms of

my contract. Really, Mr. Tanner, the only difference between
this job and any other you've taken on is that I'm paying you
to be my husband instead of my ranch hand."

She had a point there. The fact he considered it for one
second had him sweating buckets. "This is the craziest thing
I've ever heard. We don't even know each other."

Miss Northroupe rolled her eyes. "Mr. Oakes vouched for
your character, and he's one of the most trustworthy men I
know."

"Then why the hell don't you marry Ott?"

Violet storm clouds gathered in her eyes. "There's no need
for belligerence. As much as I admire and trust Mr. Oakes,
he's unsuitable." She took some bosom-expanding breaths
that had him squirming in more ways than one and favored
him with a tight smile. "Do reconsider my offer, Mr. Tanner.
You'd only be required to assume the role of my devoted husband for a month at the most, after which time you'll be handsomely paid for your services."

That damning word again. Cord gritted his teeth so hard
his head pounded. He was a cowboy. Not a whore. But she
wasn't hiring him as a wrangler. No. She wanted a husband.
Though the timing of this job couldn't have suited him better,
he damned sure wasn't about to sell himself.

"My *services* ain't for sale, ma'am."

She dug her small, white teeth into her lower lip. "Is there
nothing I can say or do to change your mind?"

"Nope." Cord pushed to his feet, not about to let her lasso
and drag him into her fool plan.

"Oh, dear." The matron pressed her round face to the
window. "Mr. Yancy has come to town."

Miss Northroupe's face turned whiter than a January bliz-
zard. "He likely has business to conduct."

Zachary moseyed over to the window and took a gander.
"He tied his horse by your surrey. He's walking down the

boardwalk. Now he's going into Lott's Mercantile." Zachary ambled back to his desk.

"Mr. Yancy is looking for you. I told you he would." The matron wrung her hands and tossed a worried glance at Miss Northroupe. "He couldn't know what you've planned, could he?"

"No, of course not." But Miss Northroupe didn't sound sure.

"This Yancy you're talking about," Cord said, unable to keep the hostility from his voice. "Would that be Gil Yancy?"

"Indeed, it is," Miss Northroupe said. "Do you know him?"

Like a brother. Or so Cord had thought. Bitter memories of being double-crossed stampeded across his mind, but he cut them off and herded his thoughts back to the here and now.

"I know him. Reckon if you offer Gil what you did me, he'll jump at the chance to be your temporary husband."

Despite the heat building in the room, Miss Northroupe shivered. "Very true, but I can't trust Mr. Yancy will abide by my wishes or the terms of the contract."

"Then don't ask him to marry you."

"If it were only that simple."

Miss Northroupe didn't come out and say she looked on Gil as her last choice, but Cord knew by her defeated tone that's what she meant. Knew, too, that she blamed him for turning her down.

Cord glanced at the contract again. He doubted Miss Northroupe would find a judge who'd honor it. Nope. Once she married, her husband could legally do any damned thing he wanted to do to her land, her stock, and her.

If she married Gil, Cord knew his longtime rival would bed the British lady before the ink dried on the marriage certificate. There'd be no getting rid of him after that.

Since Cord had no designs on the prim lady and no desire to remain in Revolt, he reckoned he was the perfect choice for the job. Temporary husband. Paid handsomely.

Tempting words to a down-on-his-luck cowboy with two choices left him: walk twenty miles to the next town packing his tack and everything he owned on his back, or ask for a job at the place he'd vowed he'd never set foot on again—Prescott Donnelly's Flying D Ranch.

"All right, Miss Northroupe. You've got yourself a deal." Cord grabbed the pen and plunged the tip in the ink.

"I promise you won't regret your decision, Mr. Tanner."

He already regretted it as he filled his lungs with air and dragged in her lavender scent. Damn! If she hadn't looked scared as a rabbit when he turned her down, or if Gil Yancy hadn't figured into this, he'd have been on his way to— Where? The Flying D for a handout?

Teeth clenched, Cord scrawled his name on the line. When this job was over, he'd have money in his pockets, a fine horse under him, and the chance to make something of himself. What more could a bastard like him expect from a respectable British lady?

He handed the pen to Zachary and watched as the lawyer added his name as witness to this leg-hobbling contract. As soon as he was done, Miss Northroupe reached for the paper.

Cord snatched it off the desk and held it above his head. "Whoa up, there. I want to know why you're hell-bent on rushing into marriage with a stranger."

Her gaze flicked from the contract to the door. "Couldn't we discuss this after the ceremony?"

"Nope."

She wrinkled her nose and mumbled something that sounded like a curse. "Very well. My grandfather refuses to grant me the title to the Prairie Rose unless I am wed."

"Let me guess. You told him you was getting hitched."

"It seemed a sound notion. However, Grandfather forbade it until he gave his approval, and I refused to obey. As we speak, he's traveling from England to meet the man I defiantly married."

Cord let out a long, low whistle and handed her the contract. "No wonder you had to hire yourself a husband mighty fast."

"Temporary husband." She spread the paper on the desk and neatly signed her name, then handed the contract to Zachary.

"You shouldn't need this document to dissolve your union. But if you do, it'll be in my safe." Zachary shot Cord a warning look. "I suggest you follow this to the letter."

Cord heard Zachary's "or else" echo in his weary head as Zachary ambled off into the other room.

Miss Northroupe sat stiffly on the chair, her smile fading. "Have you any questions regarding your duties?"

"I reckon you expect me to act like your devoted husband." Pure devilment prodded Cord to wink at her.

Her cheeks flushed apple red. "Our association will be strictly platonic. And I'll abide no philandering."

He'd expected as much. Though Miss Northroupe wasn't about to sleep with the likes of him, she wouldn't want him to find a willing woman in town either.

"You'll take up residence in my papa's room," she said. "To the world, we shall portray a blissfully married couple."

"Happy as two fleas on a fat hound," Cord said.

The old gent and matron shared a chuckle. Eyes twinkling like stars, Miss Northroupe laughed. Despite his annoyance, Cord grinned. Maybe this wouldn't be so bad after all.

He guessed her father's death was what had put the spurs to this risky plan of hers. At least she had the gumption to fight for what she wanted. Cord admired and envied her for that.

"Well, Miss Northroupe. When do we get hitched?"

"Immediately. It's imperative we formalize our bond today." She glanced at his saddle, saddlebags, and rifle stacked by the door and frowned. "Would you care to retrieve your horse before we proceed to the church?"

Anger loped across his nerves. "Don't have one anymore."

"Oh. Why ever not?"

Last night's meeting with Ott swirled in and out of his memory like smoke, but the end results remained branded on his mind. "Thanks to bootleg applejack and a pair of deuces, I lost my horse in a poker game." He saw no need to tell her that he'd also lost every cent he'd been hoarding for a year.

Miss Northroupe sucked in enough air to flutter the window curtains. "For the duration of our marriage, you'll refrain from gambling. Is that clear, Mr. Tanner?"

Cord nodded, more amused than chastised by her latest order. Certain ranch rules had a way of getting broken.

"I reckon you're opposed to drinking, too," Cord asked just to rile her a bit.

She hemmed and hawed. "I won't tolerate drunkenness. However, a drink after a trying day can be quite pleasurable."

That surprised him. He'd bet most women in this dry town would disagree with her. Hell, after what had happened to him last night at the Plainsmen's Lodge, he wasn't sure he shared her opinion.

"It's Mr. Yancy again," the matron said, staring out the window like a hawk eyeing prey. "He quit Lott's Mercantile."

"What's he doing?" Miss Northroupe asked.

The matron pressed her nose to the glass. "Mr. Yancy made one of those vile cigarettes. Now he's standing on the boardwalk, looking about and puffing away. Some ruffian came along and stopped to chat with him. Oh, dear. The ruffian is pointing toward Mr. Zachary's office."

Miss Northroupe shot to her feet and gave her ugly skirt a shake. Even standing on a box, she wouldn't be able to look over a swaybacked cow pony.

She tipped her head back and stared at him with a blend of curiosity and dread. "I suggest you deposit your equipage in my surrey, and then we'll proceed to the church."

Nervous energy shimmered off her like a mirage, niggling his own suspicions—and nudging awake his sense of compassion. He had the urge to pull her against him, tuck back the golden wisps that had escaped her bonnet, and tell her that she had nothing to fear. But touching her might scare the hell out of her. Besides, he wasn't on a first-name basis with his future wife.

For some reason Cord refused to look at too closely, he aimed to change that right now. "Cord would do just fine."

"I beg your pardon," she asked.

"Seeing as we're going to be husband and wife, you'd best start calling me by my first name from here on out."

"Certainly not! It is presumptuous to address each other with common familiarity when we're little more than strange—" She broke off and frowned at the wall, as if arguing with herself what to do now—treat him like her lover or the hired hand.

"Mr. Yancy is crossing the street," the matron said.

A frisky glint two-stepped in Miss Northroupe's eyes. "Very well, Cord. I give you leave to address me as Bea or Beatrix, my Christian name. Shall we go?"

"Yes, ma'am." But as he slung his saddlebags over a shoulder, hoisted his saddle, and fetched his rifle, he decided those names didn't fit a woman with the gumption to propose marriage to a stranger in order to gain title to her land.

The little lady took off out the door like a filly set loose to pasture after a long, hard winter in the corral. Cord chuckled and trailed his bride-to-be with the old folks pulling drag duty.

He stowed his gear in the surrey the old gent pointed out to him, then set off after Miss Northroupe. He wasn't surprised to see Gil barreling toward her from the other direction. Cord swore and picked up his pace.

"You're just the lady I've been looking for," Gil said.

She hiked her chin up. "Have you? I can't imagine why."

"I'd like to call on you." Gil was so intent on charming Miss Northroupe that he didn't see Cord charging at him. "The Bar T Ranch is putting on a shindig this Saturday, like they did nigh on a year back. I'd be right pleased if you'd go with me."

Cord had a mind to knock the big old smile off Gil's lying

mouth. But a brawl would set the tongues in town wagging. As it was, they'd gathered onlookers faster than flies to a dung heap.

"She can't," Cord said. "Ask somebody else."

Gil shot him a go-to-hell scowl. "Sticking your nose in my business will likely get you busted in your kisser."

"You threatening me?" Cord fisted his right hand.

"Just offering you a warning, partner."

"Cease this bickering," Miss Northroupe said.

"My apologies, Miz Northroupe." Gil held his hat over his heart. "The dance would give us a chance to get to know one another better. Colonel Trenton is providing rooms for single ladies to stay the night and us men will bunk in the barn. It'll be all proper like. We'd head on back to Revolt the next day."

"I'm sure it'll be a festive affair enjoyed by all as before, but I simply can't accompany you," she said.

Gil's smile wavered. "If you're worried about being alone with me and all, you could invite your housekeeper, here, to come along. Hell, bring your butler, too."

Standing behind Cord, the old gent snorted and the matron harrumphed. Cord smiled. Though the old folks weren't partial to Miss Northroupe hiring a husband, Cord had a hunch they preferred him over Gil Yancy.

"Like the lady said, she can't go with you," Cord said.

Gil's polished charm tarnished faster than the silver conchos on Cord's old saddle. "I'm warning you, partner. This ain't none of your business."

"Now there's where you're dead wrong."

"How the hell do you figure that?" Gil asked.

"It's real simple. If anybody takes the lady to that dance, it'll be me." Cord rested a hand on Miss Northroupe's rounded shoulder. She sidled up to him, and he cursed the lightning bolt of pure lust that shot right to his crotch. "Her husband."

"You're lying." Gil looked from Cord to her and back again. "Miz Northroupe wouldn't marry a drifter like you."

"Oh, but I would and soon shall." She stood her ground, defiant as a bantam hen, reminding Cord again that her Christian name didn't fit his wily bride-to-be.

"Hold up, here." The veins in Gil's neck bulged like ropes as he faced Cord. "You know damn well I saw her first."

"You're loco." But now that he thought on it, he recalled Gil setting his sights on an English lady at the Bar T. Damn!

"This is my wedding day, Mr. Yancy. It's proper to wish the bride well and congratulate the groom."

Cord applied gentle pressure to her shoulder, applauding her spunk. And, if he was honest with himself, he was publicly staking his claim to the little lady Gil had aimed to marry.

"I reckon it is." Gil chewed out his best wishes to them, though Cord knew the cowboy was lying through his clenched teeth.

"We best move on, Trixie," Cord said. "Don't want to keep the preacher waiting on us."

She whirled to face Cord, but instead of giving him a tongue-lashing for blurting out a nickname that suited her, her eyes sparkled with amusement and what looked like a glimmer of approval. The tension girthing his guts tightened another notch. She stirred some mighty powerful feelings deep inside him that he didn't aim to deal with. Ever.

"Of course. Whatever you say, Cord."

"This ain't over, partner. Not by a long shot." Gil shot Cord a look that could shred leather and elbowed past him.

Trixie rested her hand on Cord's arm, pulling his attention back to her. "What did Mr. Yancy mean by that?"

Cord shrugged, but he had a nagging feeling Gil intended to dig up the past Cord had buried and put from his mind long ago.

CHAPTER TWO

A numbing cold seeped into Bea's bones as she and Cord stood before the staid preacher in Revolt's Methodist Church with Benedict and Mrs. Mimms serving as witnesses. The ceremony seemed painfully short and to the point.

"I do." Bea forced her sacred vows out on a shiver, hoping for the best and fearing the worse.

She was taking Mr. Oakes's word as gospel and marrying Cord Tanner. A stranger. For richer or poorer. For better or worse.

All because her grandfather refused to give her the title to the home she loved because she was unmarried. Well, her autocratic grandfather had underestimated her this time. She was willing to risk much to gain what she most wanted.

Being a missus would allow Bea to provide a home for her aged retainers and her beloved horses. And should Cord refuse to abide by their contract, she'd do what she had to do to ensure she didn't remain Mrs. Cord Tanner till death do they part.

"I do," Cord said in answer to the preacher's question.

"I hereby pronounce you man and wife. Kiss if you want." The preacher turned aside to sign the marriage certificate.

Cord didn't move. Didn't say a word. Bea wasn't sure if she

was relieved or disappointed. What did she expect? Their marriage was a business arrangement.

Handing the holy document of marriage over into Mrs. Mimms's safekeeping, Bea quit the church on Cord's arm and hoped he couldn't feel her trembling. In order to maintain the upper hand, she had to remain calm and collected in his company.

A hot, dry wind whistled around the building, whipping her grosgrain mourning skirt about her suddenly weak ankles and threatening to tear the black ostrich plume from her bonnet.

The same smattering of citizens who'd strained their ears when Gil confronted Cord earlier gathered on the boardwalk before Lott's Mercantile and gawked at her and Cord. She knew the reason for their curiosity and shock.

When mourners wished to become socially active, they left cards with friends and acquaintances to signal they were anxious to receive visitors. They didn't leap from a state of mourning into the state of holy matrimony without following etiquette.

But Bea had and, in doing so, she'd trampled social mores beneath her French heels. Perhaps that would work to her advantage, though.

For Bea's stratagem to succeed, her grandfather had to be convinced she'd married Cord because she loved him and couldn't wait any longer. What better way to accomplish that goal than to present herself as a blushing bride before the town?

Outside Lott's Mercantile, the gossipmongers huddled on the boardwalk, no doubt having a field day blabbering about this scandal of the heart. Gil Yancy leaned against a porch post, rolling a cigarette and glaring at Cord.

Bea had expected her marriage would stir Gil's animosity. Gil was not one to lose graciously. How convenient he'd found a willing ear in bottle-necked Arlene Lott, reigning town gossip.

Nate Wyles's presence surprised and alarmed Bea. Her former foreman slumped against the post across from Gil, torturing her with a lewd perusal. The man was vile to the core. Seeing him here engulfed Bea in grim memories of the day her papa died.

"Don't that just beat all," Nate said in a voice loud enough to carry into the hereafter. "And here I'd always heard you can't hitch a blooded horse with a mustang."

The insult dredged a chorus of gasps from the onlookers.

Beneath her arm, Cord's muscles tensed. His clipped curse was barely audible. But Bea heard it, and his furious undertone matched her spike of anger. How dare Nate Wyles liken her to a thoroughbred and Cord to a horse of indeterminable breeding?

"Pay no attention to the lout," she said to Cord.

Gil blew out a plume of smoke and smirked at Cord. "Yep, it sure does confound a man when a lady up and decides to scrape the bottom of the barrel."

Bea longed to rap the two cowboys upside their hard heads, but common sense prevailed over her temper. It wouldn't do for her grandfather to hear that she and her husband had created an undignified scene in the street on their wedding day.

"Ignore those two," Bea whispered to Cord. "Do assist me to the surrey and we'll be off to the Prairie Rose."

Bea expected Cord to heed her order, but he didn't budge or acknowledge her. Her skin chafed with growing unease.

She cleared her throat. "Perhaps you didn't hear—"

"There's nothing wrong with my ears. I ain't one to hide behind a woman's skirts or tuck tail and run."

Cord wrapped an arm around Bea's waist and hauled her against his side, squeezing a yelp from her. Her mind went numb. Not so for her body. Every inch of her tingled, coming awake from the heat, strength, and anger radiating from him.

"I'm only gonna say this once." Cord stared straight at Gil, and his ominous tone sent fingers of dread crawling up Bea's spine. "Treat my wife with respect or you'll answer to me."

Gil pushed away from the post and ground his cigarette out under a boot heel. "Is that a threat, partner?"

"A promise." Cord's smile could freeze hot coals.

"That's right good you're standing up for your woman." Gil swaggered into the street. "But I got to tell you I never figured you'd drift back here some night and end up married to an upstanding lady by midmorning. A lady that happens to own a fine spread of land."

Cord dropped his arm from Bea and started toward Gil. "What the hell are you getting at?"

"Your bride's in mourning, partner. She ain't been courting. Ain't been receiving visitors. Ain't been to town much since her pa's death. Except for those two old servants and a couple of ranch hands, she's been alone on her ranch." Gil stopped and crossed his arms over his chest. "Makes me wonder how Miz Northroupe ended up married to a stranger."

Cord mumbled another curse. "I asked for Trixie's hand and she agreed to be my wife."

"Well, I figured one of you did the asking." Gil smirked.

Cord stiffened more than Bea thought possible. Alarm shot through her as his nostrils flared and a muscle jerked tight along his lean jaw.

Murmurs rumbled through the gathering gossips. Like a pack of hungry dogs, they smelled a juicy bit of scandal cooking. All because Gil insisted on sticking his nose in her business.

This would not do at all. Grandfather detested deceit. If he discovered that she'd resorted to trickery to gain title to the ranch and control of her dowry, he'd be so furious with her that he'd likely sell the Prairie Rose out of spite.

She'd lose everything she held dear. Everything she'd worked hard to achieve. She couldn't sit by and let that happen.

Bea lifted her hem and scurried toward Cord and Gil. Six feet of tense air separated them. She wanted to keep it that way.

"I assure you that Mr. Tanner did propose matrimony in the most proper manner." Smiling, Bea looped her arm around Cord's right one as if it was the most natural thing for her to do.

Cord's breath visibly caught, dredging a nervous giggle from Bea. Finally, he gave her the briefest of glances. The bleak look in his eyes stabbed at her heart. He didn't smile. Didn't say a blessed word. This was not going well at all.

Bea waffled between screaming in frustration and crying in despair. She didn't want Cord fawning over her, but she expected him to abide by the terms of their contract.

"Asked you to marry him proper like, you say?" Gil shook his head. "I'd have paid good money to see that."

The man was persistent beyond belief. Since Gil continued to fan the coals under a pot that should be left to cool, she had no choice but to concoct a reason for her hasty marriage. One that would silence Gil and the gaggle of gossips for good. Only one thing came to mind that didn't further tarnish her reputation.

"I assure you all that Mr. Tanner and I married so soon after meeting because we love each other deeply and couldn't bear to wait any longer to declare our hearts and souls." Bea smiled at Cord and patted his chest. "Don't we, dear husband?"

Eyes as dark and hard as walnut shells locked with hers in silent battle. Why had her clever reply infuriated Cord? She didn't dare ask now, so she continued smiling in spite of his anger and hoped he'd realize she expected him to do the same.

Bea got her wish. In a manner of speaking. Cord's white teeth flashed more snarl than smile. She held her breath, expecting he might very well growl.

"What I feel for you, my dear wife, is beyond words."

Though Cord spoke genially, one arm banded her corseted

waist and held tight while he caught her hand and trapped it against his chest. His heart thumped against her palm. Anger seethed from his pores and triggered a riot of apprehension within her.

Bea tried to tug free of his iron grasp, but he didn't let go of her. Surely he wouldn't do anything rash.

She gulped down the panic clogging her throat, leaned toward Cord, and whispered, "Do bear in mind it's not necessary for us to continue this public display of affection. This common familiarity is not part of our agreement."

A muscle jerked along his taut jaw. Seconds passed before he favored her with a smile that gave her new cause to worry.

"Reckon it's time we took our leave." Cord had the audacity to wink at the crowd. "There's no sense hiding the fact me and my bride are chomping at the bit to get on with married life."

That bold statement should've shocked her. And it did, but it also stirred the most unladylike urgings within her. My God, what had she done, aligning herself with this cowboy?

In the wake of their onlookers' collective gasps, Cord hurried her toward the waiting surrey. A chorus of low chuckles and nervous titters rose from the gathering.

Bea abandoned her subtle attempt to wrench free several shallow pants later. No doubt it'd be easier to hop from a mud puddle than extricate herself from Cord's embrace.

As if bent on tweaking propriety's nose, Cord kept her waiting beside him and ordered her servants, "Get in the back."

To Bea's shock and annoyance, Benedict and Mrs. Mimms scrambled onto the rear bench of the surrey, keeping their eyes averted from her. Her husband's huge western saddle, rifle, and saddlebags crowded the floorboards between her servants' feet.

Cord hoisted Bea onto the front seat with as much care as

he'd give a sack of grain, then followed her up. "You're forgetting yourself, Mr. Tanner."

"No, ma'am. I'm doing what you hired me to do."

"How very good of you," she said, too disgusted with his high-handedness to let his dark scowl intimidate her. "Though I commend you for putting a dose of spirit into your role, I'll not tolerate you playing the tyrant and taking charge."

Cord flung an arm across her seat back and clamped his other hand on the rail that was digging into her hip. He leaned so close that she could taste the hint of apple on his breath.

His features blurred. His scent, a mixture of soap, bay rum, and man, teased and seduced her. Her pulse pounded so loud she feared the whole town must hear it. Whatever would he do next? Ignore propriety, take her in his strong arms, and kiss her?

That fanciful dream vanished on a hot buffeting breeze as she focused on his face. His eyes darkened to an ominous black. She gulped, realizing ardor was the furthest thing from his mind.

"I don't want to hear you spread any more bullshit that we're in love." Cord spoke each word slowly. Succinctly.

Bea recoiled as if he'd struck her. True, men had never clamored for her attention. If her independent nature didn't send them running, then her temper or ordinary features would. Still, Cord had struck the bargain with plain, headstrong Beatrix Helena Northroupe. She expected him to honor his promise.

"See here, Mr. Tanner," she said, refusing to let him see her rising panic or hurt. "You signed a contract, agreeing you'd be my devoted husband. Proclaiming your love for your spouse is expected, don't you think?"

A wicked grin spread across the mouth hovering inches above hers. The gleam in his eyes bored into hers and muddled her mind. "I'll treat you kindly and with respect. But the only love I'll be a party to is the kind a man and woman revel in—in bed. So you tell me. How real do you want this marriage to be?"

Behind Bea, Benedict coughed. Mrs. Mimms muttered a litany of dire predictions under her breath.

Bea swallowed with great difficulty. She cherished her independence; Cord promised dominance. Yet the idea of having a genuine marriage, of being loved—if only physically—by this handsome cowboy, sent an alien thrill of longing through her.

But she didn't dare give in to her emotions. Not now. Perhaps never where Cord Tanner was concerned.

She wet her trembling lips and focused on what she wanted most in this world—title to the Prairie Rose. "Though our bond is temporary, it's imperative that we convince everyone our marriage is real. I'm attempting to do my part as your adoring wife. Likewise, I expect you to honor our agreement."

His devilish grin hinted of untold sins and promised untold pleasures. Instantly, Bea grew hotter than a hearthstone. Languorous. She bit her lower lip to still a surrendering moan.

"Seeing as you want a devoted husband—" Cord's breath feathered her quivering lips. "I'll do my damnedest to oblige."

Cord pulled Bea against him and kissed her full on the mouth with the whole town looking on. Her mind registered distant gasps and snorts. But as Cord's lips laid claim to hers and his tongue prowled her mouth, all Bea heard was their mingled heavy breathing and a low roaring in her ears.

There was a world of difference between the repulsive kisses she'd endured from her former fiancé and the manner in which Cord's mouth ravished hers. Indeed, she'd never believed such a kiss existed—teasing, masterful, and seductive. Though only his lips moved over hers, the heat of his body had Bea quivering with unleashed passion.

Light-headed and deliciously warm, Bea rested her palms upon Cord's hard, warm chest and kissed him back. Tentatively at first, then taking a chance and kissing him as he'd kissed her.

She forgot about Benedict and Mrs. Mimms. Forgot their onlookers were still watching. Forgot her marriage was one of convenience—not passion.

A deep moan vibrated from Cord, then his mouth deserted hers.

Bea blinked several times before she could focus on him. Her husband looked far too smug. Unease took root in her again.

"If the whole town wasn't watching, I'd tip my hat to you for a damned convincing performance." Cord straightened and took up the reins, all the while wearing an insufferable grin.

Bea struggled to regain her composure. It wouldn't do for her arrogant husband to know the passion she had exhibited was real. "Thank you. May I applaud the role of adoring husband you—dare I say—portrayed with surprising expertise."

"I wasn't aiming for adoration." Cord tipped his hat to the gathering. "Judging by their slack-jaw looks, I'd say they know damn well what that kiss implied."

Bea cringed, dreading she knew, too. "And that would be?"

"Lust, Trixie. Good ol' hot and urgent lust." With a low, rumbling laugh, Cord urged the horse into a trot.

He needn't have told Bea his kiss intimated sexual promise. Her body recognized and responded to him with an urgency that left her breathless, left her wanting more. Just like her heart warmed a bit every time he called her Trixie.

It all seemed so very natural. So very right being married to Cord Tanner. But nothing could be more wrong. A quick glance at her retainers told Bea they realized that, too.

Benedict fixed his interest on the businesses they drove past while Mrs. Mimms tried to hide her blush behind a black silk handkerchief. No doubt they wondered what social graces Bea would trample next with her husband-in-name-only.

Bea closed her eyes a blessed moment. Her plan to avoid

any intimacy with Cord would be so easy to ignore. All it would take would be a few kisses and she'd be lost again.

Logically, she had to avoid kissing him. If she adhered to her rules, he'd do likewise. It was up to her to set the example.

She drew in a bracing breath, pleased she had the courage of her convictions, and tried not to admire Cord's arresting profile. The lines fanning around his eyes bespoke of hours working in the sun. He had a crooked nose, causing her to believe it'd been broken before. As for his mouth—

He glanced at her and Bea snapped her head around, hating that Cord had caught her watching him as much as she hated the directions of her earlier lusty thoughts.

"Do bear in mind it's not necessary to display such false affection toward me in the future." That reminder should put her back into control of their association.

"I thought you wanted to con your grandpappy into thinking this marriage is real."

"I do. But my grandfather didn't witness it."

"He'll hear about it. When your grandpappy arrives in Revolt, those fine folks will flap their jaws about how I kissed you senseless in the middle of town, then hurried you back to the ranch to bed you."

Crudely stated, but the truth. Cord kissing her in public had caught and held the attention of the gossips. Since Arlene and her peers delighted in repeating anything hinting of scandal or impropriety, they'd publicize the deep affection they'd witnessed between Bea and Cord, and assume jealousy was at the root of Mr. Yancy's snide remarks.

"Which way to your ranch?" Cord asked as they approached the fork in the road outside of town.

"To the right." Bea pointed to the route that angled over the undulating plains toward the Prairie Rose.

Cord slowed the surrey and looked at her. An expression Bea recognized as melancholia came over his face.

"Is something amiss?" she asked.

"Nope." Cord stared at her mouth, then turned his attention to the road as he guided the surrey toward the ranch, his back stiff, his features guarded.

She pressed trembling fingers to her tingling lips. He had kissed her to prove a point. He didn't do it because he truly wanted to. She mustn't forget that.

Indeed, after witnessing Cord's initial reaction to her proposition, Bea was sure Mr. Oakes hadn't told Cord what she'd expected of him. If Cord had known, the meeting wouldn't have taken place. If that had happened, or if Cord had turned down her offer, she didn't know what she would've done.

True, she'd implied to Cord that his refusal to marry her left her no other choice but to propose to Gil Yancy. But she'd lied. After what had happened following her papa's tragic death, she never would've married Gil Yancy.

Bea had invested considerable effort making a stable home life for herself and creating a breeding program for her hunters since she came to America five years past. She wasn't about to allow any man to dictate how she managed either.

"It isn't much farther," Bea said, anxious to reach the sanctity of her home. "You should be able to see the Prairie Rose when we top the next rise."

Cord shifted on the padded seat. The last time he'd traveled this stretch he'd been going in the opposite direction at a full gallop. There'd been nothing but bare land between the spread at the far end of the road and the fork. No farms with sod houses. No ranches owned by foreigners. No fences. This part of the county had changed. Or had it?

As the surrey crested the hill, Cord caught sight of his bride's ranch to his left. His gaze ambled over the land where he'd hang his hat for a month. He hadn't aimed to say much, if anything, about the place, but he couldn't stop whistling in surprise at the spread before him.

Cord had figured the Prairie Rose was a cocklebur outfit,

a small ranch with a handful of stock. A good look around told him he'd been wrong.

A herd of fat Hereford cattle grazed on buffalo grass in a fenced pasture while a dozen or so thoroughbreds kicked up their heels in another one. Brown haystacks squatted on the horizon. Row upon row of corn covered another parcel.

To the south of the red barn trimmed in whitewash stretched a fine-looking orchard. Cord licked his lips. Apple, judging by the red stragglers he spied in the branches.

He never passed up the chance to sink his teeth into a juicy apple. Never turned down apple pie. Nothing chased the trail dust from his throat better than cold, sweet cider.

And nothing got him into trouble as much as those times when he'd guzzled too many glasses of applejack. Like last night.

Cord stared at the prairie he hadn't been able to blot from his mind and wondered again how Ott had convinced him to stick around. Had he struck a bargain he'd live to regret?

"Do pull up in the circle fronting the house," she ordered.

"Yes, ma'am."

Cord booted the past from his mind and guided the surrey toward the house. Before he hauled back on the reins, a short, stocky man stepped forward to take charge of the horse. The ranch hand smiled at her and the servants, but his good mood disappeared as he sized up Cord.

Giving the man a nod, Cord jumped down and took a better look at the red brick house rising two stories above the plains. He'd expected Miss Northroupe to live in a fine farmhouse, but this was a damn sight fancier than most of the homes in Revolt.

The sun glinted off the paned windows while the roofed porch kept the double front doors in deep shadow. It brought to mind another house Cord had known all too well.

Yep, a scruffy little boy could huddle under that front porch all night and half the day. He wouldn't have to listen to the pleasure and pain taking place inside. He wouldn't have to watch the comings and goings.

But Cord had. And late into the night, he'd dreamed of having a better life one day.

"Are you all right?" she asked him.

Cord shook his head and tore his gaze away from the house. When this temporary job ended, he'd be able to buy a spread far from Revolt. He'd start small and work hard. Someday he'd be a prosperous rancher. Someday he'd earn respect.

"Just thinking your pa built a right fancy place."

"Had Papa been in better favor with Grandfather, I assure you my sire would have built a grander home than this."

Cord glanced at the fine house and wondered if Trixie was satisfied with it. She was probably like her pa. Hadn't Gil accused her of scraping the bottom of the barrel by marrying Cord?

Curious if his bride would touch him now that they were back on her ranch, Cord offered Trixie a hand. Waving away his help, she presented her sweet backside to him, lifted her skirt, and commenced edging off the surrey.

"Careful you don't break your neck climbing off your high horse," he said, riled that she didn't want his help.

She let out a throaty laugh. "You'll discover I'm quite capable of managing on my own."

Oh, he was discovering a lot about her, all right. As she climbed from the surrey, he couldn't help but admire his bride's rounded backside and shapely ankles. To his surprise and annoyance, watching her stretch and shift gave him a hard-on.

She dropped to the ground and gave her ugly skirt a shake. "Papa incessantly complained about our cramped living conditions on the Prairie Rose while I continually reminded him that we were fortunate Grandfather provided funds for us to afford a decent roof over our heads."

He snorted, recalling some of the dumps he'd called home over the past ten years. "Damned fine roof, if you ask me."

"I couldn't be more pleased with my home."

She smiled so wide that twin dimples sank into her cheeks. That got him to thinking of other places a woman dimpled. Places a man liked to kiss and fondle.

Cord thumbed his hat back and swiped the sweat off his brow. He was getting harder and hotter by the minute, and his brain kept nagging him that she was his wife.

Damnation, Gil would've claimed his husbandly rights by now. That was all it took to cool Cord down. She was his temporary wife in name only. If he wanted to save himself future misery, he'd best keep that in mind.

She marched onto the porch, pushed open the doors, and whisked inside. Cord grabbed his rifle and saddlebags and trailed her into an entrance hall that dwarfed any of the rooms he'd ever called his own.

He whistled, and the echo carried up the wide staircase. "Can't imagine any man feeling cramped in this house."

"Papa was a snob through and through, believing our former manor in England with its thirty bedrooms and a staff of twenty was barely adequate. To him, the circumstances we encountered in America were far too primitive."

Her pa's highfalutin ways confounded Cord. Any man would be right proud to own this spread. "If he liked England so much, then why'd he leave it?"

"After gambling away our home, Papa had no other choice but to follow Grandfather's dictate to come here." As if she'd remembered that Cord had lost everything in a card game, Bea's mouth stretched flat. "That's why I detest gaming."

Head high, she swept through the doorway to his right. Cord filled his lungs with air and followed her into a fussy parlor.

"This place ain't been here long."

"Grandfather bought this land years ago, but he'd never done anything to it. When Mr. Turnley organized the settlement of Runnymede in Kansas and offered to teach farming to Britain's sons of nobility, Grandfather ordered Papa here."

"I heard their farming venture failed."

"Indeed it did. Mr. Turnley and most of my fellow British citizens returned to England en masse. A few of them chose to stay. Papa had no choice."

She planted herself before a big stone fireplace. He stopped beside her and took in the portrait above the mantel.

A gentleman, decked out in a black derby, red coat, fitted white breeches, and knee-high black boots, peered down at Cord from atop a horse. The stock of a black quirt protruded from under one bent arm. One black-gloved hand gripped the reins of a sinfully black stallion that appeared to be in the prime of its life.

Cord stepped closer to read the brass plaque nailed to the picture frame. "'Sherwin Reginald Northroupe on Zephyr, November 1890, Prairie Rose Ranch.'"

He glanced at her. "Your pa?"

She nodded. "And my prize stallion."

He caught the glint of moisture in her eyes and slid his gaze to the painting. Northroupe oozed power and wealth and good breeding, everything Cord lacked in spades. Yet through a stroke of bad luck, they'd both ended up stranded on the Prairie Rose.

Cord bet Northroupe would've just as soon headed back to England with the other British residents who turned Runnymede into a ghost town. Like most of those foreigners, Bea's pa had been a fish out of water here, just like Cord had been when he'd come to Revolt at age thirteen.

"How did your pa die?" he asked.

"Papa broke his neck," she said in an unusually high, cracked voice. "He and his cronies were fox hunting, though in truth, they were foxed and chasing after a poor harried coyote. According to the other riders, Papa raced ahead of the field. They saw Papa set Zephyr for a jump, but seconds before the approach the stallion went berserk and pitched Papa off." Her lower lip trembled. "Papa died instantly."

Reminded of his close call with death, Cord shrugged the shoulder he'd injured nearly a year ago. It still pained him from time to time. "What happened to the stallion?"

She rubbed her arms and let out a long, tired sigh. "Against the wishes of all, I ordered Zephyr returned to his stall instead of having him disposed of. I won't ride him due to the trauma he suffered, but his lineage is paramount to my breeding program."

The housekeeper tramped into the parlor before Cord could ask her why nobody could ride the stallion. To his way of thinking, you could ride any horse fit enough to stand at stud.

Trixie smiled at the older woman. "Yes, Mrs. Mimms?"

The housekeeper tossed Cord a guarded look. "I readied the master's room like you asked. Would there be anything else?"

"That's all." Shoulders squared, Bea marched toward the staircase. "Come along, Cord. I'll show you to your room."

Cord brushed two fingers along his hat brim as he passed the housekeeper. He mounted the flight of stairs, rifle in hand and saddlebags slung over a shoulder.

No doubt about it, the fancy rugs and furnishings reminded him of another mansion, one he'd tried to forget but couldn't.

Cord shook off those haunting memories and followed the sway of his bride's inviting hips down a carpeted hall. Spindly-legged tables cluttered with vases overflowing with paper roses crowded the hallway. Paintings of villages where plump, red-cheeked children played hung in gilded, heavily carved frames.

She pushed open a door and stepped inside. "This is— was—Papa's room. It's yours for as long as you're here."

"It's right fine." *Understatement*, Cord thought as he propped his rifle in a corner and dropped his saddlebags.

From design to size to furnishings, Cord had never seen

such a bodacious bedroom. Heavy furniture. Thick rugs. A place where a man felt right comfortable.

The stone fireplace took up one corner. The bay windows offered a good view of acres upon acres of rolling prairie.

A slow smile spread over Cord's face as he scanned the Prairie Rose. This was his ranch. Temporarily.

Rich ranch land. Fine cattle. Prize horses. Crops in the fields. And in the distance—

Cord swore under his breath. Like ash blowing off a burned-out campfire to reveal the baked soil beneath, the exact location of the Prairie Rose became clear. Painful memories lashed him. How many times had he ridden over this land that had been little more than barren open prairie? How many times had he sworn he'd never set foot on it again?

"It's a beautiful sight, is it not?"

He nodded, but his attention strayed beyond the ripe fields and fenced pastures to where the sun glinted off a tinned roof in the distance. Scotty's house.

"Is that ranch over yonder your closest neighbor?"

"My only neighbor." Her nose wrinkled as if catching a whiff of something odiferous. "Prescott Donnelly recently bought the farm next to mine, so his Flying D Ranch now borders the Prairie Rose on three sides."

"Sounds like you're not happy about that."

"I'm not." Worry lines creased her delicate brow. "Mr. Donnelly is a vulture. Whenever a farmer or rancher falls victim to bankruptcy, he buys their land. Several times, he's hired the former owner to sharecrop for him."

Much as he'd like to, Cord couldn't fault Scotty for increasing his holdings. "That's the nature of the business. Some folks succeed. Some don't."

She made a sound of disgust. "After Papa died, Mr. Donnelly offered to buy my ranch. His exact words were, 'I'll gladly take the Prairie Rose off your delicate hands.' Such rot!"

"But you couldn't sell to him even if you'd wanted to."

"That is what I told him. Mr. Donnelly wrote my grandfather, offering him an enticing sum for the ranch and the stock."

Unease trotted across Cord's shoulder blades. "What stopped your grandpappy from selling out to your neighbor?"

"Me." She held her chin high. "Grandfather was bloody well on the verge of accepting Donnelly's offer when I jotted off a hurried missive to announce my marriage."

"And that goaded your grandpappy to come here and set you to searching for a husband to hire."

"Indeed. As Mr. Oakes so aptly put it, 'Grandfather up and called my hand.' The rest you know. But in spite of our rushed association, I believe we'll get along well together."

He shook his head, hoping she was right. "Mind telling me why you don't trust Gil Yancy?"

"Because he is Donnelly's foreman." Bea slipped from the room, adding before she closed his door, "I'd be a fool to trust anyone associated with Donnelly."

Cord rubbed the bridge of his nose and swore. She put a lot of stock in trust. Which meant all hell would break loose when she found out about his past association with Scotty Donnelly.

CHAPTER THREE

Bea dashed into her bedroom, closed the door, and pressed her back against the raised panels. Her papa's chamber was twice the size of her room, and the bow windows contributed to its airiness. Yet when Cord Tanner entered the spacious area, the walls seemed to close in on them. It simply felt too intimate.

Metal chinked with the thud of heavy footsteps in Papa's, no, her husband's bedroom. Door hinges squeaked. Bea listened, recognizing the source as the door leading into the bathing chamber. The hinges squeaked again. Then the footsteps resumed. Steady. Unhurried. Crossing the bedroom.

Cord must be acquainting himself with the room. Learning what lay beyond the interior doors. There were only three.

Panic knotted between Bea's shoulders. Cord knew which door he'd entered the room by and which one opened onto the bathing chamber, so there was only one door left for him to try.

Her gaze strayed to the door connecting her room with his. She stared at the brass lock she'd secured before she left the house. Would he try the knob?

The footsteps continued midway, then stopped. The heavy door to his bedroom opened and shut with a soft clink.

Her pulse pounded in her ears. She waited for him to resume walking. Surely he wouldn't knock on her door.

He moved with the same unhurried pace. The thud of his boots and chink of his spurs grew distant. Cord was walking down the length of the hall. Away from her bedroom.

Bea took off her bonnet and gloves and dropped them on her dressing table. Though Cord had made no further advances toward her after that episode in town, she knew he might weaken tonight. He was a man, after all. If he did, she trusted the sturdy lock on the connecting door would hold tight.

Carefully, Bea removed her onyx eardrops and matching pin and placed the mourning baubles in the small jewel case on her dressing table. She stilled. Her mother's wedding band gleamed back at her. The only piece of jewelry Papa hadn't pawned.

Bea slipped the delicate gold ring onto the third finger of her left hand. She'd vowed to wear the family heirloom when she gave her heart to her husband. When she fell madly, hopelessly in love. But that hadn't happened. Perhaps it never would.

She placed the ring back in the case and closed the lid. Her marriage was a business arrangement. A temporary one at that. Though her stomach pinched at the thought of wearing the ring for appearance's sake, she'd do so when Grandfather arrived.

Two raps on her bedroom door jerked Bea from her musings. As usual, Mrs. Mimms bustled in before Bea bade her enter. She didn't object. Not that it would've done her any good.

Mrs. Mimms had attended Bea since she was a child and was more a mother to Bea than her own had been. The housekeeper's maternal bent was never more evident than at this moment.

"You were always impulsive, but I never dreamt you'd do something so rash." Mrs. Mimms's face creased with worry.

Turning her back on the housekeeper, Bea shimmied out of her dress. "It was the only choice I could live with."

Her period of mourning ended in a week, and since Bea didn't intend to go into town before then, she tossed the outgrown, outdated mourning dress in the ragbag. If only she could throw her worries aside as easily.

"But *can* you live with him?"

"Of course, I can." Bea straddled her corset chair. She rarely asked for the housekeeper's assistance, but as badly as her hands shook today, she needed the older woman's help.

"Married a stranger, you did." Mrs. Mimms set to work loosening Bea's corset tapes.

The promise of normal breathing made Bea fidgety. Or so she told herself to take her mind off her cowboy husband.

"I hired Mr. Tanner to be my temporary husband and he agreed to abide by the terms of my contract. In a month or so, our business arrangement will be nothing more than a memory."

Mrs. Mimms harrumphed as she skulked toward the oak armoire and withdrew a mauve day dress trimmed with black lace and velvet ribbons. "A grand plan you have. But what'll you do if your husband demands his marital rights, I ask you?"

The memory of Cord's lips on hers infused Bea with heat from head to toe. She glanced at the connecting door again and gulped. What would she do if his strong arms embraced her in passion? If he gazed lovingly at her?

Bea shook off any thought of having a real marriage with Cord Tanner. That path led to disaster. Though kissing him was enjoyable, she had to bar all thoughts of ardor from her mind.

"You worry too much, Mrs. Mimms. I'm quite confident Mr. Tanner will adhere to the terms of our agreement."

The housekeeper snorted. "You were 'quite confident' the earl would bequeath the ranch to you after the master's death."

Bea pursed her lips at that reminder. If Papa hadn't broken his promise to her, she wouldn't be in this pinch.

"I trusted my grandfather would abide by Papa's wishes."

"I didn't. Arms up." Mrs. Mimms dropped the dress over Bea's head. "The Earl of Arden is a shrewd old goat. Gulling him won't be easy, I tell you."

"True. But since I'm Cord Tanner's wife, I'm not actually deceiving Grandfather." Or so Bea told herself as she fastened the tiny pearl buttons on her bodice and rose.

Mrs. Mimms crossed her arms over her ample bosom. "It ain't a real marriage if it ain't been consummated."

Bea waved her concern aside. "You're quibbling over the issue. Why would anyone doubt my marriage isn't real in every sense of the word?"

Mrs. Mimms snatched up the ragbag. "Because you don't have the look of a married woman about you."

"And what might that look be?"

"The look that says you know your man." Mrs. Mimms lifted an eyebrow and added one curt nod.

Bea smiled, suspecting Mrs. Mimms was exaggerating again. "I'm quite certain by the time my grandfather makes his appearance, Mr. Tanner and I will know one another very well."

"That's what worries me. He's a bold one, kissing you in public. And you let him." Mrs. Mimms shook her head and waddled to the door. "But mind you, a woman never knows the bloke she's living with until she crawls between the sheets with him."

The housekeeper closed the door behind her, leaving Bea with a new concern. If Mrs. Mimms was right, Bea's plan was doomed. Her only chance of righting it was to consummate her marriage.

Bea trembled at the very idea. Her mama had told her she'd have to endure marital bliss one day. Bea had dreaded the thought. So why did making her marriage real in every sense of the word appeal to her now?

Cord. That's why. His kiss left her hungering for more. And admitting that weakness was what troubled her.

There had to be some means to project a familiar aura with her husband without resorting to intimacy. She simply had to find it.

Cord braced his arms on the rear balcony railing and watched his bride skedaddle down a path toward the long shed near the orchard. It took him a few moments to figure out what was different about Trixie. She'd traded in the ugly black dress she'd worn earlier for a pretty one that showed her curves.

The wind whipped her skirt around the trim ankles he'd admired. Without the godawful hat on, her golden hair blew around her head.

A fleeting memory teased his mind again. He'd seen Trixie at the Bar T Ranch. Seen that sinfully black stallion, too.

Gil's words came back to him. *I seen her first.*

Last year's rodeo. Cord had been laid up in his room, three sheets to the wind. But that hadn't stopped Gil from barging in and bragging how he aimed to marry the English lady.

So why the hell hadn't he? Because Gil was Scotty's right-hand man and Trixie wanted nothing to do with anyone connected with Prescott Donnelly.

He flexed his fingers and shifted his shoulders, watching her every step. The getup she wore would've made a right fine wedding dress. But seeing as their marriage was doomed from the start, maybe it was best she'd married in mourning garb.

A gangly cowboy ambled from the shed and met Trixie halfway. Cord reckoned the man was one of her few hands until she hooked her arm with the cowpoke's and laughed. The sweet, clear sound drifted up to Cord and slapped him in the face.

Cord called himself ten kinds of a fool. Though a preacher

had declared them married, he was nothing more than a hired hand. Trixie was the boss lady. It didn't bother him none if she made cow eyes at one of her other hands.

Trixie and the cowpoke strolled arm and arm into the long shed, looking a damn sight more cozy than a boss lady and a hired hand ought to. The man's whoop caught Cord with a sucker punch.

An imagination honed by experience gouged Cord's temper. He shoved away from the railing and hustled inside. If Trixie expected him to swear off sex for the duration of their short marriage, then by damned he'd see to it that she did, too.

Cord loped down the rear stairs. He tore out the back door and headed toward the shed the cowpoke had herded Trixie into. His long strides ate up the gravel walk in no time at all.

"Aw shucks!" A man's voice carried from the shed. "Why is it when I'm down on my hands and knees, fixing to go at it, you go and poke your tongue in my ear?"

"Honest affection, Jake," Trixie said over a dog's yip and a dull grinding sound. "Now hold still."

"I can't. It tickles something awful." The cowpoke again.

Whatever was going on in there couldn't be good. Teeth clenched, Cord stormed inside. He stopped dead in his tracks and blinked, his anger souring on his tongue.

The cowpoke Cord guessed was Jake was on his knees, all right. But he held a jug under a keg's spigot, filling it with cider. A fat tricolored hound thumped its tail and licked Jake's ear. Five roly-poly pups of mixed breed scampered around the bitch's hind legs as well as the cowpoke's.

Nearby, Trixie stood at a sorting table. Red apples covered the surface, but she appeared more interested in watching the cowpoke's and dog's antics than sorting apples.

Across from her, Ott Oakes, former Flying D cook and one of the few friends Cord had, gave his full attention to operating the apple press. Same as last night, a calico shirt hung off the old man's scrawny shoulders. His leather vest looked older than Cord's thirty years. Worn jeans couldn't hide his bowlegs. Well-oiled, mule-eared boots fit Ott's stubby feet like a glove.

Time, hard work, and personal neglect had played hell on the old wrangler. Thousands of lines crisscrossed a face baked brown by the sun. A hand-rolled cigarette dangled from the corner of his pinched mouth, looking ready to fall.

Cord knew it wouldn't. Drunk or sober, Ott had never dropped his smoke in the eighteen years Cord had known him.

He shrugged off most of his annoyance. If not for Ott and his hard-luck story about his lady boss, Cord wouldn't be here. He wasn't sure if he should thank Ott or kick his behind.

Another look at the jugs of thirst-quenching cider stacked on the floor-to-ceiling shelves on three walls and Cord leaned more toward thanking Ott for getting him this temporary job.

Cord strode toward the old man. "Don't recall you saying you'd traded in your frying pan for a cider press."

"Yep. My wrangling days are behind me." Ott clamped a gnarled paw on Cord's shoulder, and if Cord hadn't braced himself, the pressure would've brought him to his knees. "Reckon you took Miss Northroupe up on her offer."

"Said I would." Or had he? Damned if he remembered what all he'd told Ott.

"You got a snoot full last night and jabbered on and on. Most of it don't bear repeating around a lady." Ott tongued his cigarette to the other side of his mouth, looking from Trixie to Cord and grinning like a possum. "I knew Miz Northroupe could count on you to help her keep her ranch."

The hair on Cord's neck stood on end. Sure as shooting, Ott knew about her fool plan all along. Knowing Ott, he'd probably waited until Cord was skunk drunk to explain it all to him.

No sense in Cord getting his dander up over it. In a month, he'd be paid for his trouble and be long gone from here.

"Actually, Mr. Tanner proposed a better solution that ensures I'll gain the title to the Prairie Rose." Trixie sashayed over to Cord and sent him a nervous smile. "You know Mr. Oakes, of course. This is Jake, who you'll discover is an invaluable ranch hand. Well, go on. Tell them our good news."

Cord set his teeth so hard that his jaw throbbed. Ott knew this marriage was Trixie's idea. So why should Cord pretend he'd asked her to be his wife? Because he reckoned Jake didn't know Trixie had hired a husband and she wanted to keep it that way. What the hell. He'd given Trixie his word.

"We got hitched this morning."

The pups yipped and barked around Jake's feet. "What's he talking about, Miz Northroupe?"

Cord stared Jake down. "Miss Northroupe is now Mrs. Cord Tanner. My bride."

Jake gaped at him. Ott stared at the toes of his boots.

Trixie's smile looked tighter than sun-dried leather. "Mr. Tanner and I exchanged wedding vows this afternoon."

"He asked for your hand and you said yes?" Jake asked.

"She sure did." Cord winked at his blushing bride and slipped an arm around her waist. "Meeting Trixie made me realize I wanted to settle down."

Ott squinted against a curl of rising smoke and looked from Trixie to Cord. "Well, don't that just beat all."

Jake scratched a smooth cheek Cord bet had never seen a razor and turned his puppy-dog eyes on Trixie. "But you said you was gonna hire a foreman so your grandpappy'd see you could run this ranch as good as any man."

"That was my plan." Trixie let out a soft little sigh. "And then I met Mr. Tanner and the rest you know."

Jake stared at Trixie, his Adam's apple bobbing like a cork on a fishing line. "You told me straight-out you weren't gonna marry a feller you didn't love."

"I do recall saying that." Trixie paused, no doubt trying to think up a lie to console her moon-eyed, smitten cowhand.

"Folks marry for all kinds of reasons, same as they always did." Cord smiled down at his tight-lipped wife, thinking that ought to put an end to this nonsense talk about love before it got out of hand. "Time you give me a tour of the place."

Trixie dug in her heels. "I've work to do."

Cord glanced from the apples on the sorting table to Ott. "Can you finish up with Jake's help, or should my bride and I give up what's left of our wedding day and pitch in?"

Jake scowled a hole in the ground, either too riled or too embarrassed to speak. Cord didn't rightly care which.

Ott tongued his cigarette from side to side. "Me and Jake can take care of it from here on out, boss."

Trixie sucked in enough air to make the walls bow in. Guessing what had set her off, Cord nodded to Ott and hustled his bride outside before her temper blew.

"Don't get your drawers in a twist because Ott called me boss," Cord said after he'd herded her away from the shed.

She rounded on him, face flushed, hands on hips, and ripe breasts heaving with anger. "You're not the boss. *I* am!"

"Reckon that's a fact." Cord rubbed his chin, watching the stable hand glance their way as he hauled Cord's saddle from the surrey. "But do you reckon your grandpappy would want you hitched to a henpecked husband?"

She crinkled up her nubbin of a nose. "Of course not."

"Then use your head, Trixie." Cord wrapped his arms around his wife and hauled her against him.

"Let go of me." She pressed her palms against his chest.

"One of your hands is watching us, so you'd best act like a blushing bride." To Cord's surprise, she stopped struggling. "The way I see it, you've got to let me have a say in things."

"What do you propose?" She still had her back up, but Cord saw curiosity flicker in her eyes.

"Every morning, you tell me what you want done around the place and I'll relay the orders to the men."

Trixie mulled his suggestion over for less than a second. "Very well. Now, will you let go of me?"

Cord reckoned he should release her, but knowing he had a chance to do more got the better of him. "Kiss me first."

She was stiffer than a stone fence post. "Absolutely not."

"Come on, Trixie. Just one kiss'll show your stable hand we're a happily married couple."

She pressed her lips together and squinted at him. "Are you sure you aren't suggesting we do this because you're still angry with me for what I told the good citizens in Revolt?"

Cord dipped his head to hers. "I'm a mite vexed with you for tricking me into agreeing with that bunkum. But I promise you one thing has nothing to do with the other."

"I'm most surely lacking wits to consider granting you further liberties. But your argument is sound."

He dipped his head closer to hers, thinking it'd be easy to get drunk on her flowery scent and lose himself in her wide blue eyes. "Kiss me, Trixie. Just like you did in the surrey today."

She bit her lower lip and glanced behind her. And jerked free of him. "Blast you! Nobody is watching us."

Cord scanned the area and swore under his breath. "Your stable man was standing right there a minute ago."

But he was gone, same as Cord's chance of getting a kiss from Trixie. She frowned at Cord like he was a weasel sneaking into the henhouse.

He thought about telling her he'd really wanted to kiss her. But knowing Trixie, she'd probably want to know why he wanted to and damned if he could tell her when he wasn't sure himself.

"I realize you are attempting to play the role of a dutiful husband," she said, her voice brittle. "But do bear in mind public displays of affection are a fault of the common people."

Heat burned Cord's neck. Damn her. He knew she'd felt his

passion and reacted in kind. For one moment, she'd forgotten she was the upstanding lady and he was the hired hand.

"How crude of me. It must've riled you something fierce to be forced to marry me, a man on the bottom of the social ladder, so you could keep your ranch."

"I was not implying—"

The ear-splitting bellow of a horse drowned out the rest of what Trixie said. The unearthly screams bristled the hair on Cord's nape. Curses exploded from the stable, prodding his anger.

"What the hell is going on in there?"

"Something has upset Zephyr again." Trixie whirled and raced toward the stable.

With a curse, Cord ran after his wife. Whether she liked it or not, she might need his help.

Bea hurried down the aisle, terrified what she'd find inside Zephyr's stall. The demonic screams coming from it propelled her back to that horrific day ten months ago when the stallion went berserk and pitched Papa to his death.

As much as she tried, she couldn't erase the image her mind conjured of her papa lying twisted upon the ground while his prize steed pawed the air and screeched like a demon clawing its way out of the pit of hell.

She inhaled a shaky breath and looked in Zephyr's stall. Rory O'Day cowered in the far corner—mere inches from a rearing, bellowing Zephyr. Her heart skipped a beat and nearly stopped. Zephyr had her groom trapped.

Then as now, Bea couldn't fathom how the sweet-tempered stallion she'd watched emerge from a gangly colt into a prize, well-trained hunter had turned into the treacherous beast that attacked any man foolish enough to venture near him. But attack was exactly what Zephyr was about.

Foam spewed from the stallion's muzzle. Lather streaked his velvety black coat, casting hard muscles and taut tendons in vivid relief. His long tail, not groomed for ten months, arched high in the air and fanned out like a witch's unkempt mane. The horse's ears flattened for battle. His eyes blackened.

Rory's eyes went white with fright. The groom held a gentleman's saddle before him like a shield and brandished a quirt like a sword. Each time Zephyr lunged, Rory snapped the whip, which prodded the horse into a renewed frenzy.

All that kept the stallion from stomping Rory was the stout line tethering the horse in the stall. But with such powerful muscles exerting so much pressure, it wouldn't be long before the rope snapped. When it did, Zephyr would trample Rory.

"Keep your distance, Miss Beatrix." Rory pressed his back to the wall and slashed the air with the quirt. "The black devil has gone mad, I tell you. Hurry, with you, and summon Ott. You've no choice but to put the demon down this time."

That suggestion broke Bea's heart. She inched around Zephyr's shattered stall door, summoning her courage to banish her knee-knocking fear. She had to try and calm Zephyr.

Though she wanted to yell at Rory, she kept her voice low and even. "You're provoking the poor creature. Stop waving that blasted quirt about and crawl to the side."

"It's suicide you're asking of me. That beast will kill us both if you don't kill him first."

"Spoken like a true coward." Shaking from head to toe, Bea took another death-defying step toward the frantic horse.

With a whimper, Rory scooted along the wall. As she'd feared, Zephyr pawed the air a scant foot above Rory's head and continued emitting ungodly sounds.

"Zephyr is fighting the saddle. Leave it and hurry along."

Rory shoved the saddle aside. Zephyr lunged again.

Metal screeched. To Bea's horror, the hook tethering Zephyr pulled partway out of the wood. Another lunge and he'd be free.

Her heart skipped several beats. She had to grab the line

and somehow wrestle the stallion under control. If she failed, her groom would meet the same horrid fate as her papa.

Fighting panic and the frightful images that refused to fade, Bea took a teetering step forward. A strong arm banded around her waist and jerked her flush against a steely chest.

"Stay out of the way and keep quiet," Cord whispered.

She managed a wobbly nod. Her terrified gasp remained as trapped in her constricted throat as Rory was in the stall.

Murmuring soft, unintelligible words, Cord crept toward the stallion. Zephyr's head shot up. His wild eyes fixed upon Cord. Low snorts rumbled from the horse's deep, slick chest.

Bea held her breath, knowing Cord was risking his life to save Rory. She should do as Rory asked and run for Mr. Oakes and his rifle. But watching Cord splay a hand upon Zephyr's bunched haunch kept her glued to the spot. Spellbound.

Showing no fear, Cord inched toward the frenzied steed, murmuring those same mesmerizing words, sliding a gentle hand over the animal's quivering black coat. Bea gaped, marveling at the power Cord had over the stallion.

Zephyr blew, snorted, and tossed his head. But to her relief, his powerful hooves never left the ground. The stallion trembled, but didn't sidestep Cord.

Cord unclasped the line from its damaged hook and backed the stallion from the stall. "I want that saddle stowed and the stall repaired by the time I return," Cord said in that same soothing tone.

He led the jittery horse down the aisle toward the door. For the first time since Papa's death, Zephyr was led from the confines of the stable, prancing beside Cord Tanner.

Bea held up her skirt and bustled after the unlikely duo. She paused at the door, stunned. Eternally grateful.

Huffing and puffing, Rory stopped beside her. "Who's this bloke to spout orders?"

"Cord Tanner." She whirled on Rory, trembling with fear and anger. "Whatever possessed you to attempt saddling Zephyr?"

"The black beast has been docile whenever I give him leave into the corral. I thought he'd take to the saddle this time."

"It appears you were wrong. Your mistake nearly cost us the use of my finest stallion as well as risking your life." Bea ignored Rory and turned to watch Cord.

Keeping a close rein on the stallion, Cord loped beside the animal in a circle before the stable. Muscles bulged and flexed across the shoulders and legs of man and beast. The magnificent pair embodied steely grace and power, but it was abundantly clear Zephyr realized Cord was in complete control.

"Behind me back, you went and hired a new trainer, did you?"

Bea couldn't tear her gaze away from Cord long enough to glance at her indignant groom. "Cord is my husband, not a man I hired to usurp your duties. However, Cord has accomplished what you've failed to do in close to a year—gain control of Zephyr."

Rory made a strangled sound. "Married, you say?"

"Quite." A wistful smile curved Bea's mouth as Cord exercised the up-to-now wild stallion. "He's quite good with animals, wouldn't you agree?"

When Rory didn't answer, Bea turned to him. The groom was gone. From the clatter issuing from the stable, she assumed he'd hastened to do Cord's bidding.

Bea stared at Cord and the high-strung stallion prancing beside him. With soft words and a gentle stroke of his big hands, Cord had gained dominance over Zephyr.

She frowned and rubbed her arms again, but the chill went deep. The reason for it was clear. If she wasn't careful, her husband would gain dominance over her, too.

In a short period of time, Cord had taken over as boss of the Prairie Rose. In town, her servants had bowed to Cord's wishes. On the ranch, the cowboys respected and would obey him. Even indomitable Rory hastened to follow her husband's command.

But what unnerved her most was how easily Cord had managed to make her forget their association was temporary. When he embraced her in those strong arms, when his sensuous mouth bent toward hers, all rational thought deserted her.

That scared the wits out of her. Without a doubt, Cord's inclination to dominate could very well destroy her plans for the Prairie Rose. And her future independence.

CHAPTER FOUR

Cord led the stallion to the shady orchard, the tangy scent of apples drifting to him on a warm breeze. He calmed Zephyr with a firm hand and a string of words. It didn't matter much what he said as long as he kept his voice low and even.

He snatched a red apple from a low-hanging branch and bounced it in his palm. The apple was the same color as his wife's cheeks when he'd stolen a kiss from her in town. He'd embarrassed the hell out of her.

That was nothing compared to how she'd look at him when the truth came out. And it'd come out sooner or later. When she found out his family tree was nothing more than scrub brush, she'd be too shamed to show her face in Revolt.

The stallion nickered and tossed his proud head. Hell, even the horse's bloodlines were better than his.

Cord tipped his hat back, leaned a shoulder against a tree, and watched the stallion. Zephyr had damned good confirmation. Powerful legs. Deep breast. Sixteen hands tall. A sound horse except for the dozen or so white lines that marred his withers, girth, back, and haunches. Had the stallion tangled with a barbed wire fence?

Looking over the animal's sleek forelegs and muscular

thighs did away with that notion. If Zephyr had collided with a fence, he'd bear scars on his legs.

Besides, most of Zephyr's scars were thin. Whip lashes?

Maybe, but something sharp had caused three of the horse's jagged scars, and those were smack-dab where a saddle would set.

Cord chewed out a curse. Any man who abused women-folk, kids, or animals wasn't worth the sweat it'd take to bury him.

He plucked a ripe apple off a limb and clucked his tongue. The stallion's head lifted from grazing. Alert dark eyes fixed on Cord and a soft whicker vibrated his muzzle.

"Got a treat for you, Zeph." Cord set the apple in his open palm and held it out to the horse.

The stallion tossed his head and twitched his ears, leery of trusting a human. But the apple was too tempting to resist.

Zephyr inched toward Cord's hand, muzzle twitching. Cord took a step backward. The stallion blew softly, then came closer and snatched the fruit from Cord's hand.

Cord scratched the horse's neck and examined those scars. No doubt about it. A whip or quirt had made them.

"Who the hell abused you, Zeph?"

Trixie's pa? Seeing as the marks looked the same age, Cord had his doubts. A man who beat his horse did it all the time.

Cord ruled out Ott, too. The old wrangler never would abuse horses. Moon-eyed Jake didn't appear to have a mean bone in his body. The way Trixie carried on about training her horses told Cord she used a gentle hand instead of a whip.

That left the Irish groom Zephyr had nearly pounded into a mud hole. Zephyr and Rory were at odds. Cord aimed to find out why.

He led the stallion back toward the stable. The horse paced beside him, spirited but manageable. At the stable doors, Zephyr tossed his head and blew. Restless. Cord patted the nervous stallion's neck and coaxed the animal inside the stable.

At the far end of the aisle, Rory stepped from Zephyr's box. Even from this distance, Cord smelled the mick's fear.

Rory pointed a shaky finger at the stallion's stall. "That black devil wrenched the tether ring from the wood. Hanging by two screws, it is. And the wood's split, I tell you."

"How long you figure it'll take to repair Zephyr's stall?"

"A day at the most," Rory said. "Mind you don't put him on either side of the sixth stall or next to the first one."

"You got stallions in them?"

"Aye. Titan, a fine yearling. They're in the paddock now, but come night, that black brute will beat the walls down to get to them."

"It appears you're going to bed down in a different stall tonight, Zeph."

Rory pointed to a box two up from Zephyr's. "Put him in number three. The beast calms down around Cleopatra."

Cord clucked his tongue and tugged the stallion's line. Zephyr high-stepped, coat gleaming and muscles rippling from the short walk. This horse needed to be rode hard and often. Cord aimed to see to that in due time.

Handling the horse strained the muscles in Cord's arms and set fire to the old injury in his shoulder. He spoke softly and kept a tight hold. Zephyr tossed his head and pranced beside Cord, nostrils flared and scraggly tail arched high.

Anxious to land the stallion, Cord led Zephyr down the aisle to the empty box stall. He snapped Zephyr's lead onto the tether ring, then put his weight on the line to make sure it'd hold.

"Easy, boy." Cord grabbed the cloth hanging over a stall peg and commenced rubbing down the stallion with it.

Zephyr tossed his head, skittish as all get out.

White ears twitched above the top rail in the next stall and a nicker echoed through the thick plank partition. Cleopatra saying hello, Cord guessed.

The stallion lifted his head and blew a couple of times.

With a swish of his straggly tail, he nuzzled the feed box brimming with oats and dived in.

Cord slung the towel over his shoulder, released the snap on Zephyr's halter, and backed into the aisle. Rory hustled toward him with a pale of water.

"I'll take that." Cord filled Zephyr's water pan, then eased from the stall. "We need to talk," he told Rory as he secured the door.

"Aye, sir."

Cord strode from the stable and walked toward the empty corral. Tugging his hat low over his brow, he propped a boot on the board fence and studied the herd of Hereford cattle grazing in the pasture beyond. No doubt about it, they were the finest stock he'd seen in a few years.

Rory came up beside him and cleared his throat. "You saved me life, Mr. Tanner. I humbly thank you for stepping between me and the black devil when you did."

Cord eyed the nervous groom. "I want to know what the hell happened in Zeph's stall today."

"Arrogance, Mr. Tanner. Pure Irish arrogance." Rory downed his head and nudged a pebble through the red dust with the toe of one boot. "Up to now, the black brute and me were getting on just fine. Zephyr saw fit to let me lead him up and down the aisle this week. I even gave him a brisk rubdown yesterday." Stooped shoulders rose and fell. "I convinced myself Zephyr wouldn't balk when I tried to saddle him."

Cord rubbed his chin, having a fair idea what went wrong. "But the sight of that saddle set Zeph off."

Rory bobbed his head. "My fault, it'll be, if Zephyr reverts to the devil he was after the master's death. Aye, you've every right to run me off the Prairie Rose for good."

Cord couldn't tell if the mick was just groveling or if he was owning up to his blunder. "You made a mistake. Every man's entitled to a few." God knew he'd made more than his share.

"Then you're not booting me out on me ear?" A passel of hope hung on that one question.

Cord scrubbed a knuckle along his jaw, wanting to 'fess up that he couldn't fire anyone. He didn't dare.

"What's done is done. Running you off won't change a thing. Just make sure nobody lugs a saddle near Zeph for a while."

"To be sure, you can count on me to keep a watchful eye, Mr. Tanner. But mind you, so you know, gentlemen's saddles are the only ones to rouse the devil in Zephyr."

"You sure about that?"

"Aye. Every morning, the men tote their western saddles from the tack room, past Zephyr and on to their mounts' stalls. Every night when they stable their horses, they carry their saddles past Zephyr and into the tack room. Not once has the sight of them raised the devil in the black brute."

But seeing the sleek Englishman's saddle had prodded the stallion into a frenzy. "I want to take a look-see at the saddle you was trying to put on Zephyr."

"It's in the tack room."

They retraced their steps down the stable aisle to the room in back. Rory opened a panel door and slipped into a room stocked with saddles, riggings, leathers, blankets, and a passel of necessary tack. All of it hung on hooks or fancy saddle brackets. One wall cabinet held a variety of oils and dressings. A collection of veterinary remedies filled another cabinet.

Rory motioned to one of the peculiar English saddles. "This is the one that set the black brute on a tear."

Cord looked it over. The leather was smooth as butter and the corded girth strap was free of burrs.

He settled it back on the saddle tree. "Is this the one Northroupe used the day Zephyr bucked him off?"

"No, sir. That was a fine pigskin hunting saddle, it was. The master sent to New York City for it, but only used it once, God rest his soul."

Cord glanced at the sleek saddles. "Show it to me."

"That I can't do, Mr. Tanner. The saddle's gone, it is."

"What happened to it?"

Rory shrugged. "I couldn't say."

Wouldn't say, was more like it. Rory was doing his best to avoid looking Cord in the eyes. What was he hiding?

"Who put those scars on Zephyr?"

"Mr. Northroupe's foreman. A brute, he was." Rory grabbed a bottle of horse liniment off a shelf and edged to the door. "Would you be needing anything else?"

An honest answer, but Cord doubted he'd get one from the mick anytime soon. "Nope."

"Then I'll be getting back to work." Rory scampered from the tack room and closed the door behind him.

Cord pinched the bridge of his nose. Something wasn't right here. Was there a connection between Northroupe's riding accident, the missing hunting saddle, and Zephyr's scars?

Bea cringed as she entered the latest expense she'd incurred on the Prairie Rose in the ledger lying atop Papa's ornate oak desk. One hundred dollars, paid to Orson Hibbel and Sons to replace the windmill demolished in a cyclone. She could ill afford the amount, but her stock in the far pasture depended on the water pumped by that windmill.

For five years, she'd held a tight rein on Papa's extravagance and operated the Prairie Rose on the Earl of Arden's quarterly stipends. She'd bought what was necessary and paid her servants and hands on schedule. But Grandfather had withheld her last two allotments, believing that would force her to return home.

If not for Mr. Oakes assisting Bea in her enterprise these past years and having a ready buyer in Mr. Poully for the bulk of her product, she'd have been in debt. As it was, managing the ranch had been nip and tuck of late.

Grandfather's impending visit further strained her finances and her composure. He might applaud the penury she'd willingly endured since her papa's death, but if he knew she'd hired a husband in order to gain title to the Prairie Rose, he'd sell the ranch and the stock.

The earl would pay Cord for his services and make sure her marriage to him was dissolved. Mr. Oakes, Jake, and Rory could find work elsewhere, but unless her grandfather welcomed her elderly retainers into his employ, they'd have a devilish time finding suitable employment in America. And her beloved horses?

Bea gave her arms a brisk rubbing. In his recent letter, the earl made it clear that he disapproved of Bea raising hunters because it was a costly hobby. No matter how much she pleaded and begged, she didn't think he'd suffer the expense of transporting her horses to one of his holdings in England.

She could defy Grandfather and stay here in America, of course. But without the means to carry on her breeding/training program, she'd have to sell her thoroughbreds.

Ultimately, the earl's autocracy left her with two unsavory choices: find a suitable position in America, or return to England with him. Either way she'd lose her horses.

Damnation! She wasn't about to let that happen.

Lunging to her feet, Bea paced from the desk to the door, her steps muffled by the blue and white Brussels carpet. She and Cord had to project the image of a blissfully contented couple. But she had to guard against any more public arguments like the one earlier today outside the stable.

Cord shouldn't have tried to trick her into kissing him. But he had, and the only thing that popped into her muddled mind was that displays of affection were the fault of common people.

Bea knew as soon as she said it that she'd insulted Cord. She hadn't meant to. But she was terrified of surrendering to the passion his kisses stirred in her. The emotions coursing through her were too new. Too strong.

She'd intended to apologize to him, but Zephyr had screamed and the moment was lost. Now she had that fence to mend with Cord and precious little time to do it in.

Bea tapped a forefinger against her teeth. No matter. She simply had to make Cord understand that unlike her papa and the bulk of his ilk, she judged people by their worth, not their position or lack thereof in life.

Once that misunderstanding was behind them, she and Cord could become familiar with each other. In short order, they had to find a common ground on which to base their common bond.

Practicing their husband and wife roles around her retainers and Mr. Oakes seemed the wisest course. If they erred, those she trusted most could bring it to her attention. She could correct any wrongs before the Earl of Arden arrived.

Her decision made, Bea tore out of the library and went in search of her husband. Surely, Cord would applaud her new plan.

Bea dashed down the path, skirt snapping in the winds and her half boots crunching the fine gravel. Cord stood with his back to the paddock, facing the house. She took note of his rigid shoulders and dark scowl. Her steps slowed.

If Cord was still brooding over his wounded pride, perhaps she should postpone their discussion until later. Not that she had an abundance of time to squander, but it wouldn't be wise to further alienate her husband right now either.

Better to test the waters before she jumped in. Stopping at the perimeter of the lawn, Bea clutched her hands together and chanced a tentative smile.

Cord didn't return the gesture. Instead, he pushed off the fence and stalked toward her.

The stiff breeze snapped the fringe on Cord's chaps and plastered the sleeves of his cotton shirt to his muscled arms. His footfalls sounded like thunder. His jingling spurs reminded her of the ominous warning made by a rattlesnake.

As Mr. Oakes would say, Cord looked as cross as a snapping turtle.

Her first instinct was to run and hide. Avoid another verbal battle before it started. But that would solve nothing.

Spine straight, Bea lifted her chin and smiled at her husband as if nothing at all was wrong. As if her insides weren't tied into hard knots of uncertainty.

"Hey, Miz North—er, Tanner." Oblivious of the approaching storm called Cord, Jake loped across the lawn pushing their rotary mower. He stopped before her, winded and grinning from ear to ear. "When I get the grass clipped nice and short like, you want me to set up the croquet court for our evening game?"

She smiled at Jake. "Well, I suppose—"

"You'd best forget it," Cord said, fixing his dark scowl on Jake, who reddened and took a hasty step back. "My wife and I have private plans for our wedding night. Don't we, darlin'?"

She'd planned to curl up on a chair and read tonight. Alone. But a bride wouldn't do that on her wedding night, and the realization had her flushing with embarrassment and anger.

"Yes, of course," Bea said. "Perhaps another day, Jake."

Jake bobbed his head, blushing and swallowing. "Beg pardon, ma'am. With this being Wednesday, and us always playing a game on Wednesday, I just plumb forgot you got married and all today."

Cord snorted and took a wide-legged stance before her. Bea needled him with a barbed look. Why must he be so testy?

She faced Jake. "There's no need to apologize. Except for Cord lurking about, nothing is different about me or this day."

"That sure is true," Jake said. "Why, you ain't even wearing a wedding band."

A low growl rumbled from Cord. "Don't you have something better to do than take up my bride's time?"

Deciding it wise to ignore Cord's caustic remark, Bea smiled at Jake. "I took it off earlier and forgot to put it back on."

So much for putting off wearing her mother's ring until the earl arrived. She'd have to wear it all the time as well as play the role of an adoring wife. As if she truly loved Cord Tanner.

"So do you want me to clip the grass today?" Jake asked.

"That would be lovely," she said.

Cord grasped Bea's arm and guided her away from Jake, his touch gentle in stark contrast to his fierce scowl. "You and me have to talk. In private."

Bea couldn't agree more. "I suggest we adjourn to the library." Before her husband led her off, she turned to Jake. "Tomorrow, we'll resume our croquet match."

"Sure enough, Miz North—er, Tanner."

She caught the sad glint in Jake's eyes before he dipped his head and put his back to the task of clipping the lawn.

Bea bit her tongue as her husband hurried her up the path and into the house. Her vow to avoid further public arguments with Cord kept her from reminding him to cease acting the part of a tyrant and behave congenially—as a proper husband should.

Indeed, she issued the orders on the Prairie Rose. Cord merely relayed them to the men. Nothing more. Nothing less. Once they were alone, she intended to remind him of his promise.

Cord herded Trixie into the library and shut the door. A jumble of anger and jealousy swirled within him. He didn't care to admit to one of those emotions, but his wife seemed to spur the devil in him. Even now, watching her sashay to the big desk and settle on the chair behind it like a queen riled him.

Bossing, it appeared, came naturally for Trixie.

She opened her mouth, ready to fly into him.

Cord beat her to the punch. "How did Zephyr get scarred?"

"Our foreman attempted to beat him into submission."

"When did this happen?"

"The day of Papa's accident." She shivered as if chilled. "Our foreman was a horrid man."

A fact he well knew. "Nate Wyles?"

"That is him. Papa hired him. And I dismissed him."

"Because he took a whip to Zephyr?"

"Yes. I ordered that brute off the property."

No wonder Nate had insulted Trixie the day Cord married her. There was a passel of bad blood between his bride and Nate.

"What happened to your pa's new hunting saddle?"

"I've no idea. Have you asked Rory?"

Cord stared into her clear-as-a-prairie-sky eyes and knew she was telling the truth. "Yep. He claims he doesn't know what's become of it."

"I'm not surprised. The Prairie Rose was in a bloody uproar the day Papa died."

"And you had to manage without a foreman."

"Quite well, actually. Mr. Oakes has been a tremendous help to me, and he's agreed to do all he can to train Jake to one day be the foreman. Ask them what became of Papa's paraphernalia."

"Whoa, there. You're grooming Jake for the foreman's job?"

There must've been something in his tone she didn't like because she sat up poker straight. "I most certainly am."

Cord snorted, torn between cursing and laughing. "Good God, woman. Jake's barely fifteen, if I'm guessing right."

Her chin inched up another notch. "Jake recently turned sixteen. And he has pluck, a trait I admire."

"He's an inexperienced boy."

"All foremen were once inexperienced boys, I'd think."

His patience hit its limits. "Nobody in their right mind would let a boy manage a ranch. You'd best put Ott in charge."

"Mr. Oakes doesn't want the responsibility. I can assure you I haven't lost my wits."

Right now, Cord had his doubts, but he kept them to himself. "Then you'd best hire a man who knows ranching inside and out and send this boy back to his pa."

Her blue eyes darkened to violet. "Jake is a bastard and an orphan. He has no father or mother. This is his home."

"So you took him in? Like a stray cat?"

"I gave Jake a job. Not all boys have a father, you know. All they can hope for is to find a tolerant mentor."

Cord shifted, feeling like a mouse cornered by a cat. Somehow or another, she'd found his soft spot and pounced on it.

Trixie rose, the picture of elegance and good breeding—what he lacked. "Since you'll be relaying my orders to Jake, this would be the perfect opportunity for you to take Jake under your wing, so to speak. Share your knowledge with him."

"Reckon I could spend some time with the boy."

"Indeed. I suggest you begin instructing Jake on the finer points of being a foreman, as well as teach him how to work out a schedule for managing the cattle and crops."

Her orders set his back teeth on edge. Damned if he'd kowtow to her every whim. "Whoa up, there. I can give him a few pointers, but it'd take months to teach him everything."

"Of course, you're right. Do what you can, then." Trixie glanced at a shelf clock and smiled. "Dinner will be served in an hour. I suggest we adjourn to the parlor, as is customary, and practice polishing our image of a happily married couple."

"Whatever you say."

"Excellent. We'll chat a bit and enjoy a relaxing drink."

Cord scrubbed a hand over his mouth. A drink sounded good, but he wouldn't risk tossing down liquor this soon after his bout last night. Nope, he'd best stick to cider.

"That homemade brew Ott makes looked mighty appealing."

"I couldn't agree with you more." Her bright smile returned

and her eyes twinkled like stars. "I'm quite anxious to sample this latest batch Mr. Oakes racked off before our buyer arrives to claim his order."

Cord shook his head and trailed his bride, ignoring the warning waving like a bullfighter's cape in his head. Racked off? Must be some peculiarity of the British folks to use the same term for making cider as for distilling applejack.

No matter what he drank or what he did, Cord had best keep his mind on business around Trixie. She was as intoxicating as whiskey to him. But as long as he kept his head clear, he wouldn't land in another fix he'd pay hell getting out of.

CHAPTER FIVE

Hard to tell what woke Cord first, the sunlight stampeding through the bay window or the dull hammering in his noggin. He whipped his head from the blinding glare, then wished he hadn't moved so fast. The room spun like an outlaw bronco. His head throbbed so hard he feared it'd split in two.

Cord slung an arm across his eyes, blocking the annoying light that tried to drill through his pinched-shut eyelids. Hangovers were hell. Ten times worse when a fellow hadn't recovered from the last binge. This time, he had nobody but himself to blame for getting pie-eyed.

The moment Benedict had handed him applejack, Cord should've refused it. But because it riled him that Trixie had roped him into taking Jake under his wing, he'd guzzled down the liquor.

Hiring on as her husband was enough for Cord to stomach. But teaching Jake all he knew about ranching was a whole other thing.

Cord didn't cotton to the notion of wet-nursing the cow-poke. Any fool could see Jake was smitten with Trixie and she was soft on him. Did she aim to corral Jake into marrying her when the boy grew into his feet?

What if she did? What Trixie did after she paid Cord for his services shouldn't trouble him one way or the other. But it did.

So while Trixie perched on the sofa like a nosy squirrel, sipped applejack, and chattered about the bloodlines of her horses, Cord sprawled in a chair, downed a second glass of applejack, and brooded over the fact that Trixie was counting the days until she had the title to the ranch in her tight little fists.

When that happened, Trixie'd boot him off her land and out of her life for good, Cord had reckoned as he helped himself to a third glass of applejack. A spirited filly like Trixie wouldn't want to stay hitched to a maverick like Cord.

By the time Benedict announced dinner was ready, the hooch had tossed Cord on his ass like a bucking bronco. He recollected nothing after lurching to his feet. Blank. Just like he'd remembered nothing after the drinking and gambling binge in Revolt that had cost him everything he'd owned.

Cord held his head so it wouldn't tumble off his body and crawled out of the bed he'd somehow managed to fall into last night. Squinting through one eye, he shuffled in his stocking feet toward the bay windows with one thought in mind—close the damned curtains. Every step echoed like loud whams in his head.

The ranch sounds outside set his teeth to aching. Even his eyebrows hurt something fierce. The rattle of harness rings tolled like church bells. But when someone whistled, Cord winced and clutched his head.

Slumped against the casing for support, Cord shielded his eyes with the velvet curtain and looked out the window. A tarpaulin-covered buckboard pulled away from the long cider shed and rumbled down the ranch drive toward the main road.

Cord rubbed his bleary eyes, certain they were playing tricks on him. They weren't. Keene Poully, owner of the Plainsmen's Lodge, Revolt's only blind tiger business, was driving the buckboard. What was he doing here at sunup?

More than likely, buying cider to make applejack for his illegal drinking establishment.

The door to the bathing chamber opened. Cord whipped around. He didn't like getting caught in his undershirt and drawers when his revolver was nowhere to be seen. But he moved way too fast.

His head spun like a dust devil and his stomach bucked. If he'd eaten within the last twenty-four hours, he'd have lost it here with Benedict watching.

Cord fought the dry heaves and grabbed the window casing to keep from crumpling to a heap on the floor. "What do you want?"

Benedict, stiffer than one of the stone fence posts the sod busters planted across the prairie, stood in the doorway and stared at him. The older man didn't seem one bit sympathetic about Cord's miserable state.

"I've drawn your bath and laid out your clothing, sir. Do you require assistance with your toilet?" Benedict asked.

"I can manage."

"Very well." The old man didn't budge, but his broad brow wrinkled into deep furrows as he scanned the bedroom.

Cord gave the room a long gander, too. He hoped he hadn't busted something last night. The place looked the same to him.

"What else would you have me do, sir?"

"Do about what?" Cord asked.

"My duties, sir. For thirty years, I served as valet and butler to Mr. Northroupe." Benedict inclined his head a smidgen. The token respect rankled Cord. "Since you are officially the new master of the house, I feel it my duty to inquire if you desire me to retain my position of gentleman's gentleman."

Cord scratched his whiskers to hide his annoyance. The old man didn't appear any happier to wait on Cord than Cord was to have a stranger butting into his business. Besides, Cord'd been dressing himself the better part of thirty years just fine.

He opened his mouth to tell Benedict that, then clamped it shut as his gaze landed on his boots. All the barnyard muck was gone. The brown leather gleamed like they had when he'd bought them, and his spurs shone so that they hurt his eyes.

The spare jeans Cord had stuffed into his saddlebag were creased and laid on the raffia seat of a comfortable-looking corner chair. His clean drawers, undershirt, and stockings lay atop them. The other shirt he owned, a blue flannel, hung on the chair's back. His leather vest was draped over it.

On the nearby table rested his Stetson, looking freshly brushed. Beside it lay his gun belt. His silver belt buckle gleamed like it had the day he'd won it for bronco busting.

The only money to his name, two bits, lay in a silver tray on the dressing table's polished surface. Beside it sat the few toiletries he kept in his saddlebags: a pint of Oakley's Bay Rum, chipped shaving mug, soap and straight razor, horn comb, toothbrush, bone-handled pocketknife.

"What did you do with the duds I was wearing?" Cord asked.

"I took them below stairs to be cleaned, sir. Mrs. Mimms attends those duties with expert care, I may add."

Though he'd never owned more than two sets of clothes at any one time, Cord always managed their washing, simply because he was picky about his duds. But he reckoned he'd benefit in more ways than one if he allowed the old man to tend his meager possessions. God knew he needed to cultivate an ally in the house.

"Don't have much, but if you're set on seeing to them, that's fine by me." With that, Cord ambled into the bathing chamber.

Benedict trailed him. "Very good, sir."

While Benedict laid a cake of soap, sponge, and bath brush on a table, Cord stripped and sank into the tub. Warm water lapped above his waist. The soap smelled like honey instead of lye. He sighed and rested his aching head against the high, curved rim.

"Should you need assistance, just ring, sir." After setting a brass bell on a nearby chair, Benedict plodded into the bedroom.

A question popped into Cord's head, but ringing a bell would likely set his head to tolling again.

"Benedict!" he said, his raised voiced paining him.

The old gent poked his bald head into the bathing chamber. "You called, sir?"

"Who saw to me last night?"

"Mrs. Tanner sent me to the bunkhouse for Misters Oakes and Winter. They carried you above stairs, and then I took charge thereafter." Red splotches spread over Benedict's pale crinkled cheeks. "I advised Mrs. Tanner to grant me privacy to attend you. However, she insisted it was her duty to stay by your bedside until you, er, rallied. Only then did she quit the bedchamber."

Cord grimaced. No doubt there'd be hell to pay over him breaking one of her ranch rules. It wouldn't happen again.

"I appreciate what you did for me. I ain't one to drink 'cause it don't take much for me to get liquored up. Guess I'm one of them that can't hold it."

Benedict dipped his chin. "As I am possessed of a like affliction, I fully understand, sir."

Cord sure hoped so. "From here on out, I'd appreciate it if you'd see to it that there's sweet cider on hand for me to drink."

"As you wish, sir." After giving a deep bow that bellowed respect, Benedict shuffled toward the hallway door. "I shall advise Cook to ready your breakfast immediately."

Before the door closed, Cord got on with his bath. The butler seemed a right accommodating sort. Maybe Benedict was glad to have a man in the house, even if it was temporary.

Cord reckoned the old man knew Trixie was in way over

her head. This half-cocked scheme of hers to wrangle the title of the ranch from her grandfather could backfire. If it did, Cord would be out of the promised money and a horse.

And Trixie's dream of owning the Prairie Rose? Cord rubbed his chin. He'd learned early on that dreams had a way of crumbling to dust in your grasp. But he'd signed on to see hers came true.

Cord had his work cut out for him, all right. Experience had taught him that no matter how well they rehearsed their lie, someone was bound to find out the truth. That meant he'd best acquaint himself with this ranch in short order.

Finding little pleasure in relaxing, Cord finished his bath and threw on his clothes. After shoveling a hearty breakfast into his sour stomach, he strode to the long shed and stepped inside. The tang of apples teased his nose and made his mouth water.

He let his gaze drift over the sealed jugs and bushels of apples, surprised it looked as full as it had yesterday. The trough that brimmed with pressed juice was empty, but one jug sat on a table, its cork pushed half in. A tin cup sat nearby.

Cord tugged out the cork and took a sniff. He smiled. Nothing like sweet cider to quench a man's thirst.

He took a long pull of the refreshing drink, then ambled to a inner door he hadn't noticed yesterday. He opened it and stepped into the dark room. The pungent tang of alcohol hung in the cool air. He wrinkled his nose and took a better look around.

Hogsheads filled one long wall. Dates scratched on the wooden lids with a pencil proved they tended the casks at regular intervals. Several barrels racked over a year ago had "ready" scrawled over the date.

One hogshead had its bung removed, proof it was empty. The one next to it had a spigot replacing the wooden plug.

Cord crossed to it, ran a finger under the spout, and caught a drop of amber fluid. He knew what it was before he took a taste. The sweet heat burned his tongue. Applejack.

Curses tumbled from Cord as he turned in a circle, taking in the room a third time. Tubs and vats sat to one side, clean and awaiting use. A box on a shelf held corks and wires.

By a rear door sat crate upon crate of empty glass bottles. The same kind of bottles he'd seen filled with applejack at Keene Poully's Plainsmen's Lodge.

Cord thumbed his hat back and let out a long, low whistle. Sure as the sun rose every morning, his prim and proper British wife was a bootlegger, running a distillery on the Prairie Rose. Ott brewed the applejack. Keene Poully was their buyer.

If the Temperance ladies got wind of this operation, they'd tote their axes out here and tear it down. Seeing as Ott had plied Cord with applejack and coaxed him into helping Trixie in the first place, he had a mind to tap the bungs on her kegs. But he couldn't bring himself to destroy the place.

Though he was born a bastard, Cord was a man of his word. He'd agreed to play the part of doting husband. But he aimed to have a long talk with her about the danger of bootlegging.

The better part of the afternoon passed before Cord managed to corral Trixie in the library. She'd peeled her mane of golden hair into a tight knot at her nape and donned an ugly dress. This one was the color of ashes, making her look wan.

Cord stopped before her desk and hooked his thumbs under his gun belt. "I need a word with you."

"I can't imagine why."

Trixie shuffled papers on her desk, not lifting her head once. Cord took a deep breath and held his ground.

After a long silence hummed between them, she sighed and looked up. Their gazes collided. Her delicate jaw turned anvil hard and her sweet mouth pressed into a thin white streak. Her clear blue eyes accused him of untold sins.

Cord had seen that look on his stepfather's face a hundred times. The older man's disapproval had amused him, but seeing that same look on his wife's face spurred his anger.

Then as now, he didn't deserve it. It didn't help his mood none that he'd brooded all day about what he should or shouldn't do about her bootlegging.

Planting his palms on the desk, he leaned toward her. "When were you planning to tell me you was distilling and selling applejack to Keene Poully?"

Her chin snapped up. "I hadn't thought to tell you at all."

He snorted, figuring as much. "Why?"

Trixie slammed her ledger book shut and drummed her slender fingers upon the polished desktop. "The day-to-day management of the Prairie Rose has, is, and always will be my sole decision."

Not if he put his foot down, he thought, growing more vexed by the second. "Think your grandpappy'll see it that way?"

She twirled the gold ring on her left hand, a frown puckering her smooth brow. "Point taken, Mr. Tanner. Undoubtedly, Grandfather will assume you're managing the ranch now."

"Damn right, he will." Cord smiled, glad she was thinking straight for a switch.

She sucked her lower lip between her teeth and stared at her hands a long moment. "So I must ensure you not only understand how I've kept the ranch afloat, but why I've followed certain, shall we say, questionable paths."

"Like bootlegging?" At her tight nod, Cord settled onto the chair before the desk and stretched out his long legs. His gaze caught and held hers. "Go on. I'm listening."

"Did you know Prohibition was ignored in Runnymede, Kansas?"

"I heard tell most fellows had a rip-roaring time of it." As well as having the money to afford the high prices demanded by Runnymede's highfalutin drinking establishments.

"Indeed. Grandfather sent Papa a quarterly stipend, but

instead of using it to fund the Prairie Rose as Grandfather intended, Papa squandered most of it on gambling, drinking, and other lewd vices." Trixie wrinkled her nose in disgust. "Aspects of life, it would seem, you're intimately acquainted with."

He forced a smile, but it riled him that Trixie judged him to be as shiftless as her father. "I ain't a gambler or a drunk."

"Two years ago," she went on as if he hadn't spoken, "I learned Mr. Oakes was brewing small batches of applejack for his personal use. I sampled it and believed it superior to Papa's imported brandy, but Papa scoffed at the thought of drinking a common brew. I put it from my mind, until Mr. Oakes remarked how applejack sold for twice the price of cider. That was when I realized we stood at the threshold of a lucrative business."

"An illegal business," Cord reminded her.

"I'm aware of that. But with Papa's penchant for squandering money, I was in desperate need of funds to keep the ranch from failing. I told Mr. Oakes if he could find a discreet buyer for his applejack, we'd supply the gentleman with quality liquor. Mr. Poully contacted me afterward and promised he'd buy all we made. The money I earned from that agreement saved this ranch."

Cord shook his head, admiring her single-minded effort to succeed where so many had failed. "You've risked a helluva lot to keep this ranch from going under. Why didn't you take out a mortgage at the bank to tide you over, or tell your grandfather the truth and ask him for a loan?"

"If Grandfather had known the dire straits we were in, he would've ordered us to return to England two years ago and I would've lost the Prairie Rose." She tapped her front teeth with a finger. "However, even if I had clear title to the land, I'd hesitate appealing to Eli Holmes. I wouldn't be surprised if that man would foreclose on his mother should she be late with a payment."

Cord silently agreed with her, doubting Holmes had a decent bone in his body. "So you decided to chance bootlegging?"

"I decided to provide what men were importing into this state." An odd light glimmered in her eyes. "This is my home, where I intend to live out my life. I'll do anything to keep it."

"Including marrying a down-on-his-luck cowboy?"

"We struck a bargain that will benefit us both." She stared at his mouth, licked her lips, and blushed. "As I said before, I believe we'll get on quite well."

Thinking of them taking a lusty roll in the hay sent a jolt of heat to his groin. He shifted to ease his full-to-bursting feeling. Losing the battle with the applejack embarrassed him enough; he didn't want her knowing he couldn't control his body.

"About what happened last night."

Frost iced her narrowed eyes. "You need not explain."

He scrubbed a hand over his chin and cursed under his breath. He'd listened to her. She could damn well do the same for him. "I can't handle liquor, so I avoid it or limit myself to one glass. You got my word I won't get soused again."

"I should hope so, considering what you said to me last night while you were inebriated." Trixie hiked up her chin and sprang to her feet. "Now, if you'll excuse me, I'm running a tad behind schedule for my croquet match with Jake."

Cord leaped to his feet and stepped into her path. He wasn't about to sit by while Trixie played courting games with Jake, her wet-behind-the-ears foreman who got all moon-eyed whenever she favored him with a smile.

"Wait a minute. Just what did I say last night?"

High color rode her cheekbones. She wouldn't look him in the eyes. "I refuse to repeat your vulgarities."

He snorted, figuring she was making a mountain out of a molehill. "Come on. What I said can't be all that bad."

Her gaze flicked to his. "You—don't—remember?"

"Not a word." The steely glint in his wife's eyes told Cord she thought he was lying through his teeth.

"Then I suppose I should be thankful for your alcoholic stupor." Head held high, Trixie marched past him.

Cord took off after his wife. His boot heels drummed the polished wooden floor in the hallway with long, determined thuds. He stomped onto the back porch and caught sight of her crossing the yard to Jake.

The boy's big old smile made Cord's gut clench. He knew firsthand how an experienced older woman could use her charms to convince an untried young man to do anything for her—or to her. Jake was easy pickings.

Besides, Cord reasoned as he followed his wife, Trixie had hired him to be her adoring husband. It was high time he held up his end of the bargain and gave her what she'd asked for.

As Bea expected, Jake had set up the croquet court and patiently waited for her. She tried to push her humiliating scene with Cord from her mind. She couldn't. He might have forgotten his lurid remarks of the night before, but she certainly hadn't.

What Cord said he'd wanted to do to her had shocked Bea speechless. She'd fled his room, too mortified to favor Benedict with a glance, too determined to forget Cord's lusty suggestions. But in the privacy of her bedroom, imagining Cord doing those things to her had unfurled a hot ribbon of desire deep within her.

Throughout the day, what could happen between her and her husband had haunted Bea. All she had to do was welcome him into her bed. For an insane moment in the library, she seriously considered doing just that—until Cord admitted not recalling one bloody word he'd said to her last night.

It was just as well. Bea would put it from her mind, too. She stopped before Jake and forced herself to return his smile.

"Which color you want?" Jake held up the box of balls.

She reached for the blue one, then paused when a long, masculine shadow fell over her. Cord. He stopped behind her, standing so close the heat from his body burned hers. The masculine scent that was uniquely his made her senses reel.

Every carnal thing Cord had promised to do to her naked flesh trotted boldly across her mind's eye. Her mouth went dry. Against her will, her body quivered and a surrendering moan rose in her throat.

"Red," she said, picking the color that matched her mood.

"Believe I'll try blue." A powerful arm reached over her shoulder and long, tanned fingers snatched the ball from the case.

Her wits took momentary leave.

Jake gulped and looked from her to Cord, seeming ill at ease. "You're fixing to play a game with us, Mr. Tanner?"

"No," Bea said at the same time Cord said, "You bet."

Whirling around, Bea tipped her head back and glared at her husband. "Do you know how croquet is played?"

"Yep." Cord flashed Bea a positively devilish smile that brought heat rushing to her cheeks. "I look forward to playing quite a few games with you."

Mortified at the lewd ideas that took up residence in her muddled brain, she spun around and favored Jake with a trembling smile. "You may begin."

"According to the rules, red goes first," Cord said.

Jake scowled. "He's right, Miz North—uh, Tanner."

After sliding Cord an oblique look, Bea took up a mallet, set her red ball before the home stake, and gave it a solid smack. The ball expertly shot through the first two wickets.

Approaching her ball again, Bea gave it a light tap. Her ball rolled across the clipped grass and stopped behind the third hoop, putting her in an excellent position for the next round.

"Not bad," Cord said dryly.

She smiled with smug satisfaction. "Thank you."

"Miz Tanner's real good at croquet." Jake positioned his

white orb and smacked it through the first two hoops, then gave it another hit that sent his ball wide of her red ball. Purposefully missing hers, she suspected with a resigned sigh.

"I'm a fair shooter myself." After issuing that boast, Cord took his turn. As his blue ball rolled smoothly through the first two hoops, he flashed Bea a challenging smile and took great pains lining up his next shot.

Bea frowned, wondering at his move. Her mouth dropped open. Blast it all! Her husband fully intended to roquet her ball.

Cord's mallet thunked wood. Annoyance grew in Bea as his blue ball rolled across the clipped lawn, hitting her red one with enough force to send it skidding to the boundary line. His player stopped, directly in line before the next wicket.

With a solid tap, Cord sent his blasted blue ball sailing through the third hoop. It rolled to a stop, perfectly aligned before the fourth arch, she noted with admiration and disgust.

After whacking it through the fourth and fifth baskets, he gave the ball another firm tap. It landed squarely before the sixth hoop. Cord let out a smug laugh that further goaded her into action.

With blood in her eye, Bea took careful aim. Her red ball bounced across the lawn and knocked Jake's ball. Cord's mirth turned into a disbelieving snort.

Bea sent her infuriating husband a victorious smile, apologized to a down-in-the-mouth Jake, and drove her ball, which she now imagined as being Cord's hard head, through the third, fourth, and fifth arches with precise taps.

Taking careful aim, Bea gave her ball a good thwack. Her shiny red orb hit Cord's blue one and sent it skidding far off his mark. She hooted with genuine glee.

Bea batted her eyelashes at Cord and beamed. "Top that."

Cord sent her a slow, calculating grin. "With pleasure."

The game was on.

In her entire life, Bea had not played such a challenging,

cutthroat game of croquet. Cord didn't give her an inch, playing ruthlessly, playing to win. She'd never tried so hard to beat her opponent. Nor had she ever been this intentionally pulled off her game by another player, but each smug smile, laugh, clucking of tongue, or cough Cord made was done solely to distract her.

Bloody hell, but his ploys worked admirably.

As she and Cord played cat and mouse on the return route, Jake seemed more intent on helping her best her husband than paying heed to his own ball. A terrible error. Jake's obvious favoritism eroded Cord's earlier good mood.

The boy left himself in a vulnerable position and Cord took advantage. Lining up his ball to the white one, Cord gave it a hard whack. Wood cracked wood. Jake's ball shot across the lawn and road, whizzed under the white board fence, and disappeared somewhere in the pasture. Bea could only gape.

Jake's cheery expression toppled into the doldrums. "Aw, shucks," he mumbled, then ambled after his white ball.

Cord, grinning and obviously pleased with his prowess, set up his next shot. It took her a moment to realize Cord planned to send her ball the way of Jake's, even though it wasn't standing in his path.

"How dare you," she gasped.

Her husband wiggled his eyebrows and grinned. "I play to win, darlin'. Always. In everything."

With a thwack, the blue ball Bea had grown to despise skipped across the grass and hit her red one, sending it to the boundary. Cord had the gall to chuckle.

Bea bunched her fists at her sides and fumed. Like Jake, she had to waste a shot to get her ball in proper alignment for the next hoop—if she got a chance to play again. Those two barbaric plays put her and Jake far behind Cord. As he'd intended.

Play to win, indeed. Bea glowered at the blue ball as it skipped through another hoop. Cord's soft laugh grated on her nerves. Two more simple shots and her husband would win the game.

She eyed her mallet critically. Unless she stopped him.

"Looks like I'll have to wait for you two to take your turns before I win, though I doubt two more hits would do either of you a lick of good." Cord had the audacity to wink at her. "Care to concede victory to me now, darlin'?"

"Not bloody likely."

He sidled against her, his nearness doing odd things to her insides, turning them to mush. "What's the winner's prize?"

Bea gave an impatient shrug and studied the field. "She usually demands something trivial from the loser or losers," said Jake.

"I believe I'll claim a kiss from you as my prize." He wiggled his eyebrows and flashed Bea his appealing rogue's grin.

Panic swept over her in a sultry rush. With his sensual promises of last night still teasing her senses, she knew if Cord so much as touched her now, she'd melt in his arms.

Refusing to allow Cord's smirks and smiles and winks to distract her anymore, Bea addressed her ball on the boundary and estimated the power she'd need to roll it up against her husband's. Too much and she'd fly right past it. Too little and she'd waste her one chance to get even.

At this moment, getting even was the only way she could put her randy husband in his proper place.

Bea held her breath and tapped her ball. It rolled and hopped across the grass, its revolutions becoming slower, slower, slower. It kissed up against his ball with a soft tap.

She let out a rare whoop and skipped toward the balls.

"Don't do anything you'll regret, Trixie, darlin'." Cord's soft, sexy voice made her tingle, threatening to distract her. "Remember a fine lady as yourself wouldn't stoop to playing like me, a common ol' cowpuncher."

She slid her grinning husband a tight smile. "Please mind your tongue while I'm playing."

His eyes glowed like warm molasses. "Speaking of tongues, I'd be right happy having you kiss me like you did in town after I win this game."

The thought of losing herself in one of her husband's hot kisses made her knees weak. Damnation, but the man was sly. He'd succeeded in rattling her concentration again.

"If I win this match, which I'm certain to do," she said with an air of assurance she didn't feel, "I demand that you cease your obscene remarks and embrace the job that I hired you to do."

So saying, Bea rested the toe of her shoe atop her red ball and whacked it a good one with the mallet. As she'd hoped, her ball stayed in place while his blasted blue ball went flying across the court, over the clipped lawn and dirt road, and shooting into the open door of the stable.

Not daring to glance at her husband, Bea took careful aim and drove her ball through the last two hoops to win the game.

"Victory is mine. What have you to say to that?" Bea smiled smugly and looked up at Cord.

The teasing light in his eyes dimmed. "Congratulations. With your permission, ma'am, I'll busy myself in the tack room."

She frowned, not liking his too-polite tone one whit. No doubt she'd pricked his pride and he felt the need to go off and lick his wounds. Or he thought she'd change her mind.

Bea bit her lower lip. God help her, she wanted to relent, but she wouldn't. At last she'd gained a measure of control over him and this peculiar situation she'd instigated.

"An excellent notion, sir," Bea said. "Until dinner?"

Inclining his head, Cord brushed two fingers across his hat brim, laid down his mallet, and strode toward the stable.

As he crossed the court, Jake collected his ball and conceded defeat. "That's real good you won, Miz North—uh, Tanner."

"Yes, isn't it," she said, but she had her doubts about her victory as Cord disappeared into the stable.

Bea heaved a troubled sigh and hugged herself. True, she'd put her husband in his place. She should pat herself on the back. She should feel relieved. She didn't.

No matter how much Bea tried to convince herself she'd done the right thing, she couldn't squelch the disquieting notion that in doing so, she'd lost more than she'd gained.

CHAPTER SIX

The sun was peeking above the horizon when Cord reined in Ott's calico gelding by the rail fence. As he'd done three mornings straight, he unsaddled the horse, rubbed him down, then freed the animal of its bit and turned him into the corral.

Cord hooked the bridle and loose riggings over the saddle horn, picked up his saddle, and headed toward the tack room. His sore shoulder throbbed from toting forty pounds of leather, but the pain was nothing compared to the lonely ache in his gut.

Halfway down the stable aisle, Rory stepped from a stall toting an empty bucket. He stared at Cord.

Cord swore under his breath. If time hadn't gotten away from him, he'd have been back and chowing down before the crack of dawn. But he just couldn't bring himself to hurry this morning.

"Good morning, sir."

"Morning."

Cord walked by Rory. Saying more might goad the mick into asking where he'd been. He didn't aim to tell anyone, though he reckoned Ott knew where he went and why. Ott wouldn't talk.

Rory might, seeing as he was loyal to Trixie. If she knew

where Cord rode to every morning, she'd have a conniption fit. Maybe even tear her contract in two and boot him off the ranch.

Even so, Cord wasn't about to stop. But he'd be more careful from here on out. It'd been years since he'd been in these parts and, once he left this time, he didn't aim on ever coming back.

Cord slung his saddle over a bracket and spread his blanket atop it to dry. He hung the bridle on a peg, then slipped out the side door. By the time he reached the house, the sun was full up.

The smells of fresh baked bread and frying meat greeted Cord. Stomach grumbling, he ambled to the dining room. The second he took his seat at the table, Mrs. Delgado set a plate of eggs, fried potatoes, and spicy sausage in front of him.

"Eat. I baked *pan dulce*, too." Mrs. Delgado set a plate of sweet rolls on the table. "And take off your hat."

"Yes, ma'am." Cord set his hat on an empty chair, then dug into his breakfast. "Hmm-mmm. No doubt about it, you're the best cook in five counties."

"Ha! You've been talking to Ott. After eating at my table, the old coot says he can't stand to eat his own meals. I think he is just tired of cooking."

Cord had a hunch Mrs. Delgado's cooking wasn't the only thing Ott had a hankering for. He doubted it was coincidence that the widow and Ott had ended up working on the same ranch again.

"You might be right. But I've eaten many a meal out of his chuck wagon and, hands down, yours is the best."

She laughed and poured his coffee. "Next you'll be telling me that you like my *café de olla* better than cowboy coffee, *sí*?"

"Yes, ma'am, that's a fact."

Before Cord could partake of his spiced coffee, Trixie waltzed into the dining room. "Good morning."

"Morning." Cord set his cup down and rose.

"Hot chocolate, if you please," she said to Mrs. Delgado.

"*Sí*, Señora Tanner." Mrs. Delgado bustled into the kitchen.

Trixie smiled as Cord pulled out the chair opposite his and seated her. "Thank you." She helped herself to a sweet roll.

Cord took his seat and commenced eating. He was busting a gut to get his hands dirty. Work up a good, honest sweat.

"Will you be exercising Zephyr again this morning?"

"I planned to."

"Very well." Trixie blew on the hot chocolate Mrs. Delgado set before her. "After lunch, we'll resume acquainting you with the Prairie Rose ledgers."

"Yes, ma'am."

"I detected a nip in the air this morning. Did you?"

Cord eyed Trixie over the rim of his coffee cup. She nibbled on her sweet roll and sipped hot chocolate, same as any other morning. But something was different about her. Restless, maybe. Or wily as a fox. Had she seen him riding back this morning?

"Nope, can't say I did."

Her eyes took on a frosty look, as if she knew Cord was lying through his teeth, but she didn't say one word.

Cord shoveled down his breakfast. He heard her quick breathing. Felt her eyes boring holes in him. If Trixie came out and asked where he'd gone, he'd own up to a ride and nothing more.

"Reckon I'd best get to the stable and work that stallion." Cord pushed back from the table. "He's coming along right fine."

Her chin snapped up. "You've worked a miracle with Zephyr. For that alone, I thank you."

"Just doing my job."

Before he dared cinch his saddle on the stallion and swing onto its back, he needed to spend a day with the big black. But that wouldn't happen today.

Grabbing his hat, Cord hustled to the stable. He led Zephyr into the corral and worked him on the long line. Round and round in a circle. Speaking the orders sometimes, then doing nothing more than tugging the reins.

Eyes bright and ears forward, Zephyr responded to the slightest brush of the rein on his neck, smoothly switching direction. Cord flicked the line, the stallion stretched into a canter. A tug brought the horse to a trot without balking.

No doubt about it. Zephyr was smart as a whip. Yet the animal had been beaten. Why?

The question nagged at Cord hours later as he climbed the stairs and washed up. Times like now, playing Trixie's doting husband chafed him worse than the new boiled shirt he shrugged into. Somehow, Benedict had convinced Mrs. Mimms to alter a dozen of Sherwin Northroupe's fine shirts for Cord.

He was grateful, but he'd just as soon be working outside instead of wasting his time inside like a mail-order cowboy.

After lunch, Trixie herded Cord into the library like a snot-nosed schoolboy. Like they had the past three days, she explained the proper things he was to say and do in the parlor, the library, and at the dinner table so he'd impress her grandfather. All things he knew, but he didn't tell her so because he figured she'd ask him who taught him and he wasn't about to tell her.

"Let's review the ledger." She leaned close and ran a finger down the list, explaining every penny she'd put into the ranch.

Cord half listened to her. They'd gone over the numbers so many times he was ciphering in his sleep. But he didn't mind sitting close to Trixie. She said words different than most folks, but he liked that about her. And she'd done a right fine job of holding the ranch together.

Yep, Trixie had a good head on her. Gutsy, too. One day, Cord hoped to find a wife like that. One who'd share his dreams. Who wasn't afraid to take a chance. Who'd work by his side.

"Now then." Trixie snapped her ledger shut and spread rolled papers on the desktop. "We've enough time to go over the pedigrees of the thoroughbreds, beginning with Zephyr again. As you recall, we can trace his lineage back to the Byerley Turk."

Cord scanned the names. After reading them day after day, he could recite the horses' bloodlines backward and forward.

So he kept on studying Trixie instead. She'd tucked her hair into a wad at the back of her head, but bits of it worked free and curled around her pretty face. Her eyes were as blue as a prairie sky, and she smelled like flowers.

She was a fine figure of a woman. Her dark blue skirt nipped in at her waist and flared over her round hips. Her white blouse clung to her full breasts. His hands itched to do the same.

In the midst of guessing how much flesh would spill over his palms, Cord realized she'd stopped chattering. He tore his gaze from the rise and fall of her bosom and looked her in the eye.

Cord expected anger. Instead, he saw fear. Or more precisely, he guessed she feared what he might do to her.

Her reaction hit him like a slap in the face. He'd never forced himself on a woman and sure didn't plan on starting now.

But after kissing Trixie senseless in town and threatening to do it again if he won their croquet game, Cord supposed he'd given her call to suspect he'd break his word. Now, he'd been caught staring at her breasts—again.

Trixie's chin hiked up. "Though I believe you've the rudiments of the ranch well in hand, I suggest you take the remainder of the day to refresh yourself on the proper ways that a gentleman comports himself around a lady."

Cord bit back a grin. Those big words were a sure sign Trixie was more flustered with him than afraid.

"Husbands have been known to look at their wives."

"Perhaps, but I'd prefer if you didn't adopt that habit." Trixie hightailed it out of the library like a frisky filly.

It wasn't the first time she'd taken his teasing the wrong way. He aimed to apologize to her later, but he never got the chance.

Trixie stayed in her room that night. Cord picked at his dinner, feeling downright miserable.

Truth be told, he missed sharing a meal with Trixie. Missed her sweet laugh. Missed catching her staring at him when she thought he wasn't looking. Missed her getting on him when she caught him staring at her. Dang it all! He missed his wife.

In her bedroom, Bea barely touched the meal Mrs. Mimms brought up. She couldn't force food down when she was this upset.

"Are you absolutely certain nobody has any idea where Cord has ridden off to the past three mornings?"

"That I am." Mrs. Mimms poured Bea a glass of apple brandy and one for herself. "I asked Benedict, and he asked Rory, and neither of them knows where Mr. Tanner goes off to."

Bea drummed her fingers on the side table. "Since he's never gone more than half an hour, he can't go far."

"Takes a brisk morning ride to clear his thoughts, I'd say."

"You're probably right." She'd intended to question him this morning, but catching him ogling her bosom had flustered her.

At least she finally had Cord's attention. Up until that point, she suspected he'd heard less than half of what she said. What had he been thinking about all that time? Or who?

"Do you suppose Cord has a tryst with a lover?" Bea asked.

"If he does, then he's quick as a fox."

But was Cord as sly as one?

Bea doubted it. If Cord was breaking his vows, she had to put a stop to it before some husband or father caught and challenged him. Before word of his infidelity reached Grandfather's ears. Before everything that she'd risked crumbled in her hands.

Men! When would she learn she couldn't trust any of them?

After his ride the following morning, Cord wasn't in any mood to talk to Trixie. He moseyed into the room sandwiched between the bunkhouse and cook shack to eat breakfast with the ranch hands. It was high time he got some straight answers around here.

Five fat pups yelped and spilled out of their box in the corner. The tricolored hound Jake had been scratching behind its ears jumped up and saw to her litter.

Jake looked put out that Cord joined them, but Rory didn't say a word. Neither did Ott. Cord knew that unless Ott was of a mind to talk, you couldn't pry a word out of him.

Ott offered up bacon and eggs, fried spuds, and a stack of flapjacks. Like the other two, Cord shoveled it in.

Cord washed the heavy meal down with coffee strong enough to peel the newsprint off the wall and hoped Ott wouldn't clam up on him. "Why'd you leave the Flying D?"

The old man took his time rolling a smoke and puffing it to life. Hedging, for sure, Cord thought.

"Time came for me to pull freight and move on." Ott exhaled a cloud of smoke. "I ain't sorry I hired on here."

Cord had felt the same more times than he could count. "Who hired you? Nate Wyles or Northroupe?"

Ott squinted at Cord through a smoke curl. "Northroupe came into the Plainsmen's Lodge and hired four men then and there. I was one of 'em. So was Wyles. A day or two after we settled in, he more or less took over the ranch with Northroupe's blessing."

"Mr. Northroupe charged Nate Wyles with managing the cattle and the land," Rory said.

"But not the thoroughbreds," Cord guessed.

Rory puffed his bantam chest out, all beak and spurs and ruffled feathers, like a game cock tossed in the ring. "The horses belong to Miss Beatrix. She made it clear to Nate Wyles that she hired me to train them. That didn't change."

Cord rubbed a knuckle down his stubbled jaw, imagining Trixie standing her ground with Wyles before her pa died. And after.

"Can't see Wyles letting a lady boss him," Cord said.

None of the hands said a word. They didn't have to. There was bad blood between Wyles and Trixie.

"When did the other two hands leave?" Cord asked.

"Both of 'em hightailed it a few months after hiring on." Ott dug his Bull Durham pouch out of his pocket. "Jake joined us a couple years back and that took the load off. Come haying or branding time, Nate'd round up extra hands. Otherwise the work fell to Jake, Rory, and me."

Though Cord knew the answer, he drank his coffee and let tense seconds tick by before asking, "Why'd Trixie fire Wyles?"

"Because there was two ways of handling Zephyr after me, Rory, and the boy here wrangled him home." Ott's voice was scratchier than sandpaper. "Nate chose the wrong one. He had a mean streak in him a mile wide. When Miz Tanner found out what he'd done to her prize horse, she ran him off the ranch."

Jake's gaze stayed on the hound curled up in a box with her fuzzy pups. "Zephyr was so lathered up that it was late that night afore we could get close enough to drag that saddle off."

Cord tapped his fists on the table, itching to pound the foreman into a mud hole for whipping the stallion. But that beating only accounted for some of the animal's scars.

He hunkered over his coffee cup, staring straight into Jake's outraged eyes. "I'd like to take a look at that saddle."

The color leached from Jake's face. "What for?"

"Because Zephyr is scarred where a saddle sits." Cord slid a sideways look to Ott, who found undue interest in tossing scraps to the dog. "You asked me to give your boss lady a hand. I can't help her if I don't know what's been going on around here."

Ott flicked a glance at Rory who dipped his chin once. "Tell him, boy. I told you before we can trust Cordell."

Silence crackled like firebrands in the stuffy mess hall as Jake stared eyeball to eyeball with Cord. Taking his measure, Cord reckoned. If he were in Jake's boots, he'd do the same.

Jake slapped his palms on the table and pushed to his feet. "Come on. I'll fetch it for you."

The attached bunkhouse was like the dozen or so Cord had called home for eleven years—long, narrow, and low slung, reeking of dirty feet, sweat, leather, liniment, and manure. Yellowed newsprint papered the whitewashed walls. Tacked over it were cattle-breeding charts, area maps, and an occasional photograph.

Half a dozen crude cots jutted out along the long wall, but only three were in use. All of them were rump sprung.

A squat parlor stove hunkered in one corner. In another, a wooden crate belched lengths of latigo, frayed lariats, leather thongs, and buckles to repair the tack.

Bracing a shoulder against the jamb, Cord thumbed his hat back and watched Jake. The lanky boy climbed onto the crude plank table set before the lone window, grabbed hold of the ceiling joists, and hoisted himself up between them.

Fine dust rained down in his wake. Jake dropped a fancy saddle blanket onto the table, kicking up a cloud of dust. Several low grunts and more than a few muttered curses later, the boy maneuvered a gentleman's saddle between the boards.

Cord pushed away from the doorway and grabbed the saddle from Jake's hands. The pigskin leather felt buttery smooth and, despite the dust, still smelled new.

Resting the saddle on the table, Cord searched for peculiarities on a piece of tack that was mighty peculiar to a cowboy. At first glance, he saw nothing unusual. He ran a hand under the padded aprons and something sharp stuck his finger.

Cord flipped the saddle over and examined the slashed, poorly repaired leather. He cursed loud and long. Embedded under the apron were short lengths of two-line double-barbed wire.

After spreading the fancy saddle blanket in the bow of the saddle and taking a closer look, Cord snorted in disgust. Slashes in the thick wool matched the sharp barbs buried in the leather. With weight and motion, the heavy wire had sliced through the blanket and cut the stallion's back.

"No wonder Zephyr went loco. Any idea who worked spiders into this saddle?"

"There was a passel of English fellers at the ranch the week afore Mr. Northroupe died," Jake said. "But Gil Yancy was here three times that I know of, and him and Mr. Northroupe had words."

"Over what?"

"Don't know. But Gil was fit to be tied when he skedaddled out of here the last time."

Cord stared at the damaged saddle, wondering what had set Gil and Northroupe at odds. Trixie was the likely reason. Gil had been sniffing after Trixie for some time. But Cord bet Northroupe didn't cotton to a cowpoke messing with his daughter.

Not being good enough for the likes of Trixie would set Gil off. But Cord couldn't see Gil stooping that low.

Slipping a spider in a saddle was the mark of a cruel man. Though the rider took a hard fall, it was the horse that suffered. Zephyr sure had. Northroupe broke his neck.

"Who all knows about this?"

"Nobody but Ott, Jake, myself, and Marshal Ives." Rory drifted into the bunkhouse. "And the vicious cur that did this."

Cord fingered the slashes in the saddle and rubbed his chin. "I wonder why Northroupe didn't see this when he saddled up?"

"Mr. Northroupe didn't ready his own horse," Rory said. "It was my duty to saddle his mount, but when I reached Zephyr's stall that morning, I found the stallion already saddled."

"Any idea who did it?" Cord asked.

"With all the blokes and their grooms milling about that day, any of them could've done the deed." Rory shook his head, looking wind-flushed and weary. "If one of the riders hadn't broken a buckle on his saddle girth, I'd have had time to inspect Mr. Northroupe's equipage. I'd have noticed something was wrong. But by the time I'd fetched another saddle girth, Mr. Northroupe had mounted Zephyr and took off ahead of the field."

Somebody had made damn sure Rory couldn't check Northroupe's saddle. But did the no-good aim to bruise Northroupe's pride when Zephyr went loco and pitched him off? Or did he hope the fall would kill Northroupe?

Cord took in the three ranch hands' hangdog looks. "Why didn't you tell Trixie what really happened to her pa?"

"We was afraid what she'd take into her head to do when she found out," Jake said.

Rory frowned at Jake and cleared his throat. "After Mr. Northroupe died, I believed the earl would come here straight away and take care of the matter."

"But he demanded Trixie sell out and return to England, which she flat out refused to do," Cord said.

All three of them nodded.

"Miss Northroupe came to me. She had an idea how she could get her grandpappy to give her the ranch and asked me if I knew of a feller she could trust with her life." Ott dug out his makings and stared Cord in the eyes. "That's when I got word to you."

Got him drunk and let him gamble away his horse and

every red cent he had was more like it, Cord thought. He should be mad at Ott for fixing it so he couldn't turn her down. But he wasn't.

Ott was right. Trixie needed his help to get the title to the ranch and find out who'd caused her pa's death.

Late that afternoon, Bea paused studying her thorough-breds' pedigree charts and listened to the clop of hooves and jingle of harness rings. She rushed from the library and peered out a front window. Elation surged within her, fol-lowed by acute nervousness.

As she'd expected, Grandfather had arrived.

Bea tucked her charts away, then shook out her gold-striped emerald skirt and plucked at the pleats in her bodice. She gave the appearance of a proper wife. And she felt con-fident her husband would present himself as a very knowl-edgeable rancher.

All she and Cord had to do to secure Grandfather's favor was behave in a cordial, yet proper, manner toward each other.

Giving her upswept hair a pat, Bea hurried toward the front door. Her heart raced as she tried to think of anything she might have inadvertently overlooked. Nothing came to mind.

Smiling, Bea nodded to a somber-faced Benedict to open the front doors. To Bea's surprise and delight, her papa's only sister bustled inside.

The middle-aged woman wore a gray silk blouse with high stand-up collar and massive leg-of-mutton sleeves. Her navy wool skirt flared downward from the black belt banding a tiny waist.

"Oh, Aunt Muriel!" Embracing her dear aunt's uncorseted form took Bea aback. "What a wonderful surprise."

Behind a dark veil pinned to a jaunty hat, Muriel's blue eyes dimmed with worry instead of dancing with their usual mischief. "Consider me your ally through the trying times to come, my dear."

"Dash it all, Muriel," barked Bea's grandfather. "Don't get the girl in a dither out of hand."

Fletcher Northroupe marched into the spacious vestibule like a reigning monarch. The Earl of Arden's black Prince Albert suit complemented his tall, muscular frame, and the walking stick he wielded with ease enhanced his aura of unquestionable authority.

Grandfather swept his top hat off and handed it to a waiting Benedict, then ran a gloved hand through the wealth of thick silver hair crowning his head. His hand stilled, and Bea knew at once he was staring at the gold ring banding the third finger of her left hand.

Silvery mutton-chop side whiskers and a spade beard framed Grandfather's stern visage. His blue gaze homed in on hers.

"Where is he?" her grandfather asked.

Bea swallowed the panic tightening her throat and fought the urge to hide behind her aunt. "Who?"

Viscount Lambert Strowbridge swaggered into the vestibule. "I would imagine Arden is referring to your husband."

Anger and unease dueled within Bea as she stared at Lambert. Whatever had possessed Grandfather to bring her ex-fiancé along?

Lambert's thick black mustache twitched as if an unpleasant odor dared float his way. He stared down his narrow nose at Bea for a torturous moment. Then his cold gaze slid to her breasts—as usual. His thin lips pulled into a parody of a smile and a trickle of spittle oozed from the corner of his too-thin mouth.

Bea's skin crawled. She vividly recalled what had transpired the last time she'd seen that look on his face. The lecherous oaf.

"My husband's busy at present." Bea regarded Lambert with disdain, wishing she could order him off her land. But it wasn't hers yet. "Would you care for me to summon Cord?"

"Indeed, I would," her grandfather barked.

"We shall all wait to meet your husband before we dine." Muriel patted Bea's trembling hand but targeted the earl with a cutting look. "At present, I believe it wise if we settle into our rooms and rest, Father. It was a dreadfully long journey."

The earl snorted his impatience. "Very well. I shall dutifully wait to meet Bea's husband."

"Rest assured it won't be a long wait." Forcing a serene smile, Bea turned to Benedict. "Do escort Grandfather to his room, and put the viscount in the one adjoining it."

"As you wish, madam." Benedict turned and trudged up the long staircase. The earl, viscount, and two heavily laden men she remembered seeing at Revolt's livery brought up the rear.

With a sigh, Bea faced the women. A distraught Mrs. Mimms hovered behind Muriel, no doubt wondering what bed to give the unexpected female guest. Really, the solution was so logical. At least it would've been logical under normal circumstances.

Bea sent her worried housekeeper a plea for understanding, then squeezed her aunt's gloved hands. "I didn't expect you, so I didn't make arrangements. Would you mind waiting here while Mrs. Mimms moves my personal items into my husband's room?"

Mrs. Mimms's mouth opened. Some inarticulate sound emerged from her, then she snapped her mouth shut, gathered up her skirts, and huffed up the stairs.

A slight frown crinkled Muriel's smooth brow. "I don't mind waiting at all, but are you certain it won't inconvenience you to move into your husband's bedroom?"

Nervous laughter burst from Bea. "Good heavens! Why would sharing a bed with my husband inconvenience me?"

One finely arched eyebrow rose over a discerning blue eye. "Why indeed? Shall we visit in the parlor while your housekeeper makes the necessary changes?"

"Excellent idea."

Bea led the way. Aunt Muriel made herself comfortable on the blue damask sofa. Bea hurried to the sideboard and poured a sherry for her aunt. Hands trembling, she splashed a generous dram of applejack for herself.

Quaffing hers down, Bea handed the sherry to Muriel and then backed to the door. "If you'll excuse me for a few minutes, I need to speak with Cook." *And warn Cord of Grandfather's arrival and the adjustment in the sleeping arrangements.*

Muriel waved her off. "Do take your time."

Bea dashed down the hall. Like it or not, she'd share a bedroom with her husband tonight.

An image of lying beside Lambert, the man she'd expected to marry, rushed over her, filling her with old fear and new dread. She couldn't give in to panic. Surely Cord would be a gentleman about the whole thing. And if he wasn't?

Then she'd simply deal with it when the time came.

CHAPTER SEVEN

Bea paused at the kitchen to alert Mrs. Delgado of their guests and then darted out the back door. Lifting her skirts, she raced down the path to the apple shed.

She poked her head inside. "Where's Cord?"

"Last I saw, he was headed for the stable," Mr. Oakes said, not looking up from the apples he dumped into the hopper.

Bea whirled and headed for the stable at a dead run. She scurried down the aisle, slowing to check each stall she passed. In Titan's, she found Rory.

"Is Cord about?"

Rory motioned to the back, his weathered brow puckered. "In the tack room, he is. Been there all day. By the curses coming from there, I'd wager this isn't a good time to disturb him."

"I'm afraid there's no help for the intrusion," she muttered more to herself than to Rory. "Grandfather has arrived."

Not bothering to see how Rory greeted that news, Bea sprinted toward the room at the back of the stable. Taking a deep breath that did little to slow her racing heart, she lifted the latch and swept inside the tack room.

The door shut and the aroma of tanned leather enveloped

Bea like an old friend. She'd always gained a measure of comfort coming into this small masculine room, but not today.

Cord glanced up and gave her day dress a quick scrutiny. "Something I can do for you?"

She clasped her hands before her to hide their trembling. Bloody hell! If she couldn't control her nervousness now, she'd end up a blithering fool by tonight.

"Grandfather is here." When Cord didn't respond to that, she elaborated. "My aunt Muriel, Papa's only sister, accompanied him. As did Viscount Strowbridge."

Cord nodded, then presented his broad muscular back to her and continued working saddle soap onto the exquisitely tooled western saddle Papa had purchased from C. M. Moseman and Brother in New York but had never used. "Sounds like a houseful."

"Yes, quite. To accommodate our extra guest, I had to adjust our sleeping arrangements. I hope you don't mind terribly."

Cord's easy laugh belied the heavy-handed way he worked the soap into the leather. "Told you before I don't care where I bunk down. Where'd you move my belongings?"

Bea hoped her voice wouldn't quaver. "I didn't. I directed Mrs. Mimms to transfer my things into your bedroom."

The hand holding the cloth stilled. Cord's penetrating gaze shifted to hers. "What're you saying?"

Bea summoned a placid smile. "We made an agreement."

"Go on."

"The time's come for us to honor that agreement. From now on, we'll share a room. As husband and wife."

He shook his head. "No thanks. I'll sleep in my bedroll."

"No! You must sleep in the bed. Beside me."

"You're asking for trouble."

"I'm ordering you to honor your agreement." Bea paced before the well-polished saddles, trying to act as if she wasn't afraid to lie beside Cord. "Now that Grandfather is here, we must carry on as a newly married couple at all times."

Even before she finished, Cord smiled a pitying one which thoroughly irritated her. "You're not going to fool your grandfather, or anybody else, into believing that."

She planted her hands on her hips. "And why ever not?"

He ambled toward her, stopping so close her body threatened to melt from his heat. "Your eyes'll tell on you. When a woman looks at her lover, her eyes glow with desire."

"Rubbish."

"It's a fact. When you look at me, you get that tetchy look in your eyes, like you can't stand for your 'adoring husband' to touch you, much less kiss you."

"Oh, dear. Are you certain?"

"Yes, ma'am." Cord flashed a street vendor's smile. "But I know a way to put a sparkle in your eye without compromising your virtue or straying one iota from the bargain we struck."

She frowned, having serious doubts. "What do you propose?"

"Once a day, we enjoy a bout of spooning."

The thought of Cord kissing her daily made Bea's heart hopscotch with excitement. As for her husband touching her—

Experience had taught Bea she'd be the loser if she allowed that to happen. But what if Cord remained true to his word? She stared into his warm molasses-colored eyes. They promised untold pleasure. They asked for her trust.

"Very well," she said, knowing she really had very little choice in the matter. "When do we begin?"

"No time like the present."

Before she could object—not that she would—his strong arms enveloped her and crushed her against his hard, hot body. Bosom flattened against brawny chest. Belly to belly. Thigh to thigh.

One arm cradled her, holding her close. A strong hand cupped her bottom and fit her snugly against him. He lowered his head, his eyes blazing with heat and some emotion she didn't understand. His mouth closed over hers with lazy purpose, teasing, tasting, nibbling. Soft and coaxing, then with urgency.

"Come on, Trixie," he whispered against her lips, making her shiver. "This'll only work if we both do it."

With a soft moan, Bea wrapped her arms around his neck and kissed him as she'd never kissed another soul. This was a lover's kiss. Sublime. Wondrous. Addictive.

Cord's tongue darted into her mouth, shocking her. Making her nipples peak and her lower parts quiver. Making her crave more. He tasted of hot spice. Smelled of leather and man.

Her heart drummed, and a corresponding pulse pounded between her thighs. She ignored every intruding footstep and creak, each horse's whinny, clinging to him, wanting this to go on and on.

Cord pulled his mouth from hers.

She nuzzled his neck. "How will I get that sparkle in my eyes if you stop before I get into the spirit of it?"

"Not now, Trixie," Cord whispered.

She smiled up into her husband's dark eyes. "Why should we stop when we both enjoy it so?"

"Because you have an audience," Lambert said over Zephyr's sharp whickers.

Bea whirled around. Her company stood before her, gaping at her and Cord with expressions ranging from annoyance to amusement.

"I assume you're Tanner," Grandfather said, staring at Cord.

"Yep." Cord rested both hands on Bea's shoulders. "I take it you're my wife's grandfather."

Grandfather scowled. "Indeed. Fletcher Northroupe. The Earl of Arden."

"I'm Muriel, Beatrix's aunt." Muriel wore an odd smile.

Lambert's lascivious gaze fixed on Bea's bosom.

Obscene bloke! Bea whipped her arms over her breasts to

hide the evidence of the passion Cord stirred in her. How odd that Lambert made her feel dirty while Cord made her feel alive.

"While the earl and I have a talk, why don't you go on up to the house and visit with your aunt?" Cord herded Bea out of the tack room, forcing her family and a leering Lambert to retreat. "I reckon this fellow wouldn't mind joining you ladies."

"Not at all," Lambert said. "And it's Viscount Strowbridge."

Bea glared at the miserable man she'd almost married. If Cord knew what Lambert had done to her— But he had no idea.

Feigning calmness she didn't feel, Bea took her aunt's arm and strolled down the aisle. Lambert trailed them, no doubt ogling her backside. How would she endure the insufferable viscount's company?

The Earl of Arden leaned on his cane and took Cord's measure. "Name your price, Mr. Tanner, and let us be done with this charade without further damage to my granddaughter."

Cord tried to corral his anger over catching the viscount ogling Trixie and focused on the earl. He had to hand it to the old gent for sidestepping the bullshit and getting to the point.

"What makes you think my marriage to Trixie ain't real?" Not waiting for an answer, Cord went back to cleaning the fine western saddle when what he wanted to do was to go after Viscount Strowbridge. Damn the man for staring at Trixie's breasts.

The earl followed and slammed the door shut. "Dash it all! You can't gull me by tossing about that pet moniker you gave my granddaughter. I know seduction when I see it, and her impetuous marriage makes me question your motives. So if you married her to gain title to this ranch, then you've made a grave mistake."

"I didn't marry Trixie for her ranch."

The earl thumped his cane on the plank floor. "Then why did you marry my granddaughter?"

Cord thought on that a moment. "Because Trixie's got more backbone and passion for living than any woman I've met before. I wager few men could resist a combination like that."

"Indeed. Her grandmother was the same." Worry scudded across the earl's face like gathering storm clouds. "Bea is stubborn to a fault, you know."

"That she is."

"And deuced independent, a flaw you can lay squarely on her father's head," the earl said, but didn't look Cord in the eye.

Cord cracked a smile, guessing Trixie's stern grandpappy and pa had spoiled her something fierce. And that got him thinking about what brought on her pa's death.

"Something I want you to take a look at." Cord lifted the ruined saddle from a bracket and laid it upside down on the worktable. "Ever see riggings like this before?"

The earl ran a gloved finger over one of the spiders. "Blast it all! Setting this upon a horse is barbaric. Damned sadistic."

"Yep. After the barbs cut through the blanket, they dug into the horse, and it turned loco from the pain."

"And the rider?"

"I was told your son broke his neck in the fall."

"My son, the idiot, was drunk."

"Even sober, it would've been a chore keeping his seat."

The earl leaned on his cane, his nod abrupt. "Who's responsible for this sabotage?"

"Don't know. When Rory went to saddle the stallion, somebody had beat him to it." Cord fingered the sharp wires. "I'd wager whoever saddled that horse was the same one that worked these spiders in the saddle."

"My God, man! You're insinuating this was a fiendish plot to harm my son."

"Yes, sir, I am." Cord snared the earl's troubled gaze with

his own. "Besides the bastard that did this, the only ones that know about it are the hands, the marshal, and me. If it's all the same with you, I'd like to keep it that way for a while."

The earl nodded in grim agreement, his gaze narrowed on the saddle. "Have you any likely suspects?"

"Nope, but I'd say someone wanted Sherwin Northroupe hurt bad or dead." Cord tossed the ruined saddle cloth over the saddle. "It's the why that bothers me. Until I figure it out, I'm keeping this saddle out of sight."

Embracing her role of dutiful wife and gracious hostess, Bea escorted her aunt into the parlor for tea and conversation. In all honesty, Bea looked forward to the visit. Her aunt always kept abreast of current issues.

Lambert Strowbridge followed at a sedate distance. When he'd returned to England nearly nine months past, Bea had hoped she'd never see him again. She'd never dreamed he'd return as the invited guest of her grandfather. But he had and, though she was sorely tempted to toss him out, she couldn't.

Aunt Muriel perched upon the sofa and prattled about the biased laws and women's suffrage in England. Bea claimed the garnet floral side chair and deliberately fixed her attention on her aunt. Little good that did her peace of mind.

Lambert lounged in a damask wing chair, cradled his glass of whiskey in his pudgy hands, and leered at Bea's bosom. Her skin crawled. His odious presence rattled Bea so that she comprehended little of Muriel's impassioned speech.

So Bea fixed Lambert with her most censuring glower. The viscount answered with a mocking smile, then licked his thin lips and continued undressing her with his seedy gaze.

Frustration warred with Bea's anger. Clearly, her marriage didn't deter Lambert from his goal to have his lecherous way with her. Though she doubted he would dare accost her without some encouragement on her part, she thought it prudent to ensure she was never alone with the viscount.

"Take wheeling, for example." Muriel's eyes narrowed on Lambert as she continued dissecting the injustices heaped upon women. "Men have the mistaken notion the bicycle was invented for their enjoyment and benefit when it is obvious to anyone possessing half a brain that women gain physical fitness and great pleasure from the sport as well."

Lambert peered down his thin nose at Muriel. "It is the latter which concerns gentlemen. Such an exhausting sport will no doubt cause irreparable damage to women's reproductive systems."

"Fiddle-faddle," Muriel exclaimed.

"Is it?" The viscount smirked and twirled the sharp waxed tips of his black mustache.

Muriel clasped a hand over her mouth and gasped.

It took Bea a moment to understand what Lambert was talking about. When she did, Bea glared at Lambert. How dare he insinuate her aunt's inability to bear a child stemmed from her penchant for physical exercise!

Lambert kept his rodent eyes on Muriel, paying no attention to Bea. "I have heard that desperate women adjust the seat of their bicycle so as to gain a modicum of sexual gratification from the ride. That, Lady Northroupe-Flynn, is sly debauchery."

Muriel's face turned beet red, suggesting she comprehended Lambert. But Bea hadn't the foggiest notion what he meant.

When Runnymede, Kansas, had been at the height of its glory, a good deal of the women, including herself, partook of a variety of sports, bicycling included. Bea hadn't suffered any harm from wheeling. Nor had she received any carnal pleasure from the sport. Was such a thing possible?

Muriel's volatile gaze clashed with the viscount's. "My dear Lord Strowbridge. If more gentlemen took time to assure their ladies reached a voluptuous spasm, time they undoubtedly bestow upon their mistresses, then I imagine few ladies would feel the need to achieve such titillations upon their bicycles."

Purple splotches bloomed on Lambert's fleshy jowls, and lines scored the pale skin around his mean eyes. "Brazen free-thinker."

"Pompous prig," Muriel flung back without hesitation.

Latching onto the chance to put Lambert in his place, Bea leapt into the fray and applauded. "Well said, Aunt Muriel."

Cord's chuckle brought Bea's gaze swinging to the doorway.

"Don't encourage her." The earl strode into the parlor, every sharp angle of his face tense with anger. "I feared Muriel would lecture you on her bold beliefs, but I assumed she'd have the good sense to do so in private."

"I'm not a child to be cosseted." Bea's comment drew a snort from her grandfather, a smirk from Lambert, and a smile from Cord.

Grandfather fixed a damning scowl on the viscount. "When you heard Muriel sail the conversation into turbulent waters, a man of your station should have quit the room, refusing to debate such a delicate subject with my daughter and granddaughter."

The viscount's puffed cheeks resembled ripe plums. "You're correct and I humbly apologize to you and Miss Beatrix. I shouldn't have allowed Lady Northroupe-Flynn to bait me."

"But the fact remains that you did," the earl bit out.

Muriel smiled at her father, as if not the least bit offended by his reprimand. "Do bear in mind that I'm widowed and your granddaughter is a married woman."

"She has a point, Northroupe. I doubt anything said came as a surprise to Beatrix." Lambert's lascivious gaze explored Bea's bosom before lifting to her face. "Did it, m'dear?"

Shaking her head, Bea shrank in her chair and instinctively crossed her arms over her bosom, more repulsed by the trickle of spittle pooling on Lambert's thin lower lip than his question.

But Cord took exception to the query. At least that's what Bea thought when he came to her rescue.

"What takes place between Trixie and me is our business." Cord placed his hands on her shoulders, chasing away the cold brought on by Lambert's scrutiny. "I'll give you fair warning, Lord Strowbridge. Don't talk that way around my wife again."

"Couldn't agree with you more, my boy," the earl said.

Lambert turned a sickly pallor. "Do accept my humble apologies for behaving less than nobly toward either lady. You've my word nothing of the sort will happen again."

The earl snorted. Muriel sniffed and ignored Lambert.

Bea exhaled slowly, but it caught in her throat when Cord gently squeezed her shoulders—a gesture nobody saw. It had to be for her benefit. But for what reason?

Her answer came a heartbeat later in Cord's warning. "It better hadn't, because I protect what's mine."

"Ooh, how charmingly possessive," Muriel murmured.

Lambert sniffed. Grandfather chuckled.

Bea managed a weak smile, feeling far from comforted by Cord's declaration. He did an exemplary job of acting the part of her jealous husband. His overprotective stance, dominating tone, and familiar way he touched her attributed much to the ruse.

For a moment, even Bea believed their marriage was genuine. That Cord cared deeply for her. He didn't, of course.

Bea had struck a deal with Cord and she trusted him to abide by his word. She didn't worry that he'd exert his husbandly rights. He wouldn't.

And for the first time in Bea's life, an overpowering sense of longing throbbed deep inside her for the future she'd never share with her proud and honest cowboy husband.

As Bea expected, Mrs. Delgado outdid herself. The cook satisfied everyone's palate—with the obvious exception of the viscount's—with a feast of rich carrot soup, tortilla casse-role, spicy red chicken with almonds, succulent winter squash basking in syrup, and thick, hot *frijoles de olla*, ending with a rich almond pudding generously ladled with custard sauce.

"Your cook is an epicurean genius, Bea." Muriel gingerly rested the Sheffield dessert spoon she'd used on the rose and fan border of a Staffordshire plate.

Bea relaxed at the compliment. "Papa and I thought so."

"Unusual meal." Grandfather patted his rounded stomach and expelled a hearty sigh. "Dash it all, but this was the best fare I've had since leaving my home."

Cord sipped his coffee and winked at Bea, bringing a quick blush to her cheeks. "If you leave Mrs. Delgado's table hungry, there's something wrong with you. Ain't that right, darlin'?"

"Indeed." Bea smiled. The endearment tumbled from Cord so naturally, as if she and Cord were lovers.

Blushing at the thought, Bea quickly focused on her duty as hostess. "Shall we adjourn to the parlor?"

"Come now, Beatrix. Have you been stranded in this unciv-ilized country for so long that you forgot proper social con-duct?" Lambert belched and leaned back in his chair. He sent her a tolerant smile and made a shooing motion with one overly white, overly plump hand. "Off with the ladies so the gents may relax after suffering through that gastronomic dis-aster you called a dinner and savor a cigar over port."

Cord's eyes turned flinty. "Maybe I'd best ask Benedict to pre-pare you a dose of Hawley's Pepsine for your stomach ailment."

"Don't bother," Lambert said. "I'm quite certain I'll be fine after a descent night's rest."

"That settles it, then." Cord rose and crossed to Bea's chair. He grasped her free hand, surprising and pleasing her. "My wife and I like to take an after-dinner drink in the parlor and talk over the day's events. You're all welcome to join us for conversation and a sample of Trixie's homemade applejack."

Grandfather pushed back his chair and lurched to his feet. "Capital notion, m'boy. Capital."

"As they say, 'when in Rome.'" Muriel accepted her father's arm and accompanied him from the room.

The viscount threw his linen napkin upon the table and stood. "Distilling your own spirits. How utterly common."

Lambert stalked from the dining room wearing the hauteur he'd practiced to perfection. In Bea's opinion, the viscount fell short of his goal. He was still a stumpy, balding lecher with a temperament that matched his dyspeptic stomach.

As Cord escorted her into the parlor, Bea hoped Lambert would retreat to his bedroom. But the viscount joined them, sprawling in the chair he'd claimed earlier.

Cord led Bea to the sofa where her aunt perched, then left her to join Grandfather by the fireplace. A good deal of Bea's confidence fled her. Benedict trudged into the parlor carrying a silver tray bearing five glasses of amber applejack.

Panic churned Bea's stomach as she took a glass. Cord had refused to imbibe since he'd overindulged on their wedding night. Tonight, especially, she didn't want a repeat of that experience.

While Benedict served her aunt and Lambert, Bea tried to catch Cord's attention in hopes of silently reminding him of his weakness, but her husband kept his attention on her grandfather and the black leather cigar case the earl produced from a pocket.

Her grandfather said something and held the case out to Cord, offering him a cigar. Her husband shook his head and chuckled.

The deep, rich sound did odd things to Bea's insides. But her moment of pleasure deserted her as Benedict approached the pair. Grandfather took a glass and Cord wrapped long, tanned fingers around the remaining drink on the tray.

Bea breathed deeply and told herself to relax. Cord had

promised her that he wouldn't get drunk again. She had to take him at his word. Trust his judgment.

"Your marriage to Tanner shocked me," Lambert said.

She glared at Lambert, not caring who noticed. "Did it?"

"Indeed." Lambert tortured her with his reptilian perusal, triggering her internal alarm. "I enjoyed many evenings with your father and you in this very room. Yet I find it curious that when I asked for your hand in matrimony, and your father and you refused me, neither of you mentioned you were courting a man—an American at that. Nor do I recall any gossip about you and any suitor during my extended stay at the Runnymede Arms."

His innuendo that she'd plucked Cord out of thin air made Bea's face flame. His suspicions smacked too close to the truth. But she'd cut her own throat if she pursued this conversation around her grandfather, especially since she hadn't had the foresight to discuss this subject with Cord.

Bea laughed and waved his remark away as nothing of import. "I met Cord after you returned to England."

"While you were officially in mourning?" Lambert asked in an affronted theatrical voice. "A bit tacky, wouldn't you say?"

Bea pursed her lips in frustration, aware the popinjay would continue picking at her like a loose thread. Truth be told, she didn't know how to answer Lambert. To admit she'd shunned her period of mourning in favor of romance was gauche, not to mention an out-and-out lie. But since she'd announced to her grandfather that she adored her husband, what choice did she have but to invent another fabrication?

"I approached Trixie while she was in mourning." Cord's statement brought everyone's gaze swinging to his in surprise, Bea's most of all.

"And pressed Beatrix into a hasty marriage before Lord Arden could intercede, no doubt," Lambert said.

Muriel coughed. Bea braced herself, not daring to guess how Cord would react to Lambert's insult.

Cord's laugh had a lethal edge to it. "Trixie didn't require her grandfather's permission to marry me."

"I informed Strowbridge of that fact when he approached me in London. I couldn't legally give Bea to him or stop her from marrying an American." Still scowling, the earl turned to Cord. "But since my granddaughter failed to mention in her letters how she met you, I'll ask you to expound."

Bea held her breath, her eyes locked on Cord's twinkling ones. She couldn't imagine what lie he'd concoct to pacify Grandfather's curiosity and squelch Lambert's suspicions.

"Last fall, I signed on as foreman for the Bar T Ranch. They held a rodeo, and a passel of British folks came to watch." Cord grinned at her, a somewhat shy, boyish gesture that kindled warm, comforting feelings in her heart. "When I laid eyes on Trixie, I decided then and there I'd ask her out for a buggy ride."

"I attended that event, sir." Lambert held his balding head at an imperious angle, unknowingly displaying the widening center part bisecting his sparse hair. "Stayed by Beatrix's side all day. I don't recall her making your acquaintance."

"We didn't." Cord's warm gaze never strayed once from Bea's, flirting openly with her and causing heat to curl deep within her belly. "I was laid up with a busted shoulder and cracked ribs that day. By the time I got on my feet, I heard Trixie's pa had died. I kept my distance out of respect."

"If that were true, then you wouldn't have married a woman who's still in mourning." Lambert puffed out his hollow chest and thrust his weak chin forward, looking for all the world like a corpulent blackbird eyeing an earthworm wriggling from the soil.

Aunt Muriel, who'd kept her opinions to herself, chose that moment to speak her piece. "Life is meant to be lived. Did you expect Bea to retreat into a thirty-some-year mourning as our straitlaced Queen did after King Albert gave up the ghost?"

The viscount's thin lips pulled into a parody of a smile.

"And what of you, Lady Northroupe-Flynn? What living have you embraced in the decade since your husband went on to his reward?"

Muriel flinched, and her eyes darkened to violet. "How dare you question my behavior when you dove into your mistress's bed the very night you laid your wife and child to rest."

Red splotches mottled Lambert's pale face.

The earl choked on his drink. "Enough, Muriel!"

Muriel waved that order away, apparently not finished with Lambert. "And let us not forget that you approached Father and asked for Bea's hand the month after my brother died."

"Beatrix was alone in a foreign country, in desperate need of a worthy man to protect her," Lambert said.

"You're damn right. Ain't it lucky Trixie found one she could trust." Cord smiled at her with warm, laughing eyes.

Her heart skipped a beat. Emotion clogged her throat, so Bea didn't trust herself to speak. Not that she'd know what to add to her husband's story.

Cord's explanation of how they'd met was an ingenious prevarication. Most likely one of her ranch hands had told Cord how Papa had taken everyone on the Prairie Rose, Benedict and Mrs. Mimms included, to the Bar T rodeo.

It was unthinkable to believe the cowboy she'd hired to marry her, and who she'd soon share a bedroom with, had once had designs on her. Too preposterous. And far too unsettling.

CHAPTER EIGHT

Cord stood by the cold fireplace in his bedroom and watched his wife fuss with the bedclothes. He never should've confessed that he'd seen Trixie at the Bar T rodeo. And he damn sure shouldn't have made it sound like he'd gone soft over her that day. But seeing as he couldn't punch Lambert Strowbridge in the mouth for sniffing after Trixie, Cord had spread it on heavy to warn the viscount to keep his distance.

Truth be told, Cord wouldn't have noticed Trixie at the Bar T rodeo if Gil Yancy hadn't pointed her out to him.

"I aim to court that lil' filly," Gil had promised.

Cord had given the British lady a quick look and admitted she was a pretty little thing. And far above his lowly class, which is why he'd put her, and Gil's promise to court her, from his mind.

Funny how memories have a way of ambushing a man when he least expects it. Cord's mood soured the minute he escorted her into the bedroom and it dawned on him that if not for a twist of fate, Gil would be sharing this bed with her tonight.

Cord mumbled a curse, knowing full well his old friend

would've bedded Trixie long before now. Of course, Gil wouldn't have agreed to a marriage-in-name-only. But Cord had.

He'd given Trixie his word. He aimed to keep his little rustler corralled in his britches tonight and every one after it.

"Think I'll bunk down in my bedroll," Cord said.

"Absolutely not." She folded a blanket in half lengthwise and laid it on one side of the bed. "With our blankets folded thusly, we're assured of a degree of privacy while we slumber in our makeshift cocoons."

He took in the bed with the two blankets lying fold to fold and another one rolled up and marching down the middle like a soft fence. "Yep, as snug as two bugs in a rug."

She spread a quilt over the entire bed, then turned down the coverings at the tops on each side. She clasped her hands and gave a nervous smile. "Who should dress for bed first, you or I?"

"Seeing as I ain't never crawled in bed with a woman I didn't aim on having sex with, I'd best keep my britches on."

"Out of the question."

"Why? What difference will it make if I keep my clothes on?"

"Do keep your voice down." She blew out the bedside lamp, but not before he saw her fiery blush. "Bear in mind this is a business arrangement and not a love affair and dress for bed."

Trixie was greener than grass if she thought he slept in a nightshirt, but he was tired of arguing with her about the foolishness of them sharing the bed.

"Okay, boss lady. You win."

Instead of hightailing it behind the dressing screen, she stared at him all wide-eyed and curious, rousing his desire and making him wonder if she was as innocent as he'd first thought. He clenched his jaw. Her past wasn't his concern.

Cord laid his gun belt atop the dresser, then stomped to the bootjack and shucked his boots. He peeled off his socks and shrugged out of his shirt. He wanted sleep. That was all.

She made a strangled sound. "Do you intend to undress in the middle of the room? Now?"

"Yes'm, I do." Cord flipped open the buttons on his jeans and shoved them down his legs.

Before they hit the floor, Trixie galloped behind the dressing screen painted with gaudy pink and yellow roses. Yep, she was either an innocent or a prude. She'd probably keep her duds on tonight. That was fine with him.

He stepped out of his jeans. Stripped to his undershirt and drawers, he crawled into the sack and stretched out on his back.

"As worn out as I am, I'll be snoring like a choked bull by the time you get done primping."

"I assure you I don't primp."

He smiled and tugged the bedclothes to his armpits. With any luck, he'd be asleep before Trixie came to bed.

Moonlight crept through the window, bathing the room in a dim glow and casting the dressing screen in shadow. Over the years he'd had his share of women, but the only time he'd ever spent the whole night with one was the first time he had sex.

That had landed him in a fix. He'd lost what little innocence a twelve-year-old could have, and his ma had lost her job.

Trixie glided toward the dressing table like an angel and Cord forgot all about his troubled past. The shadows swallowed his wife up, but the whoosh-glide noise told him she was brushing her hair. He wondered how long it was, if the golden strands were as soft as they looked.

He caught a glint of silver as Trixie set her brush down. She rose, but instead of coming to bed, she puttered around the room, picking up his discarded clothes.

Cord's mouth went desert dry as he watched her. Her high-necked frilly nightgown covered everything but her hands and face. Her golden hair fell halfway down her back, swaying from side to side when she moved.

Trixie crossed before the window and the moonlight turned her gown transparent. Cord slammed his eyes shut. Too late. He'd branded her shape on his mind's eye. Breasts that'd overflow a man's palm. A waist he could span with both hands, and shapely legs that'd wrap around a man's flanks and hold on for the long, hard ride to glory.

Over the hammering of his heart, he heard her side of the bed squeak as she settled in and the mattress dipped. "Good night."

Cord replied with a grunt, not daring to speak. He lay still, listening to Trixie's even breathing. Tension knotted his guts and sweat soaked his brow. His pecker tented the bedclothes.

With a curse, Cord flopped onto his side. He'd be lucky if he got a wink of sleep tonight.

Sometime in the middle of the moonless night, Trixie roused Cord out of the dream that always haunted him. Not with words. Nope, her body snapped him awake in more ways than one.

He'd flopped onto his back. She'd climbed over the rolled blanket separating them and snuggled beside him.

Her head rested on his shoulder. One small hand had worked inside his undershirt to tangle in his chest hair. Her nightgown had ridden up and her long, bare leg rested atop one of his.

Cord bit back a groan. With each breath she took, her bent knee nudged his little rustler into a bucking frenzy.

"Get back on your own side," he hissed in her ear.

She moaned and moved, all right. Snuggling up beside him and sliding her leg up and down his.

Sweat soaked his body. As gently as he could, Cord grabbed her leg and moved her knee from his crotch. He meant to let go of her, but the tight muscles under her soft skin surprised him.

Cord inched his palm under her nightgown. He splayed his fingers over her soft thigh. His body burned. His breath rasped like an old hinge. Common sense told him to rein his hand in. Lust spurred him on.

He grazed the curve of her rounded hip. So soft. So firm. His hand meandered around back and cupped her sweet little bottom.

Trixie moaned softly and stirred, sliding her leg between his. Over and over and over.

The little rustler Cord tried to ignore reared its head, eager to break out of his drawers. He bit back a moan and went still as death. His gripping desire surprised the hell out of him. He couldn't remember ever feeling this aroused. Or being so close to embarrassing himself with a woman.

Trixie sighed and rolled back on her side of the bed. She wiggled her butt against the rolled blanket between them and pulled her bedclothes under her chin. Her even breathing told him she'd never roused from sleep once.

Cord gritted his teeth. He should be so lucky.

The next morning, Cord was as short-tempered as a fresh-cut steer. He'd tossed and turned most of the night, expecting Trixie to crawl on top of him again. But she didn't.

Because of his sour mood, Cord reckoned he'd best stay away from the house, Trixie's company, and Trixie in particular for a spell. So after his early-morning ride, he ate breakfast with the hands and brooded over whether he'd ever get a decent night's sleep again.

The solution came to him as he stared at the dregs in his coffee cup. He'd come right out and tell Trixie what she'd done.

Sure as shooting, she'd insist Cord curl up in his bedroll. He wouldn't have to share the bed with her anymore. Wouldn't wake up hard and horny in the middle of the night. Wouldn't have to risk he might forget his promise and slake his lust on his wife.

Ott sprinkled tobacco on a paper and rolled it up with one hand. "What set you at odds so early in the morning, Cordell?"

"Reckon I'm like the horses. I need exercising." But after last night, forking a saddle wasn't the ride Cord had in mind.

"We got hay needs baling today," Jake said. "Me and Ott could use an extra hand forking it in the baler and stacking it."

Cord looked up at the boy. He'd been Jake's age when he'd been trusted to take care of ranch business. And he'd failed.

"I'd be glad to lend a hand."

Jake tromped to the door and snatched his battered hat off the peg. "We'll get at it, then, as soon as I ready the wagon."

Jake left the bunkhouse, and Cord glanced at Ott. "How come you don't want to be foreman? Nobody knows ranching half as well as you do."

"I know it up here." Ott tapped his head with a gnarled finger. "But I ain't good at ciphering and I'm too damned old to learn how to read. Jake can do that. He's got a good head on his shoulders and he's full of spit and vinegar. He'll do fine."

"I'll take your word for it."

Cord pushed to his feet and ambled out the door, aiming to fetch his gloves from the tack room. Trixie and Muriel stood by the stable. He debated about ducking back in the bunkhouse, but his wife saw him and waved. No sense tucking and running now.

Blowing air between his teeth, Cord crossed toward them. By the looks of it, they were fixing to take a ride. Both wore riding outfits and hats. Muriel wore some sort of fancy cap.

Trixie's hat looked like a short brimmed pot with a veil, but her eyes twinkled and she looked sweeter than honey on a biscuit. She wouldn't smile so if she knew what she'd done last night.

"Morning," Cord said, dipping his chin and sliding two fingers over his hat brim.

"Good morning," Trixie said as Rory led a white mare and a frisky dun one from the stable. "I plan to show Aunt Muriel the ranch. Would you care to ride along with us?"

"I sure would," Cord lied. The last thing he wanted to do today was trail along with two women. "But I can't. I'm helping the hands with haying."

Trixie's smile fell. "Oh. Of course."

"Perhaps another time, then." Muriel moseyed over to Rory and the horses.

Instead of doing the same, Trixie smiled at Cord, like she expected him to say or do something. But what?

Hellfire! Trixie wanted him to do what she'd hired him to do. Act like her devoted husband.

Cord cupped his wife's elbow and herded her over to the white mare. "Let me help you, darlin'."

"Thank you."

Trixie stood beside the horse, right hand on the saddle and left foot forward, like she expected him to give her a leg up.

Instead, Cord grabbed Trixie's tiny waist and lifted her atop her lily white mare as if she weighed no more than a feather. Her eyes widened and she sucked in her breath. A blushing bride.

"Have a good ride." Cord patted the thigh that had plagued him last night and headed toward the stable. He'd be her devoted husband, all right. But he'd damn sure do it his way.

Bea stared at Cord's broad back and laid a gloved hand over her thudding heart. She'd been so pleased by his show of devotion that she'd wanted to kiss him. In fact, he acted so natural that she momentarily believed his affection was genuine.

Muriel clucked her tongue and heeled the mare into a trot. Bea set her heel to Cleopatra and caught up with her aunt. They both slowed their mounts to a walk.

"You're truly happy with your husband, aren't you?"

"Very." Bea patted the dense coat on Cleopatra's neck and sent her aunt a bright, if somewhat dazed, smile.

Muriel's eyes sparkled with mischief. "I trust Cord is a considerate lover, too?"

Embarrassment set Bea's cheeks on fire. "Aunt Muriel!"

Her aunt laughed. "I'm aware a lady never admits to gaining sexual pleasure, but I tell you it's a very important detail to maintaining a healthy marriage."

Panic seized Bea by the throat. She wanted everyone to assume she and Cord were intimate. They were man and wife, after all. But if Muriel peppered her with personal questions, her jig would be up in short order.

Muriel frowned. "Oh, dear. I have shocked you, haven't I?"

Much like a newborn colt latched onto its dam's udder, Bea nodded vigorously and seized the excuse Muriel provided. "It's just that I've never discussed such intimacies with anyone."

"Not even with your mother?"

A dry laugh emerged from Bea. "You're forgetting Mama was a purist who advised me to suffer my marital duty for the sole means of procreation without complaint or unseemly displays of passion."

"No wonder Sherwin crawled into the bottle." Muriel canted her head to one side and assessed Bea. "Tell me you didn't adopt that rubbish your mama prattled."

Bea grimaced at concocting another lie, but if she wanted to end this subject, she had to stretch the truth. "Not at all."

"That's the spirit." Muriel twittered with delight, then slid Bea a conspiratorial smile. "Now, do tell me. Is your handsome cowboy husband a considerate lover?"

"Extremely so." Dreading her outrageous, outspoken aunt would continue prying, Bea suggested, "Let's be off. I want to give the horses a good run and show you this wide-open prairie I've come to think of as my own."

So saying, Bea nudged Cleopatra into an easy canter. The brisk wind stole her breath and whipped at her wool skirt. She pushed all thoughts of Cord and the odd sensations he stirred in her from her mind and concentrated on what lay ahead.

Muriel kept pace atop Athena, expertly handling the dun mare. Her sapphire riding skirt flapped and her face flushed from the biting wind and exertion.

They zigzagged across a field dotted with brown teepees of dried corn shucks. They urged their mounts over a stone fence break Papa had built. Not only did it keep the cattle in the pasture, it allowed Papa and Bea to practice jumping the hunters.

Neck and neck, they raced over the gently rolling pasture. High above them, the revolving wheel on the recently repaired windmill whirred. Sun rays glinted off the tall rigging and vanes and shot an exaggerated shadow of ladder and flickering sail onto the pasture. Cattle milled around the glittering pool of cold water the wind power pumped from the deep well.

Jumps constructed of wood were scattered at intervals, but Bea avoided the route Papa had taken on his last hunt and guided Cleopatra toward the stone fence break separating this pasture from the far one. It tested horse and rider.

Papa had found it challenging. So did Bea.

As Cleopatra took the wall, Bea applied pressure with her knees and bent low over the white neck, exhilarated by the power and grace stretched out beneath her. For a moment, she and the horse soared in the air. Free. Uninhibited.

The mare set down smoothly and resumed stride. Laughing, Bea reined to a stop and patted her mount's rippling neck. A moment later, Muriel maneuvered the wide jump with ease and brought her horse to a stop beside Bea.

"You handle Athena expertly," Bea said. "Do you ride often?"

"Not as often as I would like. As for handling the mare—I credit my riding abilities to my late husband. Harlan was a master horseman. Taught me everything I know."

Though Bea's father had spoken enviously of his brother-in-law's equestrian skills, Papa complained that Harlan Flynn had been a mere Irish commoner whose tragic riding accident left Muriel a young widow. Grieving and penniless.

"I wish I'd met your husband."

"So do I. Harlan would've adored you."

Grief swam in Muriel's eyes and she looked away, but not before Bea saw the sheen of tears. Sadness seeped into Bea.

"You loved Mr. Flynn very much."

"Indeed." Muriel smiled. "Much to Father's annoyance, I've yet to meet another man who measured up to Harlan. At my age, I doubt I will. Not that I'm looking, mind you."

Bea completely understood her aunt's reasoning to remain unmarried. When Bea's brief association with Cord had ended, she intended to carry on alone. Her own boss.

Since love didn't enter into Bea's marriage to Cord, she wouldn't grieve as Muriel had done. Cord would be a fond memory. The rambling cowboy she'd impulsively married and who'd abandoned her. At least that's what he'd agreed to do. And if he didn't?

"Over yonder, Bea. Is that one of your cowboys?"

Bea looked where Muriel pointed and stiffened. Prescott Donnelly approached them at a ground-eating gallop.

"No. Mr. Donnelly owns the land adjoining the Prairie Rose."

"Ah, your neighbor." Muriel tucked a few loosened strands of hair under her jaunty hat. "Do you suppose Mr. Donnelly heard you have visitors and is coming to extend his greetings?"

"I haven't the foggiest notion why he's decided to step foot on my land." A lie, that.

The rancher wanted an audience with her grandfather and had undoubtedly heard of the earl's arrival. Her recent marriage wouldn't deter the land-grabber from offering Grandfather a tidy sum for the Prairie Rose—her ranch.

Donnelly reined his black gelding to an uncomfortably close halt before Bea and Muriel. He wore black from head to foot. His expression was as dark and hostile as the restive animal he rode. Unmanageable auburn hair hung over his collar. Thick reddish eyebrows formed a deep vee over piercing green eyes.

"Is it true you married Cordell Tanner?" Donnelly asked.

Bea returned the man's forbidding scowl. "I most certainly did. So, if you're trespassing on my land to offer me your congratulations, I suggest you do so and be on your way."

The big man crossed his gloved hands atop the pommel and snorted. "Didn't ride over here for that, though I 'spect since you've tied yourself to that tumbleweed, I'll wish you the best."

The insult to Cord infuriated Bea more than catching Donnelly on the Prairie Rose. "You're rude and arrogant beyond belief. Get off my property at once."

"That's the spirit. Give him what for," Muriel said.

"I'll head home as soon as my men round up my cattle," Donnelly stated in his don't-argue-with-me tone.

For the first time, Bea looked beyond Donnelly. Mounted cowboys separated her Herefords from Donnelly's black cattle and herded them through a break in the fence separating the Prairie Rose from the Flying D Ranch.

"Why are your cattle on my land?"

"Somebody cut five strands of barbed wire this morning," Donnelly said in a matter-of-fact voice.

Bea gaped, unable to believe it. "Are you sure?"

"Yes'm. I saw them myself. The lines were cut."

Bea looked at Donnelly's men again. One cowboy left the group and galloped toward them. She frowned, recognizing Gil Yancy long before he reined his roan gelding beside Donnelly.

Yancy thumbed back his hat, gave Bea and Muriel a curt nod, then faced Donnelly. "We rounded up the Flying D cattle, but I'd bet a dozen or so Prairie Rose white-faced cows will drop Aberdeen Angus calves next year."

Donnelly nodded, his somber gaze flicking to Bea. "Tell Cordell I'll be calling on him soon to haggle over how many calves he aims to give me for my bull's services."

That Donnelly assumed Cord gave the orders on her ranch had Bea shaking with anger, but she didn't dare set Donnelly

straight on the matter. Cord had been right. It was imperative that everyone believe he made all the decisions.

Bea took a calming breath and blew it out. "I'll tell him to
expect you, though I believe you're wasting your time. My
husband didn't cut the fence so your black bull could service
our prized Herefords and create crossbred stock."

One of Donnelly's reddish eyebrows hiked upward. "What
makes you so jo-fired sure of that?"

A sound question. Bea wished she could answer Donnelly
with confidence. But doubt wormed its way into her mind,
making her question her husband yet again. She didn't know
where Cord rode every morning or have any idea what he did.
Had he cut the fence?

No, not if Mr. Oakes's assessment of Cord was sound. Bea
put her faith in the older man. And if he'd been mistaken?

Bea hiked her chin up, refusing to consider that possibility.
"Cord wouldn't be a party to deception."

As soon as she spouted that lie, her stomach knotted with
renewed doubt. She'd hired Cord to help her deceive her
grandfather. If he'd done it once, what would stop him from
taking money to do so again?

Some emotion Bea couldn't read clouded Donnelly's eyes.
He blinked, and the expression vanished like smoke on the
wind.

"I don't aim to argue with you, Mrs. Tanner. Tell Cordell
he'll be hearing from me directly." Donnelly heeled his mount
around and trotted toward his property.

"I shan't be long. Wait here for me, m'dear." With blood in
her eyes, Muriel galloped after Donnelly.

With expert horsemanship, her aunt corralled Donnelly
near an outcropping of rock. Bea grinned, unable to hear a
word but knowing by the rapid movement of Muriel's mouth
and wagging of one finger that she was giving Donnelly a
much deserved dressing-down.

"Why'd you marry him?" Yancy asked.

Bea sighed, torn between the urge to slap Gil Yancy for keeping her doubts about Cord alive or coming up with something that would put a stop to Yancy's persistent questions.

"Cord is the image of the man I'd always dreamed of marrying, and he claims I'm the woman he'd fancied taking to wife." When Yancy snorted, Bea smoothly embellished on the lie Cord concocted. "It's the truth, you know. When Cord saw me attend the Bar T rodeo last fall with Papa, he decided to court me."

A ferocious scowl twisted his good looks. "He did what?"

She cringed, struggling for composure in the wake of his rabid fury. "Cord was immediately taken with me and planned to make my acquaintance as soon as he healed from his own injuries, but shortly after the rodeo, Papa died. Cord was forced to wait a longer interval before he approached me."

"That lying sonofabitch." A muscle ticked along Yancy's jaw. "I should've known he'd sneak behind my back and spin a yarn to get his hands on you and this spread."

A shiver of unease raced through Bea. Did Yancy know Cord had plucked that story about meeting her out of thin air? Or was he guessing? Either way, she had to settle this here and now.

"Why do you insist on doubting me?"

"I was there with Cord that day at the rodeo." Yancy jabbed his chest with a thumb. "I pointed you out to him. Told him I aimed to court you. He barely gave you a passing look."

Bea squirmed, burning with humiliation. She didn't want to believe Yancy, but she did. Cord didn't want her then. If she wasn't paying Cord, he wouldn't pretend to want her now.

"Dammit all! If Cord hadn't come along, I know we'd have been courting by now."

"You're mistaken, Mr. Yancy. Had you called on me, I would've turned down your suit."

He winced, clearly hurt by her admission. "Why?"

"You're the Flying D foreman. And Prescott Donnelly

wants the Prairie Rose for himself. So I'd never enter into a romance with a man associated with him."

Yancy gaped, as if doubting her sound reasoning. Then he laughed long and hard. In fact, he was chuckling when he rode off.

Bea swallowed hard, more shaken by his good humor than she cared to admit. Did Yancy find the irony of never having a chance with her amusing? Perhaps. But it was likely he was laughing at her. That's what troubled her most. Not knowing why.

CHAPTER NINE

Bea drummed her fingers on her crossed arms as she paced the spacious alcove off the library. "I must stop Donnelly from tossing about his wild accusations about Cord."

"As I learned, it won't be easy for you to reason with Mr. Donnelly." Aunt Muriel lounged upon a wicker chair and sipped a glass of sherry. Since their confrontation with Donnelly, the older woman's frown had yet to ease. But then, neither had Bea's.

Thankfully, nobody but her retainers knew she and Muriel were out of sorts. The Earl of Arden and Viscount Strowbridge had embarked on a jaunt into Revolt before she and Muriel returned from their ride. Cord and the hands were out in the hayfield.

Bea studied the high color staining her aunt's cheeks. "I'm curious. What did you say to him?"

"I reminded Donnelly that you'd managed the ranch quite well on your own since my brother's untimely death and, by overstepping your authority and speaking only with your husband, Donnelly was making a grievous error." Muriel wrinkled her nose and made a moue. "Donnelly laughed and said, 'Hell'll freeze over before women learn to manage more than seeing to their wardrobe.'"

"How dare Donnelly spew such a derogatory remark."

Muriel finished the remainder of her sherry. "He'd dare do that and much more. It's been my experience that devilishly handsome men such as Donnelly are excessively arrogant."

Bea frowned, wondering if her aunt's eyesight was failing. "I suppose Donnelly is attractive in a rugged sort of way."

"Indeed. His sharp, angular features mirror his hardy constitution. One can tell straight away that Donnelly is hard-bitten and untamed to the core. A man who stands by his beliefs to the bitter end. A man of supreme fortitude and will, probably prone to bouts of unbridled passions." Muriel dabbed a handkerchief to her flushed throat, and her tongue wet one corner of her mouth. "I tell you truly, there are few men of that caliber about."

"I'd rest easier if he weren't one of them."

With the windows in the alcove open, Bea heard the jingle of harness rings and crunch of wheels on gravel. She hurried to the huge panes and peered out.

"Grandfather and Viscount Strowbridge have returned."

Bea scanned the hayfield. Several haystacks rose from the dun earth, but she didn't see Cord or the ranch hands.

"What set you and Mr. Donnelly at odds?"

Bea resumed pacing. "After Papa passed over, Donnelly offered to buy the ranch. I told him it wasn't for sale. Shortly after that, I learned from Grandfather that Donnelly had petitioned him about purchasing the Prairie Rose and all its stock."

"Ah! So, Donnelly is the one who offered Father that goodly sum for the estate?"

Bea nodded grimly. "Now do you see why I must dissuade Donnelly from accusing Cord of cutting the fence?"

"Indeed, I do. If he believes Cord is dishonest, Father would likely accept Donnelly's offer." A wicked gleam lit Muriel's eyes. "However, if Father suspects Donnelly engineered this scheme to cast aspersions on your husband, Father would give Donnelly the what for and have nothing more to do with him."

"And just how do we go about implying Donnelly ordered the fence cut with the intention of blaming Cord for the misdeed?"

Muriel rose, gave her indigo blue skirt a snap to shake out the wrinkles, and plucked her white leg-of-mutton sleeves into stiff, gigantic puffs. "First, we plant seeds of doubt in the Earl of Arden's mind. Now if you'll excuse me, I believe I'll have a lengthy chat with Father."

The second her aunt quit the room, Bea slumped onto the wicker settee and buried her face in her hands. She'd thwarted Donnelly's attempt to purchase the ranch from Grandfather when she married Cord Tanner, but she hadn't expected Donnelly to retaliate and accuse her husband of vandalism.

Worse, she doubted Muriel could convince Grandfather of Donnelly's deceit. Not unless someone had seen Cord about on his mysterious morning ride, it'd be her husband's word against the rancher's that Cord had no part in the fence-cutting incident.

Boot heels scuffed in the open doorway, jerking Bea from her musings. She looked up. Viscount Strowbridge stepped into the alcove.

Panic swelled within her as she judged the distance between the door and him. It would be a close thing to escape him. Despite his girth, she knew he could move fast.

Lambert closed the door and swaggered toward her. His lecherous smile confirmed he knew he had her trapped.

"You're quite the spitfire, Beatrix. I admire you for it. But how much longer do you intend to deny the inevitable?"

"Whatever are you babbling about?"

He crossed his pudgy arms over his expanded middle and sighed. "Come, now. Have you forgotten we were affianced?"

As if she ever could. At least the ensuing brouhaha had saved her from becoming this prig's wife five years ago.

"Not at all. Nor will I forget you called off our marriage because your dalliance with an earl's daughter had gotten her with child. As I recall, Lady Delia told her father you were her lover and he forced your hand in marriage." She smiled then, and not kindly. "In America, we call it a shotgun wedding."

His reptilian eyes turned a bilious yellow. "Jealous, love?"

"Absolutely not."

"Angry, then."

"Don't be ridiculous."

Lambert sniffed. "You seek to humiliate me as I humiliated you. That's why you married the American."

Revenge was the furthest thing from her mind, but she dared not admit the truth to Lambert. The only thing larger than his ego was his cruel streak. Better to let him think what he would.

"Why I married Cord is moot. It's done and that's that."

To her shock and horror, Lambert bent over her and grasped both her hands in his fat, clammy ones. "All is not lost, love. We can still be married."

Bea jerked her hands from his and scooted as far from him as she could. But he sidestepped to keep her prisoner on the settee. "Are you deaf, Lambert? I'm married."

"An obstacle we can overcome easily." Lambert ogled her heaving bosom an uncomfortably long time before lifting his rheumy eyes to her face. "Cord Tanner's a bastard, you know. Far beneath your station. From what I overheard today in the local drinking establishment, he's a dishonest lout."

"I don't know what you've heard, but I assure you Cord's done absolutely nothing dishonest."

An evil grin twisted Lambert's thin lips. "Defensive of the chap, aren't we? And why, may I ask?" She remained stubbornly mute and he chortled. "Could it be the crude American cowboy has opened your naïve eyes to passion?"

"That's none of your business, Lord Strowbridge."

"Still playing the part of the prude, love?"

Bea's chin snapped up. "I'm a married woman."

"One who retained her maidenly charms." Drool oozed over Lambert's lower lip. "Toppling the rigors Victorian ladies place on intercourse takes a tremendous amount of time and patience. I am grateful the cowboy relieved me of that tiring chore."

"You're quite mad."

"I'm mad for you, love." Lambert dropped onto the settee, grasped her upper arms, and tugged her toward him.

Bea shoved both hands against his fleshy chest, stopping Lambert from crushing her against him. But she couldn't push or twist free of his grip. He smiled.

She kicked, landing a solid blow to his shin. Still he held tight. "Let me go, you dreadful man!"

"Divorce the American," he said, his voice harsh. "Marry me and assume your rightful place in England as my viscountess."

"I'll not divorce Cord!"

"If you don't take your hands off my wife real damned quick," Cord drawled from the doorway, "this American's gonna feel obliged to pound you into a damned mud hole."

Lambert scrambled to his feet and gave his waistcoat a tug, looking dignified and unruffled despite being the target of Cord's anger. "You've caught me in a most awkward position, Tanner."

"Damned right, I did."

Bea sprang from the settee and rushed to Cord. His hat shadowed his eyes. Grime streaked his face. He reeked of hay and sweat. But she'd never been so glad to see him.

She wrapped her arms around his lean waist and looked up into his dark, angry eyes. "How much did you hear?"

"Enough." He banded strong arms around her, pulling her to him as Lambert had tried to do. She went willingly, snuggling against his warm muscular chest, soothed by the thud of his heart.

"Yes, well." Lambert cleared his throat. "As Beatrix said,

what's done is done. I bow to her wishes. For the sake of maintaining a degree of cordiality, might I suggest you forget about this *tête-à-tête* you overheard?"

"Get the hell out of here before I forget you're the earl's invited guest and tear you apart." Cord delivered the warning in a cutting tone that made Bea tremble.

Lambert wasted no time quitting the room. The second the door shut, Cord grasped her shoulders and levered her from him. The ardor glimmering in his eyes took her breath away. Then he blinked, and like a petal on the wind, the emotion vanished.

"Your neighbor and his lapdog, Gil Yancy, rode in a few minutes ago." Cord's jaw turned rock hard. "Your grandpappy invited Scotty for supper. Scotty accepted."

The masculine Christian name gave her pause. "Scotty?"

"Donnelly. Folks in these parts call him Scotty."

Wariness seeped into Bea. If Donnelly's nickname was so well known, then why hadn't she heard it in the five years she'd lived here? More troubling, how had Cord known it?

"Where is Mr. Donnelly?"

"At the stable with the earl and Muriel. Rory's showing off what Titan can do."

Bea chewed her lower lip, debating what and how much to tell Cord. "Aunt Muriel and I chanced upon Donnelly this morning."

"I heard."

That surprised her. "If Grandfather believes you cut—"

"He doesn't," Cord interrupted. "The earl heard about it in town. When he got back to the ranch, we hashed things over."

She went very still, stunned and more than a bit confused. "Then why did Grandfather ask Donnelly to stay?"

"The earl and me got our reasons for being neighborly." Cord gently squeezed her shoulders as if trying to put her at ease, but the apprehension she glimpsed in his eyes kept her on edge. "There's something you got to know."

"What?"

He took a deep breath and let it out slowly. "Your pa's death wasn't caused by an accident. Somebody wanted him dead and used Zephyr to cover their tracks."

Bea's mouth opened, but no sound came out. Papa murdered? Preposterous. It was as inconceivable as Zephyr going berserk. But that's what had happened to the stallion.

"Trixie? You all right?"

She shook her head. Dear Papa. Murdered. It didn't seem possible. Tears blurred her vision. The room spun and a sob broke from her aching throat.

Cord whisked Bea into his arms and carried her to the settee. He sat and gathered her against him, holding her tightly.

Like Papa used to do. In her father's embrace, she'd felt protected from danger, injury, or threat. She'd felt loved. Wanted. But Mama had insisted Papa give up the practice when Bea was eight years old. Nobody had held her since.

Bea had grieved the loss. But not nearly as much as she'd missed Papa. For the second time since his death, she let her tears fall until she could cry no longer.

As she'd dreamed of doing every night, her head found a natural perch on her husband's shoulder. One palm splayed upon the steady drum of his heart. It felt natural. Comforting.

"You all right?" Cord asked again, his voice oddly gruff.

"Yes. Thank you." Bea sniffled and wiped the moisture off her face. "You're certain Papa's death wasn't an accident?"

"Dead sure. Jake showed me your pa's saddle." Cord took a chest-expanding breath and blew it out. His hand made lazy circles up and down her arm. "Somebody rigged the leather apron with pieces of barbed wire. The metal cut through the blanket in no time and dug into Zephyr's back."

"All this time I thought those scars were the result of Zephyr nearly tearing his stall down." Bea closed her eyes, recalling each bloody mark on her dear stallion. "Barbed wires imbedded beneath the saddle. No wonder Zephyr went berserk. Because Papa was drunk, he couldn't control the stallion."

"That's another thing. According to Rory, your pa was sober as a judge when he set off that morning."

Bea sat up, confounded. "But Papa reeked of whiskey."

"That's the part we can't figure out. So for the time being, I don't want you telling anybody about this, you hear?"

Bea nodded, her heart aching from the startling news. "Why would anyone want to murder Papa?"

Cord shrugged one broad shoulder. "Could be any reason. You said your pa gambled. Maybe he won something and the other feller was sore about it. Or maybe this feller wanted something of your pa's but he wouldn't part with it, so he did away with your pa."

She tapped a finger against her front teeth. "Of course. Someone who had his eye on acquiring the Prairie Rose."

"Or you."

A quivery laugh slipped from her. "Highly improbable."

One dark eyebrow lifted. "What about Lord Strowbridge?"

She wrinkled her nose, recalling the times he'd groped her breast or pinched her bottom. "In his social circle, there are women who dally outside their marriage. The viscount was merely testing the waters with me, so to speak. But I do believe you've dissuaded him of pursuing me."

"If he's smart, he will."

"You sound very convincing, husband."

"I meant what I said, wife." The seductive gleam in his eyes told her he wanted to kiss her.

Her heart galloped faster than a racehorse. She pressed her palms against his chest and inched toward him. Closer. Closer. She closed her eyes, lips puckered and seeking his.

"Ahem," Benedict interrupted.

Bea jerked back and scrambled to her feet, certain she looked as clumsy as an ox to Benedict. Or guilty as sin.

Heaven knew she felt ungainly and embarrassed at being caught sitting on Cord's lap, poised to steal a kiss from him.

"What is it, Benedict?"

"Lord Arden requests your presence on the lawn for a bout of croquet." Humor tugged at Benedict's usually stern mouth. "Lady Northroupe-Flynn has challenged Mr. Donnelly to a game."

"Has she now?" Bea smoothed her hands over her skirt and wrinkled her nose, catching a whiff of Cord's sweat as well as dried hay clinging to her blouse. "I need to change clothes."

Cord rose, standing so close that his exhalation tickled Bea's nape. "I ain't fit company right out of the field."

"I anticipated as much and have drawn your bath and laid out garments," Benedict said, his cloudy gaze fixed on the windows.

"Thanks," Cord said. "Tell 'em we'll be along in a spell."

Benedict inclined his head and quit the room.

Bea pinched her eyes shut and bit back a groan. She should say something to Cord to propel them beyond this awkward moment. But her mind was too boggled to concoct a fabrication, and she dared not tell him the truth. So she took the coward's way out.

"When you're finished," she told Cord, "knock on my door."

"Yes, ma'am."

His too-polite reply doused her with fresh humiliation. Bea rushed from the library as if her feet burned as hotly as her cheeks. Cord must think her a cold, brash woman.

After drumming into Cord's head that he adhere to the rules of their contract, she'd sat on his lap and cuddled against him. Instead of dwelling on the shocking fact that Papa's death wasn't an accident, she'd dreamed of kissing her husband. She would have, too, if Benedict hadn't interrupted them. God help her, she still ached to do just that.

* * *

A good thirty minutes later, Cord stood in the bathing chamber, slicked his damp hair back, and stared at his reflection in the mirror. Wearing clean jeans and another of Sherwin Northroupe's fancy white shirts, he looked like a prosperous rancher. Benedict had even polished his boots while he washed up. But he was still nothing more than a hired hand.

With one walloping big difference. Instead of strapping on his gun belt and spurs and spending his day in the saddle rounding up strays, he moseyed around the place like he owned it. When he wasn't pretending to be Trixie's devoted husband.

And that was the whole problem. He was hankering to cozy up to Trixie when he didn't even have to. Today, when she was at her lowest, he'd taken advantage of her. Coaxed her on. Him dirty as a pig and smelling to high heaven, yet Trixie snuggled up to him like she wanted to. Holding her felt right, but nothing could be more wrong. Just like last night in bed.

"Damn! I'll be doing good to get a wink of sleep."

Cord settled his hat on. He didn't mind leaving his spurs or gun belt behind while he and Trixie played this fool courting game with Scotty and Muriel. But he felt naked without his Stetson.

Something inside Cord cinched up around his middle, squeezing the air from him. He hadn't talked with Scotty in over ten years. He damn sure wasn't chomping at the bit to start up again. But he and the earl figured Cord had best play his cards close to his vest till they found out who cut the damned fence.

More than likely Gil did it, but Cord wanted proof. Needed to know if Gil did it on his own, or if Scotty ordered him to cut the fence. So he agreed to be civil to Scotty, though it riled him to be neighborly to the man who'd offered him a future then snatched it away from him.

He was halfway to the bedroom door when he stopped short.

The notion of walking in and catching Trixie half dressed or less sent a jolt of heat arrowing straight to his crotch.

Cord pounded on the door. "You ready?"

"Almost. You're welcome to come in." She sounded right as rain, as if she'd put what'd happened in the alcove from her mind.

He eased open the door and stepped into the big bedroom.

Trixie hurried from behind the dressing screen at the same time. Her smile blinded him.

Remembering his manners, Cord gave Trixie his arm and escorted her outside. She was all sweet smelling and wearing that pretty dress again. He spotted Gil by the stable, jawing and sharing a smoke with Ott. Their backs were to him.

Cord scanned the yard. He didn't see hide or hair of the viscount, but Trixie's grandpappy sprawled on the fancy cast-iron settee flanked by two rambling roses, watching them.

He patted Trixie's hand and grinned at her, like she meant the world to him. "Smile. Your grandpappy's looking this way."

"How good of you to notice and react appropriately." The blush on her cheeks was the same color as the roses, and her shy smile had him aching to taste her soft lips.

The Earl of Arden chuckled, reining Cord off the lusty trail his mind aimed to wander. He glanced at the earl, thinking maybe he was right pleased Cord and Trixie were getting on.

But the earl was grinning and watching Muriel and Scotty go at it. Trixie's aunt clucked away like a hen and Scotty looked madder than a rained-on rooster.

"I wonder what Muriel is talking about?" Trixie said.

"Hard telling. But whatever you aunt's saying sure ain't setting well with Scotty."

Muriel plucked a red ball out of Scotty's hand and headed toward Cord and Trixie, a mallet tucked under each arm. Her skirt snapped and sleeves billowed. Gray streaked the gold hair whipping around her cheeks. But it was her blue eyes that convinced Cord she was up to no good.

"Bea and I challenge the men." Muriel handed Bea the red ball and a mallet. "You don't object, do you, Cord?"

He laughed, knowing it wouldn't do him a damned bit of good to admit he didn't like this pairing. "Nope."

Scotty shoved a mallet and blue ball at Cord, looking as uneasy as Cord felt. "Been a long time, boy."

"Yep. Guess my luck ran out." Cord snagged the mallet from Scotty, his smile strung as tight as his patience.

Bea chewed her lip, staring from Scotty to Cord, then back to Muriel. "I'd hoped Cord and I would be a team."

Muriel's hand cut through the air. "It's invigorating when couples occasionally oppose one another. Replaying the old battle of women against men clears the air, you know."

"Balderdash!" The earl wagged a finger at Muriel. "You'd do well to expend your energies on pleasing men instead of taxing your woman's brain thinking of ways to vex them."

Muriel hiked up her chin, just like Trixie did when she was riled. "Poor Father. How your head must ache from being stuffed with pompous, bigoted beliefs. Women aren't adornments for men. Nor are we doomed to spend our days doing mindless needlework and various other domestic tasks. We have keen minds, capable of managing much more than pleasing your gender."

"Well said." Trixie smiled, looking mighty sure of herself. "Women are as competent as men to manage businesses."

Scotty rocked back on his heels. "If you're talking about hat and dress shops and the like, I reckon you're right. But a woman ain't got no call butting in on a man's doings."

Or bootlegging, Cord thought. But he couldn't bring that up, and he sure couldn't keep his mouth shut and let this set-to between the women and Scotty go much longer, not with Trixie looking ready to wallop Scotty with the mallet.

"You're welcome to your opinion, same as the women," Cord said to Scotty. "Best let it be at that."

"Reckon you're right," Scotty said.

"Indeed, he is." Trixie positioned her red ball and tapped it through the first two hoops and took a free shot.

Cord stepped forward to take his turn at the same time as Scotty. The two eyeballed each other like mad dogs.

"I aim to follow my wife," Cord said.

Scotty snorted. "Bad habit to fall into, boy."

"Reckon you'd know."

The older man winced, but the fire in his eyes reflected his anger. "I never figured you'd settle down in these parts."

Cord shrugged. "One place is as good as another."

"Reckon so, but it's mighty peculiar the fence between my spread and the Rose gets cut after you marry Miss Northroupe." Scotty lowered his voice. "Don't know how long it was down, but I reckon my bull serviced any Rose heifer or cow in heat."

"Hope not. Trixie's stock is purebred Herefords. Breeding them to your bull dilutes the blood and you end up with red Angus or white-faced black Angus. That could cut the price per head."

Scotty nodded, no longer eyeing Cord like he was itching to tear into him. "Any idea who cut that fence?"

"Nope, but I aim to find out."

Cord turned his back on Scotty and turned his attention on the game. He whacked his ball through the first two hoops as if he was knocking Scotty and the past from his mind. Another hit and his ball sidled up to Bea's with a soft clunk.

Scotty hooted and rubbed his hands together. "One good hit, boy, and she's out of the game."

"I don't see it that way."

Winking at Trixie, Cord tapped his ball. It rolled into hers, barely moving it. He took his free shot, which went wide on purpose, and then motioned for Muriel to play.

Muriel hit her ball a good one, but missed her next shot, which would've sent Cord's ball scooting to the boundary line.

After Scotty took his turn and fell short of hitting Muriel's ball, Trixie made two good plays. Cord followed suit, lining up like he was fixing to knock Muriel's ball out of play. His ball grazed hers, sending it skittering, and whacked into Scotty's.

"Hell's bells, boy," Scotty muttered, watching his ball roll out of play. "You hit the wrong one."

"Didn't mean to," Cord lied.

Muriel laughed. "Thank you for helping us poor women, Cord."

"Indeed." Trixie stared at Cord, one eyebrow arching up.

Cord grinned at her and settled his hat low on his brow. To his surprise, Trixie hiked her chin up and marched over to her red ball. Now what had got her back up?

The cutthroat game commenced then and there.

Muriel played the same as Trixie, leading Cord to think she'd taught Trixie how to play with blood in her eyes. Muriel knocked Scotty's ball out of bounds every chance she got and missed an opportunity to send Cord's off the field twice more. Scotty was just as ruthless.

Cord stayed behind his wife, taking a shot or two at Muriel and making damned sure Scotty didn't make a run at Trixie's ball. His plan worked out right fine.

Muriel and Scotty were in the middle of a heated argument near the lane. Ott leaned a shoulder against the bunkhouse, smoking up a storm and watching the couple bicker.

That's when Cord noticed that Gil was gone. Cord scanned the area. Where the hell had Gil gotten off to?

On the croquet court, wood struck wood. Cord turned and saw Trixie's ball sail through the hoops and hit the home stake.

He paused in lining up a play that'd get him out of this game to wink at Trixie. "Congratulations on coming in first, darlin'."

"With you guarding my ball, how could I, a mere woman, do anything less than finish the game first?" Trixie flung her mallet to the ground and hotfooted it into the house.

"Grave error, m'boy." The earl shook his head and heaved a sigh. "Suppose I should've told you Bea wouldn't appreciate being safeguarded. Deuced independent, she is. And stubborn. Always insisted she could take care of herself."

Cord tapped his mallet on the toe of his boot and swore to himself. "There're times when she can't."

"Right you are, m'boy. Thank God she has you to lean on."

For a spell, Cord reminded himself. Once the title was in her name, Cord would pack up and leave. That's what he'd agreed to do. What he wanted. So why did the notion that he should stay married to Trixie stick to his mind like a burr on wool?

CHAPTER TEN

Bea wasn't sure which annoyed her most, that Cord had let her win at croquet or that she'd snapped at him for doing so in front of her aunt, grandfather, and the insufferable Prescott Donnelly.

Most likely, Bea's family viewed her outburst as nothing more than a simple marital spat. She really didn't give a fig what Donnelly thought of her. And Cord?

Bea snared the hair that escaped her bun with a hairpin and jammed it back in place. "My devoted husband should know by now," she said to her reflection in the dressing mirror, "that winning means nothing to me unless I've earned it."

Rising, Bea marched from her room and joined the family in the parlor before the evening meal. She smiled at Cord as if she adored him. He returned the gesture, but fatigue deepened the lines around his eyes and mouth.

Her conscience pinched her for acting peevish, leaving her bruised with a guilty flush. Cord had worked hard baling hay for her cattle, brought the matter of her father's deadly accident to her attention and consoled her, then suffered through a game of croquet to please her aunt. And what thanks did he get? None.

"Sorry to have missed the day in the hayfield," Grandfather told Cord as he plucked a glass of applejack off the tray Benedict held. "I would've lent my back to the task as well."

Cord shrugged a shoulder and winced. "Be glad you didn't."

"Come now, Lord Arden." Lambert fingered the tips of his mustache. "Men of our station hire others to labor for us."

Bea stiffened, tempted to throw her glass of apple brandy in Lambert's insulting face. Many days she'd toiled beside Mr. Oakes and Jake in all phases of their distillery until her back screamed and her chapped hands bled.

"On occasion, I enjoy exercising more than my mental muscles," her grandfather said. "Keeps one fit."

"Indeed it does." Bea dragged her gaze from Lambert's paunch to his rheumy eyes. "Many times I've seen ranchers and farmers work side by side with the men they hire."

Muriel frowned, worrying her sherry glass in both hands. "Prescott Donnelly is one of them. He showed me a scar on his arm that he received when he was branding cattle a year ago."

Bea rolled her eyes over her aunt's obvious interest in Donnelly. Cord sipped his cider, no doubt too weary to comment.

Lambert smirked. "It seems common labor is a necessary evil men must endure in this primitive land."

"Forgive Lambert for acting cheeky," her grandfather said. "Whilst we were in Revolt, he tried and failed to rally a group for a bout of fox hunting."

An ugly flush stained Lambert's fleshy jowls. "Yes, yes. Do accept my apology."

Benedict loomed in the doorway. "Supper is served."

The Earl of Arden set his glass aside and extended a hand to Muriel. "Come along, daughter. I'm anxious to see what epicurean delights the cook has prepared for us."

"Perhaps barbequed beef," Muriel said, as she strolled off on her father's arm. "Prescott said it's a favored dish here."

Bea gritted her teeth. Was her aunt going to drag Donnelly into every conversation?

Lambert pushed to his feet and started toward Bea, clearly intending to accompany her. She shivered with revulsion at the thought of his hands on her and looked across the room at Cord. But he'd already crossed to her side.

Relief and some emotion Bea didn't dare name flooded her as Cord tucked her arm in his. "You look mighty pretty."

"Thank you." Bea smiled at Cord, dismissing the viscount as he stomped from the room. "You're quite handsome."

And he was. His hair had a dark chocolate luster and his eyes glowed like warm molasses. His sun-bronzed skin was a stark contrast to his crisp white shirt.

Bea took in the breadth of his broad shoulders under the well-tailored garment. One of her father's expensive shirts, she knew. She'd caught Mrs. Mimms altering several for Cord.

"Benedict said Mr. Tanner's wardrobe is pitifully barren, and these shirts were just taking up space," Mrs. Mimms had said.

"Very true," Bea had said, aware how much money Papa had squandered on his clothing and how soon he tired of them. "I suggest you alter any of Papa's garments that Cord can use."

Bea would rather give the clothes to Cord. It was a small bonus to him for searching out the truth behind Papa's death.

Chills stole over Bea and closed icy fingers around her heart. If Cord was right, somebody had gotten away with murder.

Cord seated Bea at one end of the table, gave her hand a squeeze, and then took the chair on the opposite end of the table. Mrs. Delgado bustled from one setting to the next, filling bowls with hearty portions of spicy stew while Mrs. Mimms placed several baskets filled with crusty spindle rolls within reach of everyone.

"I hope you made a lot of stew, 'cause when the hands get a whiff of this, they'll be knocking down the kitchen door to get at it," Cord said.

Mrs. Delgado laughed as she pushed open the kitchen

door. "They're already gathered around my table. And don't worry. There's more than enough for everyone."

Lambert scooped a chunk of beef from his bowl. "Finally a meal one can recognize." He shoveled it in his mouth.

Bea selected a roll. "The chili peppers in Mrs. Delgado's *mole de olla* add zest to the stew, don't you think?"

"Indeed. This is far from the bland fare we're accustomed to," Grandfather said after sampling the dish.

"A refreshing change from the ordinary," Muriel added.

To Bea's right, Lambert's beady eyes watered and he gasped. He grabbed his water glass and drained it in a matter of seconds. She smiled, knowing that wouldn't douse the heat of the peppers.

"Milk cools the burn some," Cord said.

Bea asked the viscount, "Should I ask Mrs. Delgado to fetch you a glass?"

"No, thank you. Never could tolerate the stuff." Lambert shuddered and resumed eating, though Bea noticed he was careful to avoid anything that remotely resembled a pepper.

Pompous prig! Bea wished the bored viscount would return to England, but she knew he'd stay until Grandfather took his leave.

Judging by the way the earl got on with Cord, Bea suspected Grandfather had settled in for a long stay. Not that she minded the earl taking an extended visit with her. In truth, she'd missed her grandfather and enjoyed being near him again.

"Prescott Donnelly is a rather argumentative sort." Muriel cooled a small portion of stew on her spoon.

Grandfather snorted. "You bring that quality out in men."

"Piffle. The man doesn't like to lose to a woman." Muriel popped her food in her mouth and chewed. "I daresay that's why he declined taking supper with us."

Bea choked on her bite of crusty roll. She didn't want

Donnelly on her ranch, nor did she care to ever share a meal with the man. Being civil to the viscount taxed her enough.

Lambert dabbed his thin lips with the napkin, rose, and gave the vest straining over his paunch a tug. "If you'll excuse me, I've letters to write this evening."

"Of course." Bea sighed, relieved to be spared an evening of Lambert's odious presence.

Mrs. Delgado served dessert and everyone enjoyed the baked apples, especially Cord. He truly had a fondness for the fruit. Afterward, they adjourned to the parlor.

The earl brought up the topic of cattle. He and Cord launched into a lengthy discussion about various breeds and the ever-changing market. Cord's theories on the industry surprised and pleased her.

Bea would've enjoyed adding her opinion, but Muriel was most curious about Revolt. To ignore her would've been rude.

"Do tell about the women's societies in Revolt," Muriel said.

"There is a quilting circle. Both churches host benevolent societies. And a few months past, Mrs. Lott established a chapter of the Women's Christian Temperance Union."

"Isn't that the group that marches on saloons and has on occasion destroyed some?"

"One and the same. At one time, Revolt had four saloons. One could walk down the boardwalk in the middle of the day and be assaulted by raucous laughter, vile talk, and the occasional fight that spilled onto the street."

"Were there any houses of prostitution?"

"Those ladies did business, shall we say, in the upper rooms of one of the saloons. But when the Temperance Union insisted the town abide by Prohibition, the saloon owners, the painted ladies, and the gamblers moved on." At least most of them did.

"That explains why I didn't see any saloons when we drove through Revolt." Muriel sipped her sherry.

Bea chewed her lower lip, debating whether to tell Muriel about the Plainsmen's Lodge. Since Muriel might mention its existence to the wrong person, Bea decided not to tell her aunt about the saloon that masqueraded as a gentlemen's club.

Gossip spread faster than a prairie fire in Revolt. If the Temperance Union ran Keene Poully out of town, Bea would lose a buyer for her applejack. She'd be back to selling cider to Lott's Mercantile and scrimping to make ends meet until she received a good price for one of her hunters.

"Father is impressed with your husband."

Bea glanced at the two men deep in conversation. "Cord's an impressive man." The honest truth.

Cord did a smashing job in his role of rancher, genial host, and devoted husband. So much so that Bea kept reminding herself that he was merely doing what she'd hired him to do. Surely Grandfather would have no qualms about deeding the ranch to them.

Muriel patted her hand. "I'm delighted you found a good man to share your heart and soul. One never knows what the future holds, so savor every moment you have with Cord."

"He's everything I could wish for in a husband."

"Is he?"

"Of course." Which was true, Bea realized with a start. "Cord is quick-witted. Hardworking. Considerate. Handsome."

And passionate. That's what scared Bea the most. When Cord touched her, kissed her, she burned in her most secret places. And she ached for more.

"I fear there's much you've yet to experience in your young marriage." A wicked gleam lit Muriel's eyes as she bent close to Bea. "The physical pleasures shared between a man and a woman are far more titillating than riding a bicycle."

Bea's face flamed and her heart pounded like hooves in her ears. "Please, no more talk about those—you know."

"Voluptuous spasms? Come now, Bea. Toss aside your inhibitions and enjoy your marriage."

"What makes you think I haven't?" Bea cringed at her too-high, too-strained voice.

"Oh, dear."

Muriel pressed a hand to her mouth and laughed softly, as if she knew Bea's secret. She couldn't, of course. Or could she?

Bea fussed with the folds of her skirt, wondering what she'd done or said to cause Muriel to suspect Bea's experience with intimacies was sorely lacking. The answer pelted Bea like a cold driving rain. As Mrs. Mimms so aptly put it, Bea didn't have the look of a married woman.

Somehow, Bea had to remedy that problem. Tonight. Before Grandfather suspected she'd yet to consummate her marriage.

Tense hours later, Cord and Bea bid the Earl of Arden and Muriel good night and retreated to their bedroom. Cord ambled to the far corner, presumably to ready himself for bed.

Bea hurried behind her dressing screen and slipped off her dress. Deciding how to affect the look of a sensually satisfied woman had her nerves skipping like fleas. Mama had taught her that any intimacy between a man and women was a perfunctory deed. But Muriel made it sound quite pleasurable. And tempting.

In the past few hours, Bea had thought of little else. She stepped out of her undergarments and dropped her pink cambric nightgown over her head. The soft fabric glided over her bare skin like a whisper, raising gooseflesh as it went.

With shaking hands, Bea fastened the tiny buttons running from her belly to under her chin. Her heart kept pace with her rising curiosity of the sexual unknown. She needed to expand her knowledge of the subject. But how far must she go?

The bed gave a familiar squeak and Bea jumped. She laid a hand upon her racing heart. The time to act was at hand. Cord had settled into bed.

Bea took two deep breaths and crossed to the dressing table

before her nerve deserted her. Perched on the tufted stool, she tore the amber pins from her hair. She argued with her morals and dragged her bristle brush through her long, fine hair, hoping her decision to court danger was sound. But doubts lingered. All she succeeded to gain was a smarting scalp and tearing eyes.

However, Bea refused to alter the course she'd set upon. She dropped the brush upon the table and crossed to the big bed and the shadowy man reposing there. She was a twenty-three-year-old virgin wife. Who better than her husband to teach her about the unknown intimacies couples share?

She slipped under the covers and lay on her back. Every inch of her quivered, partly from Cord's close proximity, partly from not knowing how to broach this problem plaguing her.

"You had a rather trying day?" she said at last.

"I've had worse."

"I imagine so." Bea squirmed in her cocoon, deciding to try a different tactic. "I apologize for snapping at you after our game today, but I was annoyed because I savor the challenge as much as the victory. Your protection denied me the former."

"Tell you what. Next time we play, we'll go for blood."

"I'll look forward to it."

"Good." Cord rolled onto his side and presented his muscular back to her, his breathing slow and even. "'Night."

"Before you nod off," Bea blurted out. "There's something I need intimate knowledge of."

"Go on."

Bea pinched her eyes shut, gathering her nerve, knowing it was now or never. "What's a voluptuous spasm?"

Cord swore and coughed. "Let me think on it."

Time ticked slowly by. "You don't know what it is, do you?"

"I know." But he didn't sound happy about having that knowledge. Or sharing it with her.

Her patience wore thin. "Muriel said a woman can achieve one from riding a bicycle, but the physical pleasures shared between a man and woman are far more titillating."

"Reckon that's true."

Bea heaved an exasperated sigh. "Would you be a touch more explicit on how a woman achieves such physical pleasures?"

After mumbling a curse she failed to catch, Cord lapsed into another lengthy silence. All she heard was his heavy breathing and the rapid pounding of her heart.

When he spoke, his voice was low and gruff, vibrating along her senses like a warm caress. "Before a man takes a woman, he'd best stroke her with his body, hands, or mouth until she comes. Then he can take his pleasure along with her."

She fidgeted with the coverlet, mulling it over, trying to picture this physical part of the marriage in her mind. Though she had the gist of it all, there were curious blank spots.

"I believe I understand," she said at last. "When a woman *comes*"—the meaning of which she didn't comprehend at all—"that is her voluptuous spasm. And the point when a man takes his pleasure is where the woman loses her virginity. Am I correct?"

He shifted on the bed. "Yep."

With Cord's assistance, she could achieve a voluptuous spasm without damaging her virtue, though the latter didn't concern her. Losing it was a small price to pay to gain her ultimate goal.

"I need to experience a voluptuous spasm tonight."

"What the hell for?"

"Because if Mrs. Mimms and Aunt Muriel don't think I look like a woman who intimately knows her man, then it's only a matter of time before Grandfather notices it and questions our marriage."

He swore. "So now you want me for stud services."

"If that is what it takes for me to look like a bedded bride, then yes." Bea puffed out an exasperated breath when he seemed on the verge of balking. "What difference will it make if we alter the terms of our marital bargain a smidgen?"

Cord released a dry laugh that shook the bed and her resolve. "None. You paid me for my services. Reckon it's time you got your money's worth."

"That's the spirit. What should I do first?"

"Just lie still, darlin'."

Cord rolled out of bed and jerked the coverlet off the bed, flinging it over the footboard. His folded blanket flew to the floor next. Before she knew what he was about, Cord snapped her out of her cocoon.

Bea squealed and crossed her arms over her bosom, scared and excited in turn. Her nipples peaked, prodding her arms. Soon, she'd know firsthand about these mysterious voluptuous spasms.

Cord stretched out on his side, facing her. His masculine scent surrounded her while the heat of him branded her from breast to hip. Her eyes closed on a shiver. Their clothing separated them, but they might as well have been naked as his hard, unyielding body pressed against hers.

"Relax." Cord dropped a kiss on her cheek, then another behind her ear before moving on to her neck.

His hand glided over her hip, across her belly, scrunching her nightgown into a wad in the valley between her quivery breasts. She burned with embarrassment and something indefinable as the seam abraded her nipples into aching nubs.

Would he pinch them? Cause her pain and humiliation?

No. This was Cord touching her. Not Viscount Strowbridge.

Cord might not be a gentleman, but he was a gentle man. He'd undoubtedly loved countless women and never hurt one of them.

The thought of Cord loving other women annoyed Bea. Refusing to acknowledge such silly jealousy, she wet her dry lips, willed herself to relax, and tried hard to smile up at Cord.

"Have you done much of this sort of thing?"

His white teeth flashed in a smile. She wanted to bite off her tongue for asking such a question. Stupid, stupid, stupid.

"I've done my share." He nuzzled her neck, making her shiver with sensual awareness.

It was nigh impossible for her to relax with his arm resting between her breasts, pulling her gown taut across her bosom. His fingers popped the first button free. Then the next. And the next. One by one until her gown lay open from throat to belly.

"I'm glad you've knowledge of these sexual intimacies," she babbled as his fingers played over her bare skin.

"Some things come naturally."

He nuzzled the sensitive skin near her ear. Pressed his open mouth against her flesh. His lips took a lazy journey to her chin, kissing and wetting her hot skin as he went.

She moaned and slid her hands over his incredibly broad, admirably muscled shoulders. He was hard. Strong.

Even through his undershirt, he was hot to the touch. So was she. Her thin gown smothered her and she longed to rip it off.

Her fingers burrowed into his shoulders. She pulled in shallow breaths, more anxious than apprehensive.

He kissed her neck and nipped her chin. He pressed one kiss between her breasts, his stubble abrading her skin.

Her body jerked of its own accord and an odd sound burst from her. His lips worked magic upon her bare skin, making her quiver from head to toe.

She grabbed fistfuls of his shirt, breathing hard. He pressed kisses beneath her breasts. Traced her ribs with his hot open mouth. Sucked the skin. Laved her stomach.

Fire licked low in her and restlessness twined within her. She squirmed and shivered, the tip of his tongue scorching her.

"That's it. Let it go. Don't hold nothing back."

He slipped a hand under her gown. His fingers meandered

up her calf while his mouth traced the damp path he had blazed between her breasts.

Her eyes went wide. An inarticulate sound bubbled from the back of her throat.

His mouth captured the tip of one breast. Bea squeaked and clutched handfuls of his thick hair. He grunted, stilling.

She clasped her hands over her eyes, humiliated she'd hurt him. "I'm sorry."

"No need to be." His lips moved from breast to breast, leaving a trail of hot kisses as he worked his way up her neck. "I like your hands on me."

Tentatively, she slid her fingers through his hair, marveling at its rich texture. He turned his head and pressed a quick kiss into her palm. She gasped, but his mouth devoured the sound.

He kissed her deeply, with such infinite care that tears sprang to her eyes. This joining of lips and tongue surpassed all others they'd shared. Passion and longing swirled and collided within her, shrinking her world to this man. This moment. This torrent of emotion.

His fingers strummed their way up her leg, playing a love song upon the moist skin of her inner thigh. The sensations thrilled her. And terrified her.

She was a marionette and he the puppeteer. A part of her warned her to hold something back, but she couldn't. She clutched at his damp broad back, squirming, demanding more.

Without hesitation, he slid a finger within her. She froze, too shocked by his bold invasion to tell if she felt pain or pleasure. One tentative move of her hips sent energy coursing through her, lifting her higher on a mysterious bubble, hinting more of the same could bring her sublime enjoyment.

His kisses grew ravenous. Still, a gnawing hunger spread within her. She ached with want.

His finger deserted her only to forge inside a second later with its brother, instigating a rhythm of charge and retreat. She gasped and writhed, prisoner to the sensations rocking her. Light flared in her mind's eye. A high-pitched sound burst from her.

Dimly, she was aware of his body stiffening beside hers. His muffled grunt sounded pained. Something hot and wet dampened her hip. A pungent odor filled the air.

For long moments they lay still, their breathing labored. Cord rolled from her, depriving her of his warmth. A soft cloth brushed her bare hip, but she was basking too much from the pleasure he'd given her to question what he was doing.

Her first voluptuous spasm. No wonder Cord had stumbled over an explanation for it. Words couldn't describe it properly.

He gathered her to his side and exhaled a ragged breath. "Tuck that away in your dreams, darlin'."

"I will." Bea sighed and snuggled against her husband.

Her head rested upon his shoulder. One hand splayed over his heart. She smiled, feeling wondrously wanton. Womanly. Loved.

The following morning, Bea reached for the cowboy who'd dominated her dreams with bone-melting kisses and lusty caresses. Her hand brushed cool sheets, proving he'd quit the bed long ago.

A sad smile played over Bea's mouth. Last night, caught in the throes of her first sexual encounter, she had convinced herself she felt genuine affection spark between her and Cord. In the light of day, she forced herself to view what happened in this bed with a calm, practical eye.

She'd asked Cord to help her achieve a voluptuous spasm and he had obliged her. Love had nothing to do with it. At least not on her husband's part, she suspected.

As for her own heart, Bea hesitated testing the depths of her emotions toward her husband. Deep affection would complicate their bond, something she hadn't considered last night.

And that realization left Bea to wonder how she and Cord would get along after sharing such an intimacy.

* * *

Dawn broke by the time Cord dragged his sorry behind out of bed. It was too late to risk taking his ride before dawn and too early for him to set to work on Zephyr.

But the longer he lay there watching sunlight dust Trixie's body with gold, the more he ached to bed her good and proper. To hell with the contract and his word that he'd keep it. He wanted Trixie under him. Right now.

So he stormed out of the house and ate with the hands. If they noticed he was a mite touchy, they didn't say. Fine by him. He wasn't in any mood to talk.

Cord snapped a lead line on Zephyr and led the big black down the stable aisle. The stallion pranced beside him, tail arched, upper lip peeled back. His nostrils flared, catching the scent of one of the mares coming in heat, Cord reckoned.

"We're in the same sorry state," he said, admitting he was prancing and twitchy this morning because he couldn't get the touch, taste, and sweet smell of Trixie off his mind.

Cord hung his head, downright shamed by the way he'd acted last night. He hadn't lost control since he was knee-high to a grasshopper. But when he was stroking Trixie and she tightened around his fingers, he jacked off then and there.

"Like a wet-behind-the-ears boy," Cord grumbled to himself.

He turned Zephyr out in the corral and trudged to the tack room. Grabbing his saddle by the horn, he hefted it on his back and winced at the dead weight dragging on his sore shoulder.

Funny how pain had a way of taking a man's mind off sex. He opened the gate, ambled into the corral, and propped his saddle against the fence. If he worked himself to the bone during the day, he'd be so tuckered out he'd drop off to sleep as soon as his head hit the pillow.

Settling his Stetson low over his brow, Cord climbed atop the fence and watched the black stallion. The minute Zephyr caught sight of the saddle, he commenced circling. His coat rippled like a black sail and his eyes glistened like black oil.

Cord waited, certain curiosity would get the best of the stallion. It did. Zephyr picked his way along the fence toward Cord. The horse nudged Cord's leg and whickered, tossing its head. But its eyes flicked to the saddle.

"Easy, Zep," Cord said, careful to keep his voice low and even. "That western saddle ain't gonna hurt you none."

Zephyr blew and edged closer, sniffing the saddle. Good. Cord wanted the horse to catch Cord's scent on the leather.

The horse ran its muzzle over the stirrup and fender. Nosed the cinch and latigo.

Zephyr flattened his ears. Tossed his head. Snorting, the stallion whirled and trotted around the corral.

Cord thumbed his hat back and hissed out his breath between clenched teeth. From the looks of things, it was going to take longer than he figured to get Zephyr used to a saddle again.

He hauled his saddle from the corral at the same time Jake came by lugging a heavy stock saddle. The boy looked like he'd taken a big old slug of sour milk.

"You heading out to ride the fence line?"

"I aimed to, but the stirrup leather broke on me." Jake kicked the worn wooden stirrup that had hit the dust.

Cord eyed the old saddle. By the looks of it, it'd knocked around since the War of Rebellion and suffered a passel of abuse before it fell into the young cowpoke's hands.

"You could get a new stirrup strap put on at the harness shop in Revolt, but you'd be tossing good money after bad."

Jake's shoulders drooped. "I ain't got the money for a new rig, so I'll have to patch this'n myself."

Cord glanced at his saddle he'd been given fifteen years ago. The leather gleamed from regular polishing and his tooled initials on the fenders remained as sharp as when the saddle was new.

Over the years, he'd replaced the twin girths on the

double-fired saddle. Except for the time Gil had borrowed it, nobody but Cord had set it. He'd sworn nobody ever would.

Cord rubbed his chin, chewing that over. Maybe Cord saw a bit of himself in Jake. Maybe the night spent holding Trixie made him soft in the head. But he knew what it felt like to own nothing more than the clothes on your back and have no home or family to turn to for help.

"Go on and use my rig today," Cord said. "No sense in you wasting time patching yours when mine ain't being used at all."

Jake's cow-brown eyes snapped wide open. "You sure, boss?"

Cord rubbed the back of his neck and grinned. "Yep."

"I'm mighty obliged." Jake swung Cord's saddle over a shoulder and hightailed it toward a hitching post where a swaybacked chestnut gelding was tethered.

Cord grabbed the lead line and headed back into the corral. He walked toward Zephyr. As frisky as the stallion was today, he had his work cut out for him. But as long as his mind was on working the stallion, he wouldn't be pondering what he was going to do about the odd ache of longing Trixie stirred in him.

A horse whickered and Jake shouted. Cord whipped around just as the gelding shied, head down and kicking. Saddle and rider flew off the swaybacked gelding.

Jake's backside smacked onto the ground, arms flung over his head, hat tumbling off. Before the red dust settled, forty pounds of saddle landed on top of the cowpoke.

The chestnut gelding bolted. Ott charged out the bunkhouse door with Rory fast on his heels. Jake didn't move.

Cord scrambled from the corral and ran toward the fallen cowpoke. He hoped Jake just had the wind knocked out of him, but getting a better look at the cowpoke had Cord fearing the worst.

CHAPTER ELEVEN

Heart in her throat, Bea lifted her skirts and raced toward the cowboy sprawled on the ground. Mr. Oakes and Rory rushed from the bunkhouse, too, their expressions grave, doubling her fears.

A loud buzzing filled her head and she faltered. She'd stepped from the house just as Cord and the saddle toppled off the horse. That he might suffer the same fate as Papa terrified her. She couldn't lose Cord. Not like this.

Out of the corner of her eye, Bea saw Cord lope from the corral to the fallen cowboy. A relieved sob tore from her soul. Cord was all right. He hadn't taken the nasty fall. So who had?

Jake! The only discernable similarity between Cord and her young foreman was their height. Cord was more muscled. More handsome. But at a distance, Bea couldn't tell the two apart.

Cord flung the saddle off Jake and knelt by his side. Mr. Oakes crouched opposite Cord. Rory stood back, watching.

She stumbled to Cord's side, but her gaze fixed on the fallen cowboy. To her horror, Jake didn't move. Didn't open his eyes.

"Is he d-d-d—" She couldn't bring herself to say "dead."

Cord stood and wrapped a strong arm around her shoulders, giving her a quick, fierce hug. "He had the wind knocked out of him but he's alive."

"Thank God. I was sure you'd been hurt."

Cord thumbed his hat back. "Seeing as someone took a knife to my saddle, I suppose me taking a fall was the idea."

It took a moment for Bea to grasp that Cord was insinuating that someone had instigated another riding mishap on the Prairie Rose. "Are you absolutely sure someone planned for this to happen when you took your morning ride?"

"Yep, but I didn't saddle up this morning."

Cord rubbed his neck, staring at Jake. Some emotion played over the hard angles of his face. Concern? Relief? Annoyance?

"Why was Jake using your saddle?"

"The stirrup strap busted on his, so I lent him mine."

Icy fear seeped into Bea's bones and she shivered. Cord had escaped injury because he didn't follow his usual routine this morning. Not so for poor Jake.

"How is he?" Cord asked.

"Out like a snuffed wick." Mr. Oakes scraped a gnarled hand over his mouth. "Seeing as that saddle horn hit the boy plumb square in the brisket, he more'n likely busted his ribs."

Jake looked as if he were napping, but Bea didn't like the grayish cast to his skin. "We should summon the physician from Revolt immediately."

"Nothing Doc can do 'cept wrap up his ribs." Mr. Oakes squinted at Cord around a haze of cigarette smoke. "Suppose it wouldn't hurt none if that cantankerous ol' sawbones what calls himself a doctor looks in on the boy."

"Agreed," Cord said. "Rory! Hightail it into town and haul Doc Crowley out here pronto."

"Yes, sir." The groom dashed off.

Mr. Oakes ran his gnarled hands over Jake's limbs. "Don't feel no breaks. Best get the boy inside."

"Let's get at it," Cord said.

Cord slid his arms around Jake's hips while Mr. Oakes got a grip on Jake's upper body. At her husband's nod, they carried the limp cowboy into the bunkhouse.

Bea followed on her husband's heels, too fretful about Jake's condition to worry if she was committing a breach of etiquette by entering the male-only domicile. Papa's foxhound roused from her bed in the corner, her ears alert. Juliet abandoned her fat pups and loped to Jake's cot. The hound sniffed his arm, whimpered, and took up a watchful post at the foot of his bunk.

Cord peeled off Jake's shirt and undershirt and tossed them aside. The cowboy moaned softly, his breath catching.

Bea bit her lower lip, hoping Jake would open his eyes. But he didn't. Perhaps sleep was best. The round bruise blossoming on his chest indicated that the saddle horn had hit him, most likely breaking ribs and causing pain with each breath.

Mr. Oakes straddled a stool by the bunk and proceeded to roll a cigarette. "I'll watch over the boy till Doc gets here."

"Give a holler when Jake comes to."

Cord wrapped an arm around Bea's shoulders and ushered her outside. As if nothing out of the ordinary had happened, Jake's horse munched tufts of dry grass near the corral. Cord's saddle was where he had left it, looking innocuous.

Grandfather and Muriel stood outside the bunkhouse, concern etched on their faces. Both were dressed in riding costumes.

"What a dreadful mishap," Muriel said.

The Earl of Arden snorted. "How's the lad?"

"He hasn't awakened," Bea said. "We sent for the doctor."

"I spoke with Rory as he was rushing off." Grandfather turned to Cord. "Was the lad's saddle tampered with?"

Cord thumbed his hat back. "Somebody took a knife to it, all right. But it was my saddle."

Grandfather's eyebrows slammed together over his regal

nose as he stared at the large cowboy saddle. Aunt Muriel's eyes widened and her mouth formed a silent O.

"Where the deuce is your groom?" A nattily garbed Lambert strode abreast of them, tapping one buff-encased thigh with a riding crop. "It's reprehensible I've been forced to stand about waiting for the bloke to ready my mount."

"If you aim to ride, you're welcome to saddle a horse yourself," Cord said.

Lambert sniffed and tugged at the sleeves of his snug-fitting jacket. "I suppose I could manage the task."

Bea wrinkled her nose in disgust. As Mr. Oakes would say, the viscount was so lazy he stunk. "Rory is off to fetch the doctor, so you'll have to make do or leave off riding."

"Has someone taken ill?" Lambert asked.

"Jake was thrown off his horse," Cord said.

"Indeed. I witnessed the entire incident from the upper balcony," Grandfather said. "It was the oddest thing. Both cinches on the saddle came loose simultaneously."

Not an iota of surprise or curiosity showed on the viscount's face. "A rather peculiar accident, wouldn't you say?"

"That was no accident." Fury darkened Cord's eyes. "Both latigos were scored. Whoever did it figured they'd bust when the horse broke into a gallop, but he cut them too deep and they snapped soon as Jake forked the saddle."

Lambert smirked. "It seems the lad's acquired an enemy. A rather brutal one, I'd venture."

Before Bea could correct his misconception, Cord stated in a flat voice, "The saddle's mine."

"Well, then. The foe must be yours, Tanner," Lambert said.

Cord studied Lambert for a long moment, then snorted, no doubt finding the man lacking more than manners. "Reckon so."

"I say, Tanner." Grandfather slapped his leather riding gloves against his palm. "Have you many adversaries?"

Cord rubbed his knuckles along his taut jaw and let out a dry laugh. "A few."

Bea mulled that over. The day she and Cord married, Gil Yancy had threatened Cord, but her husband had shrugged it off. Then yesterday, someone had cut the fence between her ranch and Donnelly's Flying D. Gil had accused Cord of doing it. And Bea knew why. Gil wanted to shift the blame from himself.

"I don't think it's coincidence that your saddle was damaged after Gil Yancy visited the Prairie Rose," Bea said.

Cord mumbled a curse and scrubbed a hand over his mouth.

"Who's this Yancy fellow?" Grandfather asked.

Bea hiked her chin up, happy to answer. "Donnelly's foreman. I wonder if Donnelly had a hand in this."

"Prescott wouldn't do such a cowardly deed," Muriel said.

"How can you be sure?" Bea asked. "You don't know the man."

"But I do, and your aunt's right. Scotty wouldn't do this." Cord blew out a heavy sigh, his eyes dark and snapping with anger. "There was a time I'd have sworn Gil wouldn't have stooped that low either. Now I ain't so sure."

"Why would Mr. Yancy wish to harm you?" Muriel asked.

Cord gave a halfhearted shrug. "Bad blood, I reckon."

It was more than that, Bea suspected. Why did Cord refuse to speak of his past association with Gil? And these secretive morning rides he took. Where did Cord go? And why?

Bea intended to find out. The best way for her to answer her questions and lay her suspicions to rest was to follow Cord discreetly when he took his predawn ride tomorrow morning.

"Tanner is wise to question this Yancy's integrity." The viscount stroked his nubbin of a chin with a forefinger. "While you were engaged in your croquet match yesterday, I took a whiskey onto the balcony. I saw this chap enter the stable. At the time I thought nothing of it. But now—"

Lambert didn't need to go on. Bea surmised everyone

knew what he was implying—Gil had slipped into the tack room and applied a blade to Cord's saddle.

"Maybe Gil did it," Cord said after a lengthy pause. "But I ain't accusing him till I get proof."

"Wise choice." The Earl of Arden turned to Lambert. "Where are you off to today?"

"This mishap has changed my mind about riding, Lord Arden. If you'll excuse me, I'll acquaint myself with your library."

"Do as you wish." Grandfather waved the prig away, a dismissal Bea suspected he did without conscious thought.

After the viscount strolled off, Cord grabbed Bea by her elbow and turned her from the others. Not a flicker of emotion showed in his eyes, releasing a swarm of butterflies within her.

"Seeing as nobody's using it, I thought I'd borrow that fancy western saddle of your pa's." Cord flashed Bea a hesitant smile, and she realized with a start he was asking for her permission.

"Of course." Bea affected a nonchalance she didn't feel. "You plan to ride this afternoon, then?"

"With Jake down, I need to run the fence line. You want to come along with me?" He flashed Bea his rogue's grin.

A peculiar thrill tripped through Bea at the thought of sharing a tryst with her husband. She wouldn't, of course. Even if theirs was a normal marriage, she needed to find out all she could about her husband's past association with Gil Yancy.

Bea kept her voice light and cheerful, though she felt anything but. "Perhaps another time. Aunt Muriel and I have plans for today."

"Enjoy yourself."

Cord brushed two fingers over his hat brim. He grabbed the saddle by the horn, swung it over his shoulder, and stalked to the stable, his steps as heavy as the lie weighing on Bea's heart.

"I believe I'll select a mount and join Tanner. It's been a deuced long time since I've inspected these lands." So saying, the earl disappeared into the stable, leaving the women alone.

"Might I inquire as to what our plans are?" Muriel asked in a conspiratorial voice.

Bea exhaled slowly. "I need to visit the Flying D Ranch. I've several questions I fear only Mr. Donnelly can answer. I was hoping you'd join me."

Her aunt clasped her hands together and beamed, seeming inordinately exuberant. "I'd be delighted to."

"Then let us be off."

Bea hoped she wouldn't regret inviting Muriel along on her impulsive visit to Mr. Donnelly's ranch or her rash decision to snoop into Cord's shadowy past.

A short while later, Bea and Muriel rode onto the Flying D land. Bea reined her spirited white mare into a sedate walk and was glad when Muriel did likewise. She'd never been here before and wanted to survey the area before she confronted Donnelly.

From the hill, Bea saw a two-story house surrounded by a white picket fence. Myriad outbuildings sat apart from the home, and Donnelly's exquisite stock grazed in the fenced pasture.

But the cemetery situated on the treeless knoll caught and held Bea's attention. It sat alone and apart from the ranch.

The final resting place embodied bleakness. A black fence divided the cemetery from the rolling prairie. The dull wrought-iron curlicues and spires of the fence absorbed the sunlight. An arch of black iron ivy above the gate bore the name "Donnelly" in bold letters.

From a carpet of brown prairie grass rose a lone monument. Despite the warm midday sun, Bea shivered. She stared at the white marble headstone. From this distance, she couldn't read the name or date, but she hesitated to dismount and enter the desolate enclosure to make a closer inspection and satisfy her curiosity.

The monument's simple cross, backlit by an autumnal sun, cast deep shadows atop the grave where patches of lichen clung to its northern side. The ground around it didn't appear to have been broken in many a year. But yellow wildflowers lay before the headstone, proving the person buried here wasn't forgotten.

Muriel broke the silence. "Donnelly's wife, I imagine."

"Perhaps." Bea had heard precious little gossip about her neighbor in the short time she'd known him. For all she knew, Donnelly could've married and buried countless wives and sired dozens of children. "Let's be off. I'm curious to see how receptive Mr. Donnelly is to uninvited callers."

They rode into the ranch yard, but Donnelly didn't notice them. The brusque rancher stood at the corral alongside several of his ranch hands.

All shouted encouragement to a cowboy clinging to a bucking horse. Gil Yancy held the reins in one hand, bending and bowing with the frenzied ride.

The horse bucked and whirled. Gil lost his seat, landing hard and kicking up a cloud of dust.

Bea hoped that would put an end to this public display of horse breaking. But the cowboys—including Donnelly—issued ungodly bets with Gil to try again.

Rising to the challenge, the arrogant cowboy brushed the dust off himself and lunged for the horse's trailing reins. A heartbeat later, Gil tweaked the horse's ear to divert its attention while he vaulted back onto the saddle. In moments, he resumed his wild ride on the unbroken horse. The cowhands cheered his pluck.

Bea released a huff born of disgust. She disapproved of this crude practice and its horde of spectators. That she was involuntarily one of the latter perturbed her.

Thankfully, the exhibition ended. The horse trotted around

the corral, sides lathered and head drooping. Gil waved his hat in the air, obviously proud to have broken the horse's spirit.

"How utterly barbaric!" Muriel glared at Gil's sweat- and dust-streaked back, unaware, and most likely uncaring, that her remark caught Mr. Donnelly's attention.

The big rancher strode over to Muriel. "Busting green broncos is a rough occupation, ma'am."

Muriel made a show of smoothing her kidskin gloves. "As my late husband, Mr. Flynn, was wont to say, 'the steed trained with patience and intelligence will be a trustworthy asset to its owner.' Your method, sir, breaks the animal's natural spirit."

"I 'spect there's some truth to that." A grin softened the hard edges of Donnelly's stern mouth, making the older man appear handsome in a rugged sort of way. "Few ranchers can waste the time and money hiring a trainer to put a fifteen-buck finish on a thirty-five-dollar bronco."

Muriel gave a theatrical sigh. "I see your point, Prescott."

She did? Bea shook her head, stunned her aunt hadn't argued the point. Why was her aunt being so agreeable?

Muriel blushed and pressed a gloved finger to her lips. "Oh, dear. I trust you don't mind me addressing you informally."

"Not as long as you let me do the same." Donnelly's eyes danced with wicked amusement.

Bea fisted a gloved hand atop the smooth pigskin horn of her sidesaddle. Good grief! Muriel was flirting with Donnelly. Worse, the rancher was returning her aunt's bold regard in kind.

That's what worried Bea the most. She doubted Donnelly's motives were honorable. Hadn't the foggiest notion what lengths he'd attempt to gain favor with the Earl of Arden. But the possibilities angered her.

"What brings you ladies to the Flying D?" Donnelly asked.

Muriel gave a throaty laugh that set Bea's teeth on edge. "Nothing more than a friendly visit, I assure you."

Donnelly's gaze explored every inch of Muriel's flushed face. "Then come inside and refresh yourselves."

"We'd love to," Muriel said.

"We haven't the time," Bea said at the same time.

"Come now, Bea. We've nothing pressing to attend to." Muriel's eyes glittered with challenge. "If I recall correctly, you wished to discuss something with Prescott."

He looked up at Bea. "What's on your mind, Mrs. Tanner?"

Far more than she was willing to share. She'd intended to ask Donnelly about Cord, but halfway here she realized she would doubt anything Donnelly said about him. But Muriel didn't know she'd changed her mind.

Bea affected a look of concern. "I'm most curious who is buried in your family plot."

To her surprise, Donnelly looked genuinely startled by the question. But before he replied, Muriel pressed the back of one gloved hand to her forehead and let out a moan of distress.

Donnelly hustled to her aunt. "Are you all right, Muriel?"

"I feel quite light-headed." Muriel moaned again and swayed in her saddle.

Before Bea could blink, Donnelly plucked Muriel from the horse. Instead of steadying her on her feet, the big rancher carried Muriel toward his house.

Bea wasn't sure what had befallen her aunt, but she certainly wouldn't leave the woman alone with Donnelly. Frustrated by the way this day had gone and worried over her aunt, Bea dismounted. She tossed her reins to the cowboy who'd rushed forward to attend to Muriel's mare and dashed into the house after Donnelly.

The big rancher strode into the garish parlor and straight toward a red and gold velvet sofa. His spurs sang out a tinny chink, chink, chink that set Bea's nerves on edge. As he stepped onto the red and black carpet covering the polished plank floor, his heavy footfalls muffled.

The gaudy opulence of the dressings did little to ease Bea's composure. Gold damask draperies held open with thick black tassel cords allowed light to spill into the parlor through two tall windows, but the dark-hued furnishings kept most of the room shadowy and mysterious.

Bea came inches from colliding with a marble-topped lyre table. She danced around a Turkish ottoman covered in a garish black and gold tapestry to position herself behind the sofa Donnelly gently eased her aunt upon.

"Can I fetch you something?" Donnelly bent over Muriel, his broad brow puckered with worry. "How 'bout whiskey or brandy?"

Muriel lifted a hand to her flushed cheek and exhaled a ragged breath. "A spot of brandy, if it isn't a bother."

"No trouble at all."

Donnelly ambled to an elaborate sideboard. Bea caught a glimpse of his drawn face in the ornately carved, gold-framed mirror before he bent to the task of playing host. Odd as it seemed, the man looked genuinely worried over Muriel.

Bea doubted there was any cause for alarm. The twinkle in her aunt's eyes as she sat up and adjusted her riding skirt confirmed the woman's vim and vigor. So why the charade? Was Donnelly the first man since Mr. Flynn's death to show interest in her and the old girl was giddy from the attention?

Snifter in hand, Donnelly plopped onto the sofa beside Muriel and pressed a brandy into her gloved hand. "Is there something I can do to help you?"

"No, you've been more than kind." Muriel sipped her brandy, then smiled at Donnelly. "Actually, I'm feeling somewhat better."

"I'm delighted to hear that," Bea said, drawing Muriel's gaze to hers. "I'm anxious to return to the Prairie Rose."

Annoyance darkened Muriel's eyes. "If you're in a hurry,

m'dear, perhaps you should go on without me. I assure you I'll be in good hands."

Bea hid her mounting irritation behind a sweet smile. If her aunt didn't have the sense to protect herself from Donnelly's beefy clutches, then Bea would do so for her.

"Dear Aunt Muriel, you know I'd never abandon you."

Donnelly cleared his throat. "If Muriel ain't up to riding, I can hitch up the buggy and take her on home, later on."

Muriel beamed at Donnelly, then waved Bea off. "There. You see, m'dear. All is settled."

Not for a second would Bea leave these two alone. Clearly, Muriel had designs on Prescott Donnelly. The ardent gleam in the rancher's eyes told her he was quite smitten with Muriel.

The thought of her enemy seducing her beloved aunt had Bea sinking her fingernails into the plush red padding of the sofa. She had to snap Muriel out of her stupor and get them out of here.

She glared at the thick, rust-colored hair curling over the back of Donnelly's neck, willing him to face her. "You never did tell me who's interred in your family plot."

The rancher went board stiff, convincing Bea she'd indeed struck a nerve. "My wife."

"I thought as much," Muriel said. "It's obvious this room has seen a woman's touch."

One with quite bizarre tastes, Bea surmised.

"Joy set to fixing up the place after we married." Donnelly removed his hat and wove his fingers through his mop of hair. "My missus said a house should reflect the owner's personality."

Bea agreed with the late Mrs. Donnelly's philosophy. But as she took stock of Mr. Donnelly in these surroundings, she realized he looked as ill at ease as she felt.

For good reason, Bea supposed. The bold colors and exotic furnishings in Mr. Donnelly's parlor simply overwhelmed one's senses. She tried to imagine the type of woman who'd consider this decor reflective of her personality. From her limited experience, nothing familiar came to mind.

Aunt Muriel, miraculously recovered, crossed to the fireplace to study a small framed photograph setting upon the mantle. The color leached from her face and she swayed.

Before Bea could round the sofa, Donnelly had surged from it. He reached Muriel in half a dozen strides. Bea stopped short.

"Easy there." Supporting Muriel with one arm, he plucked the photograph from her hand. "You'd best rest yourself a spell."

"Of course." Muriel leaned against Donnelly as he guided her back to the sofa, but her eyes were clear and bright, not at all what Bea would expect to see on a woman poised to swoon.

Muriel settled on the sofa. "Your wife, I assume?"

"Yep. That's the only picture I got of Joy." He returned the photograph to the mantle, his rugged features guarded.

"She was a strikingly beautiful woman." Muriel took a sip of brandy. "Were you blessed with children?"

"My missus had a son."

"Ah, you raised him, then?"

An odd smile played on Donnelly's mouth. "I tried, but he was the spitting image of Joy in more ways than one. And he didn't take kindly to orders."

Bea wasn't surprised. She imagined the simple fact was that the stepson refused to bow to Donnelly's domination.

"I see." Muriel toyed with her brandy. "I take it he's left the nest, so to speak."

Donnelly scrubbed a hand over his nape. "The boy's married and has a ranch of his own."

"Does that please you?" Muriel asked.

"Yes'm, it sure does."

"How do you feel about grandchildren?" Muriel's demanding tone embarrassed Bea. And why all the questions?

The big rancher gave her aunt a mile-wide smile. "I'd be right pleased if they'd fill their house with young'ns."

Muriel let out a dramatic sigh. "I envy you, Prescott. Long ago, I dreamed of having my children and grandchildren around to comfort me in my dotage."

"Same here," Donnelly said.

Emotion clogged Bea's throat. She'd had the same dream of a loving family at one time. When she was very young. Before she'd discovered a wife was little better than a brood mare. She'd be her husband's pawn, having no say in her life. Forever.

So she'd forged a new dream and come here to America. She'd be independent. She'd live her life as she wished. Alone. It's what she wanted. So why didn't it seem as appealing?

Muriel laughed, jerking Bea from her doldrums. "Perhaps I'll spoil my great-nieces and nephews, if Bea and her husband will allow it, that is."

Bea blurted out what was in her heart. "You're welcome to stay with Cord and me for as long as you like."

"Thank you, m'dear. You don't know how happy you've made me." Muriel glowed. "Now, shall we be off?"

"Indeed." The sooner the better.

Muriel laid her hand upon Donnelly's offered arm and strolled beside him toward the door. "It seems we're destined to see each other from time to time, Prescott."

"That'd be fine by me," Donnelly said.

Guilt pricked Bea. She'd made another promise she didn't intend to keep. There'd be no children. No loving family. And when that truth came out, she'd hurt the one woman she loved and respected, one who'd been denied a family she'd dearly wanted. Would Muriel forgive Bea? Equally unsettling, would Bea ever forget Cord? Or would she one day long for what could've been?

Donnelly held Muriel's dainty hand in his large callused paw, his gaze warm on hers. "The Bar T Ranch is throwing a shindig Saturday night. I'd be pleased and honored if you'd go with me."

A blush tinted Muriel's usually pale cheeks a charming pink. "I'd be delighted to have you as my escort."

The older couple strolled arm and arm outside. Bea trailed them, expecting her aunt would give Donnelly the standard "but I cannot" excuse. It never came.

Donnelly lifted Muriel onto her mount, resting his hand on her leg far too long to be decent. Instead of her aunt chiding him, as she should've done, she smiled at the big rancher as if she were some lovesick schoolgirl.

Drat it all, but Donnelly appeared equally smitten by her aunt. Bea's chest tightened at the thought of them forming a closer bond. Surely it wouldn't lead to anything lasting. But what if it did? What if Donnelly became family?

Bea would have to suffer his interference. She didn't doubt that Donnelly would insinuate himself in her business. Unless she remained married, she'd be right back to enduring the dictates of a male relative. One who coveted her ranch.

Somehow, Bea had to nip their relationship in the bud before it bloomed. But short of locking her aunt in a room, how could she stop Muriel from courting Prescott Donnelly four days hence?

CHAPTER TWELVE

For three days, Bea was out of sorts. She busied herself in the alcove during the daylight hours, either updating her horses' breeding charts or doing needlework. Jake was laid up with broken ribs, so Cord spent his days attending to Jake's duties. But nights presented Bea with a frustrating conundrum.

The thrill of experiencing her first voluptuous spasm dominated her thoughts, so much so that she was tempted to insist Cord do it again. Her unnatural appetite for desire troubled her.

Mama would be appalled to hear that Bea had enjoyed her first taste of passion. For as long as Bea could remember, her mama had preached on the merits of marital continence as well as the necessity of keeping separate beds. She'd warned Bea that women who indulged in such earthly vices became peevish, morose, and, eventually, lost their sanity.

And that is exactly what was happening to Bea. She slept fitfully, when she slept. She was tired and short-tempered. Everything and everyone annoyed her. Especially Aunt Muriel.

As she'd done every day, her aunt joined Bea in the alcove. While Bea embroidered green stems and leaves around rose bouquets on a tidy of gold pongee, Muriel made a pretense of reading.

Muriel laid her book down and sighed, her smile dreamy. "Prescott's home is rather quaint, wouldn't you say?"

"I suppose so." Bea sucked the finger she'd jabbed again with a needle, an incident that happened every time Muriel had mentioned Donnelly. "It's larger than most, like the owner."

"Prescott is a stately man."

Bea set her needlework aside and tried to reason with her aunt. "He's a shrewd man. I'd advise you to stay away from him."

"Because you fear he's trying to wrest the ranch from you."

"I know Donnelly wants the Prairie Rose. And he'll do anything to get his hands on it. You should bear that in mind."

Muriel laughed, looking and acting far younger than Bea pictured herself at that moment. "Perhaps if you'd take the time to get to know Prescott, you'd realize you've misjudged him."

"I know that man as well as I care to. Further association with Donnelly will only cause me grief."

"Hmmm." Muriel returned to her reading.

Bea strolled to the windows. Her attention swerved to the black stallion and her husband. Cord held a short line on Zephyr, walking the spirited horse in a circle around the huge western saddle in the center of the corral.

Clearly, Zephyr was wary of it. The animal's muscles rippled like black silk as he pranced at the end of the line, smoothly changing gaits at a command. It had been a very long time since she'd seen Zephyr respond so expertly.

She could thank Cord for that. That he'd managed to gain Zephyr's trust with a gentle hand instead of brute force spoke volumes about Cord's ability and integrity.

But she couldn't help but wonder if Zephyr would be obedient when Cord cinched a saddle on him. And she didn't doubt that's exactly what Cord intended to do before long.

She hugged her middle, marveling at the pair. The thought

of another fatal riding accident befalling the ranch, and especially Cord, terrified her. That was why she'd instructed her men to inspect every bit of riding equipage before using it.

Benedict trudged into the alcove and cleared his throat. "A messenger arrived, Mrs. Tanner. The chap is waiting for a reply."

Bea accepted the ivory-colored envelope Benedict held out. "Bar T Ranch" was embossed in black in the upper left-hand corner, but she guessed a bold masculine hand had scrawled "Mr. and Mrs. Cordell Tanner" upon the envelope. She opened it.

"'Mr. and Mrs. Tanner,'" Bea read aloud, "'Your presence is requested at an informal social gathering held at Bar T Ranch this Saturday, commencing at seven o'clock in the evening. Please extend my personal invitation to the Earl of Arden, his lovely daughter, and Viscount Strowbridge. Cordially, Colonel Trenton.'"

Delight glowed in Muriel's eyes. "How nice. Isn't that the same function Prescott mentioned the other day?"

"Indeed. But I refuse to socialize with Donnelly and his compatriots." Bea plucked a white linen paper from its leatherette cabinet and jotted off her and Cord's regrets. "Do feel free to help yourself to my stationery."

"Aren't you going to discuss this with Cord?"

"Not at all. He leaves these matters to me." Bea stuffed her reply in an envelope, addressed it to Colonel Trenton, and handed it to Benedict. "Give this to the messenger."

"Of course. Is that all?" Benedict asked Bea.

"Do collect Muriel's response as well."

Muriel waved a dismissing hand at Benedict, who dutifully trudged off. "There's no need to bother with one. I imagine Prescott accepted for me."

"You can't seriously consider attending with him."

"I assure you I'm quite serious," Muriel said.

Bea silently fumed. Clearly, no amount of pleading on

Bea's part was going to change Muriel's mind about Prescott Donnelly.

Two days later, the brusque rancher arrived for Muriel.

To Donnelly's credit, he asked, "You folks care to ride over to Colonel Trenton's with Muriel and me?"

"Not I." Grandfather retreated down the hall toward the rear door. "I challenged Rory to a game of chess and cannot, in good conscience, back out of the match."

Lambert twirled the waxed tips of his mustache. "Good of you to offer, old chap. However, I've arranged to meet with an acquaintance in Revolt and cannot change plans at this late date."

His excuse surprised Bea. She'd assumed the viscount's cronies had returned to England long ago. At any rate, Lambert didn't waste a second in departing.

"What about you and your missus?" Donnelly asked Cord.

"Me and Trixie got a hankering to stay home," he said.

The big rancher chuckled. "I'll be. Here I thought you had too much tumbleweed in you to settle down."

Every muscle in Cord tensed. Bea smiled, certain Cord would lambaste the rancher with a censoring retort.

Donnelly must have assumed the same thing because his humor fled. The rancher whisked Muriel out the door, leaving Bea and Cord alone in the brittle silence.

Seconds passed and Cord still didn't relax. Bea chanced a peek at him. She wished she hadn't. He'd pulled his lips into a thin, hard seam. Fury pulsed along his rock-hard jaw and sparked a forbidding glint in his eyes.

Bea voiced the obvious. "You're angry."

"I'm a mite vexed with you."

She pressed a hand to her throat and blinked. "Me? Why?"

"You told me straight up you didn't cotton to Scotty. Didn't trust the man. Didn't want a damned thing to do with him."

"And I meant every word."

"Then why did you and Muriel ride over to the Flying D?"

Bea cringed. Though Cord deserved an answer, she wasn't about to launch into a discussion right here in the hall, where Grandfather or Lambert could come upon them.

"I suggest we adjourn to the library," Bea said.

"Lead the way, Trixie."

Bea marched down the hall, her nerves jerking with each heavy step he took behind her, every chink of his spurs. She stepped inside the library and squelched the urge to dash behind the desk.

The door clicked shut behind her. Cord strode past her, rounded the massive desk, and plopped upon the leather desk chair. Her chair. Her desk.

Annoyance and astonishment volleyed within Bea. On occasion, Papa had taken the chair behind the desk, usually when he felt the need to pretend he was in charge of affairs around visitors. But Papa never gave off a reigning aura. Cord did.

"Why did you ride over to the Flying D?" he asked again.

She bit her lower lip as she paced the room, uncertain how Cord would react if she told him the truth. Not well, she feared. Cord would be angry that she'd gone to Donnelly to discover what had severed Cord's friendship with Gil Yancy. So her best course of action was to settle on a half-truth.

"Aunt Muriel grew faint on our ride and Donnelly's residence was close by, so we hurried there and begged him for help."

Cord snorted. "What'd he do? Herd Muriel in his house and give her something to revive her spirits?"

"Donnelly most certainly did. Once Muriel regained her composure, we left."

"You're saying if it weren't for Muriel feeling peaked, you wouldn't have stepped foot on the Flying D."

"Not at all."

Cord leaned back in the chair and scrubbed his knuckles along his jaw. His features were devoid of expression, save one dark eyebrow arching over one discerning brown eye. He doubted her.

"How about telling me the truth, Trixie."

She melted into a small leather chair facing the desk and feigned ignorance. "Whatever do you mean?"

"You ain't a good liar."

An unfortunate truth, Bea admitted. Her inability to tell a convincing lie was what had forced her to seek a temporary husband.

"Very well. I went to the Flying D with the intention of questioning Mr. Donnelly about you."

Except for the ticking of the mantel clock and the hammering of her heart, the room was deathly quiet.

Cord drove his fingers through his thick hair, unknowingly giving him a charming, boyish look. But she wasn't fooled. Even if she wished to, she couldn't influence Cord as she'd done Jake.

"What'd Scotty tell you?"

"Nothing." Bea took a deep breath and let it out slowly. She couldn't deceive him on this. "I didn't ask Donnelly anything about you because I believed his opinion would be skewed."

"He wouldn't whitewash the truth, least what he reckons the truth to be." Cord studied her with cool indifference. "What did you want to know?"

Everything. But she suspected that would overwhelm him, or cause him to revert back to the closemouthed man she'd wed. Better to start with simple questions and build a modicum of trust before she asked Cord what had set him and Gil Yancy at odds.

Bea twined her hands, hoping to appear calm and mildly interested. "You've never mentioned anything about your family."

"Ain't much to tell." Cord stared at her, his eyes so bleak and world-weary that her breath caught. "My ma was all I had. When I was sixteen, a fever took her."

Bea curled a hand to her chest, knowing the pain of losing parents. "What about your father?"

He shrugged, his smile crooked and fleeting. "Tanner was my ma's name. Reckon she didn't know who my pa was."

That was the last thing Bea expected to hear. She squirmed on the chair, as curious as she was ill at ease. Had his dear mother been a victim of rape? Or had she entertained lovers?

"Forgive me for asking, but why was your mother uncertain of your father's identity?"

"My ma took up her trade some thirty years back as a camp follower in the War of Rebellion. My pa could be any soldier she'd pleasured during that time."

Bea swallowed hard, digesting that startling information with great difficulty. She couldn't find it in her to condemn the woman. Nor did it shame Bea to be married to a bastard.

Heaven only knew there were more than a few shady characters perched in the Northroupe family tree. But for the life of her, she couldn't find the words to tell him that. In fact, she didn't have any idea what to say in response.

Cord splayed his callused hands on the desk, watching color leach from Trixie's checks. He'd shocked her speechless, all right. And that wasn't the half of it.

He'd spent his youth in a passel of brothels ranging from high-class to seedy. Watched his ma and dozens of other soiled doves paint up and sell themselves to men night after night. Seen and done things a boy ain't got no call seeing and doing.

He grew up a tumbleweed. A hardworking, hard-living cowboy. Raising hell and riding the range, that's where he belonged. Not sitting behind this fine desk in this fine house. He sure as hell didn't deserve to be married to a good woman like Trixie. Even for a short spell.

Cord pinched the bridge of his nose. "Reckon I should've told you before we got hitched."

"I'd imagine that isn't the sort of thing one readily volunteers when one makes one's acquaintance, but if you had, it wouldn't have changed anything."

He snorted, not believing that for one minute. "Damn it all, Trixie. Folks in these parts know my ma was a whore. Word's bound to get back to your grandpappy before long."

Her cheeks turned wind-burned. "I imagine it will, but there's nothing we can do about that now."

Cord blew out a weary breath. "If you want me to, I'll tell your grandpappy about Ma before he hears about her in town."

"Do what you wish." Trixie got to her feet and slapped at her skirt, looking everywhere but at him. "Excuse me, but I've things to attend to upstairs."

She turned and skedaddled out the door.

Cord slumped in the chair, tempted to call her back and tell her the rest of it. Since she'd been in a sour mood, he decided he'd best hold off telling her till tomorrow.

But he never got up the nerve to tell her how he'd ended up in Revolt, and why he'd left it with no intentions of returning.

Two days straight, Cord spent his days working Zephyr and tending Jake's chores. He was so tuckered out at night that he fell asleep before his head hit the pillow.

Well before the crack of dawn, he'd lie beside Trixie before taking off for his ride. He'd listen to her even breathing, finger the silky hair that spilled over her pillow. Dream of kissing her. Touching her secrets. Holding her and keeping her safe. That's what worried him most.

Someone had slipped those spiders in Northroupe's saddle and taken a knife to his. Why? Were the two connected?

Cord didn't see how. But with his past riding shotgun to the Prairie Rose, he didn't have much more time to find out.

In the wee hours of the morning, Bea sensed Cord watching her again. She feigned sleep, daring not to move. He touched her hair. Her heart raced and heat stole over her, thinking he'd go further this time. But he didn't.

Cord lowered his head, his breath fanning her cheek, coming so close to her that she thought he'd kiss her. Hoped he would. That didn't happen either.

The bed creaked as Cord slipped from it.

She listened to his bare feet slap the floor. The rustle of clothes. Clunk of boots. Jingle of spurs. Then he was gone.

Bea waited several tense minutes before springing from the bed. She tugged off her nightgown as she dashed behind her dressing screen. Heart pounding, she shrugged on chemise, drawers, and petticoat, but shunned the restricting corset to save time.

She donned a blue skirt and blouse and slipped on stockings and boots. A deep-throated whicker drew her to the window.

Bea gasped to see Cord astride Zephyr. Foreboding settled in her stomach like a leaden weight. She had confidence in his abilities as a horseman, but she couldn't dispel the worry that something horrible would happen this morning.

Rattled to the point of shaking, Bea slipped on a garnet wool jacket. She stuffed her hair under a straw hat adorned with garnet ribbons and raced from the bedroom.

Bea bounded down the rear staircase, working her fingers into her kidskin gloves as she went. She flew out the rear door and rounded the house. As she had instructed him to do, Rory stood in the shadows holding the reins to a saddled Cleopatra.

"Your husband has a goodly distance on you, he does," Rory said as he gave her a leg up.

"No matter. I'll catch up."

Grasping the reins, Bea touched her heel to the mare's flanks. Cleopatra stretched out into a fluid gallop.

The first blush of dawn cast enough light to distinguish forms. She glimpsed a rider thundering toward the Flying D.

Panic rose within her. She leaned over the mare's neck and

urged her horse to follow. The biting air stung her face and tore at her hat, but she approached the small rise at a reckless pace.

The sense of urgency clung to her like a meddlesome burr. Where was Cord going? And why?

Bea eased her horse to a trot and scanned the shadowy knoll. Silhouetted against the bruised horizon rose the cemetery's lone monument. Zephyr munched grass near the cemetery, reins trailing the ground, saddle empty.

Bea's blood ran cold. Tormented with images of Cord lying injured, she kicked Cleopatra into a gallop.

From the shadows hovering within the cemetery rose a man—tall, lean, and imposing. He settled his wide-brimmed hat on his head and turned to her.

Bea couldn't see his face, but she knew her husband all the same. Giddy with relief, she reined to a stop beside the cemetery gate. Cord was alive and well. But why was he visiting the grave of Mrs. Prescott Donnelly?

That he paid his respects to this woman was a noble gesture. That he chose to do so under the cloak of darkness smacked of dishonesty. She dared not consider the meaning behind the fresh bouquet of yellow wildflowers lying upon the monument.

But she knew. In her heart she knew. And that knowledge filled her with numbing despair.

Cord closed the gate with a grating click. He walked toward her. The hat shaded his eyes, but the first kiss of dawn detailed the grim set of his mouth.

Bea's mouth felt dryer than the parched ground. "I wasn't aware you were acquainted with the late Mrs. Donnelly."

He gave her a sad smile. "Joy Donnelly was my mother."

Bea stared at Cord, letting the truth lash her like a frigid wind. How could she have been so stupid? So naïve?

"Is this what you were afraid I'd discover if I talked with Donnelly?" she asked.

He scrubbed a hand over his face. "Yep."

Ice seeped into her soul. What little Donnelly had said about his late wife mingled and coalesced with what Cord had told her about his mother. She couldn't equate the wife of the distinguished rancher with the whore. Until she closed her eyes and recalled the garish colors predominating in Donnelly's parlor.

Anguish boiled within Bea. She'd tried so hard to keep her ranch from falling into Donnelly's clutches. She'd weathered the fierce storms, eked through financial panics, and put her back to physical tasks beside her workers. And for what gain?

She'd foolishly married Donnelly's stepson. If Grandfather titled the land upon Cord, her husband would be within his rights to merge the ranch she loved with the Flying D.

Bea blinked back tears. "Did you and Donnelly pay Mr. Oakes to betray me? Or did you threaten him?"

"Neither one." Cord strode to Bea, his features taut. "Ott came to me, saying you needed my help. You're the one who hired me to be your devoted husband."

"Don't patronize me. The fact remains I trusted Mr. Oakes and married you." Her lower lip quivered. "Donnelly's stepson."

Cord bit out several ripe curses. "I ain't in cahoots with the old man, and neither is Ott."

Oh, how she wanted to believe him. But she couldn't.

"Mr. Oakes knew how I felt about Donnelly. So did you. Why did both of you hide the truth from me?"

"I can't speak for Ott." Cord rested a hand upon her thigh, branding her through the layers of clothes. "I figured if I 'fessed up, you'd send me packing."

Bea brushed his hand away, shaken by the intense yearning his touch generated and the sincerity glistening in his eyes. "Telling me would have been the noble thing to do, you know."

"That's water under the bridge." Cord's sad smile made her eyes burn and her throat constrict. "We made an agreement and I aim to stick by it. But if you don't reckon I can do it or you don't want me around, say the word and I'll clear out."

She bit her lower lip, fighting back tears. "No! Now is not the time for you to leave."

Cord heaved a shaky sigh. "Where do we go from here?"

Bea turned her face to the biting wind and regarded the swaths of purple and pink slashing across the horizon with renewed clarity. She heaved a tremulous sigh, her heart aching. Like it or not, they were well and truly snared in a web of her making.

"For the time being, we'll carry on as before." Bea met his haunted gaze with feigned nonchalance. "It shouldn't take long for me to discover if the man I married is a trustworthy sort—or an exceedingly clever liar."

CHAPTER THIRTEEN

Cord took his time unsaddling Zephyr and rubbing him down. He could've eaten with the men, but food didn't appeal to him now. His mind was stuck on Trixie catching him standing over his ma's grave.

Sooner or later, Cord had known Trixie would find out he was Scotty's stepson. Figured when she did, she'd send him packing. But she didn't.

Trixie was holding him to their bargain, but that whipped-dog look in her eyes when she rode off this morning smarted more than tangling with cactus spines. He'd never aimed to let her down. Never wanted to hurt her. But he'd done both.

Cord wouldn't do either again. For as long as he was here, he'd pull his weight and then some.

He strode to the corral and propped the toe of his boot on the bottom rail to watch Rory cinch a contraption called a dumb jockey on Titan. The mick put the young stallion through another training session. Cord had never seen the like.

The dumb jockey sat like a giant fork on Titan's back. Lines stretched from each prong to circle the horse's tail, the reason for it being Titan would learn to hold up his tail while prancing.

Reins ran from the fork to the bridle and another pair buckled low on the girth, teaching the horse to keep his head arched. It did the trick. Titan looked every bit the prize thoroughbred.

Rory stood in the center of the corral, barking commands and working a heavy line attached to the bridle. He held a long whip in his other hand, snapping the air every once in a while to get Titan's attention, but the whip never touched the horse.

Cord smiled, admiring Rory's patience. He'd never seen a man work a horse no more than five times a day in thirty-minute sessions to break it to saddle. But this slow method seemed to work right fine.

Yessiree, Cord aimed to ask Rory to teach him how to gentle a horse this way. It sure beat getting your innards scrambled from climbing on a green horse and riding him down.

A whiff of tobacco smoke reached Cord seconds before he heard the scuff of boots. He glanced to his side.

Ott rested his folded arms on the fence, the stub of a cigarette dangling from his mouth. He squinted at Titan and Rory through a rising curl of smoke.

"Your missus looked a mite down in the mouth this morning," Ott drawled. "Reckon she followed you to the Flying D?"

"Yep. Trixie's put out with us."

Ott flung his snipe on the ground and crushed it under his boot. "Damnation, Cordell! What'd you say to her?"

"Told her we weren't in cahoots with Scotty. Told her about Ma. Thought it best to get it out in the open. Don't know if she believed me, though."

"Can't see as she'd hold your ma's past against you. But hearing you're Donnelly's stepson . . . That might be hard for her to swallow."

"Maybe too hard." Cord settled his hat low on his brow,

thinking this was as good a time as any to talk this out. "Is that why you didn't tell her the truth about me?"

"That was part of it. She needed a feller she could trust with her life, and I only knew one man what fit the bill. 'Sides that, you and Donnelly are on opposite sides of the pasture."

Cord looked at his old friend. "Why didn't you tell me Trixie was fixing to hire a husband?"

"If I had, you'd have taken off like a scalded duck." Ott jerked his makings out of his shirt pocket and rolled another cigarette. "She needs you, Cordell. This ranch needs you."

"Trixie needs me to honor our bargain. Nothing more."

"Bargain, my ass." Ott clamped a cigarette between his teeth and poked Cord's chest with a safety match. "You married that little woman. You vowed to stick by her till death parts you."

"I promised I'd be her husband until she got the title to the ranch in her hands. When that happens, Trixie wants me off the Prairie Rose and out of her life."

"She could change her mind. Or you could change it for her."

"And spend the rest of my days with that headstrong woman? No, thank you." But even as he said it, a fierce hankering to make his marriage real hit him. Could he raise a family on the Prairie Rose? Make a good life here? With Trixie?

Naw. Trixie wouldn't want to be tied to the likes of him for the rest of her days.

Lighting his smoke, Ott clambered up the fence and stared off in the distance. "What in tarnation set them cows to bawling?"

Cord climbed beside Ott and scanned the far pasture. He couldn't tell for certain, but the top of the windmill didn't appear to be turning. That'd account for the herd bawling. If the blades didn't revolve, the pump didn't draw water.

He gave Ott a sidelong glance. "When was the last time that windmill was checked?"

Ott scrubbed a gnarled hand over his mouth. "Seeing as it was repaired not long back, we ain't tended it yet."

Cord pinched his eyes shut a moment and bit back a groan. His fear of heights made mill riding his least favorite job on a ranch, but with Jake laid up, the job fell to him or Ott. He wasn't about to stand by and watch the old man climb the tower.

"Reckon I'd better go take a look at it." Cord jumped down from the fence and ambled toward the stable.

"I'll tag along." Ott scrambled after him. "I was fixing to see to the fence in the back pasture today. The buckboard's hitched and the supplies are loaded."

"Let's get at it."

By the time they reached the far pasture, dark clouds blanketed the southwestern sky. The wind kicked up, gusting every once in a while. They were in for a helluva storm.

Ott pulled the wagon beside the windmill and set the brake. As Cord figured, the giant wheel atop the tower wasn't spinning. But he hadn't expected to find the water trough overturned.

Cord stomped around it, his hackles rising. Judging by the dry ground, the milling cattle had been without water for a spell. Who'd strained their back upturning the trough? And why?

"Help me get this turned back over."

They had the trough in place in no time. But the hollow-in-his-gut feeling warned Cord they wouldn't have the same luck getting the pump working.

"What low-down sonofabitch did such a thing?" Ott asked.

He stared in the direction of the Flying D. "Could be anybody. But you can bet when I find out who did it, I'm gonna kick his ass into the next county."

Ott nodded in agreement and hobbled toward the tower. He

inspected the workings. "The main shaft appears tight. But the only way to check the gear box and workings is to climb up there."

Cord pushed his hat back and let his gaze climb some twenty feet to the small platform. He scowled, making out the shadow of something protruding upward through the blades. Whatever it was, it didn't belong there.

He crossed to the wagon and removed his gun belt and hat. Not knowing what all he'd need, he undid his bandanna and wrapped a hammer, wrench, and screwdriver up in it so he could hold the tools in one hand and still climb the tower.

Sweat slicked his shaking hands. He cursed and tucked a tin of nails, nuts, and bolts in his vest pocket.

He ambled to the windmill, telling himself if he didn't look down, he'd be all right. But as he wiped his damp palms on his jeans and skinned on his gloves, he knew that was a lie. It wasn't the climbing that bothered him as much as the coming down.

Cord sucked in a deep breath and grabbed a rung. The higher he went, the more the wind tore at his shirt and plastered his hair to his head. Dust pelted his face and he squinted, but his eyes watered and stung all the same. The tower swayed and made ominous creaks, but he gritted his teeth and continued climbing.

By the time Cord reached the platform, his heart pounded like a trip-hammer. He poked his head through the opening under the big wheel and let out a string of curses.

The gear box and motor looked fine, but some cur had nailed the business ends of two branding irons to the platform with fence staples. They'd crossed the handles and wedged them between the blades, keeping the wheel from turning and pumping water.

Cord hoisted himself onto the platform and took a closer look at the irons. His fists clenched. He knew these winged D irons like he knew the back of his hand. The Flying D brand.

Fighting the wind and his anger, Cord grabbed his hammer and set about prying the staples holding down one iron. Only a damned arrogant fool would destroy a man's property and leave his signature. Cord couldn't see his stepfather having a hand in this. Scotty was arrogant, but he wasn't a fool.

That left Gil. Cord didn't like thinking his old friend would stoop to this, but Gil was mighty sore that Cord had married Trixie. Mad enough to try killing Cord?

If Gil had taken a knife to Cord's saddle, it sure seemed that way. Gil would've been pissed off when Jake took a tumble instead of Cord. He'd have tried for Cord again.

This time Gil had rigged the windmill. He knew Cord would tend the job, even though he feared heights.

Cord worked the branding iron handle from between the blades and peered down at Ott. The old wrangler cupped his hands around his mouth, but whatever he shouted blew away on a gust of wind.

"Look out below!"

Cord waved the iron, fighting the strong wind to hang on to it until Ott scrambled out of the way. He let go of it and then commenced freeing the other branding iron.

The sky darkened and wind lambasted the tower. It swayed and the platform shook and creaked.

Cord staggered like he was booze blind. He grabbed on to one of the boards that teepeed up to the gear box and squeezed his eyes shut till the dizziness passed.

Thinking what all he'd do to Gil when he got his hands on him, Cord yanked out the last staple and jerked the iron free. The wind caught the blades, sending the big wheel into a roaring devil spin. Before he could duck, the pivot arm on the vane smacked him upside the head.

Pain exploded in his skull. He sprawled flat, losing his grip on the branding iron and hammer. They skidded over the edge of the platform, taking his bandanna and the other tools with it.

Cord knew he should shout a warning to Ott, but he

couldn't force out a sound. His head throbbed. Over the whirl of the wheel, he heard Ott yelling but he couldn't make out a word.

The platform swayed and creaked. Wind lashed Cord. The whirring grew louder, turning into a roar. A loose staple peppered his arm. Another stung his cheek.

With a groan, Cord forced his eyes open. He couldn't see much through his left eye, but the right one focused on the giant wheel. It spun on its axis. The blades revolved like a buzz saw, heading right at his head.

Cord scrambled to the center opening and dropped through it. He grappled for a toehold and ducked as the spinning wheel settled over the place where he'd been sprawled.

"Are you all right, boy?" Ott bellowed.

"Yeah," Cord lied. His head throbbed something fierce. Something wet and sticky trickled down the left side of his face and dripped off his chin. Blood, he'd bet. The wind streaked red threads of it across his vest and shirtsleeves.

His head spun and his legs wobbled like a newborn foal. The wind tried ripping him off the tower. If he didn't fight the weakness stealing over him, he'd plummet to his death.

Cord wet his parched lips and inched down the ladder, feeling for each rung, holding on so tight his hands went numb. One mistake could be his last, and would leave Trixie in a terrible fix.

The wind kicked up again, pelting Cord with dust and grit. He turned his head away and got to moving.

Dizzier than a drunk, he missed the next rung. He dropped a good foot before his hands wrapped around a rung.

Fire licked up his skinned shins. Pain galloped around his chest where his ribs banged up against the ladder. He slammed his eyes shut and hung on until the world stopped spinning. Until the throbbing in the shoulder he'd wrenched eased. Until the stampede in his head let up.

Ott's gravelly voice cut through his misery. "You ain't got much farther to go. Now, stop dawdling and get a move on."

Cord gritted his teeth and took a step. Then another. And another— All the while thinking he couldn't give up. Couldn't let his enemy win. Couldn't let Trixie down again.

Before his boots hit the dirt, a strong arm got Cord around the middle. He tried standing on his own, but his legs were like rubber, bowing out and collapsing under him.

Ott dragged Cord's good arm across his bony shoulders and held him up. "Damn it all, but if you ain't 'bout as heavy as hauling a heifer out of quicksand."

"Quit bellyaching and help me to the wagon." Cord gritted his teeth, forcing himself to put one foot in front of the other.

It seemed to take them forever. The wind gusted and the windmill hummed. Water splashed into the trough. The cattle lowed, their thirst slaked.

With Ott's help, Cord sprawled on his back on the hard wagon bed with a moan. Ott climbed up beside him and tied a bandanna around Cord's forehead.

"The irons. Did you get them?"

"You damned right I did. Hang on, boy. I'll get you home." Ott clambered onto the bench and the buckboard lurched forward.

At the thunder of hooves, Bea whipped about from tending the roses flanking the cast-iron settee. A dust cloud billowed behind the buckboard Mr. Oakes drove at breakneck speed.

He shouted something to Jake and Rory as he passed the stable. Instead of stopping, he careened up the drive. Something was horribly wrong. But what? And where was he going?

Bea looked around for Cord but didn't see him. Her heart plummeted to her toes. Hadn't he ridden off with Mr. Oakes?

Mr. Oakes brought the buckboard to a dust-choking stop at the side door of the house. Before the haze settled, he vaulted off the seat and hobbled to the rear of the buckboard. Rory reached him next. Jake trudged in a heartbeat later, hugging his ribs.

The worry lining all their features made Bea's blood run cold. She picked up her skirts and ran to the buckboard, catching what had to be the end of Mr. Oakes's explanation to the men.

"It's for damned sure if he'd passed out up there, we'd be fetching the undertaker instead of the doctor," Mr. Oakes said.

Panic clawed at Bea's throat. This was a repeat of the day they'd brought Papa's broken body home. But Papa wasn't in the wagon this time. Cord was. She knew it in her heart.

"Jake, while me and Rory haul him inside, you take the buckboard and fetch Doc Crowley out here," Mr. Oakes ordered.

With a grimace, Jake scrambled onto the buckboard's seat. He looked her way. The expression on his face reeked of sympathy.

As if caught in a trance, Bea stumbled up to the wagon and peered inside. Cord lay deathly still, his eyes closed, mouth slack. A bloody bandanna bandaged his head.

Bile rose in her throat. She gripped the sideboard to keep from collapsing. "W-w-what happened?"

"Cordell had an accident while he was mill riding." Mr. Oakes took hold of Cord's broad shoulders and motioned for Rory to grasp his legs. "Where you want us to put him?"

"In our bed, of course." Bea hurried to hold the door open, blinking back tears. "How grave are his injuries?"

Mr. Oakes avoided meeting her eyes. "I've seen worse."

That told her nothing. She grabbed Mr. Oakes's arm, stopping him. "I haven't. Please. Tell me what I can do to help?"

"If you've the stomach for it, you can wash him up 'fore Doc gets here." Mr. Oakes's gaze probed hers. "It'll do Cordell a peck of good if you're sitting by his side when he comes to."

Bea bit her trembling lower lip and nodded. She was possessed of a rather delicate disposition, but she refused to abandon Cord in his time of need. "I'll gather the necessary supplies and join you in the master bedroom."

A ghost of a grin split Mr. Oakes's weathered face. He nodded to Rory. "You heard Mrs. Tanner. Let's get a move on."

As they traversed the stairs, Bea rushed into the pantry. She stared at the shelves, but all she saw was the deadly gray pallor of Cord's skin.

Mrs. Mimms pressed a stack of bleached damask linens into Bea's hands. "You don't have to do this, you know. We can tend him."

"No. I need to be by his side." And it was true. She couldn't bear staying below while her servants and ranch hands took care of Cord.

Bea grabbed a ball of glycerin soap and dashed up the rear staircase. Benedict met her at the open bedroom door. He held a bowl of steaming water. The liquid sloshed over the sides, betraying his steadiness.

"Have you need of my assistance?" he asked.

She sent Benedict a shaky smile of gratitude. "I'd greatly appreciate your presence. And prayers."

"Very well." With that, Benedict trudged into the room.

Bea followed, her steps as plodding as Benedict's. Age and recurring bouts of rheumatism hindered the retainer's pace. Worry, fear, and a rioting stomach kept Bea lagging behind.

Benedict set the bowl on the bedside table. Bea strove to regain a semblance of composure. Nigh impossible to do.

Blood soaked the bandanna tied about Cord's head and coursed down the left side of his face. Rusty blobs dotted his leather vest. Crimson streaks stained his blue chambray shirtsleeves.

She tried to swallow the bile climbing her throat. A glance in the mirror confirmed her complexion had turned a sickly pallor.

Mr. Oakes's steel gray eyebrows inched together in either doubt or concern. "Reckon you'd best let me tend him."

"Aye. 'Tis no task for a lady." Rory stood by the foot of the bed, soft cap in hand, brow crinkled with concern.

She sank her fingernails into a towel and shook her head. "I'll see to Cord's wound, but I'd be most grateful if you'd remove his vest and shirt."

"Yes'm." Mr. Oakes set about undressing Cord, going so far as to remove his boots and jeans.

Bea's gaze lingered over her husband's form as she assured herself he had escaped further injuries. Staring at him in the light of day unsettled her nerves more than touching him had in the dead of night. Even clad in worn undergarments, he exuded strength.

Mr. Oakes untied the bandanna, and Bea knew she couldn't dawdle. She sat at her husband's side and dipped the cloth into the basin. Gingerly, she set about cleansing his head wound.

As she exposed the gash on her husband's head, a trickle of blood oozed from it. The room spun.

Bea gulped and closed her eyes, taking slow, steady breaths to regain her equilibrium. She wouldn't surrender to a swoon.

Chin up, Bea gently pressed a towel to his wound to stem the bleeding. "Exactly what happened to Cord?"

"Cordell hurt himself fixing the far mill," Mr. Oakes said.

The emotionless tone of Mr. Oakes's voice made her pause. She glanced at him. His jaw was set and his eyes sparked with anger, but he wouldn't meet her eyes. That in itself hinted he was keeping something from her—again. Just as he had after Papa's accident. The similarities unnerved her.

"How?" Bea regarded Mr. Oakes carefully.

"Cordell pried a branding iron loose from the platform, and the vane arm spun and landed him one upside the head."

She shook her head in confusion. "Why was there a branding iron atop our windmill?"

"To keep the wheel from spinning. The water trough was tipped over, too." He screwed his mouth into a knot. "Reckon you best know Cordell yanked off two Flying D branding irons."

Rage leapt through Bea like a prairie wildfire. First the fence was cut, then a knife was taken to Cord's saddle. Now this. Only one man stood to gain from her misfortune.

"Bloody hell! You retrieved them, I trust."

Mr. Oakes bobbed his head. "They're in the buckboard."

"Do hide them." She turned her attention to the gash on Cord's head. Thankfully, the bleeding had stopped. "I'll need those irons as evidence when I confront Mr. Donnelly."

"I sure hope you'll hold off doing that till Cordell gets on his feet," Mr. Oakes said.

Bea considered that as she washed the rest of the grit and grime from Cord's face and neck. She blinked, forced to face the bare grim facts. He'd yet to rouse. Hadn't given any indication he was aware of anything going on around him.

"My husband could be indisposed for quite some time." She smiled bravely. "Besides, I know what I'm about."

In all truth, Bea had a vague notion what to say and do. But she knew she had to take matters into her own hands before something else befell the ranch or someone she loved.

The clatter of an approaching wagon grew louder. Benedict trooped to the bow windows and peered out. "Mr. Winter has returned with the physician."

Rory backed to the door. "I'll send the doctor up."

"Thank you," Bea replied.

"I'll see to stowing them irons," Mr. Oakes said, making his escape on Rory's heels.

A few moments later, Dr. Crowley lumbered into the room. He fixed his somber expression on Bea. "Ott told me what happened. If you'd kindly move aside, I'll tend the patient."

Bea sent up a prayer of gratitude and gladly took her place at the foot of the bed. The doctor dabbed the wounded area with alcohol, then set about stitching together the ragged gash on the side of Cord's head.

Cord stiffened and moaned. She wanted to shove the doctor aside and take her husband into her arms, soothe all his hurts. That admission left her weak-kneed and trembling. When had this cowboy come to mean so much to her?

Bea dug her fingernails into the wooden footboard and stared at Cord through watery eyes. She'd been so certain he'd deceived her. But this latest mishap did away with that notion.

Cord was a victim of someone's vicious pranks. Someone wanted Cord out of Bea's life. She didn't know why, but she was certain that someone resided at the Flying D.

Dr. Crowley bandaged Cord's head, then washed his hands and faced her. "If he keeps the wound clean and remains calm, he'll recover faster. However, the way Cord carried on the last time I treated him, I wouldn't hold my breath on him staying quiet."

His slur on Cord's character irritated Bea, but the fact the doctor had treated him before nudged her curiosity awake. "When was the last time you were called to attend my husband?"

"About a year ago. Colonel Trenton called me to the Bar T to set Cord's dislocated shoulder." The doctor snapped his valise shut and slid Cord a look of disgust. "Rumor has it, Cord and a group of rowdies got liquored up the night before the exhibition. One of them bet your husband he couldn't stay on a particularly wild horse. Cord took the challenge—and lost."

Bea frowned, well acquainted with his inability to tolerate spirits. She could see how such a mishap could occur, especially if a rival bent on mayhem challenged her intoxicated husband.

She decided to test her theory. "Do you by any chance know if Gil Yancy was among those issuing wagers?"

The doctor shrugged on his black frock coat. "Gil was there, but I've no idea if he played a part in Cord's accident."

Inclining his head to her, Dr. Crowley took his leave.

Benedict followed the man out, leaving Bea alone with her unconscious husband. She dropped onto the bed beside him and released a tremulous sigh.

Odd how everything had changed in such a short span of time. Following her confrontation with Cord this morning, she'd feared all her well-laid plans were lost. But as the day progressed, prudence took root within her.

She couldn't fault Cord for his mother's shady past or his relationship with Donnelly any more than she could be held accountable for her mother's lack of emotion or her papa's penchant for liquor. Though Cord hadn't told her the truth of his parentage or his past immediately, he'd never meant to deceive her. That realization made her take a long look at her goals.

Without question, she wanted the Prairie Rose. But now she realized she wanted something else just as much.

Bea trailed a finger over one of Cord's black eyebrows, down his tanned cheek and jaw. She circled the deep indentation in his stubborn chin and smiled, sliding a finger down the thick column of his neck, tracing the hard muscles of his shoulders and arms.

She clasped one of Cord's work-roughened hands in hers and brought it to her lips. Closing her eyes, she kissed the back of it, each roughened knuckle, then placed a kiss in the palm.

He didn't stir. But her heart thundered like hundreds of hooves. She breathed quick and hard. Her mind settled on a bold new course of action, one that would change her life forever.

Bea glanced over her shoulder to make certain she and Cord were alone, then she smiled at her sleeping husband. Bending, she placed a feather-light kiss on his cheek, his chin, his mouth.

"My dearest cowboy, you've forced me to admit a rather unsettling truth today." She entwined her fingers with his lax ones and lowered her voice to a conspiratorial whisper. "However, I believe it prudent to keep the fact that I love you and don't wish to ever divorce you to myself for a while longer."

CHAPTER FOURTEEN

Cord opened one eye then the other. The glare of the lamp speared his eyes. He winced and turned away from the light, wondering why his head hurt like the dickens. Then it came back to him. The branding irons atop the windmill. Nearly falling.

Trixie leaned over his side, blocking out the blinding glare. "Thank God, you're awake. How do you feel? Are you in pain?"

"I've had worse." He glanced at the bay windows. Dark as pitch out. Damn! Had he slept the day away?

Trixie pressed her cool hand to his forehead and frowned. "You're a bit warm. See if you can drink some of this."

She held a glass to his mouth. Cord raised his head and drank. The cider doused the fire raging in his throat, but moving put the spurs to his pain, sending it stampeding through his noggin. He flopped onto the bed and broke out in a cold sweat.

"Mr. Oakes told me what happened." She pressed a cool cloth to his forehead, fussing over him like a mother hen, insisting he drink more cider. "Donnelly has gone too far this time."

"Don't go blaming Scotty."

"Why? The branding irons were his."

He was so plumb tuckered out, he could barely think. Barely keep his eyes open. "Somebody could've made off with them."

"Hmm." Trixie forced more cider down him. "Perhaps I should take the matter to Marshal Ives."

"No." Cord gave up fighting off sleep. He'd deal with this when he could think straight. "I'll talk to Scotty later."

Soft lips grazed his cheek and Trixie's rosy scent wrapped around him like a hug. "Of course you will. Now rest."

He did, glad for once Trixie didn't argue.

At the break of dawn, Bea slipped out of bed and gathered her clothing. She tiptoed to the bathing chamber, taking care not to wake Cord.

He'd slept fitfully. So had she, haunted by nightmares of him toppling from the windmill. Had that happened, she'd likely have ended up widowed.

That's what she'd tell Donnelly when she confronted him this morning. She suspected Gil had sabotaged Cord's saddle and the windmill, something she doubted Donnelly would condone.

The rancher was brash and arrogant, but she didn't believe he wanted Cord dead. Indeed, the more she'd thought about it, the more certain she was that Donnelly was a pawn.

He had every right to know what his foreman had done. That he'd misplaced his trust in Gil Yancy.

Bea dressed quickly in the semidark, having had the presence of mind to lay out a navy blue poplin skirt and ecru silk blouse the night before. If she awakened Cord, he'd insist on accompanying her. Or stop her from doing what had to be done.

Straw hat, wool jacket, and kidskin gloves in hand, Bea crept from the room and hurried down the rear stairs. Though her staff would be up, she didn't wish to rouse her family.

Leaving the house immediately would ensure that, but she yearned for a bracing cup of Arbuckles coffee.

The enticing scent of Maria's spicy corn muffins welcomed Bea as she stepped into the dining room. She bit back a groan. So much for her desire to slip away undetected. Aunt Muriel sat at the table, much like a reigning queen awaiting her subjects.

Resplendent in a green velvet riding habit, Muriel sipped from a delicate china cup. Bea suspected it held tea.

"Do join me, m'dear. Father called us into the parlor last eve and informed us Cord had met with foul play." Muriel regarded her solemnly. "I trust your husband is much improved."

"Cord is resting comfortably, thank you."

Muriel emptied her lungs in one dramatic exhalation. "After Father took to his bed, I had a lengthy chat with Lambert. The viscount is quite worried about your safety."

"How novel. Lambert didn't concern himself about my feelings or welfare when we were affianced." Bea crossed to the sideboard and poured a cup of coffee from the silver urn, but she declined a muffin. She suspected her nervous stomach would reject food.

"Perhaps he's had a change of heart."

Bea smothered a laugh. "I seriously doubt that."

"Whatever his reasons, it troubles Lambert to think what Cord's enemy might do to you in his quest to kill your husband."

Nothing. Cord's life was in danger. Not hers. Bea was convinced that she and the ranch were the prizes Gil sought. He wouldn't harm her. At least not physically, she reasoned.

Bea added a dollop of cream and a lump of sugar to her coffee and sat across from Muriel. "I assure you that we're prepared to deal with our adversary."

"No doubt you are." Muriel sipped her tea. "But you should be aware that Lambert implored Grandfather to whisk you back to England for your own safety."

Bea set her cup down with a clatter. "Lambert has forgotten one very important fact. I'm a married woman."

Her aunt arched one golden eyebrow. "True, but as Lambert pointed out, Grandfather would be well within his rights to sell this ranch and insist you and Cord settle on one of his properties in England, putting an ocean between you and Cord's enemy."

Anxiety strummed along Bea's taut nerves. "Cord would never consider moving to England."

"He would if he truly cared for you."

And that, Bea thought morosely, was the crux of the matter. The buds of a deep affection for Cord were flowering within her, but she hadn't an inkling if Cord felt similarly toward her.

If Grandfather heeded Lambert's advice, she'd likely never know. Their marriage was too new. In many ways, she and Cord were still strangers.

"Do excuse me, but I've a pressing matter I need to attend to." Bea pushed to her feet and hurried from the house.

She hadn't expected Muriel to follow, but her aunt was behind her. No matter. Time was of the essence. She didn't dare turn back from her set course.

"Pray tell, where are you going?" Muriel asked.

"In pursuit of justice. As Mr. Oakes is wont to say, 'it's high time to smoke the snake out of his hole.'"

Bea marched into the stable and bade Rory to ready the surrey. She'd have preferred riding her mare, but she couldn't very well do that and carry along the two Flying D branding irons.

With Muriel in tow, she went in search of Mr. Oakes. She intercepted him en route from the bunkhouse to the cider shed.

"Mr. Oakes, would you please fetch the branding irons?"

"'Fraid I can't oblige you." Mr. Oakes stuck a cigarette between his teeth and dug a wooden match from his pocket. "Jake dumped everything in the buckboard by the bunkhouse door yesterday afore he drove into town for Doc Crowley, but when I got there, all I found was Cordell's hat and gun belt."

"Somebody stole the branding irons?"

"Yep. Took Cordell's peacemaker, too."

"Bloody hell!" Bea paced, fighting the wind and her rising anger, debating what to do now. "I should've suspected that whoever vandalized our windmill would return for the evidence while we were busy attending Cord."

"I kicked myself for not telling the boy to stow them irons in the bunkhouse." Mr. Oakes shook his head. "With all of us in the house, there's no telling who the polecat was that snuck on the ranch and stole them."

"Hmmm." Bea paced, uncertain how to proceed.

Without the irons, she couldn't prove Donnelly's property had disarmed the windmill. It was Cord's and Mr. Oakes's word against Donnelly's. Still, she had to try to convince Donnelly that someone on his ranch was causing mayhem on the Prairie Rose. And that someone was likely Gil Yancy, his foreman.

"It's obvious the polecat in question hailed from the Flying D," Bea said. "I believe Yancy fetched the branding irons back to Donnelly's ranch while we were distracted."

He lit his cigarette and ground out the match into the dust. "The only way Gil would know we found those irons jammed in our mill is if he rigged it in the first place."

Bea's smile felt as brittle as her temper. "Precisely."

"That wretched man," Muriel said. "Prescott will be most distressed to hear one of his men is wreaking havoc on you."

"I do hope you're right," Bea said. "At any rate, it'll be interesting to watch Donnelly's reaction to the news."

"Hold up there," Mr. Oakes said. "I ain't partial to you riding to the Flying D by your lonesome."

"She's not going alone," Muriel said. "I'll accompany her."

Arguing with her aunt was a waste of time. Besides,

Muriel's presence might make Donnelly more receptive to reason.

Rory stepped from the stable with the hitched surrey. Mr. Oakes scrubbed his neck, clearly unsure what to do.

"We'll be fine," Bea assured Mr. Oakes. "There is no need for you to accompany us, or inform Cord of our where-abouts."

Bea climbed into the surrey. As soon as Muriel was seated, Bea snapped the reins and the horse took off at a sedate trot.

The ride was short and tension riddled. Bea brought the surrey to a stop before Donnelly's house, her thoughts swirling as thickly as the red dust. Her arrival attracted the interest of several Flying D cowboys, but none rushed forward to lend a hand. Not that she wanted their help.

She set the brake and climbed down. Head up and shoulders back, she marched to Donnelly's front door. Muriel remained one step behind her all the way.

Taking one steadying breath, Bea raised her fist to rap on the panel. It swung open. She yelped and jerked her arm back.

Donnelly filled the opening, his smile wide and welcoming. "If this don't beat all." He stepped back and motioned them inside. "Come on in. Can I fetch you ladies something to drink?"

"Don't trouble yourself." Bea swept into the house and came face-to-face with Gil Yancy.

The Flying D foreman lounged in an open doorway directly across from the garish parlor. Gil wore a smug smile, plaid shirt, and formfitting jeans. He gripped a large cup in his big hands. One sniff told her it held strong coffee.

Bea subdued the urge to slap Gil. She put a safe distance between them, focusing her attention on Cord's stepfather. "This isn't a social call, Mr. Donnelly."

The rancher's smile vanished. "Sounds mighty serious."

"Deadly serious," Bea said with a touch of acerbity.

Muriel floated toward Donnelly, wringing her gloved hands. "It's all so dreadful. Cord suffered a horrid accident."

Shock leached the color from Donnelly's ruddy face and alarm registered in his eyes, convincing Bea that he was ignorant of the latest mayhem on the Prairie Rose. In fact, he seemed genuinely worried about Cord.

Not so for Gil. He stared at the floor, as if he wasn't interested in hearing the details. Perhaps because he knew them?

Donnelly asked Bea, "What happened? Is Cordell all right?"

"Cord received a gash on his head, but he'll fully recover." Bea took a fortifying breath, watching both men's reaction. "He was removing two Flying D branding irons that had been wedged between the blades of one of our windmills."

Donnelly stared at her, brow puckered, as if he was having trouble understanding what had happened. Gil stiffened, his expression shifting from curiosity to wariness.

Finally, the big rancher snapped out of his stupor. The veins on his neck stood out like ropes as he whirled on Gil. "Why didn't you tell me somebody made off with two of our irons?"

A muscle pulsed along Gil's jaw. "Didn't know they were missing, boss. After we brand calves and our new stock in the spring, I stow the irons till we cull the herd in the fall."

"Well, that makes it real convenient for somebody to walk off the ranch with them." Donnelly jabbed a beefy finger at Gil. "I hold you responsible, Yancy."

"Any one of the hands that come and go around here could've taken those irons," Gil protested.

"What a clever ploy to cast blame on someone who's no longer associated with the Flying D," Bea said.

"What are you getting at, Mrs. Tanner?" Donnelly asked.

"The day before my papa died, your foreman visited the Prairie Rose." Bea addressed Gil. "May I ask what you were talking to Nate Wyles about?"

"Wyles owed me money." Gil's smile looked halfhearted. Forced. "I'd stopped by to collect, is all. Why do you ask?"

Bea chose her words carefully. "That day or early the next morning, someone tampered with my papa's saddle. Unfortunately, we didn't discover it until after his fatal fall from his horse."

"Hope you caught the sneaking son of a—uh, the sneaking weasel," Donnelly said.

"No, we didn't." Bea studied Gil, expecting some reaction from him, but not one emotion showed on his face. She pressed on. "The day you accompanied Mr. Donnelly to the Prairie Rose, you spent considerable time near my stables again."

Gil nodded. "That I did, ma'am. You've got the best-looking horseflesh in six counties."

"The following morning," she went on, refusing to let flattery deter her, "Jake suffered an injury because his saddle strap had been cut. Oh, did I mention the saddle was Cord's? Clearly someone intended for my husband to suffer a horrid accident when he took his usual morning ride."

Donnelly's eyes bulged, then narrowed into condemning slits. "What do you know about all this, Yancy?"

"Nothing. I saw Cord ride the wind a time or two," Gil said, confirming Bea's suspicions that he'd watched the ranch. "But I ain't messed with any saddle on her spread or any other one."

Donnelly folded his arms over his barrel chest. Though he didn't comment, he exchanged some odd look with Muriel.

"I believe you're a liar as well as a sore loser," Bea told Gil. "You had designs on me and my ranch, did you not?"

Gil plowed his fingers through his hair, but the taffy waves refused to lay smooth. "I had a hankering to court you once."

"Come now, Mr. Yancy. The day I married Cord you asked me to accompany you to the Bar T social."

"I didn't know you was fixing to marry him," Gil said.

"Are you the jealous sort?" she asked Gil.

He snorted. "No, ma'am."

Hooves pounded outside and a horse bugled. Then the front door banged open and shut. Steady footsteps and the chink of spurs rang out in the hall.

Bea flinched and her heart raced. She knew that stride. Cord. Heading straight toward this room.

She rounded on Gil while she had the chance. "Then why ever did you and Nate Wyles stand in the middle of the street in Revolt and spew derogatory remarks about my marriage to Cord?"

"When was this?" Donnelly asked as the parlor door opened.

"The day me and Trixie got hitched." Cord strode into the room, his bandage hidden by the hat pulled low on his brow.

Bea drank in the impressive sight of her husband, then spent precious moments searching his brown eyes for any sign of pain. All that flashed in their unfathomable depths was annoyance—and that emotion was directed at her.

She glanced at his bandaged head. "How do you feel?"

"Madder than hell."

Her chin came up. "You shouldn't be out of bed."

One of Cord's dark eyebrows winged upward as he crossed to her side. Bea held her ground, refusing to be intimidated.

Grandfather paraded into the room like a reigning monarch. "When Tanner discovered where you'd gone, he turned a deaf ear to my warnings. Thought it best I tag along."

"You're welcome here anytime, Lord Arden." Donnelly turned to Gil. "I know there's bad blood between you and Cordell, but you know my rules better than anybody—you insult any lady while you're working for me and it'll be the last pay you draw here."

Gil's upper lip curled. "I didn't say nothing to her but the truth. Cord married her to get his hands on that spread of hers."

A bark of laughter burst from Grandfather. "Egads, Tanner! Did you think by wedding Bea you'd inherit the Prairie Rose?"

"No, sir, I sure didn't. The last thing I was fixing to do was settle in these parts. But Trixie changed my mind."

Cord looped an arm around Bea's shoulder and pulled her against his side. His smile was secretive and his eyes glowed with warmth, as if he and Bea shared something rare and special. As if she meant the world to him. She didn't, of course.

Bea felt the tension coiled within Cord. He was doing what she'd paid him to do, and for the first time in their marriage, she longed for far more from Cord Tanner. She wanted his heart.

Cord winked at Bea, further teasing her with the pretext of a loving marriage. "Truth be told, I didn't care if all Trixie owned was the clothes on her back."

"Bullshit! If she'd known you were Scotty's stepson, she wouldn't have married you on a bet," Gil said. "And don't give me that crap that you lost your heart to her when you laid eyes on her, 'cause I was there the day you saw Miz Northroupe and her pa at the Bar T Ranch. I told you I aimed to get acquainted with her then and there and you didn't look twice at her."

Cord stepped toward Gil. "What turned your head? A pretty lil' gal in a dress as blue as her eyes, or one hundred and sixty acres of prime land and a herd of prize thoroughbreds?"

Bea had a heartbeat to savor the fact that Cord remembered what dress she'd worn that day before Gil took a swing at Cord.

Cord caught Gil's fist in his right hand. Eyes as dark and turbulent as storm clouds bored into Gil's. "If I find out you slipped that spider into Northroupe's saddle, I'll see you hang."

Surprise flickered across Gil's face, then his face contorted in anger. "You know damned well I'd never do such a low-down thing." He jerked free and then stomped toward the door.

"Yancy!" Donnelly said, bringing Gil up short in the doorway. "I got my fill of your old grudge with Cordell. Gather your belongings. Your pay'll be waiting for you by the time you're ready to clear out today."

Gil looked at Cord, back rigid and hands fisted. "Best watch your back, pard." He stormed out, slamming doors in his wake.

Fear sucked Bea's throat dry. "He threatened you again."

"Gil's all talk."

"How can you be sure?" Bea asked. "He'll lie in wait for you. Perhaps swoop down on you as you take your morning ride."

Cord shrugged. "Don't fret yourself about it."

But she did worry. They'd baited the tiger.

She was certain Yancy would pounce before long. Even if Cord was extremely cautious, Yancy might succeed in killing Cord this time. And that dire thought was what tied her stomach in knots.

Cord looked over the top of Trixie's head and took in the three people eyeing them. When he'd pried it out of Rory that Trixie was fixing to confront Scotty, he hightailed it to the Flying D as fast as he could. But he got here late.

Trixie had taken a whack at a hornet's nest and riled Scotty to the point that he'd fired Gil. Now Gil was gunning for Cord.

"I say." The earl dropped onto a tufted chair, wearing the best damned poker face Cord had ever come up against. "Bloody presumptuous of Yancy to think the Prairie Rose was part of Beatrix's dowry."

Trixie broke from Cord, as skittish as a range-bred mustang. "When I wrote you after Papa's death, I told you that he made no secret of the fact that he intended to bequeath the ranch to me."

That news twisted Cord's guts tighter than eight seconds on a wild bronco. Seeing the way word traveled in Revolt, Gil would've heard the Prairie Rose would pass on to Trixie. Sure as shooting, that's why Gil aimed to court her. But was that all Gil had done to get his hands on Trixie and the ranch? Or had his old rival had a hand in Northroupe's murder?

"Dash it all, Beatrix! It boggled my mind to imagine the rogues that would prey on an unmarried young woman who owned land and prize stock. Which is why I made it clear to you that I intended to wipe my hands of the ranch and that you were to dispose of the stock and return to England."

Trixie's chin snapped up and her chest puffed, like she was preening for a scrap. "Was that before or after Donnelly offered you a fat sum for the Prairie Rose?"

"Before, though Donnelly's offer came at an ideal time." The earl glanced Cord's way and snorted. "Or so I thought."

Cord thumbed his hat back and cleared the anger from his throat. "Reckon that's about the time I called on Trixie."

"Indeed it was," Trixie said, sidling up to Cord again. "I couldn't bear the thought of leaving my home. Or you."

"Bloody convenient Tanner came along when he did," the earl said. "Tell me, Tanner. Were you aware of the rumor I'd heir the Prairie Rose to Beatrix?"

"Nope. Never heard about it till now."

Cord met the earl's eyes straight on. If he didn't play his cards right, he'd cost Trixie her ranch and end up on foot and dead broke. It'd be a long walk to the border, shouldering his gear and regrets.

The earl stroked his beard and took Cord's measure. Cord hoped the earl didn't find him lacking.

"Seeing as Cordell ain't been around these parts the past ten years, I tend to believe him," Scotty said.

Cord couldn't believe his ears. He could count the times on

one hand that Scotty had stood by his side. Seeing as they'd been at odds for years, Cord couldn't figure why Scotty was doing it now. Was Scotty fixing to gain Cord's trust? Or the earl's?

"I'll take you at your word," the earl told Scotty, stropping a razor's hone on Cord's suspicions that Scotty was up to no good.

"Dear Grandfather, please afford me the same courtesy," Trixie said. "Surely you can see Cord and I are well suited."

The earl chuckled. "So it seems. But know this, Beatrix. If I detect Tanner is a slacker or a reckless manager, I'll not grant you title to the Prairie Rose."

"Fair enough." Cord took Trixie by the arm and guided her toward the door. "Come on, darlin'. We'd best get on home."

"Splendid notion."

"If you've got the time," Scotty told the earl as he made to get to his feet. "I'd like a word with you and Mrs. Flynn."

"Time I have." The earl dropped back on the chair.

Muriel settled on the sofa like a setting hen. "As do I."

Trixie balked at the doorway. "We shouldn't go off without Aunt Muriel and Grandfather."

"They don't need us seeing them home." Cord herded his wife out of the house.

Trixie batted at his hands. "Stop it. I came with Muriel and I'll go home with her."

"You're leaving with me."

Outside the sprawling bunkhouse, Cord spied Gil slinging a saddlebag on his roan gelding. His old friend glanced his way, looking red to the brim with 100-proof rage.

Cord itched to have it out with Gil here and now. But he didn't want to drag Trixie into a brawl, and he didn't want her rushing back into Scotty's house and stirring up more trouble. Best he take her home and deal with Gil later.

Rory was minding Zephyr, the earl's black gelding, and the

mare Rory had ridden over. The horse harnessed to Trixie's surrey was tethered to the hitching post.

Cord rubbed his chin. Unless he was willing to wait around for the earl and Muriel, one of the women was going to have to fork a saddle going home. As fidgety as Zephyr and Trixie were getting, he wasn't about to hang around here any longer.

"See Mrs. Flynn home in the surrey," Cord told Rory.

"Aye, sir."

Cord grabbed Trixie around her little waist and set her atop Zephyr. She landed sideways on the saddle with a muffled "oomph." Before the stallion or his wife kicked up a fuss, he gathered the reins and swung up behind her.

"There's no need for you to get high-handed," Trixie said, turning her head so the feather on her hat tickled his chin.

"There's no call for you to get into an argument with your grandpappy about the title to the ranch, but you did anyway."

"I lost my temper."

Cord could understand that. He was sore as a saddle boil at Trixie for confronting Scotty in the first place.

"I just hope to hell your set-to with your grandpappy doesn't land us both in a fix." He corralled her in his arms and heeled Zephyr into a trot. "Hang on."

Trixie's shoulder slammed against his chest. The feather on her hat snapped in two and her hat bobbed over her eyes.

She mumbled under her breath, righting her hat with one hand and grabbing the saddle horn with the other. "Must we race home?"

Cord didn't know whether to laugh or groan. Her butt slapped the saddle and the breasts he'd dreamed of fondling spanked his left arm and set his blood on fire.

"The sooner we get home the better." Still, Cord slowed Zephyr to a walk so the ride wouldn't scramble his wife's innards too much. "You'd fare better if you'd fork the saddle and lean back against me."

"Ladies do not ride astride."

He scanned the golden prairie. "True enough, but there ain't a soul in sight to catch you if you do."

Trixie bit her lower lip, no doubt mulling that over. "I don't suppose there'd be any harm in riding that way once."

"Not a damned bit."

She fidgeted. "Oh, very well, then." She hiked her skirt and petticoat to her knees and swung her leg over Zephyr's neck.

Cord got a gander at her small fancy boots, black stockings skinned up long legs, and the ruffled hem of her white drawers. She slapped her skirt and petticoat down, muttering all the time.

The stallion tossed his head and blew.

Cord felt like doing the same. Hot memories of stroking her bare legs broke him out in a cold sweat. He should've known better than to get this close to her when his temper was up. But the only way out of his misery was to get her home fast.

He wrapped an arm around her middle. Her soft middle. Damn! Knowing there wasn't much but cotton between her skin and his arm shot a bolt of lust to his crotch.

Cord pulled her against him and heeled Zephyr into a gallop. Trixie yelped and grabbed the saddle horn. The wind tore her hat off and whipped her skirt up to her knees. But what fired his blood was the way her breasts rode his forearm.

"Had I known I'd be riding a horse at breakneck speed, I'd have taken more care this morning and bound my bosom," she said.

"It ain't good for you to flatten yourself that way."

"I can't believe this bouncing is good for me either. And must we ride so fast? I've already lost my hat to the wind. My skirts are soon to follow."

Her skirt was flapping against his legs like wet wash, but he didn't aim to slow down. Nope. He was lusting for Trixie and the longer they were spooned together, the worse it'd be for him.

So Cord did the only thing he could think of to stop her bellyaching. He pressed his arm over her full breasts.

She sucked in a lungful of air. Her breasts stopped their wild bouncing, but her nipples grew rock hard against his arm.

Lust grabbed him by the balls. "That help?"

"I believe so," she said in a throaty voice that set his blood to humming. "Do you recall the night you allowed me to experience my very first voluptuous spasm?"

He seined air between his teeth. That memory haunted his dreams. "I remember."

"Could we do that again?"

Hell, yes, they could. But as the Prairie Rose came into view, Cord reminded himself that getting his fingers wet in his wife's heat was just going to torture him into wanting all of her.

"That's selfish of me to suggest such a thing," Trixie said. "You certainly didn't receive the same thrill as I did."

"Wrong again, darlin'." He'd never gotten that hot or gone off that fast from feeling up a woman. The touch and taste of Trixie stuck with him like a burr, making him hunger for more.

"Besides, you're recovering from a horrid accident. I wouldn't want you to do anything to cause you more pain."

"Trixie, you've worked me into a lather. If you change your mind now, I guarantee that'll hurt me a helluva lot more than a toss in the hay."

"So you would like to do it again?"

His little rustler reared up and let out a whoop, drowning out the whispered warning from his brain that he'd best keep his hands and mouth to himself. "I sure as hell would."

Holding his wife to his thundering heart, Cord focused on the stables dead ahead. The stallion flew through the opened doors and raced down the aisle, spooking the stabled horses and kicking up a blinding cloud of straw and dust.

Cord hauled back on Zephyr's reins. The horse sat back on his powerful haunches, tossed his head, and bugled.

Before the red dust settled, Cord vaulted off the horse and ground reined him. He snatched Trixie from the saddle and carried her into the tack room, which reeked of leather and liniment.

"You're a deliciously amorous cowboy, Mr. Tanner." She sent his hat sailing and drove her gloved hands through his hair. Her smile was downright sexy, her eyes were dancing with wicked delight, and her body was soft as butter in his hands. "Do kiss me like you did the last time."

"Yes'm, I sure will."

Cord covered her mouth with his and kicked the door shut. He braced his back against it, crushing his enticing wife in his arms. His elbow flipped the latch home, locking nosy parkers out.

He kissed her deeply and thoroughly, coaxing her to let herself go. Teaching her what a man's mouth could do to fire up a woman. Trixie gave as good as she got, heating him up to the point he reckoned smoke was pouring off him.

She squirmed in his arms and wriggled against his length. Her gloved fingers tore at the buttons on his shirt. Frantic little sounds bubbled from her throat.

Aroused to the point of pain, Cord tore his mouth from hers. He took in the cluttered room. Dim light filtered through a paned window set high on the wall. Stacked beneath the window were the horse blankets he'd meant to put away but hadn't got to yet.

Cord pushed away from the door and stumbled to them. It wasn't fancy, but it'd do. He laid Trixie atop the makeshift bed of blankets. Rocking back on his heels, he tore off his gloves and flung them aside. He didn't want anything between his fingers and her hot flesh.

Trixie sprawled on her back—chest heaving and dreamy-eyed. She bit the tips of her gloves, tugged them off, and tossed them.

Like he dreamed she'd do, she opened her arms to him.

With a groan, he came to her. His tongue delved into her sweet mouth while his hands bunched her skirt and petticoat to her waist. He tugged at her drawers. Haste made him clumsy as an ox in a garden plot.

Agonizing moments passed before he shucked her drawers off her and flung them over his shoulder. He stretched out beside her. His mouth made love to hers while his fingers stroked the tight little bud buried in the nest between her legs.

She bloomed instantly. Burying his face in her hair, Cord crushed her to his chest and savored every ripple, shiver, and sigh she made. She was so honest and pure in her passion that he knew holding her would cleanse his soul.

Her fingers tore at the buttons near to bursting on his jeans. "Make love to me."

The little rustler was chomping at the bit, but Cord set his teeth. "Making love ain't part of our bargain."

"I don't care a fig about our bargain."

"I do." He sat up and drove shaky fingers through his hair. "I won't risk getting a baby on the woman I've agreed to leave."

She trailed one hot finger across his thigh, setting off a line of flash fires. "That won't happen."

Cord clamped a hand over her tormenting one. He ached to rip off his pants and bury himself in her. But he didn't dare move until he was absolutely certain his wife meant what she said.

"You know how to keep from getting in the family way?"

She nodded. "Years ago, when I was affianced to Lambert, Mrs. Mimms instructed me on how to avoid getting with child."

There were a passel of them. But the women he'd known that practiced those ways were soiled doves. Not ladies like Trixie.

Didn't she want children? Or had Lambert forced himself on her and she didn't want the shame of getting in the family way before her wedding? A wedding that never happened.

He curled one hand into a fist, aching to drive it into the high mucky-muck viscount's face. Sure as shooting, the viscount had got to Trixie. And then left her high and dry.

"Please." Trixie slipped the buttons free on her blouse and beckoned to him with her eyes. "Make love to me."

Cord wet his lips and stared at the breasts straining against the thin cloth. His gaze drifted to her soft, creamy thighs and the gold nest between them that he ached to stake claim to. She was offering it all to him. Pleasure with nothing binding him to her.

How could he refuse? He might not be the first man to have sex with Trixie, but he damn sure would be the first one to make love with her.

He freed himself and stretched out beside her, bringing her to the brink of pleasure with hot kisses and hotter caresses. His blood pounded like a stampede in his ears and he was hard enough to drive nails. He moved her hands where he ached for her touch. She drove him wild with sultry murmurs and exploring strokes, not the least bit shy.

With a groan, he settled between her thighs. She arched her back and moaned, driving him wild with wanting her.

One deep thrust and he buried himself in her wet tight heat. And got the surprise of his life.

She went board stiff under him and let out a squawk that had his ears tolling like bells. He reckoned that was normal for a virgin. A virgin, damn it all!

Her eyes were pinched shut. She pressed her sweet lips into a thin line. Her breasts were rising and falling too fast.

He swore under his breath, calling himself ten kinds of a low-down cur for hurting her. Much as he wanted to ease his ache, he reckoned he'd best pull out before he caused her more pain.

He rocked back, aiming to ease from her slow like. She wrapped her legs around him and dug her fingernails into his butt.

Like a hair trigger, he went off. He spent himself and collapsed on her, weak as a kitten. She wrapped her arms around him and held on for dear life.

Cord waited for his breathing to return to normal, then he levered himself on his elbows and looked down at his wife. She stared up at him with big round eyes. Innocent eyes.

Something was dead wrong here. "Suppose you tell me how you aim to keep from getting with child."

Bea blushed and toyed with his collar. "I don't aim to do anything because it's my mid-cycle. At least I think it is."

Cord flopped on his back and flung an arm over his eyes. How many times had he heard of this tried and failed method? Trixie might as well douche with alum for all the good it'd do keeping her from getting knocked up. Neither way was foolproof.

But she didn't know that or she wouldn't have egged him on.

He sighed. "What's done is done. Best thing to do is to forget it happened and hope to hell I didn't get a child on you."

She gasped and scrambled off the blankets. Clothes rustled. He waited, expecting her to tear into him any second.

He heard a sob. Her feet hit the floor at a run. The door flew open and banged off the wall like a gunshot.

Cord lurched to his feet and hightailed it to the door, looking past the stallion who'd wandered into his stall. Trixie raced from the stable like she couldn't bear the sight of him.

He kicked the door shut. The lonesome part of him wanted Trixie to bear his child. The trail-weary part of him knew she'd hate him for it. Hell, she probably hated him already.

CHAPTER FIFTEEN

Bea slammed the door to the bedroom she shared with Cord and slumped against the heavy panels. Except for her burning eyes and the ache deep within her, she felt numb. And so very much alone.

She'd welcomed the moment of pain without complaint, thinking Cord would cuddle her against his heart afterward. Certain he'd whisper love words in her ear. Instead, he'd rolled from her and suggested they forget what they'd just shared. How could something as wondrous as making love for the very first time come to such a wretched parting of the ways?

Because she'd expected too much from Cord. Caught in passion's web, she hadn't considered he'd be averse to the prospect of fathering a child. Though he lusted after her, he wanted nothing to bind him to her.

As much as his rejection pained her, Bea respected Cord for his honesty. He'd followed her contract to the letter. It was she who'd broken it. She'd seduced him. Now she had to suffer the consequences of not having her love returned and grapple with the question plaguing her. Did she want more from Cord?

Bea buried her face in her hands. A week ago, all she desired from Cord was temporary assistance. But the longer she was around him, the more she grew to care for him.

No, that wasn't entirely true. Bea loved Cord. But did she want to forge a future with him? The hollow ache in her heart said yes. The fear of giving any man control over her life screamed no. What ever was she going to do now?

By late afternoon, Bea ventured from the bedroom. She'd spent hours alone, mulling over her dilemma, and failed to reach a decision she could live with.

Bea found Mrs. Mimms and Mrs. Delgado in the kitchen. Mrs. Mimms was spooning red powder in jars while Mrs. Delgado added a small piece of camphor to each and filled them with apple brandy.

"Have you expended your supply of pain elixir?" Bea asked.

"*Sí*, Señora Tanner." Mrs. Delgado wiped the jar tops and pushed in corks. "Ott just took my last bottle. Young Jake used up his supply. Ott said my elixir did away with Jake's pain and didn't make him sleepy like the doctor's laudanum did."

"I see." Bea strolled to the window and scanned the stable area. "Did he say how Jake was?"

"He is much better."

Rory was usually working Titan this time of day, but the paddock was empty. Nobody was about. Inside or out.

Worry clomped across Bea's shoulder blades. "Grandfather and Aunt Muriel should have returned by now."

"They're taking supper with Mr. Donnelly." Mrs. Mimms dug a folded paper from her side pocket and handed it to Bea. "One of those blokes from the Flying D brought this over."

Bea read the short message aloud. "'My dearest Beatrix, Prescott graciously invited Father and me to dine with him this evening. I do hope you and Cord manage to suffer Lambert's presence without much difficulty. Lovingly, your aunt M.'"

"Before you ask," Mrs. Mimms said. "The hoity-toity viscount is spending the day with an old chum in Revolt and said he wouldn't return till late."

Bea paced the short space between the door and the kitchen table covered with jars. "Lambert is the least of my concerns. I'm worried about Muriel's infatuation with Mr. Donnelly."

"And why is that?" Mrs. Mimms asked.

Because if Donnelly charmed her aunt into marriage, Grandfather might gift Muriel with the Prairie Rose. But she said, "I don't want to see her hurt."

"Lady Muriel knows what she's about," Mrs. Mimms said.

"*Sí*," Mrs. Delgado chimed in.

"I hope you're both right."

But as she pitched in to assist Mrs. Mimms and Mrs. Delgado with the pain elixir, Bea was plagued with doubts.

That evening, Mrs. Delgado prepared an intimate supper for Bea and Cord. Unfortunately, Cord didn't join her, so she barely touched the meal.

It wasn't like Cord to miss supper. Was he still stewing about making love to her? Or had some ill befallen him?

She pushed her plate away and went in search of Cord. A silver slipper moon cast enough light for her to reach the stable. Inside, one lit lantern illuminated the aisle.

Bea checked the stalls for Cord. She found him in the tack room. A lantern on the table burned low, spilling dim light over the cowboy sprawled upon the horse blankets they had shared.

Cord was snoring so loudly the windowpanes rattled. An empty jar of Mrs. Delgado's elixir lay nearby. Bea's drawers pillowed his stubborn head.

Fury boiled in her. If Cord was in pain, he should have come to her. But no. He chose the stable over her company and guzzled down a remedy that put him in an inebriated state. The fool.

Bea doused the lantern, whirled on her heels, and stormed from the room. She marched down the aisle and extinguished

the other lantern, then darted from the stable and collided
with Mr. Oakes.

The older man stumbled back. "Beg pardon, ma'am."

"It is I who should apologize. I should've been watching
where I was going." Bea tried to smile, but her lower lip trembled. At least in the semidarkness, she didn't believe Mr.
Oakes would notice the tears stinging her eyes.

"Is something ailing you?" Mr. Oakes asked.

She sniffled. "Not at all."

Mr. Oakes shuffled from foot to foot, looking ill at ease.
"Is Cordell around?"

Bea pursed her lips so tightly they went numb. "He's in the
tack room. Asleep. Whether it was by design or accident, it
appears he drank an entire bottle of Mrs. Delgado's elixir."

Mr. Oakes whistled. "That packs a helluva wallop."

"Indeed it does. Whatever you have to say to Cord will
have to wait until morning. Late morning, no doubt."

He snorted. "Hell, me and the boy'll have it fixed by then."

Unease skipped up her arms. "Have what fixed?"

"The tarpaulins. Some rowdy went and cut the ropes on
every one of our haystacks. Most of the tarps have blown off."

Bea hugged herself against the chill wrapping around her.
She hadn't anticipated another malicious act to come so soon
on the heels of the last incident. But after Donnelly had dismissed Gil, she should've expected Gil to retaliate.

Mr. Oakes scanned the star studded sky. "It don't appear
like rain, but my old bones are telling me it's coming. Reckon
I'd best wake the boss early so he can help me and the boy."

That did it. She was the boss here. Not Cord.

"As I'm certain my husband will be indisposed, I'll do as I
have in the past and help you and Jake with this task. We'll
set to work at sunup."

"Yes, ma'am."

Before the crack of dawn, Bea roused from a fitful sleep.
She refused to dwell on what could have been or what should

have been between her and her stubborn husband. Cord had made his choice and now she was making hers.

Just in time, too. Mr. Oakes was right. Low gray clouds hung on the horizon, promising rain.

Bea dressed in her old bicycle suit that Muriel had sent years ago. She'd given up riding a wheel, but the outfit came in handy for certain strenuous ranch chores.

After donning a pair of common button boots, she grabbed her bonnet and leather gloves and hurried to the stable. The air had a damp bite and the breeze barely ruffled her bloomers. Halfway there she saw a tall cowboy hitching a horse to the buckboard.

Bea faltered and her heart gave an odd little kick of delight. Cord? He turned and waved. She laughed at the mistake she'd made again. It wasn't Cord but Jake. At this distance and in the faint morning light, she could barely tell them apart.

Out of the corner of her eye, Bea saw the viscount emerge from the stable leading Esprit, the chestnut stallion he rode daily. She teetered to a stop and fought the urge to laugh.

Lambert had stuffed his corpulent body into spiffy garb that would have complimented a slimmer physique. Unfortunately, all that he wore with aplomb was his air of haughty indifference.

"Good morning, m'dear." Lambert swaggered toward her.

"Morning." She met him halfway. "Where are you off to?"

"Revolt. I find that stretch quite exhilarating." An odd sheen lit Lambert's gaze as he ogled her and a trickle of spittle oozed from his thin lips. "I'm surprised to see you've adopted such radical attire as bloomers."

Bea's skin crawled under his scrutiny. "Are you? They're quite functional around the ranch."

A muffled thump drew their attention to the buckboard. Jake picked up a heavy tarpaulin and tossed it in the bed. Another muffled thump split the still air.

"Your husband appears to have regained his stamina."

Bea opened her mouth to correct him of his misconception and then thought better of it. If he knew the cowboy was Jake and that Cord was sleeping off a drunk in the tack room, Lambert would insist on tagging along with her and Jake.

"Yes, hasn't he?" Bea didn't feel one bit of guilt for playing Lambert for a chump.

Lambert glanced at Jake's back and his expression curdled like Mrs. Delgado's crock of cottage cheese. "If Tanner has no objections, I'd be honored if you'd join me this morning."

"Thank you, but we're off to the far hayfield—" She paused, choosing her words with care. She didn't want Lambert to follow them. "We're anxious for privacy. I'm sure you understand."

He snorted and mounted the restive stallion. "You need not explain more. When I was married, I enjoyed occasional trysts with a very special viscountess."

According to the gossips, the viscountess hadn't been his wife. Bea thanked the heavens that she'd escaped marriage to him. Lambert was an unfaithful lout and a blustering tyrant.

Lambert adjusted the belt of his charcoal gray Norfolk jacket over his paunch, his expression bored. "If you'll excuse me, I'll be off on my solitary jaunt." He gave her a curt nod and urged Esprit into a trot.

"Do enjoy yourself." Though in all truth, she didn't give a fig if Lambert had a pleasant day.

Bea watched her corpulent ex-fiancé ride out of sight, then crossed to the buckboard. "I trust we're ready to be off."

"Yes, ma'am." Jake tossed a coil of rope in the wagon bed and then brushed off his gloves on his denim-clad thighs. "Here. Let me give you a hand up."

Bea climbed onto the high seat, wincing at the new tenderness between her legs. Jake laid a rifle in the wagon bed and then vaulted up beside her. She caught his slight grimace and cringed, knowing his ribs still pained him. He wasn't ready to do hard physical labor yet.

Her gaze drifted to the open stable door. But neither was Cord. Both men had suffered accidents. Even if Cord was fit, it was her responsibility to attend the problems on her ranch. She couldn't afford to get into the habit of relying on a man who was eager to leave her.

Jake snapped the reins and clucked his tongue. The buckboard jerked forward at a lumbering pace.

Bea grasped the arm of the bench. "What about Mr. Oakes?"

"He told me to go on. Said he'd be along directly."

Jake guided the buckboard past the apple orchard on a worn trail, then diagonally across the cornfield toward the far hayfield. Neither spoke a word the entire time.

Not that Bea cared to talk. She was too lost in her own worries about the feud between Cord and Gil to press Jake for conversation. And she'd helped Mr. Oakes and Jake cover the haystacks last year, so she didn't need to be schooled in what to do.

A breeze toyed with her bonnet ties, carrying with it the scent of fresh-cut hay and rain. Unease feathered across her skin like a warning. She scanned the darkening ribbons unfurling across the sun-kissed horizon and knew they'd have to work fast to beat the rain and wind.

Jake pulled the buckboard to a stop on the south side of the first haystack they came to. He set the brake and climbed onto the back. In a matter of minutes, he'd unfolded a tarpaulin and begun tying ropes through the two corner grommets.

Bea climbed down from the high seat and strolled around the haystack, scanning the field. Mr. Oakes was correct. Every haystack was devoid of its tarpaulin.

"Holler when you're ready and I'll toss the ropes over the top to you," Jake shouted.

"I'm ready. Get on with it."

The wagon creaked, and two ends of rope arched high over the haystack and snaked down the side. Bea grasped one and then the other just as a gust of wind plastered her bloomers to her legs and threatened to rip her bonnet off.

"I have them," she shouted over a chill gust of wind.

Jake joined her and took one rope, pulling it hand over hand to drag the tarpaulin over the top of the stack. Bea did the same, though she wasn't nearly as fast as Jake. He secured his end and came to help her.

"I'll finish this side while you tie down the other."

"You sure?"

"Of course. Take a look at that sky. We can't dawdle."

Jake hesitated, then hurried around the stack. Bea tugged and pulled. Sweat popped out on her upper lip and her arms burned from exertion, but she was determined to do her part to help. Not that they could afford to wait for Mr. Oakes to help them. The sky was growing angrier by the minute.

Bea worked the rope through the grommets and secured it to the stakes in the ground. She glanced back at the ranch. What was keeping Mr. Oakes?

The crack of a rifle split the air, echoing across the field. The horse whinnied and the buckboard rattled.

"Jake?"

Only the moaning wind answered her.

Heart in her throat, Bea crept around the haystack. Jake sprawled behind the wagon, deathly still. Bright red blood trickled from a gash aside his head.

"No!"

She dropped to her knees beside him. Her hand trembled as she searched for Jake's heartbeat. Its strength surprised her—Jake's pulse was steady and strong. She gasped out the breath fear had trapped in her lungs, but her relief vanished as a whinny echoed from the nearby ravine.

Panic clawed at Bea's throat like talons as she scanned the wooded area sloping toward the creek. A swatch of color flashed among the dense brush. Whoever had shot Jake was there. Watching. Waiting for another victim.

Hoofbeats drummed the ground, closing the distance between the ranch and the field. It must be Mr. Oakes. And he was riding into a deadly trap.

Bea scrambled to her feet and snatched the rifle from the buckboard. Shortly after Papa's death, she'd sought Mr. Oakes's tutelage in shooting the thing. A woman living alone couldn't be too careful.

Biting her lower lip, she levered back the hammer and took cover behind the buckboard. Fast-approaching horses and her heartbeat thundered in her ears.

Color flashed amid the trees again. Bea aimed at it and squeezed the trigger.

The boom roared in her ears. The horse spooked, rocking the wagon. The discharge knocked her off her feet.

She landed hard on her bottom. The shoulder she'd braced the rifle against throbbed.

Hoofbeats bore down on them from behind. Horses—not a horse. Jake groaned and managed to sit up. She struggled to her feet, feeling exposed and stupid and scared out of her wits.

Mr. Oakes galloped past her first. He leaned low over a stocky brood mare, his revolver drawn. Her grandfather sped by next, then reined to a stop at the buckboard and steadied the restless horse fighting the harness. Only then did she see the rifle the Earl of Arden brandished with surprising prowess.

Zephyr came to a dust-choking halt beside her. Bea hugged herself and stared holes in the ground. She knew the rider would be Cord. And she knew he'd be furious with her for going off without him this morning. Not that it mattered. She'd done what she had to. Surely he'd understand that.

His boots banged the ground like gunshots. Silver spurs sang out an ominous tune that twanged along her nerves. Long denim-clad legs braced wide before her.

Bea hiked her chin up and faced Cord. She'd not allow any man to intimidate her. No matter that his fists bunched at his sides or that fury flamed in his eyes, which had gone nearly black.

But try as she might, she couldn't stop her lips from trembling or blink away those damnable tears stinging her eyes. All because she knew she was responsible for Jake getting shot. Gil Yancy had retaliated this morning, erring as she and Lambert had in thinking the young cowhand was Cord.

Cord thumbed his hat back. "Start talking, Trixie."

She marveled her husband could speak civilly, considering the way he had set his jaw. The firm lips that had roamed freely over her body last night were now pulled into a grim slash.

Her shoulders slumped. "Someone shot Jake."

That got Cord's attention away from her and onto the cowhand. He knelt by Jake's side. "You all right, boy?"

Jake groaned. "My head's pounding like a stampede and I'm bleeding like a stuck hog."

"Hold still while I bandage it." Cord reached inside his shirt, tugged out a rather large white cloth, and gave it a shake. Bea identified the garment. Her drawers. Heat scorched her face. "This'll do till we get you back home."

Cord tied the snowy white garment around Jake's head. Jake must have seen the ruffled hems and guessed what they were, too, because he flushed a deep red to the roots of his hair.

Mortified speechless, Bea batted the dry grass off her bloomers and silently groused that Cord had the audacity to wave her drawers about, as if he wanted everyone to know they'd made love. Odd behavior for the man who'd told her to forget the intimate interlude had occurred.

"I say, Tanner," Grandfather said. "Would that be ladies', er, unmentionables you've tied about the lad's head?"

"Yep. Trixie's drawers." Cord skewered Jake with a piercing gaze. "Did you see who shot you?"

Jake hung his head. "All I saw was the sun glinting off a

rifle barrel in the brush by the creek. Before I could grab my rifle and find cover, he got a shot off."

"You're damned lucky he just grazed you." Cord faced Bea. "Why did you order Ott not to tell me somebody had cut the ropes on the tarpaulins?"

"Considering your condition last night and my uncertainty of it this morning," Bea said, "I decided it would be best for me to attend the matter myself."

Cord snorted. "Now why don't that surprise me."

"What's this about a condition?" Grandfather asked.

"Had a rip-roaring headache last night," Cord said. "Ott gave me a remedy and it knocked the props out from under me."

An overwhelming wave of guilt washed over Bea. Why hadn't she considered that Cord would still be suffering from his fall last night? Why hadn't she thought to ask about his health then? Why had she naturally assumed the worst of him?

Because she was angry and hurt. She had behaved more like a petulant child than a woman in love. Unfortunately, Cord didn't share that tender emotion with her. She had to accept that.

Mr. Oakes rode up to the buckboard, jerking her thoughts away from her misery. "Lost his tracks in the grass."

Cord rubbed his nape and sighed. "Figured as much. Best take Jake back to the house."

Bea thought that was a sound notion. Jake shouldn't be driving the wagon.

While Mr. Oakes climbed off the mare and Cord helped Jake into the buckboard, she retrieved Jake's hat. Grandfather trotted past her with Mr. Oakes's horse in tow.

No matter. Though she was wearing her bloomer outfit, she didn't care to ride astride. But with Jake and Mr. Oakes claiming the buckboard bench, she'd be forced to ride in the back.

She handed Jake his hat. "Are you in great pain?"

"My head hurts something fierce." Jake gripped his hat but refused to look at her.

She didn't take offense. It embarrassed her no end that Cord had used her drawers to bandage Jake's head. That's when she noticed Cord watching her.

He wore the strangest expression. Nervous, almost. Perhaps leaning toward the hesitant. And underneath it all, anger. That's what he directed squarely at her.

She marched to the rear of the buckboard, intending to climb in. The wagon jolted off before she made four good steps.

"Don't fret yourself none," Mr. Oakes said to her. "Cordell's bark is worse'n his bite."

"I shall bear that in mind." She turned to Cord. "Do you intend to engage in an argument with me?"

He grabbed Zephyr's reins and strode toward her. "I hope to hell not. But we've got things to settle between us."

He was going to leave her high and dry. She just knew it.

"I don't think we do. You signed a contract that details our common bond to the letter. Remember?"

"How could I forget?"

He snared her around the waist and hoisted her atop the stallion. The animal whickered, drowning out her wince.

Cord vaulted up behind her and set Zephyr to an easy walk. Instead of holding her close, he caged her within his arms.

Anger emanated from him in scorching waves. "I've done some thinking since last night."

She stiffened, fearing the worse. "Have you?"

"Damn right." Cord's warm breath fanned her ear, sending shivers of dread coursing through her. "I want a change in our marriage agreement right here and now."

Oh, dread. "Why ever would I do that?"

"Because you ain't got a choice."

Bea bit her lower lip, aware Cord could do anything he

wished with her or the ranch. So why did he seek her acceptance? "What do you propose we change about our agreement?"

"If I got a child on you, there'll be no divorce."

Had she heard him correctly? "Are you serious?"

His hands tightened slightly on the reins. "Yep."

Her mind reeled. If she was with child, they'd stay married. She'd win his heart in time. And if she didn't?

She shivered at the thought. "A fair arrangement, but—"

"Fair or not, I ain't gonna sire any bastards. Any kid of mine will have his ma and pa and a place to call home."

The anguish vibrating in his voice brought tears to her eyes. He'd had nothing growing up. No father. No home. She suspected he'd received very little affection. Those slights left deep scars.

As much as she detested being stuck in a loveless marriage for the rest of her days, she couldn't deny Cord the family he so very much deserved. He'd be a good father. A good husband. And she'd do everything in her power to be a loving mother and wife.

In fact, the more she thought about it, the more she realized she ached for a family of her own. A husband. Children. A home. She had it all right here. Cord. The Prairie Rose. She laid a hand over her midsection. And perhaps a baby growing within her.

"Very well. If I'm with child, we'll remain married."

He was silent for the longest time. "You've got my word I'll keep my hands to myself from here on out. What happened between us last night won't happen again."

She smiled to herself. That's where Cord was wrong. They'd make love again. She'd make certain of it.

"Did you see who shot Jake?"

"No. But I'm positive it was Gil Yancy."

"What makes you so sure of that?"

"Gil has a grudge against you. Did you realize that from a distance, Jake resembles you?"

He chuckled low. "Nope, but I've always thought one cow-poke pretty much looks the same as the next."

Bea rolled her eyes, wondering if her husband was blind or if he truly didn't realize how he stood out among men. Cord was tall and oozed strength. And he was exceptionally handsome.

She sighed. "So whoever shot Jake thought they were shooting you. Since I believe Gil Yancy damaged your saddle as well as disabled my windmill, I'm convinced he's the culprit. Will you go out after him now?"

"Nope." Cord reined in Zephyr by the house. He swung down, plucked Bea from the saddle, and set her on her feet.

"Why ever not? Gil will try to kill you again, you know." She clutched his shoulders, her eyes searching his dark ones. "What will we do?"

"*We* go on as before, except I don't want you leaving the ranch without me or your grandpappy."

Bea bristled at his order. "And what of you? Do you intend to continue taking predawn forays to the cemetery?"

"I can take care of myself." Cord vaulted onto the saddle and tugged his hat low over his brow, no doubt oblivious to the fact that he radiated sensuality. "Tell your stubborn aunt not to leave the ranch unescorted, either. No more gallivant-ing to Scotty's in the middle of the night."

That snapped Bea from her risqué musings of Cord. "Are you suggesting Muriel has visited the Flying D after dark?"

Cord dipped his chin. "She did last night."

"Are you certain?"

"Yep. Caught her sneaking home this morning right after you lit out with Jake. When I asked her where she'd been, she said she rode to Scotty's last night after everybody was asleep. She owned up to spending the night with him." A muscle throbbed along his jaw, proof Cord was annoyed with Muriel's amorous interlude.

"What a bloody muddle!" Bea whisked inside to think this

through, fearing if she didn't squash Muriel's impulsive affair with Donnelly, she'd never be rid of Donnelly's interference.

Wanting no part in the coming scuffle between Muriel and Trixie, Cord headed toward the bunkhouse. He needed to check on Jake, then find Gil and have it out with him.

Cord still couldn't imagine his old rival would stoop to murder. But stranger things had happened. Hell, look how much he'd changed in the few weeks he'd been hitched to Trixie.

Oh, she still put him in a sod-pawing, horn-tossing mood from time to time. But more often than not, she brought out yearnings that scared the living hell right out of him.

Cord ached to stay married to her more than anything, but as things stood, he'd be moving on—unless he'd knocked her up. Chances of that happening the first time he got to her were damned slim. And if he didn't catch the bastard out to plug him, Trixie would end up wearing her faded widow's weeds.

He tied Zephyr to a corral rail and ambled into the bunkhouse. He thumbed his hat back and grinned.

The earl was reading the papers and breeding charts tacked to the walls. Jake slouched on his cot while Ott wound a cloth around his head. Juliet and her fat pups milled at Jake's feet.

Trixie's drawers lay in a heap on the cot. The snow white cloth with its ruffles and lace shone like a tin roof in the sun.

He'd embarrassed the hell out of her and Jake when he plucked them from his pocket. At the time, all he'd had on his mind was bandaging Jake up. Now, it made Cord a mite red-faced and uneasy to see his wife's fancy drawers on another man's bunk.

Cord plucked up the drawers and shoved them in his pocket. "Your head still pounding?"

"Some," Jake said. "I ain't walking real steady either."

"If that snake was a better shot, you wouldn't be here." Ott tied off the bandage. "I'll fetch you more of Mrs. Delgado's elixir. That'll take your mind off your aches and pains."

Knock him out was more like it. That's what it'd done to Cord. But he figured the boy could use a couple days' rest.

"I say, Tanner," the earl said. "I've business to attend to in Revolt and would greatly appreciate your company."

"When you plan on going?"

"Immediately."

Cord wondered what the earl had up his sleeve. "Fine by me."

"Smashing! After I retrieve an item from the house, we'll be off." The earl marched out of the bunkhouse at a good clip.

"Keep an eye on things while we're gone," Cord told Ott.

"Sure thing, boss."

Cord strode to the stable and down the aisle. He found Rory mucking out Esprit's stall. "While the earl and I are gone, I want you to help keep a close watch out. Don't hesitate to use a gun if you have to. Whatever you do, don't let the women leave the ranch alone."

"You can depend on me, you can. But just to even up the odds, when the viscount returns from his morning ride, I'll be certain to apprise him of the happenings and enlist his aid."

Rory would get about as much help from the viscount as he would from the horses, but Cord didn't waste his breath saying so. "Just keep an eye out while we're gone."

Cord strode to the tack room. He took a clean bandanna from his saddlebags and stuffed Trixie's drawers in the pouch. He reckoned he should've taken them back to the house then and there, but he didn't want to waste the time. In here, they were hidden.

As he expected, the earl was saddled up and waiting. He'd learned this morning the earl was a force to be reckoned with, the kind of man he'd be damned glad to have on his side in a fight.

The earl showed no fear or bravado. Just raw courage. Cord suspected Northroupe had been one helluva scrapper in his day.

Cord tied his bandanna around his neck and then swung onto Zephyr. "Ready?"

"Indeed, I am, m'boy. This morning's calamity has convinced me it is time for me to wipe my hands of this ranch."

CHAPTER SIXTEEN

It would've been easier to rope a bobcat with meat string than to get the earl to spit out what he aimed to do with the Prairie Rose. Least that's what Cord was left thinking by the time they rode into Revolt close to an hour later. Try as he might, he couldn't get Trixie's grandpappy to tell him a damn thing about his plans.

All asking outright got Cord was, "You'll see, m'boy."

His nerves screeched louder than a dry axle. He had to give it another shot while he had the chance. "You know Trixie loves that ranch. Losing it'd break her heart."

The earl barked a laugh. "Egad! Have a modicum of patience, m'boy. I'm not about to toss you and Beatrix out on the streets."

Cord breathed a mite easier, taking the earl at his word.

They trotted past the brick bank. Eli Holmes stood in the doorway and eyed them. Disgust churned Cord's gut. The banker was an old buzzard, lending hardscrabble ranchers and sod busters enough money to give them hope and then circling them. Soon as they were late making a payment, Holmes foreclosed on them.

Next to the bank rose Lott's Mercantile, taking up the space of three regular-sized buildings. The false front was as yellow as the sunflowers dotting the prairie. Big and flashy, like a drummer peddling snake oil.

From the window, Cord spied Arlene craning her neck to get a gander at them. He bet that in less than ten minutes, word would spread that he and the earl had come to town. No doubt speculation would run higher than a rain-swollen river.

The earl reined up before Security Land and Legal and dismounted. He tethered his horse to the hitching post, then brushed dust from his black frock coat.

Cord swung down and tied Zephyr next to the earl's gelding. He glanced toward the Plainsmen's Lodge and swore. Nate Wyles leaned against one porch post. Gil Yancy took the other one. Both cowboys appeared to be spoiling for a fight. So was he.

He had a mind to have it out with both cowpokes, but the earl's voice stopped him from taking a step. "Business first, Tanner. Mr. Yancy will be there when we're finished."

"The weasel on the right is the foreman Trixie fired."

"Is he now? After I've taken care of my business, I'd very much like to speak with the chap."

Cord ground his right fist in his left palm. "Then I'll wait till you're done talking to him before I plow into him."

"That's the ticket." The earl clapped Cord on the back and chuckled. "After Zachary sets things to rights for me, we shall give those cheeky devils the what for."

Picturing the earl in a brawl had Cord grinning. He shook his head at the tomfoolery of it all and trailed Trixie's grandpappy into the lawyer's office.

Zachary motioned to the chairs before his desk. "Good to see you, Lord Arden. Tanner. What can I do for you two gentlemen?"

The earl removed his top hat, dropped onto a chair, and pulled a wad of papers from his inside coat pocket. He plunked them onto the desk. "As I said in my letter, I'm eager to wipe my hands of the American property I hold title to."

"Like I told you before, I know of someone who's interested in buying the Prairie Rose." Zachary reached for the title.

The earl dropped a gloved hand atop the papers. "Deuced foolish of me for not making my wishes clear." He flashed the lawyer a smile that would've made a confidence man's pale in comparison. "You see, my good man. I wish to sign the land over to Tanner, my grandson by marriage."

Relief swelled in Cord. Then reality splintered into him. He'd have the title, all right. But unless Trixie was packing his kid, he'd sign it over to her and be on his way.

It's what he'd agreed to do. Put Revolt behind him. Head out west and settle on a strip of land. And try to forget how right it felt to make love to Trixie.

Zachary leaned back in his chair, his cool gaze sliding to Cord. Cord managed a smile. Everything was working out as Trixie had planned. If Zachary didn't say something to screw this up.

"I feel it's my duty to ask you to carefully consider your granddaughter's welfare." Zachary smiled at the earl and spread his arms wide. "Once the title is in Tanner's name, nothing can stop him from selling the land and absconding with the profits."

"I wouldn't do that," Cord said to the earl. "But if you doubt me, have Zachary put the title in Trixie's name."

Surprise flickered in Zachary's eyes. "Are you serious?"

"Damned right, I am," Cord said.

The earl stroked his spade beard. "I rather think Bea would relish that, say what?"

Would she ever, Cord thought. "It's no secret she's kept the ranch going through some mighty tough times."

"Indeed, Bea is resourceful," the earl said. "Too much so at times to place the title solely in her name."

Zachary cleared his throat. "With careful wording, the land can be owned equally between Mr. and Mrs. Tanner. It couldn't be sold unless both parties agreed. But, in the case of death, the survivor would have full ownership."

The earl clapped his palms together. "Smashing notion. Have you any qualms about joint ownership, m'boy?"

"Not a one." He wouldn't be surprised if Trixie dogged him into getting the title switched to her name before the ink dried.

"Take care of it, Zachary. As usual, I'll see you are handsomely recompensed." The earl rose and Cord followed suit.

"It'll take me a day or two to finalize it." Zachary faced Cord, acting leery. "Would you prefer I keep the title in my safe until you retrieve it or should I send it out to the ranch?"

Cord didn't have to think on this one. It'd be easier to walk away from later if he didn't have to see his name on the title now. "You'd best keep it here."

The earl put on his top hat and gave it a pat. "I trust what transpired today shall remain in strictest confidence."

"You have my word on it, your lordship," Zachary said.

"Excellent." The earl strode to the door.

Cord trailed him outside, feeling as if they could take Zachary at his word. He'd seen the lawyer handle sticky matters at the Flying D and keep his mouth shut. So far he hadn't said a word about the damnable contract he'd drawn up for Trixie.

Before they reached the horses, the earl shrugged out of his fine coat. "All that remains to be done is to sign over Beatrix's dowry to you. But I'd prefer taking care of that matter after Zachary updates the title. Have you any objections?"

"Not a one."

"I pray you won't tell Beatrix about our business transaction this morning. I'd like to surprise her with the news when I give you and Bea the title as my wedding gift." The earl folded his coat and draped it over his saddle, then set his hat atop it.

"I'll keep my mouth shut." He frowned. "What're you doing?"

"Preparing to have a chat with those rounders." The earl nodded toward the Plainsmen's Lodge as he tugged off his gloves. He tossed them into his hat, then removed his fancy white tie and stuffed it in next. "Having second thoughts, are we?"

"Nope. But you'd best keep in mind that cowpokes tend to talk mighty hard with their fists."

"Think I am a duffer, eh?" The earl bobbed up and down, pumped his arms and clenched his fists. His shirt tightened over muscle. "I assure you I'm quite adept at fisticuffs."

Cord didn't doubt that for a minute. He took off his gun belt, hooked it over his saddle horn, and dropped his hat atop it. "How long has it been since you bruised your knuckles?"

"Shortly after we arrived in America. I ran into a bedchamber thief in a hotel in New Orleans. One blow put the bloke out, but his cohort proved to be quite the scrapper."

Cord grinned, having a hunch the earl had got in more than a few good licks. "Ready to beat the truth out of those two mavericks?"

"Indeed I am, m'boy."

Cord kept his eyes on Gil and Nate as he and the earl ambled over to the Plainsmen's Lodge. The cowpokes' sunken eyes hinted they'd had one helluva bender last night. Judging by the stench of stale whiskey and sweat drifting to him, both needed a bath.

Nate's dark hair hung in greasy hanks past his collar. His long, drooping mustache hid a weak chin. The white scar angling from his left earlobe to chin topped off his mean look.

Remnants of a meal clung to Nate's flannel shirtfront and leather vest. The grimy string of a Bull Durham bag dangled from a breast pocket. Cord guessed Nate had found work, because he sported a new Stetson and fancy boots.

Not so for Gil. The cowpuncher looked like he'd been bunking on the open prairie. He had two days' growth of brassy whiskers. His clothes were sorely in need of a washing.

Cord glanced at Gil's roan gelding. Its coat was damp, hinting it'd had a recent run. Nate's sorrel looked the same.

Anxiety cinched up Cord's gut. These two cowboys had done some recent, hard riding. To the Prairie Rose and back?

Cord stared into Gil's angry, bloodshot eyes. "Appears you had Rhubarb out for a morning run. Mind telling me where to?"

Gil's mouth twisted. "That ain't none of your business."

"I think it is. Someone paid a visit to the Prairie Rose this morning." Cord curled his fists at his sides. "Thought maybe it was you."

"You thought wrong, pard." Gil unbuckled his gun belt and dropped it behind him.

Nate cackled, doing the same. "Ol' Gil spent the night with a sporting lady in Wichita. You know the place, Cordell. It's the last parlor house your whore mama worked in."

Cord's gut tightened up another notch. He'd stopped fighting men who'd called his ma a whore years ago. But when a no-account like Nate insulted her, the rage in Cord coiled, ready to strike.

"I say, is this hooligan implying your mother was a prostitute?" the earl asked.

"Yep. The Golden Plume is a whorehouse," Cord said.

The earl coughed. "I see."

Gil pushed away from the post and strode into the street, planting himself five feet before Cord. "The upstairs gals asked about you, pard. I told them you wouldn't show your face at the Plume till you had the title to the Prairie Rose in your name." He tossed a glance toward Zachary's. "Damnation, but you're good, Cordell. You charmed that lil' lady into marrying you so you'd get your hands on her prime land and horseflesh. Or did you screw your wife out of it?"

"I'm gonna drive those words down your throat." Cord started after Gil, but the earl laid a hand on his shoulder to stay him.

Lord Arden's blue eyes glinted like flint. "Mr. Yancy, a

gentleman never bandies about a lady's name in a gaming hall, a house of ill repute, or in the middle of the street."

A dull flush darkened Gil's features. Cord doubted it stemmed from humiliation. His old friend had always gotten out of sorts whenever Scotty chewed him out. Seeing that he'd clamped his mouth shut, Cord knew Gil was madder than hell.

"You must be Northroupe's pa—the earl of something or another," Nate drawled, fixing the earl with a squinty-eyed stare.

"The ninth Earl of Arden." The earl squared his shoulders and jutted his chin out. "I understand that my son hired you as foreman on the Prairie Rose."

Nate bobbed his head. "Me and Northroupe got on just fine."

The earl gave Nate a quick once-over and snorted. "Due to the fact you're no longer employed on the Prairie Rose, I gather you and my granddaughter did not get on."

Hatred honed the sharp angles in Nate's rangy face. "She ne'er did cotton to me none. After her pappy bit the dust, she got all up in the air 'cause I was fixing to put a bullet in that devil stallion what throwed her pappy to his death."

Cord clenched his teeth so hard his jaw throbbed. "That horse wouldn't have gone loco if it hadn't been whipped and tortured, but then, I reckon you two already know that."

"I told you I never put a spider in any saddle," Gil said.

Tension burned across Cord's shoulders like a whiplash. "Did you try to part my hair with a bullet this morning?"

"If I shot at you," Gil said, "I wouldn't have missed."

It was a fact. Gil was a crackerjack shot. He wouldn't have grazed Jake; he'd have killed him.

Cord turned to Nate. "Where were you at dawn?"

Nate smiled, showing yellowed teeth. "Screwing a whore. Like Gil said, we ain't got nothing to do with the troubles you've been having on your spread."

"I'm not convinced of that," the earl said. "Mr. Yancy bears a grudge with Tanner, and from the gossip I heard at this lodge, you vowed to get even with my granddaughter for firing you."

Nate's eyes slitted. "Best watch what you accuse a man of doing, old man, or you'll get whopped good and proper."

"Don't be too certain of that, you cheeky squirt." The earl moved like lightning and drove a fist into Nate's pug nose.

Nate bellowed and staggered back. Blood streamed from his nose. With a roar, the wily cowpuncher charged the earl.

Gil sprang at Cord a heartbeat later. The impact knocked them to the ground, but Gil ended up on top.

Fire licked through Cord's left shoulder and he shifted, trying to protect the old injury. Gil took advantage of catching him off balance. He drove a fist into Cord's jaw and followed it up with a quick jab to the ribs.

Another punch came flying at Cord's nose. Cord caught Gil's fist in his palm. The muscles in his arms burned. Before Gil jerked free, Cord walloped him aside the head with his free hand.

Gil grunted and lurched to his feet. Cord scrambled up and lunged at his old rival.

They tore into one another like a couple of cowboys hitting town after a long cattle drive, drawing blood with piledriving fists, kicking up dust and kicking ass.

Cord hurt in places he forgot he had. He couldn't see out of his right eye. His left shoulder throbbed like it'd been twisted out of the socket. The knuckles on both hands burned something fierce. Breathing deep was pure torture. But each grunt Gil let out gave Cord another boost of energy.

He grabbed Gil by his vest and yanked him to his feet. Gil landed another jab to Cord's middle before he sent Gil sprawling with a teeth-rattling punch. Gil didn't rouse this time.

Panting for breath, Cord turned to the fistfight between the earl and Nate. The Englishman sent Nate staggering backwards through the door to the lodge. The cowpuncher's arms windmilled, but he couldn't catch himself.

The earl dusted his hands and marched after Nate. Downright surprised by the older man's agility, Cord hugged his sore ribs and staggered toward the saloon.

A horse's bugling brought Cord up short. That demon's cry was Zephyr's, but with folks gathering around to watch the fight, Cord couldn't see what had riled the stallion.

Cord pushed his way to Zephyr. By the time he reached the stallion, he'd quieted. Nobody was even close to the horses.

Still, Cord aimed to take a closer look. A heavy hand clamped onto his shoulder. Figuring it was Gil, Cord spun on his heels and drove his fist toward his old rival's face.

Only it was Marshal Ives behind him. Not Gil.

The marshal ducked the punch and let loose one of his own. Bone cracked bone.

Cord's head snapped back. Pain stampeded through his noggin. He crumpled to his knees and sprawled on his back. Right before his eyes rolled back in the sockets and the world went black, he saw the marshal's shadow standing over him.

Cord awakened with a groan, hurting from head to toe. The lumpy straw mattress under him didn't cushion his aches and pains. The sour smell filling his nostrils was enough to set his gut churning. Where the hell was he?

He pried open the eye that didn't throb and took in the bars surrounding him. He slammed his eye shut and cursed. Revolt's one-room jail. He'd spent enough nights here to recognize it.

"Good afternoon, Tanner. I trust you enjoyed your forty winks." The earl's voice rumbled with disgust.

"Hardly." Cord forced his eye open again. The earl slouched on the lumpy cot across from him. Gil sprawled on the one near the bars. He didn't see Nate. "What happened to Wyles?"

The earl slid Cord a sour look. "The ruffian pulled a shiv on me and made good his escape. I informed the marshal of such when he arrested me for brawling. At first, I feared Ives had turned a deaf ear to my petition. But after his men carried you and that bloke in here, he dispatched two men after Wyles."

Cord sat up and cradled his aching head. "I'm sure as hell sorry I got you tangled up in this mess."

"You're the one sporting the mouse, m'boy. Not I," the earl said. "Nor am I the least bit sorry I joined you in the fray. Since I suspect Wyles had a hand in my son's demise, I rather enjoyed giving him the what for. It was a damnable fluke the hooligan slipped away."

The front door creaked open and Marshal Ives lumbered into the jail. He dropped his hat onto a rough desk, hitched up his baggy trousers, and shot the three of them a look of disgust.

Lord Arden rose and crossed to the barred door. "I trust you procured our bond from Mr. Zachary, as I instructed."

"'Fraid not, your lordship. He lit out afore I could talk with him." Ives plopped onto his oak swivel chair, leaned back, and stacked his boot heels atop the desk. "You best think on somebody else to help you out."

The earl stroked his beard and paced the cramped space. "Any other time, Strowbridge would avail himself of the spirits offered at the gentlemen's club."

Ives checked the time on his pocket watch. "Well, like I told you an hour ago, if the viscount did come into town today, he didn't stick around long."

"I would wager Strowbridge is at the ranch," the earl said.

"Just say the word and I'll send a boy out to the Prairie Rose to fetch him," Ives said around a fat wad of chew he'd stuffed into his mouth.

"No!" the earl and Cord barked in unison.

The earl gave the cuffs of his blood-smeared shirtsleeves a tug. "We don't wish to upset the ladies."

"Suit yourself." Ives's boots hit the floor with a bang. The sound tore through Cord's head like an explosion, but Gil didn't flinch. "I got a notion you'll change your minds by the time I come back from making my rounds."

"A moment, please." The earl scowled at Cord. "I say, Tanner. You must know someone who can get us out of this coil."

Cord locked gazes with Ives, then muttered a curse born of defeat and frustration. "Send for Scotty."

"Ah, yes. Mr. Donnelly." The earl waved a dismissing hand at Ives. "Well, my good man. See to it."

Grinning like a possum staking claim to a pile of garbage, Ives set his big hat onto his small head and strode out. A lonesome silence settled over the jail.

The earl nudged Gil's shoulder. Gil didn't stir. The earl returned to his cot and plopped down. "I gather there is some truth to this bloke's aspersions on your character."

Cord rubbed his throbbing forehead. He might as well explain it all to the earl before someone else did.

"I'm the bastard of a prostitute Scotty Donnelly married when I was twelve. Scotty adored her. He tolerated me." Cord looked up at him. "I know I ain't good enough for Trixie, what with her coming from a good family and all, but—"

"Allow me to tell you the truth about Beatrix's good family," the earl said. "My son and his wife were so bloody proper about everything. When Bea was born, her mother sought to impress the Queen by naming the baby after Victoria's daughter, Princess Beatrice. But my son's vapid wife was too indisposed to see to it." He chuckled. "My son was in his cups at the christening and dubbed the child Beatrix. His wife never forgave him."

Cord grinned. "Trixie suits her better."

"Indeed, it does." The earl sighed. "Bea's parents would have detested it, and they would've been appalled to know their daughter married someone born on the wrong side of the sheets."

"What about you? Are you saying my past doesn't bother you?"

"Not in the least. You're not the first baseborn person to marry a Northroupe and I warrant you'll not be the last." The earl leaned back and smiled. "Bea is the very image of her grandmother, my countess Helena. She was of humble birth and too independent by half, I tell you. Led me on a deuce of a chase before I trapped her in the bonds of holy matrimony."

"Any regrets?" Cord figured there was a long list of them.

"Only that I outlived her." The earl blinked rapidly, but Cord spied moisture gleaming in the earl's eyes. "I'd like to hear the truth, Tanner. Why did you marry Bea?"

He blew out a weary breath. He wouldn't lie to a man who'd bared a part of his own heart and soul to him.

"Trixie made me an offer I couldn't refuse."

The earl snorted. "I suspected as much. Out with it."

He glanced at Gil. His rival was sprawled on the cot, sawing logs. Cord kicked the cot to make sure. Gil kept on sleeping.

In a low voice, Cord told the earl about the contract Trixie had offered him. He admitted he'd signed it partly to honor his word, and partly to best Gil. That he'd kissed her because she'd goaded him into acting like a doting husband and swore he'd kept his distance afterward because he'd liked holding her and kissing her too damned much. Finally, he'd 'fessed up that he was wary of sharing a bed with her and struggled to keep his hands to himself.

The earl cleared his throat. "I take it you failed the latter, that Bea is your wife in every sense of the word?"

"Yep." Cord's face heated up like a boy's. "We struck a new bargain—if I got a child on her, there'll be no divorce."

"I see. Was that your idea or Bea's?"

"Mine."

"Sound notion. Tell me, did Bea argue the point with you?"

He rubbed his nape and frowned. "She agreed to it."

The earl tipped back his head and let out a knee-slapping belly laugh that dredged a chuckle out of Cord.

"A word of advice, m'boy," the earl said between dying laughs. "When a Northroupe lady turns unaccountably biddable, you can lay odds she's set to finagle something from you."

Cord had the notion the older man was right. What he couldn't figure was what else Bea wanted from him.

Outside, a horse snorted. Agitated voices rose and fell. Footsteps tapped a fast path across the boardwalk. Cord rose and braced himself, expecting Scotty to barge in and rake him over the coals for landing in jail.

The door swung open. Instead of his stepfather, Trixie burst into the room with a swish of her dark blue skirt.

Her gaze locked with Cord's. A cherry red flush rode her cheekbones. Panic flickered in her expressive eyes.

He tore his gaze from Trixie's and frowned at the open door. Nobody from the Prairie Rose made an appearance. Unease gnawed at him, with anger dogging its heels.

Cord crossed to the bars and wrapped his fingers around the cool metal. "If you rode into town alone—"

"Mr. Donnelly insisted he escort Muriel and me into Revolt," she said.

Cord swore under his breath. "I should've known he'd bust a gut telling you I was behind bars."

"Mr. Donnelly had little choice. The lad the marshal sent to the Flying D was redirected to the Prairie Rose, where Donnelly was keeping company with Aunt Muriel." She jabbed a finger in Gil's direction, but her gaze stayed on Cord. A tear slid from one glistening eye, and Cord flinched like he'd been gut punched. "You told me you were not going to seek him out. You lied to me."

"Calm yourself, Bea," the earl blustered. "A man cannot always know when he'll be drawn into a fracas."

Trixie crossed her arms over her bosom. "Piffle! Why else would my husband come into Revolt if not to fight with Gil Yancy?"

Wild horses couldn't have dragged the truth out of Cord. But it went against his grain to lie to her, too.

"I'd say the lil' wife has got you by the short hairs, pard." Gil sat up and yawned, and Cord wanted to knock the smirk off his rival's battered face. "What did bring you to town?"

The earl shot to his feet and towered over Gil. "We had reason to believe you attempted to kill Tanner this morn."

"I told you it wasn't me." Gil drove his fingers through his mop of gold hair. "Ask Arlene Lott. She was out sweeping her boardwalk when Nate and I rode into town at sunup."

"How convenient for you," Trixie said.

"I believe him." Cord read the truth in Gil's eyes.

Gil might've snuck on the Rose last night and cut the ropes on their tarpaulins out of pure meanness, but he didn't shoot at Jake. But Cord still couldn't figure Gil hanging around the likes of Nate. Were they drinking buddies? Or were they partnered in something on the wrong side of the law?

The door opened and Marshal Ives lumbered in. Muriel and Scotty trailed him.

Scotty dug into his pocket and tossed a couple of gold pieces on Ives's desk. "This cover bail on the three of them?"

"Sure does." The marshal raked the money into a drawer, then snagged the ring holding a long brass key off a hook and fit it into the lock on the metal door. It swung open with a screech. "Get on with you. This time keep your noses clean."

"Thank you, Marshal Ives. I shall heed your advice." The earl strode to the wall where his coat and hat hung on a peg.

Gil started through the opening, but Trixie planted herself before it and barred his exit. He glanced at Cord, then smiled at Trixie and winked. "You know, if ol' Ott hadn't conned Cord into helping you out, I bet you'd have hired me to marry you."

Damn it all to hell and back! Gil had been playing possum. He'd heard every word Cord said to the earl.

Trixie tossed a wide-eyed look around the jail and then whirled on Gil. "Don't delude yourself. If Cord hadn't helped me, I'd have sooner wed Ott Oakes than the likes of you."

Gil flinched, but Trixie paid him no mind. She was looking down her nubbin of a nose at Cord like he was a turncoat. But the tears swimming in her eyes knocked the wind from him.

"How could you?" She sashayed out the door without giving him time to answer.

Just as well, since he didn't know what to tell Trixie. He'd let her down. Broken his word.

Before Gil skedaddled, Cord leaned close to him and bit out, "If I see you or Wyles sneaking around the Prairie Rose, I'll make damned sure the both of you regret it."

"I'll keep that in mind." Gil strapped on his gun belt and jammed his revolver his holster. "But instead of you wasting your time wondering what I'm up to, you'd best figure out who's out to kill you before he gets the job done."

CHAPTER SEVENTEEN

Bea paced the library, her emotions seesawing from anxiety to anger. It was late afternoon, yet Grandfather and Cord hadn't returned to the ranch. But what annoyed her was that Donnelly hadn't taken his leave after escorting her and Muriel home.

"Donnelly's chivalry doesn't fool me," Bea told Mrs. Mimms who was wielding a feather duster across the bookcases. "He wants the Prairie Rose. What better way to achieve his goal than to fawn over dear love-starved Aunt Muriel."

Mrs. Mimms turned to look at her. "You can't be thinking the earl would sign over the ranch to Donnelly and Muriel instead of you and Mr. Tanner?"

"Indeed I am." She bit her lower lip, heartsick that Cord had told Gil about their contract. "If Gil Yancy knows I hired Cord to marry me, then Grandfather likely has heard about it, too."

Mrs. Mimms pointed the duster at Bea. "I told you the earl wouldn't be easy to gull. Now what'll you do, I ask you?"

Bea slumped on a chair. "Make Grandfather understand that though I chose Cord for a reason other than love, my marriage differs little from the ones my descendants were forced into."

"Does it now?" Mrs. Mimms returned to her dusting with renewed fervor.

"Of course." She'd been wedded and bedded. Surely Grandfather realized that. Surely he'd honor Papa's wishes now.

The door opened and Benedict trudged in carrying a note on a silver tray. "A message came for you."

Bea took the note and read it, relieved it was good news. "Viscount Strowbridge is riding into the next county to visit friends and won't return until tomorrow." She'd had no idea Lambert had so many acquaintances in the area, but she was glad she didn't have to suffer his company. "Do inform Mrs. Delgado."

"Yes, madam." Benedict left.

Laughter floated from the parlor where Muriel was entertaining Donnelly. Clearly her aunt was smitten with the rancher, but Bea feared he was only toying with Muriel.

Bea tapped her front tooth, growing more perturbed by the moment. "I wager my aunt and Donnelly are engaged in something more intimate than a rousing game of chess."

"Would you be thinking they're doing what you and Mr. Tanner did in the stable last night?" Mrs. Mimms asked.

Her cheeks burned with embarrassment. "How did you know?"

"I tend the laundry, mind you. This morning, the proof you'd given up your virginity stained your petticoat. Then there was the curious fact that your husband spent the night in the barn, but plucked your drawers from his shirt and bandaged poor Jake."

"What of it? Cord and I are married."

"Aye, and I'm thinking if fortune smiles on us, you and Mr. Tanner will stay married." Mrs. Mimms quit the library.

Bea slid a hand over her flat stomach. She yearned to bear Cord's baby. But she hoped it wouldn't happen yet. She wanted Cord to stay married to her because he loved her, not because he felt obligated to raise the offspring he'd never wanted.

She was well aware of the pain a child felt from knowing a parent didn't love them. Oh, Papa adored her. There was no doubt. But Bea's mother had very little to do with her.

Mrs. Mimms had taken care of Bea. Scolded her. Pampered her. Taught her things a woman should know. And loved her.

Sick with worry she'd end up without child, ranch, or husband, Bea stole onto the enclosed alcove off the library. She plumped a seat cushion, then curled onto the settee. After her papa's death, she found she could forget the trials of the world out here. She could forget her sorrows of the moment by admiring the land she had come to love.

Bea trailed a finger over the cushion's vines and grape clusters and studied the vista of rolling hills. Some thought them barren, but to her they glowed a rich gold.

Shadowed ravines hid shallow streams. Trees were few and far between. During the summer, hot dry gusts sucked the moisture from skin and soil. Winter's howling blasts of glacial air chilled man and beast to their marrow.

With wise planning, a dose of luck and prayer, the ranch survived brutal blizzards, killing droughts, and devastating tornadoes. Thanks to Mr. Oakes's guidance, Bea had discovered how to endure and prosper in this variable land. If only she knew how to weather the storm brewing within her own house.

The soft clearing of a throat snapped Bea from her doldrums. One glance to the doorway confirmed Muriel's presence. She noted her aunt's eyes sparkled and a flush stained her ivory cheeks.

Bea forced a smile. "You look exceedingly chipper. I take it you spent a pleasant afternoon in Mr. Donnelly's company."

"It was the finest day I've enjoyed in years." Muriel floated toward a willow chair and perched on its tufted cushion. "Prescott asked for my hand in marriage and I accepted."

Panic and fear welled and collided in Bea. "How can you marry a man you barely know?"

"Perhaps I should ask you the same question."

Determined to avoid any discussion of her marriage to Cord, Bea quickly switched tactics. "After your arrival here, I recall you said you'd never consider marriage again because you loved Mr. Flynn so very much and treasured your freedom."

A sad smile curved Muriel's mouth. "I did say that. And I did adore my husband. But throughout my years of widowhood, the thing I miss most is having a companion by my side."

"You're lonely?" At her aunt's nod, Bea shrank against the settee, painfully reminded of her own yearnings to have someone to stand beside her, to share her joys and sorrows. "But you've led a full life with your causes."

"No amount of crusades can take the place of the man you love holding you late into the night. Surely you understand that?"

Bea plucked at the ruffled edging of a cushion, understanding all too well. "I do. Though I'd never thought cuddling could make one feel so wondrous."

"I gather Lambert never exhibited that simple affection?"

She grimaced, longing to forget those brief distasteful encounters. "Lambert groped and pinched. I'd suspect gently embracing a woman is foreign to him. The few kisses he forced on me were quite repulsive."

"I can well imagine. But I gather you enjoy Cord's kisses?"

"Oh, yes. When we kiss, whatever I've been thinking about deserts me and I find myself clinging to him, certain if he doesn't stop his assault soon I'll swoon, and equally certain if he does stop kissing me I'll die." Bea dragged in a shaky breath and resisted the urge to fan her flushed face. "The sensations are quite overwhelming to the senses."

"How interesting. Prescott has the same effect on me." Muriel smoothed golden wisps back into the bun at her nape—hair Donnelly had undoubtedly freed earlier. "You love Cord."

"Yes. Very much."

"And does he love you?"

Bea couldn't force out the lie. "I don't know."

"Come now. Many men find it difficult to say what's in their hearts, but a woman knows when her man loves her."

Did she? Bea had little experience with love or lovers. Her parents had acted like strangers to each other. Though Papa swore his parents had adored each other, Bea's grandmother had died long before Bea was born. So had Mr. Flynn, the young love of Muriel's life. The rest of her married relatives were virtual strangers. So Bea truly had no idea how a man in love behaved.

"Cord is good and kind and gentle," Bea said after a long pause. "He's a wonderful husband."

"Is he? Prescott is worried that Cord isn't fully prepared to settle down to married life."

"Mr. Donnelly worries too much." Bea wanted to put an end to this conversation. "Pray tell, do I have the pleasure of your company because he has taken his leave?"

"Not at all. Prescott went to the stable the second Father and Cord returned."

Bea shot to her feet, excited and apprehensive. "When?"

"Quite some time before I sought you out." Muriel rose and floated to the door. "Oh, and Prescott is staying for dinner. The dear man insists on gaining Papa's consent to wed me."

She sent Muriel a pained smile. Unless something miraculous happened to change her aunt's mind, Donnelly would become her uncle as well as her stepfather-in-law.

"What will you do if Grandfather doesn't give his blessing?"

"Oh, he'll give it, m'dear." Laughing, Muriel flounced out. Sinking onto the settee, Bea gnawed on her thumbnail and stared at the prairie. Before Donnelly appealed to the Earl of Arden, she had to have that talk with her grandfather.

Once she convinced the earl that she and Cord were deserving caretakers for the Prairie Rose, the only crucial task ahead of her was to win her husband's heart.

Bea was pacing the foyer when Grandfather marched into the house with Donnelly at his side. "I'd like a word in private with you," she told her grandfather.

"It will have to wait till later, Beatrix. I've something of great import to discuss with Donnelly."

The men closeted themselves in the library. She paced the hallway, fretting over what they had to discuss of such importance. Donnelly's desire to marry Muriel? The small fortune Muriel must have? The Prairie Rose?

Whatever it was, the two men had been talking for close to an hour. Thanks to the thick doors, Bea couldn't hear a word of their conversation.

The back door swung open and the chink of spurs rang over the thud of boots. Bea turned, locking gazes with Cord. She smiled. He nodded, tugged his hat low over his eyes, and bounded up the rear stairs. Was he avoiding her?

Of course he was, drat it all. Cord had to know what was afoot between the Earl of Arden and Donnelly. Something the men didn't want her to know about. Their avoidance made her all the more determined to find out what was so bloody secretive.

Bea hiked up her skirt and sprinted up the rear staircase. She burst into the bedroom and teetered to a stop. Benedict was the only occupant, and he was trudging toward the bathing chamber door with a stack of garments draped over an arm.

"Where is Cord?"

Benedict paused at the door and looked at her, his expression stoic. "Enjoying his bath."

She hesitated, knowing she should wait for Cord to finish. But she wanted to know what was going on now.

"Mr. Tanner bade me to inform you he would join you in the parlor, albeit a tad late." Benedict trudged into the chamber and closed the door in her face with a resounding click.

Bea set her teeth and fumed. They'd locked her out.

She wheeled around and hurried back to the library. She'd wait for Donnelly to take his leave of the earl and then she'd rush in and confront her grandfather. But the library was empty.

Growing more frustrated by the second, Bea followed the drone of voices toward the parlor. What a cozy little group. Muriel, Donnelly, and Grandfather were enjoying a drink before dinner and chatting like old friends.

"Ah, there you are," Muriel said, face flushed like a girl's.

Grandfather smiled at Bea. "Would you care for a sherry?"

"I'd prefer applejack." Bea headed toward the sideboard.

Donnelly beat her there. "Let me do the honors." He poured a glass for Bea and handed it to her with a too-large smile.

"Thank you."

Bea dropped onto a chair and took a thirsty drink, then another, her eye on the clock, her nerves stretched to their limit. She didn't wish to suffer through another evening with Donnelly, but short of taking to her room, she had little choice.

"How about you, Arden?" Donnelly hefted the decanter.

"Indeed, my good man." Grandfather ensconced himself in the gentleman's chair beside Bea. Approval glowed in his blue eyes as Donnelly attended him.

Bea tossed back the rest of her applejack and welcomed the heat blazing a trail down her throat. Damn the rancher's interference. This was her house! Or rather, it should be.

She held her empty glass out to Donnelly. "If you please, I should like a spot more as well."

"Yes, ma'am." Donnelly filled Bea's glass to the brim and returned the decanter to the sideboard.

Muriel perched on the sofa and Donnelly joined her, the

picture of a cozy couple, the image Bea had hoped to project with Cord. "As I was saying, Prescott is a ruthless chess player."

"Smashing news," Grandfather said. "I'm quite anxious to get up a cutthroat game. Perhaps tomorrow evening?"

"Fine by me," Donnelly said.

Of a sudden, Bea sensed someone watching her. She turned to the doorway and gaped at the handsome image her husband presented.

Cord wore fitted black trousers and a sinfully black shirt with a pleated linen bodice, garments she recalled Papa had purchased shortly before his death. Items they could ill afford.

Again, Mrs. Mimms had altered the garments to fit Cord's lean shape. As Bea hadn't seen the white leather vest and white satin string tie before, she assumed they belonged to Cord.

His damp hair gleamed black. In fact, all that detracted from his handsome appearance were the cut on his lip, the bruising along his jaw, and the swollen, angry flesh around one eye.

Cord strode toward the sideboard. "Evening."

Grandfather, Donnelly, and Muriel returned his greeting, then resumed their discussion of chess. Did Cord know the game? Had Grandfather bothered to ask him?

Bea blocked out the chatter and watched her husband pour a glass of sweet cider. But he only stared into his glass. He didn't drink it.

A chill crept up her spine and she warmed herself with another gulp of applejack. More than his appearance had changed. Just what had transpired in town today?

Donnelly rose, glass in hand. "If I may?" He looked to the earl, who nodded his consent. "Muriel has agreed to marry me."

"Pray tell when this wedding will take place?" Bea asked.

The rancher's eyes glowed as they met Muriel's glistening

ones. "Two days from now. We'll have the ceremony in Revolt and hold a shindig out at the Flying D."

"Congratulations." Cord lifted his glass for a toast.

"Best wishes to you both." With effort, Bea smiled.

She longed to ask Donnelly if he truly cared for her aunt or if he was using Muriel's affections to gain what he'd coveted all along—the Prairie Rose. But now wasn't the time.

Grandfather raised his glass. "Hear, hear. I'm relieved Beatrix will no longer be without family in America."

She finished the remainder of her brew and stifled the urge to belch. This was too much. Grandfather made no secret of the fact that he admired Donnelly and approved of this match. That he expected the older couple to watch over her and Cord.

Benedict trudged into the room. "Dinner is served, madam."

"Splendid." Bea shot to her feet and took a teetering step. She longed to get this meal over with so she could have a long chat with her grandfather. "Shall we adjourn to the dining room?"

Cord was beside her in an instant, taking her arm and steadying her until the room ceased spinning. "Easy, darlin'."

He spoke so softly, Bea doubted the others filing past them heard. "I arose too fast."

One dark eyebrow lifted. "Appears to me you belted down too many glasses of tangle-foot."

"Fiddlesticks." To her shock, she slurred her esses and her head spun like a wheel.

He was right. Merciful sakes, she was in her cups! But if she remained her usual cheery self, surely nobody would notice.

Cord guided her into the dining room, seated her at the hostess chair, and took the one to her left. As he'd done since his arrival, Grandfather presided over the group from the host's chair. Muriel sat to his left, Donnelly to his right.

Bea frowned at the trio. Donnelly was doing his best to get in good favor with Grandfather. And Muriel was helping him.

Cord speared a piece of golden chicken and deposited it upon Bea's plate. A spicy chunk of sausage came next, followed by generous portions of fried potatoes, peppers, and candied carrots.

"You need food in your gut," Cord mumbled.

His concern brought tears to Bea's eyes. What a good man Cord was. Handsome and strong. And such a gentle lover.

Sighing, Bea leaned toward him, reached a hand out, and patted his cheek. "You're such a good man."

Ignoring her husband's scowl, Bea affected a bright smile, then dug into her meal. The spices fired her appetite, reminding her she hadn't eaten all day. No wonder she was a bit tipsy.

"Muriel tells me that you run Herefords on your spreads in England," Donnelly said to her grandfather as the rancher loaded his plate with meat and potatoes.

"Indeed I do. However, after watching your black Angus herd fatten, I'm seriously considering purchasing a herd of them from Scotland for my estates."

The men launched into a discussion of the declining price of cattle and the increasing difficulty producing a decent crop on this arid land. Muriel seemed a touch miffed by the topics.

Bea looked on the conversation as a means for her to regroup her wits. As she munched a dessert of spicy mashed pumpkin tucked within a sweet crust, she listened intently to her husband.

"For the Prairie Rose to prosper, we'd best go easy on crops and concentrate on producing a sizable herd of prime cattle," Cord said in an authoritative tone that had her puffing up with pride.

"I couldn't agree with you more, m'boy," Grandfather said.

Her hopes rose with her impatience. Perhaps her grandfather would settle her dowry on Cord and sign the title to the Prairie Rose over to her without further delay.

But in case the earl questioned Cord's ability to manage, she decided to embellish on their earning potential. "Let's not forget the profit to be made from the apple crop and applejack."

Grandfather stared down the length of the table at Bea. "Interesting you should mention that. I was quite shocked to hear from the gent who operates the Plainsmen's Lodge that my only granddaughter has been distilling spirits for quite some time."

Bea's chin came up. "Papa was a poor manager, and we found ourselves short on funds more often than not. So I used the resources available to me and turned a small profit."

"You've eked out a living bootlegging, which is illegal, mind you, and something you ain't gonna keep doing," Cord said. "You can't depend on an apple crop to get you through the lean times. One cyclone hits the place and your orchard turns to kindling."

"I am well aware of that possibility," Bea said, trying her best to make Grandfather believe they both had the best interest of the Prairie Rose at heart. "Are you forgetting we'll profit from the occasional sale of a well-trained hunter?"

Cord snorted. "You've yet to get an offer on any of them."

"The bulk of the hunt clubs in America are situated in the East and haven't heard of my thoroughbreds as yet," Bea said.

"They probably won't hear tell of them, either." Cord flashed a smile. "Any way you cut it, you and your thoroughbreds are smack dab in cattle country."

She wagged her fork at him to prove her point, refusing to surrender her dream. "If we place advertisements in a few Eastern newspapers, I'm sure we'll reap a much larger reward from a few wealthy buyers."

"It's a short-term profit." Cord met Bea's gaze head-on, and the intensity and fervor in his warm brown eyes had her heart pounding and her cheeks flushing with heat. "Easing into the cattle business will keep us from going under while those horses are getting a finish and buyers for them are located."

Grandfather's shrewd gaze locked on Cord. "Do you think

it wise to concentrate on expanding the herd when the price for cattle is plummeting?"

Bea held her breath, looking from one tense face to another. If Grandfather agreed with Cord's plans for the Prairie Rose, he would be more inclined to put Cord in charge. But that would never happen if he felt Cord's intentions would bring ruin to the ranch.

Cord leaned back in his chair and fingered the carved rose on his silver fork. "Making a small profit off beef is a damn sight better than losing your investment in crops ruined by drought. Too many grangers lost everything this year. You can hold on to animals till you get your price. You can't do it with crops."

"I say. Can't find any fault with your sound logic, m'boy." The earl smiled at Bea. "Heed your husband. I trust Tanner won't squander your fortune as your wastrel father did his."

"Good of you to finally notice." Despite her relief, Bea's stomach roiled with anxiety. "Now, I pray you'll cease shilly-shallying and sign over the Prairie Rose to me."

Muriel gasped. Donnelly stared at his empty plate.

"Trixie," Cord said in a low, warning tone.

"Do not attempt to chastise me!" She ignored her husband and stared down the length of the table at her autocratic grandfather. "I'm the one who has put her heart and soul in this land. Not you. Not Papa. This is my home, and your refusal to grant me the title is beyond cruel. Can't you understand that?"

"Were you not squiffy-eyed," her grandfather said in a tone that could cut glass, "you'd know better than to bring up this topic at dinner."

"I wouldn't have brought it up now if you hadn't avoided me all day. And I'm not inebriated." Bea pushed to her feet so fast the room spun and she swayed.

"You're damned close." Cord leapt to his feet and settled Bea against his side, squeezing a squeak of surprise from her. Eyes as dark and rich as chocolate probed hers. "Let's get you to bed. You can hash all this out with your grandpappy tomorrow."

Bea batted at his hands, but he held her fast. "Stop playing the tyrant. You're my husband. You're supposed to help me."

"I am, darlin'. More than you know."

She glanced at the others. Shock best described Muriel's and Donnelly's expressions. But Grandfather was livid with anger. Well, so was she.

"You know I'm right," she told her grandfather.

A snort was his reply.

"Come on, Trixie." Cord guided her from the room.

Bea was too weary to keep up the battle tonight. As they climbed the front staircase, she slid an arm around his lean waist and welcomed his assistance into their bedroom, where several lamps burned oh-so-intimately low.

"You need help undressing?"

She shook her head. "I can manage, thank you."

"I'll turn down the bedding." Cord held her a second longer, then released her and strode toward the bed.

Bea stumbled behind the dressing screen and tore at her clothes. Tonight hadn't gone at all well. Now she wondered and worried what the morrow would bring.

The soft creak of the bed announced Cord had stretched out upon it. Anxious to do the same, Bea dropped her nightdress over her head. She fastened the tiny buttons in haste, then glided to her dressing table, tore out her hairpins, and began the tedious process of brushing the tangles from her fine hair.

She studied the mirror's reflection of Cord. He'd tugged the covers to his armpits and folded his arms across his chest.

Though she was annoyed with his high-handedness, he was a handsome man. And for the moment, he was still her husband.

Bea tossed her silver brush on the dressing table and made straight for her side of the bed. She wanted nothing more than to snuggle against his warm muscular length, slide her fingers inside the openings of his soft nainsook undershirt, and explore his broad chest sprinkled with crisp hair.

She slid under the covers. "Good night."

"Night." Cord extinguished the light on the bedside table, plunging the room into darkness.

Her hand stole toward him and met a wall of bedding from head to toe. It took her dazed mind a moment to realize he'd folded their blankets into separate cocoons, like she'd done that first night they'd shared this bed. She could imagine one reason why he'd do such a thing now. He didn't want to touch her.

His rejection brought hot tears to Bea's eyes. Everything was falling apart at once. She loved her ranch but could lose it to Donnelly. She loved Cord, but he'd soon ride out of her life.

"Why did you do this?" She poked at the wall of blankets.

"You made an ass out of yourself tonight in front of your family," Cord said in a rough-edged voice. "I'm just making sure you don't do something else you'll regret in the morning."

She dabbed at her eyes and sniffed. "Whatever made you think I was attempting a seduction?"

Cord let out a dry laugh. "I was raised in a whorehouse, Trixie. I know when a woman is hungry for a man."

"I see. I take it you're not hungry for me."

"I want you, but not this way." He trailed a finger down her flushed cheek. "One day you'll thank me for doing this."

"I doubt that." She captured his hand and held his callused palm to her cheek. "I don't want any barrier between us."

"You don't know what you're saying."

"Oh, but I do." She kissed his palm and heard him suck in a sharp breath. "Would you at least hold me until I fall asleep?"

He moaned as if in great pain. "Reckon so."

Bea closed her eyes and cuddled as close to her husband as the blankets would allow. His strong arms held her tight. She rested her hand atop his heart and felt its rapid beat. She smiled. Her nearness did affect him.

As a chorus of I love yous sang within her heart, Bea felt certain her seduction wasn't a total failure after all.

CHAPTER EIGHTEEN

Cord planted his right foot on the bottom fence rail, crossed his arms on the top one, and watched Rory put Titan through his paces. But his mind kept wandering from the training session to the restless night he'd spent holding Trixie close to his heart. Before she'd dozed off, she'd whispered those three words that drove all thoughts of sleep from his mind.

I love you.

He'd been knee-high to a grasshopper when he'd first heard those words. He and his ma lived in a highfalutin parlor house in Dodge City, but she was too busy working to pay him much mind.

Every night men called on her. Every night she'd hide Cord in the old pine wardrobe in her bedroom. He'd sit in the dark, cramped space, listening to the creaking bed ropes and the grunts and groans coming from the string of men she serviced.

She'd say those words to every man she screwed. When Cord asked her how she could love all those fellows, she'd laughed and said she told them that because that's what men wanted to hear.

As the years and countless men wore on his ma, she went from being the belle of the gilded palace to a used-up whore living in a filthy crib in back of a saloon. No matter if the men paying for her services praised her or beat her, she'd toss out those three damned hollow words.

I love you.

Sporting women had whispered that to Cord from time to time, but he wasn't fooled. The soiled doves he'd paid to screw him didn't like him half as much as what he did to them, taking his time to make sure they'd been pleasured, too. The simple fact was nobody had ever given a damn about Cord Tanner.

I love you.

Cord rubbed the taut muscles in his neck and swore. Women said those three words after having sex with a man. It was as simple as that. So why the hell did Trixie pick last night while he held her close to his heart to say such a thing to him and keep her pretty little mouth shut when they'd made love?

Applejack. That's why. It'd loosened her tongue. Any other reason was too damned frightening to ponder.

The clop of hooves and rumble of wheels stampeded into Cord's thoughts. He turned around and took a gander up the drive. A fancy black buggy was heading toward the front of the house.

Cord squinted at the scrawny man driving it. He bit out a couple of ripe curses. Eli Holmes. It was a crying shame the tightfisted man pulled the purse strings at the Revolt bank.

If Marshal Ives hadn't been pulling drag on a piebald gelding, Cord would've hightailed it into the stable and let Trixie and her grandpappy deal with Holmes. But it was possible Ives was bringing word on Nate Wyles.

Cord muttered another curse and set off to the house. He didn't care to speculate what had prodded Holmes to visit the Prairie Rose. Or why Strowbridge sat beside the banker, or why the stallion he'd ridden off on wasn't tied to the buggy.

A white sling cradled the viscount's left arm against his

flabby gut. Red dust covered his fine clothes. His fancy shirt was torn and he'd ripped his yellow-checked jacket.

"What happened?" Cord asked as he reached the buggy.

Ives rested his beefy hands atop his saddle horn. "Lord Strowbridge was ambushed this side of the county line. On his way back from foreclosing on a farm, Eli happened on him. He took him into town and had Doc Crowley patch him up."

"I daresay this has been the most horrendous experience of my life." The viscount winced as he climbed out of the buggy. "One moment I was trotting along, savoring the bracing bite in the air. The next instant, a lone rider crests the hill and shoots me."

"You're damned lucky he just winged you," Ives said.

Strowbridge went white as milk. "There is that. However, it grieves me that while I lay in the ditch, writhing in excruciating pain, the highwayman galloped off with Beatrix's stallion."

"Did you get a good look at the horse thief?" Cord asked.

"The ruffian wore rough clothes much like yours, but a red bandanna covered most of his face." Strowbridge dabbed the sweat and dirt off his forehead with a fancy kerchief. "Thank you, Mr. Holmes. I'm in your debt."

Holmes's beady eyes gleamed. "I'm glad I could oblige."

Cord waited until Strowbridge waddled into the house before turning to Ives. "Any idea who did this?"

Ives snorted and shifted his bulk in the saddle. "Not a one. From the sounds of it, the feller who robbed the viscount looks like every cowpoke and drifter in the whole damned state."

Holmes poked his lean face out of the buggy's shadow. "Even so, shouldn't you be out rounding up a posse?"

"By now that trail is about as clear as mud." Ives turned his attention on Cord. "Tell me what this here blooded horse of yours looks like and I'll telegraph the towns in these parts so the lawmen can keep an eye peeled."

Cord described Esprit as best he could to Ives, but he didn't hold out much hope they'd find the stallion. Hell, whoever had stolen Esprit probably had a buyer lined up. The horse would be sporting a new brand and be across the border or heading west by now.

"Any idea where Wyles is holed up?" Cord asked.

"I ain't seen hide nor hair of him since the fistfight." Ives brushed his hat brim with two fingers, then wheeled his black and white spotted gelding around and trotted toward Revolt.

Expecting the banker to leave, Cord stepped back from the buggy. "Much obliged you gave the viscount a hand."

"Think nothing of it." Holmes cocked his head to one side and surveyed the ranch. "You've done quite well for yourself, Tanner. Of course, I should have realized you'd be as clever and enterprising as your mother."

Rage boiled in Cord and he jammed his fists in his pockets to keep from punching Holmes. But damn if he'd talk about his ma to the man who'd left bruises on her and countless other whores who worked the cribs behind the Golden Plume.

"If you've got something to say, spit it out." He had a mind to drag this cruel sonofabitch out of the buggy and give him a taste of the pain he'd caused so many women.

Holmes's cunning eyes put him in mind of a buzzard circling a dying cow, waiting for it to draw its last breath. "If you're ever in need of funds, come see me at the bank. Now that you have collateral, I'd gladly lend you money."

"I hear tell from James Zachary that a friend of his is fixing to open a new bank in Revolt next month."

"Nothing more than a risky venture," Holmes said. "Revolt can't support two lending facilities."

"That's what I figured." And why he'd urge Trixie to place her money and trust in the new banker.

Bidding Holmes adieu with a nod, Cord strode to the house. The clomping of hooves told him Holmes was leaving.

Cord reckoned the tightfisted bastard was chomping at the

bit, eager to foreclose on several more struggling settlers and grangers before the day was out. He wouldn't be surprised if one of them put a bullet in his black heart someday.

Putting Holmes from his mind, Cord headed for the library. He reckoned Trixie would be busy writing up an advertisement for a newspaper back East, offering Esprit for sale. He'd best tell her about the viscount's mishap and that the stallion had been stolen.

Not bothering to knock, Cord ambled into the library and came up short. The earl sat before the desk, drumming his fingers on his knee and looking mad enough to bite a nail in two.

Trixie slumped behind the desk, elbows propped on its surface and palms cupping her chin. Except for the red streaks in her eyes, she was pale as milk. He reckoned she was battling a toe-tapping, heel-stomping hangover.

Benedict approached Cord. "The viscount bade me to inform the earl and Mrs. Tanner of his recent *misfortune*."

"I ain't surprised," Cord said, though he'd just as soon have been the one to break the bad news to Trixie.

"Indeed. If you'll excuse me, sir, I shall see to Lord Strowbridge's bath." Benedict left the room.

The earl faced Cord. "What do you suppose the chances are of the authorities finding the steed?"

Cord shook his head. "Slim to none."

Trixie pulled a stack of greenbacks from a drawer and slapped them on the desk. "Well, Grandfather, as you can see, the stallion you wished to purchase is no longer in my possession. So take your money back and return the stallion's papers to me."

"The deuce I will! I purchased that stallion before any of us knew it had been stolen." The earl shoved the money toward Trixie. "Never let it be said the Earl of Arden would welsh on a deal. The money is yours. The horse is mine."

She pushed the money back at her grandpappy, her sweet

little mouth pinched in pain, anger, or both. "The horse was stolen, so the deal is off. Do collect your money, sir."

"Bosh!" The earl crossed his arms over his chest. "Take the damned money, Beatrix."

"Absolutely not." Trixie flopped against the chair back and stared him down with bleary eyes.

Cord thumbed back his hat and sieved air through his teeth, knowing this standoff between these two hardheads could go on for hours. He was right proud of Trixie for refusing the handout, but it riled him that the earl was being so contrary.

Deciding he'd best settle this, Cord hooked a leg over the edge of the desk and faced the earl. "If you're dead set on owning one of Trixie's horses, we'll take your money now and ship you the horse of your choosing when Rory gets done training it."

"Titan has exquisite lines, if you recall," Trixie added.

The earl's eyes twinkled from either glee or mischief. Sure as shooting, the Northroupes Cord had come to know were full to the brim with both traits.

"I rather fancied a mare, you know. Perhaps the dapple filly with the white blaze and stockings. She's quite fleet of foot."

Cord played a hunch. "You're gonna race that filly."

"Steeplechases, to be precise. At my age, I prefer being a spectator at the race where I can make a few pounds off the winner instead of braving the elements chasing about after a fox."

"Empress would be an excellent choice," Trixie said.

The earl stroked his beard, and this time Cord saw the glint of amusement light the older man's eyes. Damn, but the earl was teasing his granddaughter.

Cord bet it wasn't the first time the earl had done it. Bet it wouldn't be the last.

At that moment, Cord envied Trixie something fierce for having a grandparent who cared enough to pull her leg for fun.

"What do you think, Tanner?"

Itching to play along in this game, Cord locked gazes with Trixie. "To be honest with you, Lord Arden, I'd considered keeping that filly for myself."

Trixie clasped Cord's hand with both of hers. Desire snaked through him like a lazy, sun-warmed river.

"You could choose another," she said. "We have two mares with foal. Esprit covered the sorrel mare, but Cleopatra's lines are impeccable."

Cord's heart commenced galloping in his chest. The game had turned serious.

Trixie knew damned well he'd have to stick around to get that foal. Was she that desperate to satisfy her grandpappy? Or that desperate to keep Cord around?

The longer he stayed, the harder it'd be to leave. And if he'd knocked Trixie up? There'd be no riding out.

His thumb drew lazy circles on the back of her pale hand while he took in her golden hair and delicate features. Would their child take after Trixie? Would she gift him with a sweet little girl with sun-kissed hair and dreams dancing in her eyes?

"Which stallion covered Cleopatra?" Cord heard himself ask in a voice that had dropped way too low.

"Zephyr." A deep blush stained Trixie's cheeks, but her gaze locked on his, seducing him, sucking him in deeper and deeper.

"Cleopatra and Zephyr. Wonder which color will dominate?"

"Perhaps neither. Perhaps they'll blend together."

Light and dark. Sunshine and shadow. That was Trixie and him in a nutshell. Different as night and day. Yet they shared a common bond that he didn't much understand.

"You thinking that foal will be worth my wait?"

"I truly do," she whispered.

Cord swallowed hard. She wasn't talking about foals or babies any more than he was. Her eyes had gone violet. Her breath came in short, breast-jiggling puffs. Her fingers stroked his palm, spurring his little rustler to rear.

"I'll take the foal Cleopatra drops." He stared into her eyes and grazed her palm with his thumb.

She trembled and leaned toward him, her sweet mouth parted. "You won't regret it."

The earl coughed, breaking the sensuous thread Trixie had roped Cord with. She jumped back, face flushed and eyes wide.

Cord ran a shaky hand over his face and stood, keeping his back to them until he reined in the lust galloping through him. If he and Trixie had been alone, he'd have dragged her onto the desktop and fit his body to hers. Here and now. Slow and deep.

"Now that you have reached a decision," the earl said, "I'll await the foal sired by Esprit. With any luck, the get will run as swiftly as the stallion."

"That would, of course, depend upon the dam." The viscount swaggered into the library, looking as bored as ever. "If you'd show me which mare Esprit covered, I'll endeavor to give you my unbiased opinion on the foal's worth on the track."

"Didn't know you were an expert on horse racing," Cord said.

The viscount twirled the waxed tips of his mustache and smirked. "My good man, Strowbridges have been renowned for their blooded horses for generations."

"As I recall," Trixie said. "You owned thoroughbreds, hackneys and Clydesdales, but I don't recall you showed any particular interest in the Derby or the Ascot."

Strowbridge frowned and picked at the linen sling supporting his arm. "I was attracted to the sport after the untimely death of my viscountess. In the ensuing two years, I have endeavored to refine the bloodlines in my stable."

"With smashing results, if I may be so forward as to add," the earl said. "You have acquired quite a reputation with the racing set, both as patron and breeder. However, I wonder if you erred when you sold that bay stallion, which finished second at Epsom Downs, before we set off for America."

"The sum offered was too tempting to reject out of hand." The viscount pulled a leather wallet from an inside pocket of his fussy checkered jacket and smiled at Trixie. "My dear Beatrix, I accept full responsibility for the loss of the stallion and am here to tender compensation to you."

Trixie gaped at Strowbridge, looking as stunned as Cord felt by the viscount's offer. "How generous of you."

"But unnecessary." Cord kept an eye on the viscount like he would a rattler, knowing his next words might rile the Englishman into striking. "Unless you had a hand in Esprit's disappearance."

Strowbridge's face turned as purple as a roundhouse bruising. "How dare you insinuate that I am a thief."

The earl slapped his palms on the arms of his chair and laughed. "Use your noggin, Strowbridge. I warrant Tanner is merely pulling your leg and producing splendid results."

"Of course." Trixie bolted from her chair and scrambled to Cord's side, wrapping both arm's around his right arm and branding his soul. "Weren't you, darling?"

Cord forced a grin. "Yep, I was just joshing with you."

The viscount tugged on his too-short waistcoat. "A bit of an offending spoof, say what?"

"I've heard worse," Cord said.

"I would imagine you have." Strowbridge turned his attention on Trixie and fixed her with that oily smile that riled Cord. "If you'd be so kind as to show me which mare to inspect?"

"Athena is the sorrel mare," Trixie said. "If she isn't in the paddock, you'll find her in stall number six."

"I shall attend the task immediately." The viscount strode from the library as if his pride hadn't been ruffled.

Trixie dropped her hands from Cord and stepped in front of him, hands on hips. "You weren't joshing, were you?"

"I don't trust him as far as I could toss him."

"You don't like him."

"Nope." Cord crossed his arms over his chest. Wild horses couldn't drag it out of him that he was jealous to boot.

A smile teased Trixie's inviting lips. "Neither do I."

"Strowbridge is a royal pain in the posterior," the earl said. "But he did offer to reimburse Beatrix for the horse that had been stolen out from under him."

"Right good of him." So why couldn't Cord shake this feeling of impending doom that clung to him like a wet blanket on a cold night? Sure as shooting, trouble brewed on the horizon. But who posed the biggest threat? Strowbridge, Nate Wyles, or Gil Yancy?

"Now that our business is settled, I shall take my leave." In a smooth motion befitting a younger man, the earl got to his feet. "With Muriel's nuptials close at hand, it's imperative I arrange for a suitable wedding gift."

All the color seeped from Trixie's face. "Please, tell me you won't give the Prairie Rose to Mr. Donnelly and Muriel."

"Cease your worries, granddaughter." The earl held up a hand when Trixie opened her mouth to say more. "If you promise not to harangue me about this ranch, I'd very much like for you to join me on my jaunt into Revolt."

Trixie bit her lower lip and stared at the money lying on the desk. She lifted her gaze to Cord's. "I saw an exquisite bowl at Lott's Mercantile that I wish to purchase for Muriel and Mr. Donnelly. From us, of course. If you think we should, that is."

He would've never thought "us" and "we" would make him feel so damned good inside. He would've never guessed a lady would ask his opinion on such a simple domestic matter.

Cord snatched the money off the desk and pressed it into her hands. "Whatever you decide is fine by me. But you'd best buy yourself something nice, too."

She fidgeted with the money. A blush stained her cheeks. "Would you like me to bring you something back from town?"

Just you, Cord thought, but he shook his head in answer.

"I say, you could join us," the earl said to Cord.

Cord shook his head. "Told Rory I'd lend him a hand."

The smile slipped from Trixie's face, and Cord's heart gave an odd kick. On impulse, he bent toward his wife with the notion of dropping a kiss on her flushed cheek.

Trixie turned her head at the same time. His lips settled over hers. She tasted like apples and spice and sweet tomorrows.

A powerful hunger gnawed at him, tempting him to take all she offered. But his vow to keep his hands to himself stampeded through his thoughts.

Cord aimed to make the kiss short and sweet. Until Trixie wrapped her arms around his neck, tugging him closer.

He gripped her waist, aiming to set her back from him. But her tongue flicked in his mouth, bold as brass and hotter than a firebrand. Flames licked through him.

With a groan, Cord crushed her to him and kissed her like no man should kiss a lady in front of her grandpappy. Of course, it didn't help his control any that she didn't behave like a lady. The way she kissed, pawed, and squirmed had his little rustler straining to bust out of his britches.

Cord had a mind to sweep her up in his arms and pack her to their bed. He ached to tear her clothes off, caress every inch of her with his hands and mouth, and beg her to do the same to him.

At the tap on his shoulder, Cord tore his mouth from Trixie's to find himself staring at the earl. The older gent stood beside them, beaming like a gambler who'd just won the fat jackpot.

The earl winked. "Perhaps Beatrix has changed her mind."

Cord didn't know whether to laugh or cuss. Since Trixie was stuck to him like wallpaper, he reckoned it was plain as window glass that she was itching to make their bed ropes twang. It was the why that had him sweating bullets.

He needed to sort this out in his head, when he was away

from her and could think again. As gently as he could, Cord pulled away from her.

"Enjoy your outing, darlin'," Cord said.

She licked her kiss-bruised lips and smiled at him dreamy-eyed, confounding him even more. "I shall."

Cord managed a grin, dipped his chin to the earl, and lit out of the library. He took off out the rear door, welcoming the chill bite in the air. Titan, Cleopatra, and Empress were grazing in the paddock with Ott's and Jake's horses.

Zephyr was kicking up dust in the corral on the other side of the stable. Probably got the scent of one of the mares.

Damn it all, but he was in the same fix. Even out here in the fresh air he caught a whiff of Trixie's rosy bouquet. Maybe a hard ride would wring the piss and vinegar out of him and Zephyr.

He headed down the aisle to fetch his tack. As he neared the sixth stall, he heard Strowbridge muttering under his breath.

Cord stopped in the opening and watched the viscount go over Athena with an eye for detail. "What do you think of her?"

The viscount hiked one shoulder in a lazy shrug. "On the surface she's an impressive dam. Deep-chested, strong legs, and alert. But I would like to inspect her papers. The least flaw in bloodlines would lessen her worth and her gets, don't you know."

Cord snorted, knowing all too well the importance some folks put on good bloodlines—in animals and people. "The earl didn't seem concerned about her lineage."

"Arden isn't up to snuff on racers, nor is he interested in educating himself overmuch. To him, it's merely a diversion." He wiped his hands on a snow white cloth. "Fortunately for the earl, he has ample time and money to waste on his hobbies."

"I take it you're in it for the money," Cord said.

"One needs deep pockets to live a goodly life."

The viscount swaggered into the aisle and tossed the rubbing cloth into a wooden bucket at the same time Rory entered the stable from the opposite end leading Zephyr. The stallion let out an ear-splitting bugle and reared.

Cord took off toward Zephyr at a dead run. Rory threw his weight on the leather tie line, but he was no match for Zephyr's strength. Powerful muscles quivered along the stallion's black flanks and bunched in his haunches. Cord would have sworn by the ungodly sounds coming from the horse that he was being tortured.

Cord snatched the leather line from Rory. "Easy, Zeph."

Hand over hand, Cord inched his way down the taut line to the stallion's halter. He grabbed it and forced Zephyr's head down.

The horse blew and sidestepped, crowding him against the wall. But the animal didn't try to rear again.

Cord stroked Zephyr's quivery muzzle. "You ain't supposed to let a damned towel spook you."

Zephyr's coat rippled like a black curtain snapping on a clothesline. Panic glittered in the stallion's eyes, convincing Cord the animal was too damned frightened to reason with.

He tugged the line and led Zephyr toward his stall. To his relief, the stallion lunged into it.

Cord eased from the stall and closed the slatted door. He thumbed his hat back and watched the riled stallion stomp.

It annoyed the hell out of him that something as simple as a flash of white could set Zephyr off on a tear. Hell, for all he knew, the snap of a petticoat had spooked the stallion in Revolt.

It'd take time to work with the stallion, get him used to sudden sounds and sights again. Time Cord might not have.

Unless Trixie was in the family way, Cord would collect his pay and move on. No way could he wait around for Cleopatra to drop his promised foal. No way could he live close enough to see Trixie off and on and keep his hands off her.

Backhanding the sweat off his brow, Cord strode down the aisle to where Rory stood. "You'd best keep your distance from him the rest of the day."

Rory nodded, eyes wide and face ghostly pale. "To be sure, I won't go near the black devil."

"If you're wise, Tanner, you'd reconsider keeping such an uncontrollable beast standing at stud," Strowbridge said as he swaggered from Athena's stall.

Cord leaned a shoulder against the wall. "Torture made Zephyr go wild, not his blood. Only thing he'll mark his foals with is a damned fine conformation and an unbending spirit."

"Perhaps, but it's highly conceivable the stallion will pass on his ungovernable traits." Strowbridge cradled his bum wing in its sling. "You're a fool to take this lightly. That horse is a killer. One day your luck will abandon you before you can escape the beast's tirade."

Now why did that sound like a threat instead of a word of warning? Because he'd had a belly full of the viscount and his interfering ways. That's why.

"Is that why you told Trixie she'd best let Nate Wyles shoot Zephyr after he pitched her pa to his death?"

"In the heat of anger, I suggested that to her. However, I'd view that as a last resort now. The animal is valuable, if only for its impeccable lines."

"You thinking of buying Zephyr?" Cord asked.

"Absolutely not. I'd never own such an unmanageable beast." Strowbridge let out a nasty laugh that lifted the hairs on Cord's arms. "But I'm sure Beatrix could find a fool willing to pay a goodly sum for that four-legged killer."

Zephyr bugled, as if highly offended by that remark. The viscount slid a squinty-eyed glare in the stallion's direction.

"Trixie would never sell Zephyr," Cord said.

"Well, then. That is that. If you'll excuse me."

The viscount marched out of the stable, but a long time passed before Zephyr quieted down. Had everything that had happened to Zephyr spooked him so that he was close to turning wild?

Cord didn't think so. He grabbed the towel and stormed to Zephyr's stall. The stallion stared at him, eyes alert.

He flapped the towel. Zephyr shied, then tossed his head, stomped a foot, and went back to munching oats.

Something was damned screwy. That towel should've spooked Zephyr again, but it didn't. So what the hell had set him off?

CHAPTER NINETEEN

Late that day, Bea and her grandfather left Lott's Mercantile laden with packages. The boxes he'd shipped from England over a month ago had arrived. Bea hadn't a clue as to their contents.

Neither did Arlene Lott, though she tried her best to persuade Grandfather to satisfy her curiosity. Arlene did succeed in shrewdly talking him into buying an epergne of extravagant proportions for a wedding gift.

Bea took her time browsing and chose a canary-tinted berry dish to give her aunt and Donnelly. While Arlene wrapped it for Bea, she selected an indigo linen shirt with collar and cuffs a shade lighter for Cord. She could barely wait to see his broad shoulders fill out the garment.

For herself, Bea purchased a blue linen shirtwaist with high ruffled collar and leg-of-mutton sleeves. It was the first new clothing she'd bought in over a year.

She felt giddy and guilty for splurging. After all, Grandfather hadn't signed over her dowry. Though she longed to ask him about it, she'd keep her promise to not bring up the subject today—but tomorrow she'd beg him to cease his dithering.

"I owe you an apology," Grandfather said once they'd gained the surrey and were clomping down the street.

Bea glanced at her stern-faced grandfather. "Whatever for?"

"For doubting you. When I received your letter, stating you were staying in America and would soon wed, I nearly suffered a fit of apoplexy." Concern scored his face. "I feared the man you intended to marry was a scoundrel who'd trifled with your affections so he could fatten his own purse."

"That's a reasonable assumption. You didn't know Cord." Not that she had either, but Grandfather need not know that.

He coughed. Or was that a stifled laugh? Bea glanced at her grandfather, but he stared at the road, his features reserved.

"If you'd mentioned Tanner before, I wouldn't have grieved so. But your intention to marry was completely unexpected."

Indeed it was, but his ultimatum left her no other choice she could live with. "I'm sorry I caused you undue worry."

"At least it turned out well. Tomorrow I'll finally marry my headstrong daughter off." The earl smiled. "And you're happily married to Tanner, a good man who'll provide well for you."

But for how long, Bea wondered.

The amber sun was sinking below the bruised horizon when she and Grandfather returned to the ranch. Summer was a fond memory. Unless she was with child, her marriage would be the same.

Bea stepped onto the back porch at the same time Cord galloped to the stable on Zephyr. An odd thrill coursed through her. She waited at the door, package in hand, anxious to see his face when she gave him the shirt.

Cord vaulted off Zephyr and ran into the bunkhouse, only to emerge moments later with Mr. Oakes. Her eagerness turned to fear. In short order, Mr. Oakes saddled his calico gelding, then he and Cord galloped toward the far pasture. Something was wrong.

Bea raced from the house and met Jake halfway across the yard, coming toward her. "What's happened?"

"Two heifers are having trouble birthing. Mr. Tanner told me to tell you not to wait supper on him."

"I should take Cord and Mr. Oakes their supper—"

"Mr. Tanner don't want you coming out this time of night," Jake interrupted, surprising Bea with his authoritative voice. He seemed so much older. Wiser.

"You'll come get me if Cord needs my help, won't you?"

"Yes'm." Jake tugged his hat low over his brow, just like Cord always did, and then ambled back to the barn.

Bea busied herself in the library in case Cord wanted her assistance. She shivered at the howl of coyotes and the moan of the wind. But Cord never sent for her.

And sometime in the wee hours of the morning, she fell asleep fearing he never would seek her out.

The next morning, a horse's bugling echoed into the bathing chamber and jerked Bea from her lethargy. She scrambled from the tub and peered out the window. Cord and Mr. Oakes had returned.

She dried as fast as she could, dressed, and hurried down the steps to the back door. It opened before she got there.

Cord strode in. Blood and muck smeared his shirt and jeans. Dark stubble shadowed his lean jaw. Lines scored his tired eyes.

"Dear God, you look ready to drop in your tracks," she said, heart pounding with worry and relief.

His crooked grin tore at her heart. "Been a long night. Had to pull both calves. Thought for sure we'd lose one of the heifers and her bull calf, but we saved them."

"I heard the coyotes." And imagined all sorts of horrors.

"They smelled blood. Ott and me guarded the heifers all night till they could manage on their own."

"You need rest." Bea wanted to hurry him to bed and watch over him as he'd watched over her cattle last night. "Muriel will understand if we don't attend her wedding today."

Cord was shaking his head and climbing the rear stairs before she finished. "A good washing and I'll be fine."

Benedict puffed his chest out and trudged after Cord. "I'll draw your bath, sir."

Mrs. Mimms huffed down the stairs moments later. "Lady Muriel wants you to help her ready herself after you've dressed. Would you need my assistance?"

"I can manage alone, thank you."

Bea returned to her bedroom and slipped behind her dressing screen. She shook with nervous energy, expecting Cord to finish his bath and walk in any second before she was dressed.

After donning her new blouse and dark blue skirt with a deep flounce, she added a straw hat with wide blue ribbons. She studied her reflection in the cheval glass, surprised the blouse's color deepened the blue of her eyes.

Her brow puckered. She should've worn this the day she and Cord had exchanged vows. But her heart hadn't been involved then, she admitted as she stepped into her kidskin opera slippers.

Bea fetched the shirt she'd bought for Cord from its hiding place behind her dressing screen and laid it on the bed. She knew he'd see it, but she hadn't a clue if he'd wear it.

After one last check in her mirror, Bea stole into Muriel's room to lend her assistance. Her aunt was dressed in an elegant garnet ensemble trimmed in cream-colored Egyptian lace.

Bea marveled at the lace-edged drapery. "You're ravishing."

Her aunt smiled, the image of a radiant bride. "I bought this for your nuptials. How odd it'll serve as my wedding suit."

Far better than mourning garb, Bea thought with renewed regret. "Mrs. Mimms said you wished for my assistance."

Muriel waved a hand. "I wanted a word with you. It's my fondest wish you'll develop a close friendship with Prescott."

"I'll grant him the respect due a male relative."

Muriel sent her a sad smile. "Pray tell, would you feel the same had Prescott and Cord not been at loggerheads?"

"Perhaps." Bea hugged her middle. "I've lived in this house for five years and Donnelly has yet to ingratiate himself with me. If you remember, he tried to buy this ranch from Papa, and when that failed he petitioned Grandfather."

"Yes, yes. And Father ordered you to return home, but you'd found true love and refused to leave here." Irony tinged Muriel's voice. "Do tell, has Cord given any indication how he truly feels about his stepfather becoming his uncle by marriage?"

"None at all." Bea looked askance at her aunt and grinned. "But it's a rather peculiar twist of fate, wouldn't you say?"

Muriel giggled and perched a white straw leghorn hat adorned with garnet roses, cream beadings, leaves, and lace upon her head. "It seems Cord is destined to be a relative of Prescott's."

But for how long, Bea wondered as she preceded Muriel to the parlor where the men awaited them.

Though advanced in years, Grandfather still cut a distinguished figure in a black Prince Albert suit. A top hat adorned his silver head.

Bea had to bite back a laugh as she turned to the viscount. Lambert wore a cutaway jacket and trousers of pale green and black check, emphasizing his rotund form and turning his amber eyes a bilious hue. His small derby more resembled a pot than a hat.

Muriel paraded into the room and both Englishmen heaped praise on the bride-to-be. In truth, Muriel did look radiant and far younger than her forty-odd years. Cord's softly spoken compliment was less effusive, but just as sincere.

Not that Bea could tell him so. The sight of her husband rendered her mute. His warm brown eyes locked with hers and her heartbeat raced. He strode toward her, and her lips parted from a mixture of astonishment and invitation.

Cord had slicked his dark brown hair off his forehead. The

damp strands glistened black in the lamplight. The indigo shirt she'd given him fit his broad chest to perfection. He'd added the white vest and white ribbon tie, but carried his same hat.

Bea admired how the black trousers made his legs look longer and leaner. His boots gleamed from a good polishing.

Stopping before Bea, Cord clasped her wrists and spread her arms to the side. His hot gaze licked over her body, making her burn with sensual delight.

"You're beautiful, darlin'," he said in a low, intimate voice that made her shiver and clench her legs together.

She wet her tingling lips. "You, sir, are quite the charmer. An exceedingly handsome one, at that."

In one swift motion, Cord tugged her to him and bent his head to hers. "Thanks for the shirt."

Before she could think of a single thing to say, Cord dropped a kiss on her forehead. It was so gentle, tender, and fleeting that tears sprang to her eyes.

Bea blinked them away and smiled up at Cord, but he had released her and turned to Muriel. "Scotty's a mighty lucky man."

"How odd." Muriel slipped an arm through Grandfather's offered one and giggled. "Prescott said the same of you and Bea."

Cord flashed Muriel a quick smile and settled his Stetson low on his brow. "We'd best get going. I reckon Scotty's worn a path in the church's floorboards by now."

"Indeed. Let us be off before he changes his mind," the earl blustered. "I've been waiting ages for some chap to take my opinionated daughter off my hands."

Everyone laughed at the jest. But as Cord handed Bea onto the front seat of the surrey, she had an unsettling premonition their gaiety wouldn't last throughout the day's festivities. She'd no sooner thought it when Lambert groused about sharing the rear bench of the surrey with Muriel and Grandfather.

The drive into Revolt passed without incident. Lambert strolled into the Methodist church, looking exceedingly bored. Cord escorted Bea inside while Grandfather attended the bride.

Bea trembled, recalling the sacred vow she'd made that day she'd wed Cord. He gave her hand a squeeze, then cleared his throat and shifted his feet.

The nervous action somehow comforted her. Was he remembering their wedding day, too?

The town's scions had already crowded inside the church to witness the marriage of Lady Muriel Northroupe-Flynn, daughter of Earl Arden, to Prescott Donnelly, prosperous rancher.

The preacher nodded to the organist.

Arlene held her head at a regal tilt and pounded the keys like one possessed. Cord flinched. Bea winced at the assault on her ears, shocked that Arlene's rendition of the Bridal Chorus sounded like a funeral dirge.

"Bloody hell, let us get on with it so that infernal woman will cease that ghastly racket," Grandfather whispered to Cord.

"Come on, Trixie." Tucking Bea's hand in the crook of his arm, Cord guided her down the aisle.

Out of duty and love, Bea had agreed to serve as Muriel's matron of honor. She didn't know what Donnelly had said or done to gain Cord's cooperation, but she was grateful Cord was acting as best man.

The reverend and Donnelly stood to one side. Bea stared at the man who'd soon be her uncle by marriage.

Donnelly looked dignified in his black sack coat and matching trousers. He'd managed to somewhat straighten his wavy reddish hair. Open adoration replaced his usual somber expression.

Bea frowned. She'd doubted Donnelly capable of showing love. The look on his face proved her wrong. What she wouldn't give if Cord would look on her with such ardent affection.

Grandfather escorted Muriel to her intended. As her aunt and the rancher exchanged vows and the preacher intoned solemn words over the couple, Bea peeked at Cord. Lines furrowed his brow.

Did it fluster him they'd promised to love and honor each other till death do they part? Cord did respect her, but love—

Bea caught her lower lip with her teeth. Love was the only common ground that would make their common bond endure the test of time. But Cord distrusted love. And she yearned for his heart more than anything else in this world.

Once the vows were sealed and the newlyweds received well wishes from the citizens of Revolt, Bea, Cord, Lambert, and Grandfather piled into the surrey and trailed the buggy Donnelly and Muriel were riding to the Flying D. Scores of whooping celebrants followed them.

Food and spirits flowed freely all evening. Bea lost sight of Cord and ended up perched on a sofa in the garish parlor with the women, most strangers to her.

After two hours of enduring their chatter, Bea went in search of Cord. Donnelly's raised voice boomed from the room he employed as his office. She inched closer to eavesdrop.

"The boy has got flaws," Donnelly barked, "but cowardice ain't ever been one of them."

"Hell, I know that, Scotty," came Marshal Ives's rumbling baritone. "But finding Wyles's carcass in the draw that angles by the Prairie Rose looks bad for him."

"For the last time, I didn't kill Nate Wyles last night."

Recognizing Cord's soft-edged drawl, Bea shoved open the door and rushed into the room. "Of course you didn't."

Marshal Ives faced Bea, his expression as wary as his stance. "No offense, ma'am. But I reckon you'd swear that whether your husband was guilty or not."

"I'm telling the truth, sir." Bea smiled at her tight-lipped husband and her stomach seized up. Had he shot Wyles? No! He wasn't a cold-blooded killer.

"On and off all night, me and Ott were up to our armpits in shit and blood, pulling calves and tending the heifers a good three miles from that draw."

Ives scratched his beard and nodded. "I tend to believe you. It appears Wyles was fixing to torch your haystacks, but one of his enemies dropped him first. Reckon with him dead, the shenanigans on the Prairie Rose will stop."

"That depends on who put a bullet in Wyles's back." Cord drove a hand through his hair. "If he and Gil were partners and Wyles double-crossed him—"

"Hold on, there," Ives said. "Gil's been a guest in my jail the past two days. Ain't no way he could've plugged Wyles."

Cord scowled. "What did Gil do to land in jail?"

"He got hooched up and picked a fight with me when I made my rounds. I tossed him in jail for the night." Ives shook his head. "Same thing happened today, so I locked him up again."

Donnelly stared at his clasped hands. "Tell Yancy if he wants his old job back, it's his for the asking."

"I'll tell him. Congratulations to you, Scotty." Ives lumbered to the door, then paused. He glanced at Cord. "Don't suppose your gun or them branding irons ever turned up?"

Cord snorted. "Not a sign of them."

"Good evening, Marshal Ives." Muriel swept into the room, clearly oblivious to the tension crackling in the air.

"Evening, ma'am." The marshal tipped his hat to Muriel in farewell. "My best wishes to you."

Muriel beamed. "Thank you."

Closing the door in the marshal's wake, Muriel hurried toward Donnelly and set a silk-plush dressing case before him. "Do forgive me for the delay. Mrs. Lott detained me."

"Think nothing of it, sweetheart." Grief shadowed Donnelly's face as he touched a finger to the padded lid of the chest. "I reckon you recall this, Cordell?"

A muscle worked along Cord's jaw. "Yep. Like yesterday."

Muriel floated to Cord and clasped his big hands in her small ones. "I told Prescott I believed Bea should have this dresser case. Have you any objections?"

Cord frowned. "Nope."

Donnelly handed it to Bea. "Cordell gave this to his ma the Christmas before she passed on. It's been stored ever since. I'd be honored and right pleased if you'd take it."

Bea accepted the case with trembling hands. The crushed silk felt ominously cold against her skin. "Thank you."

"Time to call it a night, Trixie." Cord's voice remained calm, but his features quivered with tension.

Bea couldn't agree more. "I am quite ready to leave."

A ghost of a smile touched Cord's mouth. "Let's round up the earl and Strowbridge and head for home."

They located Grandfather in the bunkhouse embroiled in a poker game with Mr. Oakes, Jake, and two Flying D cowboys. The Earl of Arden had discarded his Prince Albert coat, top hat, and white silk tie and had rolled his white shirtsleeves to the elbows.

A stack of crisp American banknotes and a glass of whiskey sat before Grandfather. The lock of silver-white hair brushing his forehead gave him a gambler's air.

"Lambert joined a few chaps in search of a bit of muslin diversion. I do not expect him to return tonight." Grandfather grinned as the king of spades was dealt him. "Now off with you two. I'll return to the ranch with Jake and Ott when I'm ready."

On the ride to the Prairie Rose, Cord didn't say one word. Neither did Bea. She sat beside him huddled beneath a shawl, clutching the dressing case he'd given his mother long ago.

His withdrawal chilled her more than the cold bite in the moonless night air. She didn't know if he was reliving heartfelt memories or felt bedeviled by ghosts. Though she yearned to comfort him, she feared he wouldn't welcome it.

Cord drew the surrey to a stop beside the side door of the

house and jumped down. He helped her to the ground, his touch brief and indifferent. Uncertainty burrowed her skin. She shivered again and clasped her shawl around her.

He leaped back into the surrey and took up the reins. She panicked, sensing the chasm between them yawn wide.

"I'll await you in the library."

"Don't. I'll be a while." With that, Cord cracked the line over the horse's rump and the surrey rumbled toward the stable.

Her spirits plummeted. She was tempted to race after him and ask that he not leave her alone this night, but it'd do no good.

Cord had shut her out of his life, and no amount of tears or insisting or begging would let her back in. Worse, she had no way of knowing when, or if, he'd return to her.

Despondency weighed upon her shoulders as she trudged into the bedroom. Benedict had thoughtfully lit a lamp and started a fire in the hearth to chase away the chill.

Last night, Bea would have welcomed this romantic setting. Now, it mocked her for her failure to lure her husband to her bed.

Depositing the cursed case on her dresser, Bea draped her shawl over the dressing screen and slipped behind it. She discarded her clothes in a heap and donned a flannel nightgown.

Bea inched from behind the screen. The loneliness in the room overwhelmed her. She shivered and hugged herself, then chided herself for acting like a ninny.

Eventually Cord would be along. But if he didn't, she'd manage. Until she had moved into his bedroom, she'd gone her entire life sleeping alone. She could very well endure a night without his presence. Couldn't she?

Determined not to wallow in self-pity, Bea squared her shoulders and marched to the hearth. She built up the fire, then whisked to the dresser and sat upon the tufted bench.

Bea tugged the crimped pins from her hair, humming a

nameless ditty Mr. Oakes was wont to whistle. She abandoned the cheerful tune as she brushed her hair. The white bristles scraped her scalp and tore tangles from her fine mane. Tears smarted her eyes. Still she brushed her hair from scalp to ends until the golden tresses snapped with electricity, until the ache in her head took her mind off the one in her heart.

Equanimity continued to elude Bea. The unknown contents of her mother-in-law's burgundy dresser case dominated her thoughts.

Bea set her brush aside and pulled the case in front of her. Inexplicable foreboding filled her heart. Her thumbnail toyed with the brass clasp for an undecided moment.

She flipped it open and lifted the lid, which cradled a celluloid-framed hand mirror. The cloying scent of roses escaped the interior, making her breath catch.

Biting her lower lip, Bea stared into the ecru satin-lined case. A crystal scent bottle nestled on one side. Niches on the other held manicure implements. In the square center section lay a crimson silk handkerchief. It had a black silk scalloped edge. The name "Joy" was embroidered in a corner with the same floss.

With trembling fingers, Bea plucked the handkerchief from its nest and set it aside, revealing a silvery linen handkerchief with vermilion flowers in its center and a matching border. Beneath it she found a raspberry handkerchief trimmed with black tatting.

Bea lifted the last one and her breath caught. She admired the blue handkerchief edged with fine ecru lace. It looked new.

"How beautiful." She fingered the soft mull.

The butter-soft muslin caressed her flesh like a whisper. This was her favorite, suiting her taste completely.

"I gave that one to Ma the second Christmas after she'd married Scotty," Cord said, startling her.

Bea stared at his reflection, but he wasn't looking at her. He peeled off his new shirt, folded and tucked it into a drawer. His soft undershirt molded to his powerful back and broad shoulders. Excitement stirred within her as he strode toward her, but his gaze never lifted from the handkerchief she clutched.

He touched one blunt fingertip to the fine fabric and then jerked his hand back as if burned. "Ma never used it."

"Perhaps she thought it too elegant for everyday use."

Cord pulled his mouth to one side. "It wasn't red."

She frowned at the three brightly colored handkerchiefs. "Yes, I can see your mother was partial to the color."

"Ma said red made her feel alive." Cord stalked to the bay window, braced an arm high on the casing, and peered out at the inky night. "Scotty would've skinned me alive if I'd have bought her anything red. But when I saw that wine-colored dresser case at Lott's, I reckoned he wouldn't kick up much of a fuss."

Bea traced the rim of the case with a finger. "It's a truly lovely accessory any woman would be proud to own."

His laugh was bitter. "Ma said it wasn't personal enough."

"She actually told you that?"

"Yep." Anguish reverberated in that one word.

Bea's mouth fell open, then closed with an angry snap. "That was a perfectly horrid thing for her to say to you."

"I'd heard worse." Cord stood so stiff and proud and withdrawn that her heart literally ached for him.

Bea knew firsthand how it felt when your mother treated you without a grain of compassion. As hard as she'd tried, she'd never been able to please her mother in word, deed, or appearance.

Too angry to see reason, Bea laid the blue handkerchief aside and resumed her search of the case. Her eyebrows lifted at the sight of two black hairpins the shape of daggers. As she studied the cameo pin depicting three scantily clad Grecian ladies frolicking upon a chariot, her cheeks burned and her mouth gaped. She'd not realized anything so risqué existed.

Bea plucked out a bracelet with peeling silver plating and wrinkled her nose. Its small bangles—a horseshoe, shamrock, fiddle, bottle, and heart—were of an inferior quality and badly worn.

The dim light caught the facets of two gems buried deep in the case. Bea fished them out and gasped. Two large diamond ear screws winked up at her from her palm.

"These are absolutely gorgeous jewels," Bea said in awe.

Cord crossed to her in six long strides. "I'll be damned. She kept them anyway."

Bea glanced from the ear screws to the disapproval lining her husband's face. She paled and stared down at the gems.

Their beauty captivated Bea. "As well she should have. These diamonds are quite exquisite."

Cord snorted. "The day Scotty married Ma, he asked her to get rid of those earrings. She promised she would."

"Pray tell, why would he demand such a thing of her?"

"Because another man gave them to her."

"But surely Donnelly didn't expect your mother to give back every gift a gentleman gave—" Bea broke off, understanding dawning in a heartbeat. "Oh, dear. These weren't a gift?"

A muscle pulsed along Cord's lean jaw. "Ma got those from the owner of the first parlor house she worked in as payment for services rendered. It's possible he was my pa."

Bea gnawed her lower lip and made a rash decision. "In that case, I'll keep them for myself."

"Like hell you will."

His domineering order chafed her pride. "Need I remind you Donnelly gave this case and its contents to me."

"So he did." Cord bent close to her ear and fixed her with dark, unreadable eyes. "But I'll be damned if my wife wears the baubles some no-account pimp gave my ma for pleasuring him."

Her gaze flicked from the sparkling gems to her husband's angry face. "Even if he was your father?"

"Especially if he was my pa." Raking a hand through his hair, Cord stalked to the window. "Any man who'd turn his back on his child and force his woman to whore for him isn't worth the powder to blow him to hell."

"I couldn't agree with you more." Without an iota of regret, Bea dropped the ear screws into her oval hair receiver for Mrs. Mimms to dispose of and resumed her search of the dressing case.

She frowned, confused. The upper compartments were attached to all four sides, but their shallow depth suggested there was another compartment below. A hidden one.

With her lower lip clamped between her teeth, Bea glided her fingers around the case, searching for a catch. She found it in the side beneath the padded silk covering.

Bea pressed her thumb against the tiny button and heard a soft click. One side of the bottom shelf rotated outward; the other half sank into the slit in the case.

Grasping the edge of the shelf, Bea pulled. It opened midway and stopped. She frowned, peering inside.

A white celluloid hairbrush and matching comb nestled in satin niches. Certain one or both was preventing the drawer from opening, she inched them out and set them aside.

Still, the shelf refused to fully open. Bea muttered to herself as she crouched on her stool and squinted into the slot.

Something white was wedged between the case and its semicircular shelf. She stuck two fingers in the narrow opening and tried to remove the obstruction, but her digits were too short to grasp the block.

Chewing her lip, Bea used her mother-in-law's dagger hairpins to work it from its confinement. It was a sheet of paper, tightly folded. She smoothed it out and read the delicate script.

"What did you find now?" Cord asked.

"A letter. It's addressed 'My Dearest Joy.'"

Cord snorted. "Probably from one of Ma's old cronies."

Bea read the note. Fingers of dread tightened around her heart. "Oh, my God!"

"What's wrong?"

Bea clutched the letter to her bosom, unable to answer. Disbelief and shock churned within her. She closed her eyes, but those damning words blazed in her mind's eye.

Cord rested a gentle hand on her shoulder. "Trixie?"

She swallowed hard and stared into Cord's troubled eyes. "Was your Aunt Anne a trustworthy sort?"

"Aunt?" He shrugged. "Didn't know I had one."

"I feared as much."

Bea sighed. Nothing would be gained by keeping the truth from him a second longer. But she wished she knew a way to soften the news, wishing she could spare Cord more heartache.

Cord loomed over her, his face drawn with concern. "What the hell's the matter? You're white as a sheet."

She swallowed hard and forced out the words. "Your Aunt Anne wrote your mother, begging her to tell Donnelly the truth."

He scowled. "Which is?"

"Prescott Donnelly is your father."

The color leached from Cord's face. He sucked in a sharp breath, his gaze bleak. His features looked as hard and cold as stone. Without a word, he balled his fist at his sides and stalked to the door.

Bea leapt to her feet and raced after him. She couldn't guess what he intended to do, but she loved him far too much to allow him to suffer this shock in solitude.

CHAPTER TWENTY

You stick by Scotty and he'll pass this here ranch on to you, his ma had told Cord right before she died.

At the time, Cord had figured his ma aimed for him to hornswoggle the ranch from Scotty. Now he wasn't so sure. Had his ma been trying to tell him that Scotty was his pa? Had Scotty known the truth all along and kept it from him?

Cord damned sure was going to find out. He jerked his hat off the peg and stormed to the door.

"No!" Trixie tackled him and slammed him against the door.

He swore and twisted to get free, but she banded her arms around his waist, twined her fingers at his belly, and held on tighter than a tick.

Cord set his jaw. "Let go. I've got to talk to Scotty."

"We'll call upon Donnelly tomorrow."

"I ain't gonna wait that long." Cord wrapped his hands around her spindly wrists and tried to pry her loose without hurting her. She sank her teeth into his back. "Ouch, damn it! Why'd you bite me?"

"To gain your attention." She pressed her mouth to the smarting spot and a hot shiver ripped through him. "You can't barge in on a man when he is in the midst of his honeymoon."

Cord clunked his forehead against the door and pinched his eyes shut. He'd been so damned mad and confounded that he'd plumb forgotten all about Scotty's wedding. "I'll call on him first thing in the morning."

"Yes, we shall."

Trixie pressed against him. Her hard nipples poked his back, striking a different kind of fire in him.

She nuzzled his back and stroked his belly with a thumbnail. Sweat beaded his forehead. His blood roared in his ears. His little rustler got harder than an anvil.

"Would you care to talk?"

He'd just as soon bury himself in her heat and forget his ma had let him live a damned lie for thirty years. Or had she?

"Ain't nothing saying this Anne is telling the truth."

"True, but if this is all fabrication on Anne's part, and she was intent on flinging muck, then why did your mother keep this letter? Why not burn it?"

"Who knows? If Ma was dead set on keeping her secret, it makes no sense that she held on to that letter."

"Perhaps it does," Trixie said. "It's possible your mother was afraid to tell you or Scotty the truth, so she kept the letter, hoping that one day one of you would find it and the truth would finally be out."

"You don't reckon Scotty knows I'm his—" Cord swallowed, not able to think of himself as Scotty's son yet. "Knows the truth?" he finished in a voice gone gruff with anger and hurt.

"I rather doubt it. From what little I know about Prescott Donnelly, had he realized you were his son, he would have proclaimed it to any and all who'd listen."

Trixie was right. His ma had done wrong by lying to Scotty and him. But why'd she do it? Was she so pissed off at Scotty that she denied him his only son? Did he go off and leave her no other choice?

Or was his ma afraid that Scotty would yank Cord away

from the vile life of growing up in a whorehouse? He fisted his hands on the door. That was probably it. Scotty would've given Cord a home. A family.

He hissed a weary breath through his teeth. "Damn her."

Trixie trembled against him. "Don't say that."

He turned around and grabbed her shoulders, tempted to shake her and tell her he had every right to cuss his ma to hell and back. But worry, and some other emotion he couldn't bring himself to think about, shone in her big blue eyes and stopped him cold.

"You're shaking," he said. "You'd best go warm yourself."

Trixie scurried to the hearth and bent to the fire, rubbing her hands. The soft flannel nightgown hugged her sweet bottom. His hands itched, yearning to do the same.

"According to your aunt," she said, tormenting him with her lush curves, "your mother left Donnelly at the altar."

Cord dropped on the chair, braced his elbows on his knees and stared at the tips of his boots. Maybe he could piece together his past, make some kind of sense of this, if he didn't stare at his enticing wife.

"Ma told me she almost married once but he died in the war. Lost her family then, too." Cord snorted. "But I reckon that was another damned lie."

"Odd, isn't it? You weren't aware your aunt existed, yet Anne knew of the tie between your mother, Donnelly, and you." The hem of Trixie's gown swayed as she paced before the fire, giving him a peek of her bare feet. Even they were perfect. "Perhaps we could locate Anne."

Cord ground his palms against his eyes and took deep breaths. "What the hell for?"

"Anne is family."

His laugh was as bitter as the memories haunting him. He'd grown up a tumbleweed, rambling with his ma and getting by on lies and handouts most of his life. Living a step above a guttersnipe.

Oh, there was those five years that he and his ma had lived under Scotty's roof. That'd been the closest he'd come to seeing how a real family lived, until he'd hired on as Trixie's husband.

Though she'd tormented the hell out of him with her bossy ways and crazy attempts to seduce him, being her husband had been the best damned thing that'd ever happened to him.

If he hadn't gotten a child on her? He'd divorce her and move on like he'd said he would. Oh, she might fancy herself in love with him, but would she feel the same years from now? Would she hate him because he'd knocked her up and forced her to stay hitched to him? Would she resent their young'ns?

He downed his head, miserable to think of living his life without her but knowing he'd have to. Hell, he couldn't even stick around these parts, because it'd drive him loco to see his Trixie marry another man.

"What a damned mess."

Trixie stopped in front of him. Her fingers dug into his shoulders, loosening one tension only to yank another bowstring tight. "Concentrate on something pleasant. Something you find immense pleasure in doing."

He gulped and pinched his eyes shut, trying damned hard to recall the time he'd won the silver buckle for bronco riding instead of the night he'd ridden her in the tack room. It might've been her first time in the saddle, but she'd broken him just the same.

She inched closer between his spread legs. Her gown brushed his arms, feeling as silky soft as her skin. Her legs grazed his knees and her hands glided over his shoulders, down his spine.

She snaked her hands beneath his undershirt and slid it upward, baring his back. Rubbing it. Stoking the fire in him.

He forced his eyes open. Her toes peeked out from under

the hem. Slowly, he let his gaze drift up her white nightgown to the shadow between her legs.

Cord sucked in a ragged breath, ready to bust his britches. Her nearness, her touch, branded him—drove him wild. He broke out in a cold sweat, shaking inside, wanting her more than he'd ever wanted anything.

"Are you feeling better?"

Hell, no. He was close to exploding. But he forced a lazy grin and looked her square in the eyes. "I feel right fine."

She took her hands off him and tipped her head to one side, staring at him for so long that he feared his false smile would crack his face. "Would you like me to hug you?"

That knocked the grin off his face. He dug his fingernails into the padded arms of the chair to keep from dragging her onto his lap and giving her a taste of what he wanted. Holding her would be pure hell, but one look at her clear blue eyes told Cord that's what she needed right now.

He hissed out a breath. "If you want to."

"I truly do." Trixie perched her soft bottom on his left thigh and wrapped her arms around his neck. "It's a balm for the soul, you know."

"If you say so." Felt more like kerosene thrown on a fire.

She took in a bosom-puffing breath and let it out. "When you hold me, I feel as if nothing or nobody can ever harm me."

He thought about warning Trixie she was treading on dangerous ground. "That's 'cause you're safe with me."

Trixie squirmed on his lap until she rested her head on his shoulder. He had to snap his thighs together and clamp a hand upon her knees so she wouldn't tumble to the floor.

"How do you feel when I hug you?" Her warm breath scorched his neck and fanned the flames raging below his belt.

"I'm hotter'n hell, Trixie."

"Hmm. I feel the same. On hot summer nights, when the air was stifling, I'd lock my door and lay abed nude." She freed the buttons on his undershirt and worked it off him in a matter of seconds. "Have you ever slept without your clothing?"

He stared at her, desperate to guess her intent, but she never lifted her gaze from his chest. Her hands stayed on him, too, and those exploring fingers had his heart dancing a hoedown. If she was bent on seducing him, she was doing a damned good job.

"Yep. When I lived at the Flying D," he managed to say.

Her fingers circled his nipples, then slid lower at a snail's pace. "You haven't done so since?"

"Nope." Damn, he was going to burn to a cinder.

Her fingers reached for the top button on his jeans. Cord caught her hand, but couldn't stop the groan rumbling from him.

Wide eyes lifted to his, questioning and challenging at the same time. "Do you intend to sleep with your pants on?"

He had a hunch he wasn't going to get much sleep whether he kept them on or shucked them. "I'll come to bed. Like always."

"Very well." She scooted off his lap and sashayed toward the bed. "While you undress, I'll turn down the bedclothes."

Cord crossed to the washstand and splashed cold water in his face. He could've sworn it sizzled as it ran down his chest.

As much as he hated to confront Scotty tomorrow, he reckoned it'd be easier than sharing a bed with Trixie tonight. He heeled off both boots at the jack and tugged off his stockings. Yessiree, it'd take all the willpower he could rustle up to keep his hands off her.

Resigned to a fitful night, he shucked his jeans and draped them over a chair, then padded to the hearth. Once he found his undershirt, he'd shrug into it, snuff out the lamps, and crawl into bed. He wouldn't think about the enticing woman lying beside him.

Cord frowned. "What did you do with my undershirt?"

"I have it."

Something in her honeyed voice warned Cord she had him by the short hairs again. He eyed the bed. His blood boiled. The little rustler reared.

Trixie knelt smack dab in the middle of the bed, her golden hair draping her shoulders and tumbling down her back. She'd folded her hands primly upon her thighs. If she hadn't taken off her nightgown, she would've looked the picture of prim and proper.

But she'd tossed her gown aside and shrugged into his worn undershirt. She hadn't bothered to button it, either, so he got an eyeful of full, creamy breasts. The shirt's length left most of her long legs exposed, yet managed to hide her secrets.

He took a hobbling step toward her. "Why'd you do that?"

"I thought I'd feel cooler wearing your shirt, but I'm still terribly hot." She leaned forward. The longing in her eyes got his heart racing. "Surely you feel the same."

"What if I do?"

She glanced at his groin, and her mouth curved into a lusty smile. "You'd be wise to remove your drawers."

His fingers fumbled with the buttons on them before his brain kicked in. He stopped, not about to make the same mistake.

"Do you want me to beg?"

Her voice was low. Sultry. She leaned forward a bit more, offering herself to him, as if she knew he was so hungry for her that he couldn't pass up another touch. Another taste.

His laugh came out as raw as his need. "Nope. But there's no turning back, so you'd best be sure what you want."

Her eyes glowed with invitation. "I've no doubts."

Cord sure as hell did, but he flipped the buttons free on his drawers and sent them to the floor just the same. Over the thud of his own heart, he heard her soft gasp.

He strode toward her, wondering if seeing him hard and hurting would send her running. He should've known better. She sat still, eyes wide and darkened to a smoky violet.

Resisting the urge to push her onto her back and satisfy them both, he lay on his back and tucked his hands under his head. Even if it killed him, he'd let his wife look her fill.

He pulled his mouth to one side. "I'm all yours, Trixie."

Of all the scenarios Bea had considered, this hadn't been one of them. Donning his undershirt had been the extent of her seductive ploys. She'd hoped Cord would take the initiative and seduce her as he'd done in the tack room.

That he offered himself to her thrilled her beyond words. She quivered with restless energy, anxious to explore the myriad angles and planes of his fascinating muscular body. The mental picture she'd drawn of his naked form had been sketchy at best. Reality was much more intriguing. And arousing.

He exuded the power and pride of a thoroughbred, but she knew an unbridled passion lay beneath his calm demeanor. She pondered what she should do to unleash it. Kiss him or touch him.

Emboldened by the desire smoldering in his eyes, she scooted toward him. "Would you believe I'd convinced myself you were far too bashful to disrobe before me?"

His lips twitched. "What gave you that notion?"

"You kept your pants on when we made love."

She scrutinized his jutting manhood and judged her husband to be a magnificent specimen of masculinity. He definitely exhibited thoroughbred lines. No wonder she'd experienced a twinge of pain during their first coupling.

He stretched like a cougar rising from his nap, exuding power and prowess. "There's a damned good reason why we didn't shuck our duds. We went at it like a couple of mustangs."

"It was a rather spontaneous engagement." She frowned as she recalled one unsettling detail concerning the consummation of her marriage. "But as I recall, it was over and done with before I got into the spirit of things."

"You shouldn't have run off so soon."

She glared at him. "You didn't encourage me to stay. In fact, you suggested we forget the entire thing happened."

His dark inscrutable eyes searched hers. "Did you?"

"Of course not." She inhaled a shaky breath and splayed her hand on his hard, flat belly. "I've yearned to touch you."

His breath caught and his dark eyes glittered like jets. "Have you, now?"

She nodded, her bravado wavering a tad. But she refused to let him see her uncertainty. He'd shown her great pleasure could be had from intimately touching a lover, but due to the differences in their bodies, she wasn't certain how to give him the ecstasy he'd afforded her. She'd simply have to improvise.

Slowly, she glided her hand toward the nest surrounding his engorged maleness. The coffee-brown hair was crisp and damp. His flesh burned her palm, making her temperature rise.

She chanced a peek at his strained expression and suppressed a shiver. It occurred to her if she'd an inkling to back down, this would be a splendid time to do so. Though her knowledge on sexual matters was minimal, she intended to be his wife and lover.

For the rest of her life.

She glided her fingertips up the hot velvety-smooth length of his impressive male organ. He inhaled sharply and stiffened. His eyes blackened. Oddly enough, his long legs jerked once.

Fearing her light touch had been more tickle than caress, she decided to wrap her fingers about him and try again. He exhaled a raspy breath, but didn't relax.

A glance at his face further disheartened her. Tension contorted his features. She heaved a sigh of defeat and unconsciously grazed the swollen tip with her thumb.

He let out a low moan and covered her hand with his. "Whoa, darlin'. I want you too much to take any more exploring tonight."

Excitement spiraled through her in a dizzying rush. She'd had the right of it all along.

"Yes, I can see you're quite stimulated." Her thumb stroked him again, eliciting a ragged moan from him. "Tell me what to do to give you pleasure. Tell me what you want of me."

He tugged her wrist. She tumbled onto his brawny chest with a squeal of surprise. Her breasts spilled through the opening in the shirt, flattening onto hot skin and crisp hair. Her nipples tingled and ached. Her woman's place literally wept.

Desire smoldered in his eyes. "Do what comes natural."

Since she ached to feel the strength of his body pressed against hers again, stretching out upon him seemed quite the thing. Gripping his shoulders, she did precisely that.

She lifted her face to his, expecting a dominating kiss. He gifted her with soft, plucking ones that made her sigh with glee, alternating with slow, deep ones that made her moan with need.

His kisses intoxicated her. His hands drove her wild as they skinned the undershirt from her and roamed over her body, caressing every inch, promising untold sensuous delights.

She squirmed atop his hot, hard length, quivering from the tremors of excitement building inside her, gliding her hands over him. Her soft legs parted to straddle his hard ones.

The hard tip of his arousal prodded her woman's place. He bucked his hips. His fingers played over the sensitive skin of her inner thighs and inched higher, higher, higher.

"That's it, darlin'." His husky voice vibrated against her neck. "You're headed in the right direction."

Wanting to sound worldly, she opened her mouth to deliver a similar quip. He slid two fingers into her heat, retreated, and thrust in again. Some unearthly sound escaped her.

He groaned his pleasure and captured her lips with his. The kiss turned wet, deep and deliciously erotic, sharing the same breath, the same driving need. His fingers plied her with bold strokes while his body gyrated beneath her like a boiling sea.

Pressure coiled within her, winding her tighter. Just when she thought she'd die, the tension burst into a spellbinding blur of sensations.

Tearing her mouth from his, she buried her face against his neck and hung on for dear life as spasms rippled through her. Before the last one shimmied to an end and that glorious lethargy claimed her, he grasped her hips and made them one.

For the longest time, he didn't move. His impressive size stretched her to the limits. She refused to move an inch, fearing the pressure would turn into pain again.

He lifted her off him a bit, then brought them together with a rumbling groan of satisfaction. A jolt of delight shook her from head to toe. She gasped, reveling in the feelings of being joined to the man she loved.

"Ride me, darlin'." He drew her knees to his waist, grasped her arms and levered her off his chest ever so slowly.

The position drove him deeper within her, setting off lightning bolts of fiery vibrations. The feelings were so intensely wondrous that she tossed her head back and bit her lip to keep from screaming out her excitement.

"Aw, hell. Did I hurt you?" The gruff concern in his voice brought tears of joy to her eyes.

Blinking them away, she smiled down at his anguished face. "No, love. Not in the least."

Shaking off the last of her timidity, she planted her palms on his chest and levered herself up his length. Flashes of desire chased the worry from his eyes, making them glow like hot coals.

Inching herself down on him revived the stirrings of another voluptuous spasm. She hesitated and slid him a questioning look.

He wriggled his eyebrows and grinned wickedly.

Straddling the cowboy who'd lassoed her heart, she clutched his waist and increased her rhythm. She caught a glimpse of their reflection in the cheval glass and faltered, shocked by the wicked image she presented.

Large work-roughened hands cupped her bosom. Her breath caught. He held her breasts as if they were priceless treasures, as if he, too, was branding this special moment in his memory.

Her qualms vanished. She surrendered to the desperate need bubbling within her, to this man she loved with all her heart. As he slid in and out of her, letting her set the pace, she spiraled higher on wings of promise, sensing this mating would surpass carnal gratification. This would be emotionally phenomenal.

He grasped her hips and bucked beneath her. She shrieked as spasms rippled through her, bonding her body, soul and heart to him for all time. He whispered her name on a ragged groan and eased out of her, clasping her to him as if he'd never let her go.

Bea collapsed atop his sweat-slicked body, too weak to wiggle, too blissful to care. His heart hammered against her breast. She felt a slight tremor in the hand stroking her back.

She lifted her head and searched his face. His molasses-hued eyes held a flicker of caution, suggesting he wasn't quite as relaxed as he'd like her to believe. Not knowing why was enough to dim her radiant glow of pleasure.

Stacking her hands on his chest, she propped her chin on them and stared straight into his wary eyes. "Tell me the truth. Did you prefer me straddling you?"

"I liked the view." He squeezed her bottom. She gasped and surged forward, dragging a soft chuckle from him. "But before I make a choice, we'd best give the old-fashioned way another try."

Excitement swirled in her belly, but fear of seeming overly anxious made her hedge. "When?"

He wriggled his eyebrows. "Now."

In one swift movement, he flipped her onto her back and

sprawled atop her. His kiss was incredibly tender, but too brief for her liking.

"You got any objections to that, darlin'?"

She pouted as if truly debating such a silly thing. "Hmm. The kiss or the lovemaking?"

He growled and nuzzled her neck, then caught her earlobe in his teeth and lightly tugged. "Well?"

The mirror detailed his powerful form covering hers and she squirmed with eagerness. "I haven't one single objection." She slid her arms around his neck and clung to him. "In fact, I believe I like this position, too."

He obliged immediately, his laugh throaty. A heartbeat later, she gasped at the glide of skin against skin as he swept her away on another journey of passion.

The blinding glare from a late-morning sun poured into the bedroom. Cord lay on his back, shading his eyes with one arm while cradling his wife to his side with the other.

He smiled, unable to recollect a time he'd lollygagged this long in bed. Hell, he couldn't recall having such a rollicking good time with a woman.

Too bad it all had to end. But this morning he had to face his past—and somehow come to grips with what he had to do.

Cord glanced at the fancy dresser case and the folded letter proclaiming Scotty was his pa. Unease churned in his gut.

He wouldn't be surprised if Scotty refused to believe Anne's claim. Hell, he wasn't sure how he felt about the whole thing. For all he knew, Anne Tanner Brody was as good at spreading tales as her sporting sister had been.

Two short raps sounded on the bathing chamber door. It opened a crack.

"Is anything amiss?" Benedict asked.

Cord tugged the covers over Trixie. "Nope."

Benedict mumbled something he couldn't catch, and then Mrs. Mimms's voice joined the old man's. "Very well," he said.

The door opened a bit farther. A gray head, and a frizzy carrot-colored one, poked around the door.

"Forgive my interruption, sir," Benedict said. "But Misters O'Day, Winter, and Oakes feared something was amiss when you did not arrive at the stable at your usual time."

"It ain't like you to stay abed this long," Mrs. Mimms said. "We were all concerned."

"Whatever did I do to deserve this deplorable lack of privacy?" Trixie asked. "As you can see, we're quite all right."

Mrs. Mimms harrumphed. "Would you look at the clothes strewn about the room?"

Benedict cleared his throat. "Will there be anything you wish me to do for you this morning?"

Cord scraped a hand over his jaw. "I could use a shave."

"And a bath," Trixie hissed at him.

"And a bath," Cord repeated, though he reckoned by the twinkle in the old man's eyes that he'd heard Trixie.

"I shall see to it immediately." Benedict shut the door.

Trixie tossed the covers aside and scrambled off the bed. Cord caught her around the waist and tugged her onto her back.

He drowned out her squeal with a quick, hard kiss and settled himself between her thighs. "It'll take Benedict a while to fill the tub, so there's no sense in rushing."

"True." She looped her arms around his neck, then shocked the hell out of him by wrapping her legs around his hips. "Have you any idea what we could do in the interim?"

His pecker went rock hard. "One or two." He slid into her slick core, then paused. "Unless you got something better to do."

"There's nothing else I'd rather do."

As if to convince him she meant every word, she arched her back and welcomed him home. He obliged on a groan.

CHAPTER TWENTY-ONE

Right after breakfast, Cord and Trixie set out for the Flying D. He'd aimed to have the horses saddled, but Trixie was moving a mite slow, even wincing when she sat down at the table.

Since he was to blame for wearing her to a nub in bed, he hitched the surrey and brought it around. She clutched her shawl tight around her and sent him a peculiar smile as he helped up her, but didn't say more than two words on the ride over.

He didn't know what to make of her silence. Had he hurt her when they'd made love? Or was she as worried as he was how Scotty was going to take the news?

Cord lifted Trixie from the surrey and guided her to Scotty's front door. He wanted to get this over with.

"What will you do if Donnelly denies Anne Brody's claim?" she asked, her face as pale as buttermilk.

His mustered up a smile. "Not a damned thing. I've lived thirty years without knowing my pa. Don't reckon I need one now."

But deep inside, Cord's heart pounded like a war dance tom-tom. What the hell was he going to do if Anne Brody was right and Scotty owned up to being his pa?

Instead of knocking, he grabbed Trixie's hand and barged into the house. He followed the rumble of voices to the parlor.

For the first time he could recall, the heavy draperies were pulled back. Light spilled into the parlor. Instead of making it look cheery, the wash of daylight made his ma's tawdry trappings stand out all the more.

He sighed. Hopefully, Scotty would let Muriel put her touch on the house. He had a hunch his aunt-by-marriage—or was it stepmama?—would dress the room in soft colors. Something on the lines of the homey things Trixie favored.

As he took in the expressions of the occupants of the room, his mood soured a bit more. Muriel slumped on the settee and fidgeted with a hankie. Behind her, a scowling Scotty dug his fingers into the sofa back. Both glum faces fixed on Gil Yancy, who grinned at the couple as if he'd spent the day gambling and had just won the fat pot.

No one noticed their arrival. Feeling like an intruder in the house he'd called home, Cord opened his mouth to say howdy.

Trixie beat him to the punch. "Dear me. I trust we haven't come at an inopportune time."

"Not at all, m'dear." Muriel patted the place beside her on the settee. "Do join me."

Trixie hustled to the settee and eased down, frowning at Gil. "Am I to assume you're employed at the Flying D again?"

"No, ma'am. I'm heading west."

Scotty snorted. "I still say you're a damned fool to take off out west with winter coming on."

"You worry too much," Gil said. "I aim to hole up this side of the Divide before the snowballs start flying. When the outfits start hiring in the spring, I'll be first in line."

"You and a passel of other cowpokes." Scotty scrubbed a hand over his face. "If things sour on you, just remember you'll always have a bunk here at the Flying D."

That old familiar emptiness swelled in Cord. He was on the

outside looking in again. Scotty made no bones about caring for Gil. While these two had gotten close, Cord had drifted.

He'd spent years looking for a place to call home. Now that he'd found it, he feared it'd slip through his fingers like sand.

Gil eyed Cord, looking as guilty as a gambler caught with three aces up his sleeve. "Something I gotta tell you." He faced Scotty. "Both of you. That time you were laid up, and me and Cord drove the cattle to the railhead in Caldwell? You always blamed Cord for getting rip-snorting drunk and leaving me alone to fend off that bruiser who broke into our hotel room, knocked me out, and made off with all our money."

"I remember," Scotty said. "What of it?"

"Well, the fact is, I was liquored up. It wasn't a big man who robbed me but the little soiled dove. I figured you'd be madder than hell at Cord, but you wouldn't fire him like you would've done me. Never thought you two would get in a fight, or that Cord would pack up and ride out for good."

Cord tipped his head back and swore under his breath. All these years he'd stayed away, blaming himself for leaving Gil alone, feeling responsible for losing Scotty's profit and his trust. For letting down the best friend he ever had.

"You're right. I'd have sent you packing then instead of a week back," Scotty said. "What's done is done. My offer stands."

Gil ambled over to Scotty. "Thank you kindly, but it's high time I moved on. It'll take me a spell, but I aim to pay you back that money I lost."

"You don't have to do that," Scotty said.

"Yeah, I do. It's ate at me too long as it is."

"Be careful, boy." Scotty threw his arms around Gil and gave him a bear hug. An odd pang of jealousy speared Cord.

They parted. Gil tipped his hat to the ladies, then strode to Cord. Tension coiled like a rattler in his gut. He wanted to hit Gil. Wanted to thank him for finally telling the truth.

"You don't know how damned sorry I am for lying about what happened," Gil said.

"Reckon we both had some growing up to do."

He nodded. "I won your buckskin last night playing five-stud draw. He's in the corral. Take care of him this time, ya hear?"

"I'll pay you—"

Gil held up a hand, stopping him. "Nope. That horse is yours. And you won the lady fair and square." He glanced at Trixie, and the old teasing glint lit his eyes. "Who knows, pard. Maybe we'll both end up on top this time."

Gil settled his hat on and walked out the door. A few moments later, the clip-clop of hoofbeats faded into the distance.

"I'm so glad you paid us a visit this morning," Muriel said, drawing Cord's attention back to the newlyweds.

Trixie squirmed on the sofa and winced. "I hope you still feel that way once you hear what we discovered last night."

"What the hell happened now?" Scotty asked.

Cord met Scotty's piercing gaze. "We need to talk."

"This sounds mighty serious, Cordell."

"Oh, it is." Trixie flipped the catch on her handbag and pulled out the damned letter. "Mr. Donnelly, do you recall making the acquaintance of Miss Anne Tanner Brody?"

"Sure did. Anne was Joy's only sister. Joy said the fever took Anne during the Rebellion." Scotty scratched his bushy side whiskers. "Don't recall her saying Anne married, though."

Cord inhaled a ragged breath. "According to that letter Trixie's holding, Anne Brody was alive in April 1879."

Frosty green eyes narrowed on the letter, then homed in on Cord. "That can't be."

"'Fraid it is. I take it Ma had written Anne shortly after you made an honest woman out of her." Cord pointed to the letter. "That's Anne's reply to Ma."

Scotty swiped a hand through his hair and mumbled a curse. "Where'd you come by it?"

"I found it in the dresser case you gave me," Trixie said before Cord could open his mouth. "Am I correct to assume you weren't aware of its existence?"

Scotty shook his head slowly at first, then faster in denial. Cord braced himself for the explosion.

"Something's damn wrong here. Why in the hell would Joy hide the fact her only sister was still living?"

Trixie bristled like a bantam hen. "The date on the letter proves Joy lied to you. The content herein explains why."

"Read it and see for yourself," Cord told him.

"Believe I will." Scotty snatched the letter from Trixie's hand, and stomped back to the window to read it.

Cord told himself he didn't give a damn one way or the other if the older man believed it or not. But it didn't work. He cared all right, more than he wanted to admit.

Still clutching the letter, Scotty dropped his hand to his side and stared out the window. Cord shuffled his feet, not sure what to do or say. He glanced at the women, thinking Muriel or Trixie would pipe up. Neither did. Muriel stared at Scotty, worry lining her face. Trixie frowned at her clasped hands.

"Midway through the Rebellion," Scotty finally said, his voice gruff and broken, "I asked your ma to marry me. Joy insisted we wait till the war was over. I did, but it was the longest wait of my life. When I went back to Missouri to marry Joy, she was gone. Fourteen years passed before I found her working in that dirty crib in Wichita."

"Sick and barely able to support us." Cord let out a dry laugh, remembering the filthy room and the filthier men his ma welcomed into her bed. He'd never forget the day the big redheaded rancher happened on his ma and moved them from that hell on earth to this piece of heaven on the prairie. "Knowing what you did, seeing what she'd become, why'd you ask Ma to marry you?"

Scotty's eyes bored into his. "It's simple, boy. I never stopped loving your mama."

Some odd emotion got a stranglehold on Cord's throat. Of all the reasons Scotty could've given him, he hadn't figured on a declaration of love. "Now that you know the truth?"

"Joy will always hold a special place here." Scotty thumped a beefy fist on his chest, then cleared his throat and sent Muriel a crooked smile. "According to my first wife's sister, I got a child on Joy during the Rebellion. Anne was an honest sort, so I believe her when she claims Cordell is my son."

Muriel clapped her hands together and held them to her bosom. Tears poured from her wide blue eyes so much like Trixie's. "Oh, my. How wonderful."

"I believe that makes you my mother-in-law." Trixie opened her arms, lips trembling and eyes brimming with moisture.

Not hesitating, Muriel enfolded Trixie in her arms. "I never dreamed by coming to America I'd gain a family in one fell swoop."

Sobs mingled with the women's laughter. Cord tugged his hat off and drove his fingers through his hair, feeling skittish as all get out. Scotty looked just as uneasy.

The older man mumbled a curse and strode toward Cord. They sized each other up, each watchful, wary.

Finally, Scotty thrust his huge paw toward Cord. "If you're game, we've got a lot of catching up to make up for lost time."

Nothing could be said or done to blot out Cord's troubled youth, but he'd be damned if he'd do as his ma had done and turn his back on the only family he had. "Sounds good to me."

A broad smile, more dazzling than a Kansas sun, lit Scotty's face. He shook Cord's arm like he was priming the red pitcher pump beside the Flying D's tin sink. About the time Cord feared his arm would rip out of the socket, Scotty jerked him against his barrel chest and squeezed the dickens out of him.

The cold that had surrounded Cord's heart for years began melting, filled by a warmth he'd never felt before.

Out of the corner of his eye, Cord saw Muriel stroll toward him and Scotty. "Excuse me, husband dear, but I do have something of import to say to your son."

"Sure enough." Scotty ambled back and swiped at his eyes.

Muriel stepped before Cord. Instead of holding his hands, she stood on tiptoe, reached up, and cupped his cheeks. The gentle touch made Cord's breath catch in his throat.

"I realize I cannot take the place of your mother in your heart, but I'd be honored if you'd let me dote on you from time to time." Muriel sent him a tentative smile.

Cord hadn't expected that, but it made him feel damn good. Made him feel wanted. "Reckon I'd enjoy a bit of mothering."

"Splendid, m'boy." Muriel placed a feather-light kiss on his cheek, smiled through her tears, and retreated to the settee.

The maternal gesture had Cord grinning like a fool, but one glance at Trixie and his pleasure fled. Worry set his insides to churning. She sat poker stiff, staring at her hands, looking wan.

Having grown up around bawdy women who didn't hide anything from a growing boy, Cord had a hunch he knew what ailed Trixie. And if he was right—

Muriel plopped beside Trixie and took her hands in her own. "Is something amiss, m'dear?"

Trixie squirmed, then leaned close and whispered something to Muriel. The older woman's mouth turned down.

Muriel stood, tugging Trixie up with her. "You must see the spectacular view of the Prairie Rose from our boudoir windows."

"I'd enjoy that." Trixie trailed Muriel toward the stairs.

Cord stepped in front of Trixie, forcing her to look at him. He flashed her a teasing grin. "Want me to tag along?"

"No!" Trixie flushed and stared at the polished floor. "There is a personal matter I wish to discuss with my aunt."

She raced from the parlor. Cord watched her, his heart as heavy and cold as an anvil, as she trotted up the staircase with Muriel nipping at her heels.

Cord's skin crawled and his knees threatened to buckle. This was it. Sure as shooting, Trixie was having her woman's time. There'd be no baby. No reason for them to stay married.

Scotty's big paw landed squarely on Cord's shoulder. "Don't work yourself into a fret. Muriel will tend your missus. Let's go on in my office and talk. I could use a whiskey."

So could Cord. Hell, he felt like drowning himself in liquor right now. Maybe it'd dull the pain knifing through his heart.

Like he'd done countless times, Cord trailed Scotty into the ranch office. He dropped his hat on a low table and plopped onto a leather chair before the desk.

Without a word, he took the glass Scotty offered him. So tempting. But he didn't want it. He wanted Trixie.

"So the Tanners hailed from Missouri?" Cord asked, setting the full glass of liquor on Scotty's desk.

Scotty sat across from him and took a swig of his whiskey. "The northwest corner of the state. Your grandpappy, Cy Tanner, owned a nice little spread there. He joined the Union Army the second year of the Rebellion, leaving Anne and Joy to work the farm. That year, my unit spent the winter on the Tanner place."

"That when you got acquainted with Ma?"

"Yep. Joy was the prettiest lil' thing I ever saw. In the evenings, we'd sit on her porch and talk. Lost my heart to her right then and asked her to marry me. She refused. A month later, word came that bushwhackers had killed her pappy." Scotty frowned and twirled his glass in his big hands. "I comforted her and well, hell, one thing led to another and we ended up in bed."

Cord smiled, knowing how a man could lose his good intentions around a willing woman. "You asked her to marry you."

His pa nodded. "She promised she would after the Rebellion was over. The rest of it you know."

"In all its ugly glory." Cord fisted his hands, recalling the string of brothels and men his ma had chosen over a life as Scotty's wife. "I don't understand how you could've loved Ma."

Scotty shook his head and chuckled. "I've asked myself that countless times. But sometimes a man's heart doesn't give him a choice in the matter. Mine sure as hell didn't."

"But Ma said that to everyone."

"Yep, I know." Scotty's voice rasped with bitterness and regret. "Your ma never understood what love was. But that didn't change how I felt about her."

"What about your feelings for Muriel?"

"I love her in a different way than I did Joy." Scotty poured himself another whiskey. "Muriel understands. She loved her first husband but found a place in her heart for me. I tell you, boy, I'm damned lucky Muriel came into my life."

Cord felt the same about Trixie. Marrying her was the best thing that had ever happened to him, but he didn't have any idea how a man knew if he loved a woman. Didn't know if he was capable of feeling that way. Didn't know if he was worthy of Trixie's love now, or if he'd ever be.

Muriel whisked Bea above stairs to attend her needs, giving her clean drawers, unwell cloths, and offering a tonic to ease her cramps. Bea declined the latter.

She mopped at her tears. "I'd so hoped I was with child."

"You are fretting overmuch." Muriel embraced Bea. "You haven't been married a month yet. Give yourself time."

Muriel's commiseration did not lessen the ache in Bea's back or lift the heaviness from her heart. Cord had promised to remain her husband—if he got her with child.

Throughout the long day at the Flying D, Bea struggled to

feign a cheerful air. Not an easy task. Embroiled in her miseries, Bea half listened to the conversation between Cord and Donnelly. Even on good days, she found discussing cattle boring.

When the sumptuous meal was served, Bea picked at her food and refused to meet Cord's keen gaze. She blamed Donnelly for her distress. His hints of a family dynasty further depressed her.

By the time Cord suggested they leave, dusk had fallen and Bea had worked herself into a dither. She didn't look forward to telling Cord she wasn't pregnant.

Cord tied the horse he'd lost gambling to the back of the surrey, then lifted her onto the seat and climbed in beside her. As she had feared, Cord didn't mince words. "What's wrong?"

"Nothing at all." Bea pasted an overbright smile on her face. "Donnelly took Anne Brody's claim quite well, don't you think? And Aunt Muriel. Well, anyone can see she's quite elated to acquire a son in marriage."

"She'd make a right fine mama."

Bea could've bitten her tongue off for bringing up the topic of children. "Wasn't the roast beef delicious?"

"Yep. So why didn't you eat much of it?"

"I wasn't overly hungry."

Cord slid Bea an assessing look that flooded her face with heat in a matter of seconds. "Why's that?"

She heaved a defeated sigh, focused on her clasped hands and forced the truth to escape her dry mouth. "Delicately put, I'm temporarily indisposed."

"You mean you ain't in the family way?"

"Precisely."

Bea wished Cord would expound on her announcement so she'd know how he felt about it. But he kept his thoughts to himself.

By the time he guided the surrey onto the lane leading to the Prairie Rose, the repetitive chink of harness rings and the steady clip-clop of hooves had given Bea a brutal headache. She rubbed her aching temples, her raw nerves a jumble.

"Reckon you're anxious to get the title to the ranch."

The lack of emotion in his voice roused her worst fears. He didn't sound particularly concerned one way or the other.

She decided it best to hide her true thoughts on the matter. "Gaining title to the Prairie Rose is most important to me."

His smile was grim. "That's what I figured."

Cord pulled the surrey beside the back porch and set the brake. Jumping down, he reached out to help her to the ground. His touch was far too brief, his features shadowed and unreadable in the dusky twilight.

"While I tend the horses, ask the earl to meet us in the library." He cleared his throat, his expression so remote she wanted to bawl. "It's best we settle everything tonight."

Cord climbed back into the buggy and set off toward the barn. Bea watched until tears blurred her vision, then she fled into the house. She wouldn't gainsay Cord if pride goaded him to uphold their original bargain to the letter. After all, it was time Grandfather signed the ranch over to Cord.

But after the question of the land and her fortune were settled, Bea intended to do everything in her power to strike a new and hopefully long-lasting bargain with Cord. She wasn't about to let her cowboy husband go without a fight.

Bea found Grandfather in the library, brooding over a glass of whiskey. Lambert lounged on a sofa doing likewise.

She faced the viscount. "Do forgive the interruption, but Cord and I wish to speak with Grandfather in private."

"Let me hazard a guess." Lambert twirled the waxed tips of his mustache until they resembled hat pins. His low chuckle had a nasty quality to it. "Your husband has asked you to appeal to the earl for the title to this ranch."

Her shoulders snapped back. "This ranch is my home."

"Don't be a fluff-headed goose, Beatrix." The viscount's fleshy jowls vibrated as he leaned forward. "Tanner is a penniless drifter. No doubt the bloke married you because he had his eye set on owning your stable and this property."

Bea shook with outrage. "Odd, but I had suspected that was the very same reason you'd sought my hand in marriage."

"A moot point, since you are another man's wife." The earl set his glass down with a clunk and glared at Lambert. "However, I'd like to know why you wished to wed Bea."

"Above all, your granddaughter is an enterprising lady. As you know, fattening one's holdings are commonplace in our world." Lambert's lascivious gaze slid over Bea, making her shiver. "My dear Beatrix. When will you come to your senses, rid yourself of Tanner, and become my viscountess as was intended from the start?"

"Never," Bea said.

The viscount tossed down his whiskey and faced Grandfather. "I venture if you'd dispose of this ranch, Tanner will show his true colors and abandon Beatrix immediately."

"You're barking up the wrong tree, Strowbridge." Cord's voice was controlled and calm. Too much so. "Even if he wanted to, the earl can't sell the Prairie Rose."

"You sound terribly sure of yourself." The viscount smirked.

Cord strode into the library, crossed his arms over his chest, and smiled. "I am. The earl signed the Prairie Rose over to me. And I ain't about to sell out."

Shocked speechless, Bea dropped onto a straight chair and gaped at her husband. She didn't doubt Cord's claim for a second. But for the life of her, she couldn't fathom why Cord and Grandfather had kept the truth from her.

Lambert lurched to his feet. "Bloody hell, Arden. I suppose you have handed Tanner her fortune as well?"

Grandfather's blue eyes sparkled with an unholy gleam. "I intend to do so on the morrow. Tanner is Bea's husband."

Lambert slid a pointed glare at Cord, then fixed his imperious gaze on her. "I should have realized you cared nothing of maintaining bloodlines when you allowed that fine fox-hound of Sherwin's to whelp those worthless mongrels."

Bea leapt to her feet, shaking with outrage. "You've over-stayed your welcome, Lambert. Get out of my house."

"As you wish. I shall leave immediately." With a dip of his weak chin, the viscount marched from the room.

Grandfather swore. "I should have never extended an invitation to the cheeky bloke to accompany me here."

"Why did you?" Cord asked.

"Strowbridge convinced me I would need an ally in America. His accounting of Bea's situation was grim at best. Clearly the viscount thought I'd take one look at you and have you dispatched, and then he'd make a grand play for Beatrix's hand."

Bea wrinkled her nose. "Lambert is an arrogant fool."

"Yeah, he's that," Cord said. "But I reckon Strowbridge could strike like a rattler, if he's got a mind to."

"One never knows what a man or woman scorned will stoop to do." The earl pushed to his feet and pressed a paper into her hand. "Or a desperate one, for that matter. Now I must find my bed. Last night reminded me I am not the dashing blade I once was."

As the earl strode from the room, Bea glanced at the marriage contract in her hands and cringed. Dear God. Grandfather knew.

"When did Grandfather give you the title?"

"When we went to town. Zachary put the ranch in our names. Said it'd be easy to change. Reckon we can do that tomorrow."

She searched his eyes for a hint of affection, a smidgen of desire. She saw nothing but resigned wariness. Her heart ached so badly she could barely draw a breath. But she forced a smile.

"I believe I'll go to bed. It's been a trying day."

"Night," Cord said. "I've got a mind to stay up awhile."

He didn't have to say he wasn't coming to bed until he was sure she was asleep. She knew that's what he intended to do.

Bea escaped the library and stumbled down the hall. She scrambled up the rear stairs and into the bedroom, letting her tears fall on the contract. Had she gained exactly what she'd set out to achieve only to lose the one man she'd ever love?

CHAPTER TWENTY-TWO

Cord jolted awake, heart pounding. He scanned the dark bedroom for the source of the sound that had roused him. All was quiet. Nothing appeared out of place.

Deciding he'd had a nightmare, he closed his eyes. Trixie sighed in her sleep, rolled over, and cuddled against his side.

He smiled, feeling warmth spread through him, thaw the coldness that had kept him pacing the library until he was sure Trixie was asleep, wondering what the hell he should do.

It was anybody's guess if his ma's cold blood or Scotty's forgiveness flowed in his veins. But in the wee hours of the morning, with Trixie snuggled up beside him, he knew nothing in his life had ever felt as right and natural.

He didn't aim to leave her. Since he wouldn't force her hand, he was going to have to win her heart. That wasn't going to be easy. He wasn't good at discussing feelings—especially ones he didn't understand. Like this mystery called love. But somehow he had to make her see they belonged together.

A muffled scraping came from below. His hackles bristled—a sure sign of trouble. What the hell was going on?

Cord crawled from bed and padded to the chair where he'd shucked his jeans. He shrugged into them, grabbed his boots

and rifle, and slipped into the bathing chamber. After jamming
on his boots, he picked up his gun and eased into the dark hall.

He stole down the rear stairs, keeping his back to the wall.
He searched the house room by room. Nothing stirred in the
kitchen, dining room, or parlor, but a sliver of light drifted
onto the floor beneath the closed library door.

Swearing under his breath, Cord eased toward the room
that held the ranch's records and floor-to-ceiling bookshelves.
He pressed an ear to the door, catching faint noises: the
squeak of a drawer opening and closing, papers rustling, the
shuffle of feet.

Shaking off the last of his sleep, Cord shouldered his rifle
and burst into the room. A lamp burned low on the desk, casting a mellow glow upon Strowbridge, hunched over a stack of
papers. The viscount yelped and raised his hands, palms up.

Cord lowered the rifle. "What the hell are you doing here?"

Strowbridge slid a nervous glance around the shadowy
room and dropped his hands to his lap. "Beatrix keeps exemplary documents, don't you know. Few horse breeders bother
to trace the lineage of their stable."

"Trixie is particular about things like that." Cord stomped
to the desk and reached for the breeding charts. "She was nice
about ordering you off her land. I ain't so inclined. Get the
hell off the Rose before I blow a hole in you."

"I'll leave, but not without taking what I came for."

Before Cord could blink, Strowbridge cocked and aimed a
revolver at Cord's heart. A quick look told Cord the firearm
was his own stolen gun. Son of a bitch! His enemy had been
right under his nose all this time.

"This ain't the first time you've set out to kill me."

"You are quite astute, Tanner. I failed to anticipate you'd
allow Mr. Winter to use your saddle, or that I'd scored the
girth straps a bit deeper than necessary." Strowbridge pulled
his mouth into a mockery of a smile. "After that error, I had
to resort to more ingenious methods to dispose of you."

"Such as crippling our windmill with branding irons?"

"I must admit it was Nate Wyles's idea to sabotage the mill. But due to the fact you and Beatrix were at odds with Mr. Yancy, I insisted Wyles use Flying D property."

"Which he stole and rigged for you."

Strowbridge nodded. "Wyles cut the fence, keeping the Flying D cowboys occupied rounding up their cattle. With the Flying D deserted, Nate had no difficulty procuring the branding irons."

Cord stared into the viscount's rabid eyes and shivered. "That morning Jake was shot. You thought that was me with her."

"Correct again. Regrettably, when I attempted to eliminate you, or who I assumed was you, my aim was off." Strowbridge flexed his left arm and winced. "Thankfully, so was Beatrix's."

Cord smiled. She'd winged the viscount, all right. He decided he'd best teach Trixie how to shoot. If he came out of this alive. Right now, the odds weren't in his favor.

A chill slid down Cord's spine as he pieced together what he knew as fact with what he suspected. He played a hunch. "Nate did your dirty work last year, helping you kill Trixie's pa."

The refined mask slipped from Strowbridge's too-round face, revealing a man straddling the razor's edge of panic. "If Northroupe had simply forced Beatrix to marry me at the time, I wouldn't have had to resort to extremes."

Cord flexed his fingers, chomping at the bit to surprise Strowbridge and yank the gun from him. "But Trixie's pa bowed to her wishes instead of yours, so you put spiders in his saddle."

"You must credit Wyles for that bit of handiwork. Though I admit I was quite uncertain my plan would work when Northroupe refused my proffered flask of whiskey."

"If he didn't drink, then why did he reek of liquor?"

Strowbridge gave a dry chuckle. "I emptied my flask into his mouth. Everyone believed Northroupe was in his cups."

"Was he dead when you poured rotgut down his throat?"

"No. Northroupe had merely broken his neck. Since the sot was unable to move, I strangled him and spared him from living the remainder of his miserable life as a cripple."

The cold-blooded murder of Sherwin Northroupe spurred a stampede of rage in Cord. He corralled it. He had to keep the viscount talking and wait for a chance to disarm him before Strowbridge took it into his head to put a slug in Cord.

"Who beat Zephyr?"

"Wyles. But plying the whip increased the animal's frenzy and it broke free. By the time we'd summoned a wagon for Northroupe and returned to the ranch, the cowhands, as you call them, had subdued the stallion. I assumed when Beatrix heard what had happened, she would gladly dispose of the beast." Strowbridge snorted. "But Beatrix refused my advice, my assistance, and my suit. She even had the cheek to discharge Nate Wyles."

Cord smiled, proud as all get out of Trixie. "So you returned to England with your tail between your legs and fed a pack of lies to the earl. With Northroupe dead and Trixie in America on her own, you felt damn sure her grandpappy would sell the ranch and force her to marry you."

"It was the logical conclusion. Unfortunately, I failed to consider Beatrix would marry an American out of spite."

The gun barrel dipped, pointing at Cord's gut. Strowbridge's trigger finger shook, and an evil smile contorted his thin lips. A heartbeat later, he raised the gun to Cord's chest.

Despite the cool air, Cord broke out in a sweat. "You went to a lot of trouble trying to marry Trixie. Tell me, Strowbridge. Did you ever love her?"

"Indeed not. Beatrix has a hefty dowry that would go far to replenish my dwindling assets." The viscount got to his feet, keeping the gun trained on Cord's heart. "Roll the papers on the horses and hand them to me."

Cord shuffled through the papers at a snail's pace, desperate for a way to get out of this alive. He took his time laying one paper atop the next. If he could just rouse the earl.

"I should've guessed you had your eye on the horses all along." Cord raised his voice, hoping it'd carry upstairs.

"I'd like nothing better than to ship Beatrix's thoroughbreds to my depleted stables in England, but my creditors in America insist I hand them over to them. Esprit merely satisfied one individual I owed."

Cord shook with tension and a damn good dose of fear. The viscount had a bad habit of murdering those who got in his way. And Cord was smack dab in the way of him rustling horses.

Time to make his move or get shot. "Why'd you kill Nate?"

"Mr. Wyles made the fatal mistake of blackmailing me. Do hurry, Tanner. I'm not a patient man."

Muscles coiled to strike, Cord held the papers a foot short from Strowbridge's hand. The viscount reached for them.

Cord dropped the papers and grabbed the viscount's gun hand. Strowbridge lurched backward, dragging Cord over the corner of the desk. Papers scattered.

Cord held on but couldn't pry the gun from the viscount. His muscles strained. The old injury in his shoulder ached like blue blazes. Sweat dripped in his eyes. For a man who looked and acted like a nancy boy, Strowbridge was strong as an ox.

The viscount's face purpled. Blood lust gleamed in his eyes.

In that split second, Cord stared eyeball to eyeball with death. He thought of Trixie lying sweet and helpless in their bed and forced Strowbridge's arm up. The gun barked.

Red-hot pain tore through Cord's upper arm. He faltered but didn't let go of Strowbridge. The viscount squeezed the trigger. Five metallic clicks sounded in rapid succession, but instead of bullets tearing into Cord, chamber after empty chamber came up.

Bellowing like a fresh-cut steer, Cord grabbed Strowbridge's shirtfront and drove a fist into his face. Bone cracked
and blood spattered. The viscount yelped.

Cord reared back for another swing at the same time the
viscount slammed the revolver aside Cord's head.

Pain roared in his noggin. Lightning flashed behind his eyes
before blackness dropped over him and his knees buckled.

Bea jolted awake and reached for Cord. "Did you hear—"

Her question died in her throat as her hands slid over the
empty space beside her that still held his warmth. She tossed
the bedclothes aside and sprang from the bed.

Cord hadn't been out of the bed long. Had he, too, heard
the shot? Had he gone to investigate its cause?

Of course he had. There was no good reason why anyone
would be discharging a gun this time of night. It could only
mean trouble. She wasn't about to let Cord face his enemy
alone.

Heart pounding, Bea threw her white wrapper around her,
stepped into her slippers, and raced from the room. As she
sped down the hall, a door opened and slammed behind her.
Heavy footfalls fell into step behind hers.

"Stay here while I see what is amiss," the earl said.

Bea ignored that order and bounded down the staircase.
Her heart felt lodged in her throat. A voice inside her urged
her to hurry. Heeding it, she charged down the hall, beckoned
by the light spilling from the open doorway of the library.

A sense of dread slithered across her shoulders. Bea sprang
into the room and froze, clamping a hand to her mouth. Cord
lay in a crumpled heap directly in front of the desk.

"Bloody hell!" Grandfather dashed around her toward
Cord.

A calf-length white nightshirt exposed Grandfather's bony
ankles and long, narrow feet stuffed in maroon velvet slippers. Gold embroidery on the vamps depicted the Arden coat

of arms—a laurel of ivy framed a sleeping hare with two bears rampant.

For one moment Bea thought to turn her head in deference to her grandfather's state of undress. But when he laid the revolver he carried upon the desk and knelt beside Cord, all thoughts of propriety fled her mind. She flew to her husband.

Curses tumbled from her grandfather as he turned Cord onto his back. Cord was deathly still. Another revolver lay nearby.

A scream rose in Bea's throat. Tears burned her eyes. Blood streamed down her husband's arm. She dropped onto her knees and pressed a trembling hand upon his pale cheek.

"Fetch cloths for bandages," her grandfather barked.

Bea refused to leave. She ripped the wide gathered hem off her wrapper and pressed it into his hands. "How is he?"

Grandfather tore off a length from the soft cloth and formed a square pad. "The bullet grazed him. He has lost a good deal of blood, but nothing more serious than that. However, this nasty lump on his head tells me that Tanner was coshed."

Bea glanced at the papers regarding the breeding history of the cattle strewn upon the desk and floor. "It seems somebody was rifling through my records. But why?"

"Perhaps a thief assumed you had a stash of money they hoped to relieve you of. Tanner most likely surprised the bloke in the act." Grandfather pressed the pad upon Cord's upper arm, drawing a muffled moan from him. "Do fetch the whiskey, m'dear."

Scrambling to her feet, Bea snatched the bottle off the desk and pressed it into her grandfather's hands. The earl poured the amber liquor over the wound, eliciting a groan from Cord.

A watery sound escaped Bea and she blinked her burning eyes. An awful ache of fear swelled inside her.

Grandfather cleared his throat and tossed her a scowl. "Buck up, Beatrix. Hold this tight to the wound while I bind it."

She did as bidden, but her stomach roiled as Cord's warm blood coated her fingers. He couldn't die. She wouldn't let him.

"Open your eyes, Cordell Tanner!" Her face was inches above his. "You must be awake when I tell you I love you. Do you hear me? I refuse to confess my feelings to a sleeping man. Now open your eyes!" Her lips trembled. "P-p-p-lease, Cord."

Cord moaned. "You're asking for a helluva lot, darlin'."

She swallowed a sob of joy and kissed his forehead and cheek, thankful he was awake. "Don't try to trick me into pouring out my heart. I'll not tell you I love you until you look at me."

A ghost of a smile played over his firm mouth, then his dark eyelashes fluttered open a smidgen. "I'm looking."

"I love you."

Cord rewarded her declaration with his old look of unease. That he had trouble accepting her vow told Bea his condition was not grave. She couldn't be happier. Clearly if he was on his deathbed, he might make promises he didn't mean or understand.

"Who shot you, m'boy?" her grandfather asked.

Cord's eyebrows snapped together. "The viscount."

Her grandfather tied off the bandage with a curse. "Why the deuce would Strowbridge shoot you?"

"Trixie's horses. He aims to rustle them to pay off his debts." Cord swallowed and locked gazes with the earl. "Strowbridge admitted he killed your son. Sherwin wasn't drunk."

The accusation tumbled from Cord at the same time the frantic whickers and screams of horses sliced through the chill night air. Rage emboldened Bea. Lambert had killed Papa and shot her beloved husband. She wouldn't stand by while he stole her horses.

Grabbing the revolver lying upon the floor, Bea leapt to her feet and raced from the library. As she sped down the hall and out the rear door, Grandfather's shouts and Cord's curses faded.

The screeches issuing from the stable rose, more frenzied, devilishly fierce. The agitation came from several horses, but the one she recognized above all the others was Zephyr.

As he had the dark day her papa had died, the stallion emitted unearthly sounds. Injuries the horse had suffered that day had turned him into a demonic beast. She dreaded to discover what Lambert had done this night to cause the stallion to regress.

Bea bounded though the open stable door. She slid to a stop. Midway down the aisle, Lambert threatened her beloved mare with a riding crop. Cleopatra's white coat quivered. Tendons strained in the horse's long, elegant legs. A low continual whinny vibrated from the mare, whose gentle eyes had gone wild.

Without hesitation, Bea aimed the heavy revolver at the viscount. "Unhand my horse!"

"Go to Hades, you interfering bitch!" Lambert swung his right arm around, pointing a rifle at Bea.

A hand snagged Bea's arm and jerked her from the doorway just as the rifle fired. She heard a bullet whiz by her ear and flinched. Lambert fired again. The stable door splintered.

Her spine slammed into a brawny chest, knocking a squeak from her and a curse from her bandaged hero. "Cord!"

"Remind me to give you a whipping when this is over." Despite the anger in Cord's voice, his hold remained gentle.

Tears spilled from her eyes. "He lashed Cleopatra."

"She'll be all right, darlin'." Cord pried the revolver from her shaky hands and tossed it onto the ground.

Bea frowned. "Aren't you going to shoot Lambert?"

"Not with an empty gun." Cord peered into the darkness. "Can you get a clean shot at Strowbridge?"

"No. He's too close to the mare," her grandfather replied.

The Earl of Arden stood on the other side of the doorway,

more in shadow than moonlight. Wind snapped his nightshirt about his legs and tore at his silvery hair. But the hand holding his revolver remained steady. Without a doubt, he looked as wild and dangerous as her dear horses sounded.

The frenetic shrieks from the stable intensified. Hooves pounded the ground again and again. Wood groaned, then cracked.

Lambert bellowed a torrent of vile curses. A moment later, Cleopatra burst through the doorway, trailing reins and kicking free of a gentleman's saddle before disappearing into the dark.

"Whoa up, girl." Mr. Oakes's calm voice echoed from the shadows, joined by a chorus of murmurs from Rory and Jake.

Cleopatra whickered, then let out a series of nervous snorts. Bea released her breath in a whoosh, thankful her mare had broken free, relieved her men had come to their aid.

A frenzied clamor exploded from Zephyr. Lambert shouted. A whip cracked the air. Hooves ripped at wood.

Athena and Titan galloped from the stable next, both trailing a lead line. "I got them," Jake and Rory shouted in unison.

Bea wrung her hands. But what of Zephyr?

Wood splintered like lightning strikes. The whip snapped like a gunshot again. Lambert cursed.

She clutched Cord's arm. "Please. It's unbearable being unable to see what that abominable lout is about."

Cord nodded. "Then let's take a look-see."

Side by side, Bea and Cord inched toward the open door. A glance across the opening showed Grandfather approaching from the other side, gripping his revolver.

"I shall personally make certain Strowbridge hangs for the crimes he has wrought," Grandfather said over Zephyr's bellows.

"I got a hunch you ain't gonna get the chance," Cord said.

Bea peeked around the door's edge and gasped. Jagged boards littered the aisle. What little remained of the door panel on Zephyr's stall hung by one badly bent hinge. The stallion had obviously kicked it to smithereens.

Within the stall, Zephyr faced the opening the viscount stupidly tried to block with his portly form. The stallion reared, pawing the air above Lambert's head. The restraining hook had been torn from the wall again and swung from the horse's line.

The viscount cursed, lashing the stallion with the whip. Lather flew off Zephyr in white streaks. His hooves pounded the ground again and again, making it tremble.

To Bea's shock, Lambert lunged for the line. Zephyr reared on powerful haunches, lashing lethal front hooves in the air. Light flashed off his metal shoes like lightning.

The stallion let out a deafening screech. He thrust his head forward, ears flattened, baring large teeth. The dark eyes fixed on the viscount mirrored a restless spirit.

An icy dread seeped into Bea's bones, chilling her more than the brisk night air whipping around her bare legs. She shivered and clasped Cord's hand, terrified to watch, yet unable to tear her gaze away. As if understanding her dilemma, Cord wrapped his arms around her and tucked her close to him.

Spewing a torrent of vile oaths, Lambert gave the stallion's rope a hard jerk. Zephyr balked, tossing his head, ripping the line from the viscount's grasp.

Lambert stumbled backward. Zephyr reared and danced on hind legs toward the retreating man, herding him against the wall.

"Run, Lambert!" Bea shouted.

She doubted he heard her above the stallion's screeches. Not that it mattered. Lambert's chance for escape had come and gone. Zephyr had trapped him.

The stallion's front hooves struck Lambert's shoulder. Bea stuffed a fist in her mouth, swallowing a scream. The viscount dropped to his knees, then rolled and scrambled to his feet.

For a split second, Bea thought Lambert had a chance of

surviving. Instead of dashing down the aisle to freedom, the fool looped Zephyr's line around his arm.

Lambert brought the stallion's head down. The viscount must have assumed the shorter line gave him control, because he reared back and cracked the whip across the horse's scarred shoulder.

Zephyr bellowed. His coat rippled like wet black velvet. He reared, standing tall on powerful hind legs. The viscount dangled from the line, legs flailing, shrieking curses.

As if realizing his peril, Lambert released the line. He stumbled, dropping on his hands and knees. Zephyr came down, his front hooves hitting the viscount's spine. Lambert screamed.

Cord stiffened. Bea winced. Bile rose in her throat.

As if bent on seeking vengeance, Zephyr went for the kill. His hooves pounded Lambert. Over and over.

Bea whipped around and buried her face against Cord's chest, unable to watch Lambert's broken body lurch with each drubbing of hooves. She cried, but in truth her tears were more for her papa than the man who had engineered his death and tried to kill Cord.

The stallion's frantic noises gave way to quivering nickers. He snorted. Blew. Over the thundering of her heart, Bea heard slow, steady clip-clops grow closer and closer.

"Stand back. Give the stallion room," Grandfather ordered.

The muscles in Cord's chest tightened against her bosom, but he didn't budge. "Don't move, darlin'."

A wet muzzle nudged Bea's shoulder. She sucked in a sharp breath, dragging the pungent scent of earth, lathered horse, and death into her lungs. Her legs quaked.

"Easy, Zeph," Cord murmured.

The stallion let out a series of low rumbling whickers. He nudged her shoulder again, and she whimpered, afraid she'd faint.

Cord gripped her upper arms and moved her aside, putting

himself between her and the stallion. "Go on up to the house, darlin'. Me and the hands will take care of things here."

Things being a dead man and a stallion one would be a fool to trust. But stopping Cord was out of the question.

He grasped Zephyr's line and led the animal away into the night. A chill that had nothing to do with the cool air settled into her bones. Even in the moonlight, dark splotches stained Zephyr's chest, legs, and hooves.

Bea knew it was blood. Lambert's.

"Jumping Jehoshaphat, but I ain't never seen the like," Mr. Oakes muttered to Rory as the groom led Cleopatra into the stable.

Jake trailed him, leading Athena. "I rightly don't care if I ever do again."

Her heart heavy with worry, Bea blinked back tears and silently echoed Jake's wish as her husband and the sinfully black Zephyr disappeared into the darkness.

CHAPTER TWENTY-THREE

Cord and the men had just hoisted Lambert's bloody carcass into the buckboard and covered him with a tarpaulin when Trixie brought Cord's hat and shirt to him. He ached to take her in his arms and chase away the fear prowling in her eyes, but he shooed her back to the house. She'd seen enough. God knew he had.

He reckoned it was nigh on four in the morning before they mucked the mess from the stable and got the horses settled. He sent the earl to the house to rest and Jake into Revolt to fetch the marshal. Then he set to washing the blood from Zephyr.

Since the big black had ripped his stall to smithereens, Cord stabled him in Esprit's box. Zephyr didn't balk, even when Cord dabbed Humphreys's Veterinary Cure Oil on the open whip marks. Truth be told, the stallion was as mild as buttermilk. It was as if attacking Strowbridge had quenched Zephyr's thirst for revenge.

Dawn was chasing the night across a bruised sky when Jake and Marshal Ives rode up. Cord could hardly put one foot in front of the other. He rubbed the taut muscles in his neck, wondering if Trixie had gotten a wink of sleep, wishing he could crawl into bed with her. But that wouldn't happen anytime soon.

"What happened last night?" Ives asked Cord as the earl moseyed from the house to join them.

"Viscount Strowbridge shot Tanner," the earl said.

"He's the one who stole my revolver." Cord rolled his stiff arm, knowing he was damned lucky he'd come out of his showdown with a flesh wound and nagging headache.

The earl went on at length and told the marshal how he and Trixie had found Cord, and then Cord told Ives the rest of it. Ives scowled, taking it in.

"Ott found the Flying D branding irons wrapped up in a horse blanket in the stable." Cord glanced at the earl, and the older man looked aside and swore.

Ives hooked his thumbs under his gun belt and rocked back on his heels. "Reckon this Viscount Strowbridge aimed to take them irons back to England as mementos."

"That's what I figured," Cord said. "They were stowed beside two valises stuffed with his clothes."

Ives scrubbed a hand over his mouth. "I'd have never figured that fancy Englishman on teaming up with Nate Wyles."

"That's what Strowbridge counted on." Cord snorted, angry at himself for being duped. Maybe if Trixie hadn't dominated his thoughts every day and his dreams every night, he'd have seen the viscount was up to no good. "Strowbridge was proud of himself for outwitting us. Reckon that's why he decided to brag about it, rub it in before he plugged me and made off with the horses."

The marshal grunted. "In the West, horse thieves tend to end up being the guest of honor at a necktie party."

"Hanging is a helluva lot quicker than getting stomped to death." Cord rubbed his tired eyes, but the viscount's grisly death was branded in his memory.

"I'm thinking Strowbridge would've ended up dead either way." Ives ambled to the buckboard and lifted the tarpaulin. He dropped it, whirled, and grasped a wheel, giving in to a bout of dry heaves. "You sure that feller's the viscount?"

"That's him," Cord said.

But if he hadn't seen Zephyr beat Strowbridge into the ground, it would've been damn hard to identify him. The horse's hooves had turned the viscount's fine clothes to rags and rendered his face unrecognizable.

The earl cleared his throat, his features grave. "If you would permit me, Marshal Ives, I shall accompany Mr. Winter into town and provide for Strowbridge's interment."

"Right kindly of you to offer, Earl Arden. By all means, see to his burying." Ives sighed, no doubt glad the county would be spared the expense of laying out the viscount.

"It is the least I can do for a fallen countryman," the earl said in a somber, dignified tone.

"Then I reckon there ain't nothing more for me to do." Ives climbed onto his bay gelding, then dipped his chin and brushed two fingers over his hat brim in farewell.

As the marshal trotted down the lane, Cord clapped a hand on Jake's shoulder. "Are you up to heading into town with the earl and help him see to Strowbridge's burying?"

Jake looked a mite green, but nodded solemnly. "Yes, sir."

"Hit the sack when you get back, then." Cord turned to Ott and Rory and nodded his gratitude. "It's been a long night. You'd both best take it easy the rest of the day."

Neither argued. Jake clambered onto the buckboard, took up the reins, and waited for the earl to join him.

The earl turned to Cord. "Seek out your wife, m'boy. Beatrix has worn a path in the carpet waiting for your return. God knows you look ready to fall on your face."

Cord smiled. If he looked as puny as he felt, Trixie would pounce on him the second he staggered inside. Just as well. Last night he'd done a lot of thinking about what lay ahead of them.

Years ago, Scotty had warned Cord that when a woman drags a loop, she won't go far till she finds a man willing to jump into it. Fool that he was, Cord had jumped in with both feet. But right now, he didn't feel foolish. He felt lucky. And damned nervous.

He aimed to sit Trixie down and tell her he wanted to forge a new contract with her—a permanent one. Since she loved him, that ought to be the easy part.

The hard part would be telling her why he couldn't leave her.

Seeing Cord trudge toward the house, Bea raced from the alcove in search of Benedict. After ordering him to draw a bath for Cord, she rushed into the kitchen and instructed Mrs. Delgado to prepare a hearty breakfast.

Heart pounding, Bea took up a post by the back door. She considered waiting in the library until Cord had cleaned up, eaten, and rested, then thought better of it. She'd waited to see her husband far too long as it were.

She snapped the wrinkles from her blue linen skirt, fussed with the high lace collar on her white blouse, and smoothed her hair back into the knot at her nape. Satisfied she looked presentable, she folded her hands before her and smiled.

Cord opened the door and stepped inside. Bea gasped. She hadn't expected him to look so haggard. Or so withdrawn.

His dark gaze skimmed over her, but deftly avoided meeting her eyes. "We need to talk, Trixie."

The lack of emotion in his voice sent dread coursing through her. "Why don't you take your bath first and—"

"That can wait." Cord heaved an exhausted sigh and motioned for her to precede him. "Let's go into the library."

Bea did as he bade. She told herself Cord was somber because of all he'd endured last night. But she had a nagging feeling that something more than lack of sleep and his wound plagued him.

She inched toward the desk, her nerves jumping with each heavy step Cord took behind her. He closed the library door, assuring them of privacy. Heart racing, she forced a cheery smile and faced the man who held her future in his capable hands.

Cord stared at the patterns on the blue and white Brussels carpet as if he were trying to read a message within the myriad curlicues and swirls. He looked confused. Or scared to death.

"What would you care to discuss?"

An enormous indrawn breath expanded his powerful chest to impressive proportions. He blew it out between his teeth.

"The time's come for us to end this common bond we made."

Bea gaped, unable to believe that after all they'd been through together, Cord still considered their marriage to be a cold business deal. She stalked around the desk and jerked open a drawer. Her hands shook as she yanked out the damnable marriage contract she'd insisted Cord agree to.

She fought back tears and thrust the paper at him. "You're free to divorce me after the ranch is in my name. Then there's my dowry to settle, and the horse you want isn't even born yet."

He thumbed back his hat, and a slow smile curved his sensuous mouth. "What'll you do if this cowboy decides he ain't gonna saddle up and ride away?"

Love him till she drew her last breath. But she wasn't sure if he was serious or if he was teasing her.

"Our contract states—"

"I could tear that paper up," he said. "Zachary wouldn't kick up a fuss. Neither would your grandpappy. It'd be my word against yours that you hired me to marry you. What would you do?"

She blinked and stared into his warm brown eyes, seeing an odd calm lurking behind his weariness. Dared she hope?

"There's little I could do."

"You could kick me outta your bed."

"Yes, I could do that." Bea smiled when his grin turned into a frown. "But I wouldn't."

"I'm mighty glad to hear that." Cord took the contract from

her, tore it in two, and winked. "If we keep going at it like we did the night before last, we'll have a houseful of young'ns."

"One can only hope, but I could take after Aunt Muriel and never conceive." She bit her lower lip. "What if I'm unable to give you a child?"

"Not having kids won't change how I feel about you." Cord loomed over her, eyes wary and muscles tensed. "Why the hell are you arguing about us staying married?"

Exasperation whirled within Bea like a Kansas tornado. "For a rambling cowboy turned astute rancher, you can be quite daft when it comes to matters of the heart."

"The hell you say. I know how you feel about me." Cord nodded once, a curt I-got-you-there look that made her teeth ache. "You've told me twice you love me. Once in bed, and last night when you thought I was dead."

"And I meant it both times." Bea pressed a palm over his heart and searched his face. "What are your feelings toward me?"

He frowned. "Same as you feel about me."

"Then say it."

"All right." His throat worked, his mouth opened, then he downed his head. "Tonight."

When they were in bed, she realized.

Bea stalked to the window and hugged herself, furious his mother had left such deep scars on his heart. "You still view professions of love as a thank-you for lovemaking. Am I right?"

"No!" But his perplexed expression told her he wasn't sure.

"I love you. For now and always. With all my heart and soul. With every breath I take."

"I know." Cord crossed to her in three long strides, his gaze clearly pleading with her to accept him as he was.

Though she ached for his touch, Bea held up a hand to stop him from taking her in his arms. "Come no closer. I love you and shall say it often when we are at arm's length, but never again when you hold me. Or when we're intimate."

A groan rumbled from him. "Why the hell not?"

"I don't want you to confuse love with seduction."

His jaw quivered. The tendons in his neck grew taut. "I don't. Not now. Hell, you know how I feel about you."

"Do I?"

Bea blew him a kiss. Some primal sound issued from him and she smiled. Yes, she knew how he felt, but she wanted to hear him say it. Wanted Cord to hear himself say those words. She was sure if he mastered that, he'd escape the demons plaguing him.

He opened his arms, his eyes glowing with an emotion Bea had never seen before. "I want to hold you when I say it."

Excitement rippled through her. "Why?"

"Because I just do, is all." He scowled fiercely.

"Very well." Bea smiled and stepped into his embrace, but alarm filled her when her palm touched the sticky dampness below his bandaged shoulder. "You're bleeding."

"Some."

"I should bandage it and—"

"Later."

His breathing was ragged, his face pale. His eyelids drifted downward, threatening to close, scaring the life from her.

"I love you, Trixie."

Before Bea could savor his heartfelt declaration, Cord moaned and crumpled to his knees, taking her down with him. His hat brim dipped low, casting his face into shadow. She snatched his hat off and pressed the back of her hand to his cool forehead, then caressed his bristly jaw and searched his eyes.

Panic spiked her voice an octave and set her heart to galloping. "Oh, Cord! Are you in pain?"

"Naw. I'm just weak as a newborn calf." Cord braced his back against the wall and gave her the laziest of smiles.

"I'll summon the men to help you to our bed." Bea dropped

a kiss on his forehead, then made to rise. Cord tugged her hand. With a yelp, she tumbled back onto his lap.

He chuckled, albeit a weak one. "Sit your sweet little butt down, woman. I ain't done talking to you yet."

One strong arm curved around her and pulled her close. She snuggled against him and fought back tears of joy. The sincerity in his warm molasses-colored eyes chased the frigid fear from her.

"I love you, Trixie." Cord kissed her, a tender but thorough bonding of lips and dueling of tongues. "You can bet as soon as I'm on my feet and you ain't indisposed, I'll spend every night showing you just how much."

Letting her love for him shine in her smile, Bea plopped his discarded hat on her head and thumbed it back—just as he always did. Cord's eyes twinkled and his lips quirked at the corners.

"Cowboy," Bea said in an exaggerated lusty drawl, "you can bet your sweet butt I'm gonna hold you to that promise."

EPILOGUE

One year later

Cord stood at the bay window in the big bedroom he shared with Trixie and took in the Prairie Rose with a mixture of pride and hope. They'd ricked a good supply of hay, stowed the corn in silos, and got a good price on their cider from Lott's Mercantile. The cattle were fat, and the foals frisked in the paddock.

He had a passel of things to be thankful for and damn few regrets. It riled him they'd never found the stallion Lambert Strowbridge had made off with. Esprit had plumb disappeared.

Same with Anne Tanner Brody. Cord wished he'd been able to locate his aunt, but according to the folks back in Missouri who'd known her, Anne had moved from their small town in 1881, two years after she'd written to Joy. Nobody knew where she'd taken off to, so there was no way of knowing if she'd been telling the truth.

Cord sighed, wishing he'd favored Scotty instead of his ma. But he was tall and lean with dark hair and eyes and a blade of a nose while Scotty was squat as a beer barrel with a mane of wild red hair, a pug nose, and snapping green eyes.

Nope, it didn't matter to Cord if Scotty was his pa. He was

the only one Cord had ever known. And sure as shooting, Scotty believed Cord was his son.

So did Muriel and Trixie. Both women were mighty quick to point out the similarities between Scotty and Cord—the good traits and the bad ones.

So Cord didn't balk when Scotty, Muriel, and Trixie urged Cord to change his last name. Legally, Cord was a Donnelly. But deep in his heart, Cord had doubts.

Up until one month ago, that is.

Now he knew he was Prescott Donnelly's son.

Scotty's two-seater surrey rumbled down the lane toward the house, followed by a Flying D wagon loaded with trunks and crates, kicking up a mile-high dust cloud. Cord smiled. Even from here he knew the tall fellow sitting beside Scotty was his grandpappy-in-law, the Earl of Arden.

Cord strode to the rocking chair where his beautiful wife sat nursing their month-old son. "They're here, darlin'."

"I do hope Grandfather enjoyed a pleasant trip. To think he came all the way to America for the christening."

Trixie handed the baby to Cord, and then set about putting her bodice to rights, hiding the soft milky breasts from his hungry eyes. She sent him a smile that melted his heart and crossed to the cradle. He admired the curve of Trixie's sweet butt as she bent to lift their sleeping daughter from her crib.

Cord blinked the sudden moisture from his eyes and gazed at the baby boy cradled in his arms. His spitting image, he thought as he trailed a finger over his son's dark mop of hair.

"You've made me the happiest man on earth, Trixie."

"And you, dear husband, have made me the happiest woman alive." Trixie sashayed to him and raised her mouth to his.

He lowered his head, expecting a brush of lips. The kiss was greedy and left him hungering for more.

With a saucy smile, she strolled from the room. Settling his son in his arms, Cord blew out a shaky breath and followed his wife. He liked trailing Trixie. Birthing their babies had put a swing in her backside that had him aching to make love to her.

But until he was damn certain making love wouldn't cause her any pain, he'd bide his time and watch her.

Trixie swept into the parlor. The twins' doting grandparents and great-grandfather swarmed her like bees to a full-blown rose.

"You grow more stunning as the days pass," the earl said.

"And you, sir, don't look as if you've aged a day in over a year." Trixie settled on the settee and Muriel joined her, fussing with her granddaughter, as usual. "You're well, I trust."

The earl puffed out his chest. "Indeed. Though had I been on my deathbed, I would have rallied and made the journey to see my great-grandchildren. I say, Tanner. Are you hiding the lad beneath that fussy shawl?"

"You'll be pleased to know Cord and I agreed on his name." Trixie smiled at Cord. "We named him Fletcher Prescott Donnelly."

Scotty flashed a mile-wide smile. "I'll be."

"A noble moniker," the earl said, looking right pleased they'd decided to name the boy after him and Scotty.

Cord tugged the shawl off his son's head. "Fletch, say howdy to your great-grandpappy."

The earl chucked Fletcher under his chin. The baby's dark brown eyes twinkled as he blew a spit bubble and gurgled.

"Handsome lad," the earl said. "The image of you, m'boy."

With emotion clogging his throat, Cord could only nod.

Scotty hunkered by Muriel and smiled at his granddaughter. "Now, I wager you this here is the prettiest baby girl I've ever seen in my life. Why, she's sure to steal every man's heart."

"You got that right." The first time Cord held her, she'd lassoed his heart. Laid to rest his lingering doubts, too.

His darling baby girl, Hannah Muriel Donnelly, was

blessed with Trixie's fine bones, milky smooth skin, and kiss-able little bow of a mouth. But she'd inherited Scotty's pug nose, laughing green eyes, and wild mane of red hair.

Cord smiled at his family, his heart near bursting with love, his restless soul finally at peace. Yep, no doubt about it.

He was the luckiest cowpoke in the whole wide world.